The Complete Escapades of The Scarlet Pimpernel

Volume 4

The Complete Escapades of The Scarlet Pimpernel
Volume 4

Sir Percy Hits Back

and

A Child of the Revolution

Baroness Orczy

LEONAUR

The Complete Escapades of The Scarlet Pimpernel
Volume 4
Sir Percy Hits Back
and
A Child of the Revolution
by Baroness Orczy

FIRST EDITION

First published under the titles
Sir Percy Hits Back
and
A Child of the Revolution

Leonaur is an imprint of Oakpast Ltd

Copyright in this form © 2018 Oakpast Ltd

ISBN: 978-1-78282-736-8 (hardcover)
ISBN: 978-1-78282-737-5 (softcover)

http://www.leonaur.com

Publisher's Notes

The views expressed in this book are not necessarily
those of the publisher.

Contents

Sir Percy Hits Back

Contents

Chapter 1

On the spot where the Hôtel Moderne now rears its more ambitious head, there stood at that time a cottage with sloping red-tiled roof and white-washed walls. It was owned by one Baptiste Portal, an old peasant of the Dauphiné, who dispensed refreshments to travellers and passers-by, as his father and grandfather had done before him, in the shape of somewhat thin *vin du pays* and an occasional glass of *eau-de-vie*, while he spent his slack time chiefly in grumbling at the fact that the new posting-inn on the high road had taken all his trade away. He did not see the necessity of the posting-inn, did not old Baptiste, nor for that matter that of the high-road or the post-chaise. Before all these new notions had come into the heads of the government people up in Paris, travellers had been content to come squelching through the mud on the back of a good horse or come ploughing through inches of dust in the old *coche*. So why not now? And was not the old wine of Les Amandiers as good and better than the vinegar dispensed at the more pretentious posting-inn?

The place was called Les Amandiers because at the back of the house there were two anaemic almond-trees with gaunt, twisted arms which covered themselves in the spring with sickly blooms, and in the summer with dust. In the front of the house, up against the white-washed wall, there was a wooden bench on which Baptiste's privileged customers were wont to sit on fine evenings, to drink their *vin du pays* and join the old man in his wholesale condemnation of the government "up in Paris" and its new-fangled ways. From this vantage-point a glorious view was obtained over the valley of the Buëche, and beyond Laragne as far as the peaks of Pelvoux: whilst to the right towered in the distance the grand old citadel of Sisteron with its turrets and fortifications dating from the fourteenth century, and the stately church of Notre Dame. But views and winding rivers, snowy peaks, and medieval fortresses did not interest Baptiste Portal's customers nearly as much as the price of almonds or the alarming increase in the cost of living.

Now, on this particular afternoon in May the mistral was blowing mercilessly across the valley from over the snows of Pelvoux, and the cold and the dust had driven all of good Portal's customers indoors. The low-raftered room, decorated with strings of onions which hung from the ceiling together with a bunch or two of garlic, of basil and other pot-herbs, and perfumed also with the aroma of the *pot-au-feu* simmering in the kitchen, had acquired just that right atmosphere, cosy, warm, and odorous, beloved of every true man born in the Dauphiné. It was a memorable afternoon, remembered long afterwards and retold by the gossips of Sisteron and Laragne in all its dramatic details. But at this hour, nothing more dramatic had occurred than the arrival of a detachment of soldiers, under the command of an under-officer, who had come up from Orange, so they said, in order to fetch away the young men who were wanted for the army. They had demanded supper and shelter for the night.

Of course, soldiers, as soldiers, were very much disapproved of by those worthies of Sisteron who frequented Les Amandiers, more especially now when what they did was to fetch away the young men for cannon-fodder, to fight the English and prolong this awful war which caused food to be so dear and hands for harvesting so scarce. But, on the other hand, soldiers, as company, were welcome. They brought news of the outside world, most of it bad, it is true—nothing good did happen anywhere these days—but news nevertheless. And though at the recital of what went on in Paris, in Lyons, or even as near as Orange, the guillotine, the tumbrils, the wholesale slaughter of tyrants and *aristos*, one shuddered with horror and apprehension, there were always the lively tales of barrack-life to follow, the laughter, the ribald song, and something of life seemed to infiltrate into this sleepy half-dead corner of the old Dauphiné.

The soldiers—there were a score of them—occupied the best place in the room, as was only fitting; they sat squeezed tightly against one another like dried figs in a box, on the two benches on either side of the centre trestle table. Old Baptiste Portal sat with them, beside the officer. Some kind of lieutenant this man appeared to be, or other subaltern: but, oh dear me! these days one could hardly tell an officer from the rag-tag and bob-tail of the army, save for the fact that he wore epaulettes. Now this man—but there! What was the use of comparing these ruffians with the splendid officers of the king's armies in the past?

This one certainly was not proud. He sat with his men, joked, drank with them, and presently he convened friend Portal to a glass of wine: "À *la santé!*" he added, "*de la République*, and of Citizen Robespierre, the great and incorruptible master of France!"

Baptiste, wagging his old head, had not liked to refuse, because soldiers were soldiers and these had been at great pains to explain to him that the reason why the guillotine was kept so busy was because Frenchmen had not yet learned to be good Republicans.

"We've cut off the head of Louis Capet and of the widow Capet, too," the officer had added with grim significance, "but there are still Frenchmen who are bad patriots and hanker after the return of the tyrants."

Now Baptiste, like all his like in the Dauphiné, had learned in childhood to worship God and honour the king. The crime of regicide appeared to him unforgiveable, like that mysterious sin against the Holy Ghost which M. le Curé used vaguely to hint at, and which no one understood. In addition to that, Baptiste greatly resented His Late Majesty King Louis XVI and his august queen being irreverently referred to as Louis Capet and the widow Capet. But he kept his own counsel and silently drank his wine. What his thoughts were at the moment was nobody's business.

After that, talk drifted to the neighbourhood: the *aristos* who still clung to the land which by right belonged to the people. Neither Baptiste nor his customers—old peasants from the district—were a match for the lieutenant and his corporals in such discussions. They did not dare argue, only shook their heads and sighed at the coarse jests which the soldiers uttered against people and families whom everyone in the Dauphiné knew and esteemed.

The Frontenacs, for instance.

The talk and the jests had turned on the Frontenacs: people who had owned the land for as long as the oldest inhabitant could remember and God only knows how long before that. Well! it appeared that in the eyes of the Republic the Frontenacs were bad patriots, tyrants and traitors. Didn't Citizen Portal know that?

No! Portal did not—he had never been called "citizen" before, and didn't like it: he was just Baptiste to those who knew him, *quoi?*—nor would he admit that the Frontenacs were traitors. There was *Monsieur*, who knew more about cattle and almonds than any man for leagues around. How could he be a bad patriot? And *Madame*, who was very good and pious, and *Mademoiselle* who was so ill and delicate. But on this there followed an altercation—stern rebuke of Baptiste from the officer for talking of "*Monsieur*", of "*Madame*" and "*Mademoiselle*". Bah! there were no *aristos* left in these days.

"Aren't we all citizens of France?" the lieutenant concluded grandiloquently.

Silence and submission on the part of all the groundlings which followed the lieutenant's rebuke, somewhat mollified the latter's aggressive patriotism. He condescended to relate how he had been deputed to make a perquisition in the house of the Frontenacs, and if anything was found in the least compromising, then the devil help the whole brood: their lives would not be worth an hour's purchase. In fact, in the lieutenant's opinion—and who better qualified to hold one?—the Frontenacs were already judged, condemned, and as good as guillotined. He held with the "law of the suspect" lately enacted by the National Assembly, did Lieutenant Godet.

Again, much wagging of heads! "The Committees in all Sections," Godet now goes on airily, and proceeds to pick his teeth after that excellently stewed scrag-end of mutton, "the Committees in all Sections are ordered in future to arrest all persons who are suspect."

No one knows what is a Committee, nor yet a Section: but they are evidently fearsome things. But no matter about them: the thing is, who are the "suspect" who are thus arrestable?

"The Frontenacs are suspect," the lieutenant explains whilst sucking his tooth-pick, "and so are all persons who by their actions—or—their writings—have become—er—suspect."

Not very illuminating, perhaps, but distinctly productive of awe. The worthies of Sisteron, those who are privileged to sit close to the centre table and actually to put in a word with the soldiers, sip their wine in silence. Just below the tiny window at the end of the room, two charcoal-burners, or wood-cutters—I know not what they are—are lending an attentive ear. They dare not join in the conversation because they are comparative strangers, vagabonds really, come to pick up a few *sous* by doing menial work too lowering for a local peasant to do. One of them is small and slender, but looks vigorous; the other, much older, with stooping shoulders, and grey, lank hair that falls over a wrinkled forehead. He is harassed by a constant, tearing cough which he strives in vain to supress out of respect for the company.

"But," the worthy Portal puts in tentatively, "how does one know *Monsieur le*—I mean, citizen officer, that a person is in verity suspect?"

The lieutenant explains with a sweeping gesture of the tooth-pick: "If you are a good patriot, Citizen Portal, you are able to recognise a

14

Suspect in the street, you can seize him by the collar then and there, and you may drag him off before the Committee, who will promptly clap him in prison. And remember," he added significantly, "that there are forty-four thousand Committees in France today."

"Forty-four thousand?" somebody exclaims.

"And twenty-three," Godet replies, gloating over his knowledge of this trifling detail.

"Forty-four thousand and twenty-three," he reiterates, and claps the table with the palm of his hand.

"One in Sisteron?" someone murmurs.

"Three!" the lieutenant replies.

"And the Frontenacs are suspect, you say?"

"I shall know that tomorrow," rejoins the other, "and so will you."

The way he said those last three words caused everyone to shudder. Over at the far end of the room, the charcoal burner, or whatever he was, had a tearing fit of coughing.

"'Tis little Fluerette who will weep her eyes out," good old Baptiste said with a doleful shake of the head, "if anything happens to *Mad*—to the citizens up at the *château*."

"Fluerette?" the lieutenant asked.

"She is Armand's daughter—Citizen Armand you know—why?"

He might well stare, for the officer, for some unaccountable reason, had burst into a loud guffaw.

"Citizen Armand's daughter, did you say?" he queried at last, his eyes still streaming with the effort of laughing.

"Yes, of course. As pretty a wench as you can see in Dauphiné. Why shouldn't Armand have a daughter, I'd like to know."

"Do tigers have daughters?" the lieutenant retorted significantly.

Somehow the conversation languished after that. The fate which so obviously awaited the Frontenacs, who were known and loved, cast a gloom over the most buoyant spirits. Not even the salacious stories of barrack-life, on which the men now embarked with much gusto, found responsive laughter.

It was getting late, too. Past eight o'clock, and tallow was dear these days. There was a cart-shed at the back of the house, with plenty of clean straw: some of the soldiers declared themselves ready for a stretch there: even the voluble officer was yawning. The regular customers of Les Amandiers took the hint. They emptied their mugs, paid over their *sous*, and trooped out one by one.

The wind had gone down. There was not a cloud in the sky, which

15

was a deep, and intense sapphire blue, studded with stars. The waning moon was not yet up, and the atmosphere was redolent of the perfume of almond blossoms. Altogether a lovely night, Nature in her kindest, most gentle mood. Spring in the air and life stirring in the entrails of the earth in travail. Some of the soldiers made their way to the shed, whilst others stretched out on the floor, or the benches of the room, there to dream perhaps of the perquisition to be made tomorrow and of the tragedy which would enter like a sudden devastating gust of wind into the peaceful home of the Frontenacs.

Nature was kind and gentle: and men were cruel and evil and vengeful. The Law of the Suspect! No more cruel, more tyrannical law was ever enacted within the memory of civilization. Forty-four thousand and twenty-three committees to mow down the flower of the children of France. A harvest of innocents! And lest the harvesters prove slack, the National Convention has just decreed that a perambulating army shall march up and down the country, to ferret out the Suspect and feed the guillotine. Lest the harvesters prove slack, men like Lieutenant Godet with a score of out-at-elbows, down-at-heels brigands, are ordered to scour the country, to seize and strike. To feed the guillotine, in fact, and to purge the Soil of Liberty.

Is this not the most glorious revolution the world has ever known? Is it not the era of Liberty and of the Brotherhood of Man?

Chapter 2

The perambulating army had now gone to rest: some in the cart-shed, some along the benches and tables or floor of the inn. The lieutenant in a bed. Is he not the officer commanding this score of ardent patriots? Therefore, he must lie in a bed—old Portal's bed—whilst old Portal himself and his wife, older and more decrepit than he, can lie on the floor, or in the dog's kennel for aught Lieutenant Godet cares.

The two wood-cutters—or shall we call them charcoal-burners?—were among the last to leave. They had petitioned for work among the worthies here present: but money was very scarce these days, and each man did what work he could for himself and did not pay another to do it for him. But Papa Tronchet, who was a carpenter by trade and owned a little bit of woodland just by the bridge, close to Armand's cottage, he promised one of the men—not both—a couple of hours' work tomorrow: wood-cutting at the rate of two *sous* an hour, and then he thought it dear.

And so, the company had dispersed: each man to his home. The

16

two vagabonds—wood-cutters or charcoal-burners, they were any-how vagabonds—found their way into the town. Wearily they trudged, for one of them was very old and the other lame, till they reached a narrow lane at right angles to the riverbank. The lane was made up of stone houses that had overhanging eaves, between which the sun couldn't ever penetrate. It was invariably either as damp as the bottom of a well, or as dry and wind-swept as an iron stove-pipe. Tonight, it was dry and hot: broken-down shutters, innocent of paint, creaked upon rusty hinges. A smell of boiled cabbage, of stale water and garlic hung beneath the eaves; it came in great gusts down pitch-dark stair-ways, under narrow doors, oozing with sticky moisture.

The two vagabonds turned into one of these doors and by in-stinct seemingly, for it was pitch dark, they mounted the stone stairs that squelched with grease and dirt underneath their feet. They did not speak a word until they came to the top of the house, when one of them with a kick of his boot threw open a door; it groaned and creaked under the blow. It gave on an attic-room with sloping ceiling, black with the dirt of ages, and with dormer window masked by a tat-tered rag that had once been a curtain. There was a wooden table in the centre of the room, and three chairs, with broken backs and ragged rush-seats, dotted about. On the table a couple of tallow candles gut-tered in pewter sconces.

One of the chairs was drawn close up to the table and on it sat a young man dressed in a well-worn travelling-coat with heavy boots on his feet, and a shabby tricorn hat on the top of his head. His arms were stretched out over the table and his face was buried in them. He had obviously been asleep when the door was so unceremoniously thrown open. At the sound he raised his head and blinked drowsily in the dim light at the newcomers.

Then he stretched out his arms, yawned, and gave himself a shake like a sleepy dog, and finally exclaimed in English! "Ah! At last!"

One of the vagabonds—the one namely who at Les Amandiers had appeared with bent shoulders and a hacking cough, now straight-ened out what proved to be a magnificent athletic figure and gave a pleasant laugh.

"Tony, you lazy dog!" he said, "I've a mind to throw you down-stairs. What say you, Ffoulkes? While you and I have been breaking our backs and poisoning our lungs with the scent of garlic, I verily believe that this villain Tony has been fast asleep."

"By all means, let's throw him downstairs," assented the second vagabond, now no longer lame, whom his friend had addressed as Ffoulkes.

"What would you have me do but sleep?" Tony broke in with a laugh. "I was told to wait, and so I waited. I'd far rather have been with you."

"No, you wouldn't," Ffoulkes demurred, "for then you would have been dirtier than I, and almost as filthy as Blakeney. Look at him; did you ever see such a disgusting object?"

"By Gad!" rejoined Blakeney, surveying his own slender hands coated with coal-dust, grease and grime. "I don't know when I have been quite so dirty. Soap and water!" he commanded with a lofty gesture, "or I perish."

But Tony gave a rueful shrug.

"I have a bit of soap in my pocket," he said, and diving into the capacious pocket of his coat he produced an infinitesimal remnant of soap which he threw upon the table. "As for water, I can't offer you any. The only tap in the house is in the back kitchen which *Madame*, our worthy landlady, has locked up for the night. She won't have any-thing wasted, she tells me, not even water."

"Fine, thrifty people, your Dauphinois," commented Blakeney, wisely shaking his head. "But did you try bribery?"

"Yes! But *Madame*—I beg your pardon, Citizeness Marlot—im-mediately called me a cursed *aristo*, and threatened me with some committee or other. I couldn't argue with her, she reeked of garlic."

"And you, Tony, are an arrant coward," Blakeney rejoined, "where garlic is concerned."

"I am," Tony was willing to admit. "That's why I am so terrified of you both at this moment."

They all laughed, and since water was not obtainable, Sir Percy Blakeney, one of the most exquisite dandies of his time, and his friend Sir Andrew Ffoulkes, sat down on rickety chairs, in clothes sticky with dirt, their faces and hands masked by a thick coating of grime. Down the four walls of the small attic-room fillets of greasy moistures trick-led and mingled with the filth that lay in cakes upon the floor.

"I can't bear to look at Tony," Blakeney said with a mock sigh, "he is too demned clean."

"We'll soon remedy that," was Ffoulkes' dry comment.

And behold Sir Andrew Ffoulkes at close grips with Lord Antony Dewhurst, and this in silence for fear of disturbing the rest of the house and bringing attention on themselves. It was a sparring match in the best style, Blakeney acting as referee, its object—to transfer some of the grime that coated the clothes and hands of Sir Andrew on to the immaculate Lord Tony. They were only boys after all, these men, who even now were risking their lives in order to rescue the innocent from the clutches of a bloody tyranny. They were boys in their love of adventure, and in their hero worship, and men in the light-hearted way in which they were prepared for the supreme sacrifice, should luck turn against them.

The sparring match ended in a call for mercy on the part of Lord Tony. His face was plastered with grime, his hands as dirty as those of his friends.

"Tony," Blakeney said finally, when he called a halt, "if her ladyship were to see you now, she would divorce you."

Vent having been given to unconquerable animal spirits, there was a quick return to the serious business of the day.

"What is the latest?" Lord Tony asked.

"Just this," Sir Percy replied: "That these hell-hounds have sent out detachments of soldiers all over the country to ferret out what they are pleased to call treason. We all know what that means. Since their iniquitous "Law of the Suspect", no man, woman, or child is safe from denunciation: now with this perambulating army, summary arrests occur by the thousand. It seems that at any moment any of those brigands can seize you by the coat-collar and drag your before one of their precious committees, who promptly sends you to the nearest guillotine."

"And you came from a detachment of those brigands, I suppose."

"We have; Ffoulkes and I spent a couple of hours in their company, in the midst of fumes of garlic that would have reduced you, Tony, to a drivelling coward. I vow the smell of it has even infested my hair."

"Anything to be done?" Tony asked simply. He knew his chief well enough to perceive the vein of grim earnestness through all this flippancy.

"Yes!" Blakeney replied. "The squad of brigands who are scouring this part of France are principally after a family named Frontenac, which consists of father, mother and an invalid daughter. I had already found out something about them in the course of the day, whilst I carted some manure for a farmer close by. Beastly stuff, manure, by the way! I tried to get into touch with *Monsieur*, who is a stubborn optimist, and does not believe that any man could mean harm to him or to his family. I went to him in the guise of a royalist agent, supposed

19

to have inside information of impending arrests. He simply refused to believe me. Well! we've met that type of man before. He will have a terrible awakening tomorrow."

Sir Percy paused for a moment or two, a deep frown between his brows. His keen intellect, alive to all those swift tragedies which he had devoted his life to countermine, was already at work envisaging the immediate future, the personages of the coming drama, husband, wife, invalid daughter; then the perquisition, the arrest, summary condemnation and slaughter of three helpless innocents.

"I can't help being sorry for the man," he said after a while, "though he is an obstinate fool! but it is the wife and daughter whom we cannot allow those savage beats to capture and to kill. I caught sight of them. The girl is pathetic, frail and crippled. I couldn't bear—"

He broke off abruptly. No need to say more, of course; they understood one another, these men who had braved death so often together for love of humanity and for love of sport. Blakeney silent, one firm, slender hand clutched upon the table, was working out a problem of how to rescue three helpless people from that certain death-trap which was already laid for them. The other two waited in equal silence for orders. The League of the Scarlet Pimpernel! pledged to help the innocent and to save the helpless! One to command, nineteen to obey: the two who were here, in this filthy, dark attic-room, were the chief's most trusted officers; but the others were not far away!

Seventeen others! scattered about the countryside, disguised, doing menial work in order to keep in touch with the population, spying, hiding in woods or huts: all of them under orders from their chief, and prepared for the call from him.

"Tony," Blakeney said at last, "you'd better find Hastings and Stowmaries at once and they must pass the word round to others. I want three of them—they can draw lots for that—to go to the Four Oaks and there to remain until I can send Ffoulkes to them with full instructions. When you've done that, I want you and Ffoulkes to spend the night in and about Les Amandiers and gather what you can of the projects of these brigands by keeping your ears open. I'll keep in touch with you from time to time."

"You think," Ffoulkes put in, "that we'll have trouble with the Frontenacs?"

"Not with the ladies, of course," Blakeney replied. "We'll get them safely out of the way before the perambulating army of jackals arrives. With God's help we ought to have enough time to gather a few valuables together. The problem will be with that obstinate, tiresome man. I feel sure he won't move until the soldiers are hammering at his door. Anyway, I shall know my way in and about the *château* by tomorrow morning and will then get into touch with you both at Les Amandiers."

He rose: a tall, straight figure on whom the filthy clothes of a vagabond sat with strange incongruity. But even in this strange garb which was grotesque as well as degrading, there was an extraordinary dignity in the carriage of the head, the broad shoulders, the firm, long Anglo-Saxon limbs, but above all in the flash of the eyes beneath their heavy lids and in the quiet, low-toned voice so obviously accustomed to be heard and obeyed. The two others were ready on the instant to act according to instructions: to act without argument or question. The fire of excitement was in their eyes: the spirit of adventure, of sport for sport's sake, had them in its grip.

"Do I go with you now, Blakeney?" Ffoulkes asked, as his chief had remained for a moment standing, as if following a train of thought.

"Yes," Blakeney replied. "And by the way, Ffoulkes, and you too, Tony, while you are at Les Amandiers try and find out about this girl Fleurette the old innkeeper spoke about. He said that the girl would cry her eyes out if anything happen to the Frontenacs. You remember?"

"I do. He also said that she was as pretty a wench as could be found in the Dauphiné," Ffoulkes put in with a smile.

"Her father is named Armand," Blakeney rejoined.

"And the lieutenant called him a tiger, rather enigmatically I thought."

"This Fleurette sounds like an engaging young person," Lord Tony commented with a smile.

"And should be useful in our adventure," Blakeney concluded. "Find out what you can about her."

He was the last to leave the room. Ffoulkes and Lord Tony had already gone down the stone staircase, feeling their way through the darkness. But Sir Percy Blakeney stood a minute or two longer, erect, silent, motionless. Not Sir Percy Blakeney, that is, the elegant courtier, the fastidious fop, the spoilt child of London society, but the daring adventurer, ready now as so often before, to throw his life into the balance to save three innocent people from death. Would he succeed? Nay! that he did not for a moment doubt. Not for a moment. He would save the Frontenacs as he had saved scores of helpless men, women and children before, or leave his bones to moulder in this fair land where his name had become anathema to the tigers that fed on the blood of their kindred. The true adventurer! Reckless of risks and dangers, with only the one goal in view: Success.

Sport? Of course, it was sport! grand, glorious, maddening sport! Sport that made him forget every other joy in life, every comfort, every beatitude. Everything except the exquisite wife who in far-off England waited patiently, with deadly anxiety gnawing at her heart, for news of the man she worshipped. She, perhaps, the greatest heroine of them all.

With a quick sigh, half of impatience, half of longing, Sir Percy Blakeney finally blew out the tallow-lights and made his way out into the open.

Chapter 3

The house where Fleurette was born and where she spent the first eighteen years of her life, still stands about halfway down the road between Sisteron and Serres and close to Laragne, which was then only a village nestling in the valley of the Buëche. To get to it you must first go cautiously down the slope at the head of the old stone bridge, and then climb up another slope to the front door beside the turbulent little mill stream, the soft gurgle of which had lulled Fluerette to sleep ever since her tiny ears had wakened to earthly sounds.

The house is a tumble-down ruin now, only partly roofed in: doors and shutters are half off their hinges: the outside staircase is worm-eaten and unsafe, the white-washed walls are cracked and denuded of plaster; the little shrine above the door has long been bereft of its quaint, rudely painted statue of St. Anthony of Padua with the Divine Child in his arms. But the wild vine still clings to the old walls, and in the gnarled branches of the old walnut tree, a venturesome pair of blackbirds will sometimes build their nest.

A certain atmosphere of mystery and romance still lingers in the tiny dell, and when we fly along the road in our twentieth-century motorcar, we are conscious of this romantic feeling, and we exclaim: "Oh! how picturesque!" and ask the chauffeur to halt upon the bridge, and then get our Kodaks to work.

Perhaps when the plate is developed and we look upon the print, we fail to recapture that sense of a picturesque by-gone age and wonder why we wasted a precious film on what is nothing but a tumble-down old cottage, and why so many tumble-down old cottages are left to crumble away and disfigure the lovely face of France. But a century and a half ago, when Fluerette was born, there was an almond tree beside the front door, which in the early spring looked as if covered with pink snow. In those days the shutters and the doors and the outside staircase were painted a beautiful green, the walls were resplendent with fresh white-wash every year. In those days too, the wild vine turned to a brilliant crimson in the autumn, and in June the climbing rose was just a mass of bloom. Then in May the nightingale often sang in the old walnut-tree, and later on, when Fluerette was tall enough, she always kept a bunch of forget-me-nots in a glass, in the recess above the front door, at the foot of St. Antoine de Padoue, because, as is well known, he is the saint to appeal to in case one has lost anything one values. One just made the sign of the cross and said fervently "*St. Antoine de Padoue priez pour nous!*" and lo! the kindly saint would aid in the search, and more often than not the lost treasure would be found.

All this was, of course, anterior to the horrible events which in a few days transformed the genial, kindly people of France into a herd of wild beats thirsting for each other's blood, and before legalized cruelty, murder and regicide had arraigned that fair land at the bar of history and tarnished her fair fame forever. Fluerette was just eighteen when the terrible events came to pass that threatened to wreck her young life, and through which she learned not only how cruel and evil man could be, but also to what height of self-abnegation and heroism they could at times ascend.

Fluerette's birthday was in May, and that day was always for her the gladdest day of the year. For one thing she could reckon on Bibi being home—Bibi being the name by which she had called her father ever since she had learned to babble. Fleurette had no mother, and she and Bibi just worshipped each other. And of course, Bibi had come home for her eighteenth birthday, and had stayed three whole days, and he had brought her a lovely shawl, one that was so soft and fleecy that when you rubbed your cheek against it, it felt just like a caress from a butterfly's wing.

Old Louise—who had looked after the house and watched over Fluerette ever since Fluerette's mother had gone up to heaven to be with the *bon Dieu* and all the Saints—old Louise had cooked a delicious dinner, which was a very difficult thing to do these days when food was scarce and dear, and eggs, butter and sugar only for the very rich who could bribe M'sieu' Colombe, the *épicier* of the Rue Haute, to let them have what they wanted. But no matter! Old Louise was a veritable genius where a dinner was concerned, and M'sieu' Colombe, the grocer, and M'sieu' Duflos the butcher, had allowed her to have all she asked for: a luscious piece of meat, three eggs, a piece of butter, and this without any extra bribe. Then there were still half a dozen bottles of that excellent red wine which Bibi had bought in the happy olden days; and he had opened one of the bottles, and Fluerette had drunk some wine and felt very elated and altogether happy—but for this there was another reason of which more *anon*.

Of course, the latter part of the day had been tinged with sadness, again for that one reason which will appear presently: but not only because of that, but because of Bibi's departure, which it seems, could not be postponed, although Fluerette begged and begged that he should remain at least until tomorrow so as not to spoil this most perfect day. *Le bon Dieu* alone knew when Fluerette would see Bibi again, his absences from home had of late become more frequent and more prolonged.

Mais voilà! on one's eighteenth birthday one is not going to think of troubles until the very last minute when it is actually on the doorstep. And the day had been entirely glorious. Not a cloud: the sky of such a vivid blue that the forget-me-nots that grew in such profusion beside the stream looked pale and colourless beneath it. The crimson peonies behind the house were in full bloom, and the buds of the climbing rose on the point of bursting.

And now dinner was over. Louise was busy in the kitchen washing up the plates and dishes, and Fluerette was carefully putting away the beautiful silver forks and spoons which had been brought out for the occasion. She was putting them away in the fine leather case with the molleton lining, which set off the glistening silver to perfection, and little Fluerette felt happy and very contented. She worked away in silence because Bibi had leaned his darling old head against the back of his chair and closed his eyes. Fluerette thought he had dropped off to sleep.

He looked thin and pale, the poor dear, and there were lines of anxiety and discontent around his thin lips: his hair too had of late been plentifully sprinkled with grey. Oh! how Fluerette longed to have him here at Lou Mas. Always and always. It was the only home she had ever known; dear, beautiful, fragrant Lou Mas. Here she would tend him and care for him until all those lines of care upon his face had vanished. And what more likely to bring a smile to his lips than dear old Lou Mas with its white-washed walls and red-tiled roofs, with its green shutters and little mill streams beside which, for nine months of the year, flowers grew in such profusion; violets, forget-me-nots, and lilies of the valley in the spring, and meadowsweet throughout the summer until an early frost cut them down?

As for this room, Fluerette knew that there could not be in the whole of France, anything more beautiful or more cosy. There was the beautiful walnut side-board, polished until it shone like a mirror, there were the chairs covered in crimson rap, rather faded it is true, but none the worse for that, and there was Bibi's special armchair adorned with that strip of tapestry which Fluerette had worked in cross-stitch, expressly for his birthday the year of her first communion. Never had there been such chairs anywhere. And that beautiful paper on the walls, the red and yellow roses that looked as if you could pick them off their lovely chocolate-coloured ground, and the chandelier with the crystal drops, and the blue vases with the gold handles that adorned the mantelpiece, not to mention the print curtains and the pink and blue check cloth upon the table. Oh, Fluerette loved all these things, they had been the playthings of her childhood and now they were her pride. If only Bibi would smile again, she felt that the whole world would be like heaven.

And then all at once everything went wrong. Fluerette had got her beautiful new shawl out of its wrappings and draped it round her shoulders and rubbed her cheek against it. Then she had said quite innocently: "It is so lovely, Bibi, and the wool is so soft and fine. I am sure that it came from England."

And it was from that moment that everything went wrong. To begin with, and quite by accident, of course, Bibi broke the stem of the glass out of which he had been drinking, and a quantity of very precious wine was spilt over the beautiful tablecloth.

Whereupon, unaccountably, because of course the table cloth could be washed, Bibi pushed his plate aside quite roughly and suddenly looked ten years older; so wan and pale and shrivelled and old. Fluerette longed to put her arms round him—as she used to do in the happy olden days—and ask him to tell her what was amiss. She was grown up now—eighteen years old today—quite old enough to understand. And if Bibi loved her as she thought he did, he would be comforted.

But there it was! There was something in the expression on Bibi's face that checked Fluerette's impulse. She went on quietly—very quietly, like a little mouse—with her work, and for a while there was silence in the cosy room with the beautiful roses on the wall that looked as if you could pick them off their chocolate ground: a silence that was unaccountably full of sadness.

Chapter 4

Bibi was the first to hear the sound of footsteps coming up to the door. He gave a start, just as if he were waking from a dream.

"It's M'sieu' Colombe," Fluerette said.

At once Bibi reproved her, a thing he hardly ever did: "Citizen Colombe," he said sternly.

Fluerette shrugged her plump shoulders: "Ah well—!" she exclaimed.

"You must learn, Fluerette," Bibi insisted, still with unwonted severity. "You are old enough to learn."

She said nothing more; only kissed the top of his head, the smooth brown hair, of late so plentifully tinged with grey, and promised that she would learn. She stood by the sideboard intent on putting the silver away, with her back turned to Bibi so that he could not see the soft tone of pink that had crept into her cheeks, as soon as she perceived that two pairs of feet were treading the path outside the door.

Now there was a vigorous knock against the door, and a cheery, raucous voice called out loudly: "May one enter?"

Fluerette ran to the door and opened it.

"But certainly, certainly," she said, and then added, seemingly very astonished: "Ah! and M'sieu' Amédé, too?" From which the casual observer would perhaps infer that the pink colour in her cheeks had been due to the arrival of M'sieu' Colombe, the *épicier* of the Rue Haute, rather than to that of his son Amédé. It was no doubt also that worthy *épicier* with his round, florid face, dark, twinkling eyes, and general air of ferocious kindliness that caused the pink colour to spread from Fluerette's cheeks down to her neck and the little bit of throat that peeped out above her kerchief.

The good Colombe had already stalked into the room and with a familiar "*Eh bien! Eh bien!* We did contrive to come and drink Fluerette's health after all?" had slapped Bibi vigorously over the lean shoulders. But Amédé had come to a halt on the mat in which he was mechanically wiping his boots as if his very life depended on their cleanliness. Between his fingers he was twirling an immense posy of bright pink peonies, but his eyes were fixed on Fluerette, and on his broad, plain face, which shone with perspiration and good temper, there was a half-shy, wholly adoring look.

He gulped hard once or twice before he murmured, hoarse with emotion:

"Mam'zelle Fluerette!"

And Fluerette wiped her hot little hand against her apron before she whispered in shy response:

"M'sieu' Amédé!"

Not for these two the new-fangled "*citoyen*" and "*citoyenne*" decreed in far-off Paris. To their unsophisticated ears the clamour of a trumpet-tongued revolution only came as an unreal and distant echo.

Amédé appeared to have finished cleaning his boots, and Fluerette was able to close the door behind him before she held out her hand for the flowers which he was too bewildered to offer.

"Are those beautiful flowers for me, M'sieu' Amédé?" she asked.

"If you will deign to accept them, Mam'zelle Fluerette?" he replied.

She was eighteen and he was just twenty. Neither of them had ever been away more than a few hours from their remote little village of Dauphiné where they were born—she in the little house with the green shutters, and he in the Rue Haute above the shop where his father, Hector Colombe, had sold tallow-candles and sugar, flour and salt, and lard and eggs to the neighbours, ever since he had been old enough to help *his* father in the business. And when Amédé was four, and Fluerette two, they had made mud pies together in the village street with water from the fountain, and Amédé had warded Fluerette against the many powerful enemies that sometimes threatened her and caused her to scream with terror, such as M'sieu' Duflos, the butcher's, dog, or Achille the *garde-champêtre* with his ferocious scowl, or Ma'ame Amélie's geese.

They had sat together—not side by side, you understand, but the boys on the right side of the room and the girls on the left—in the little class-room where *M. le Curé* taught them their alphabet and subsequently the catechism; and also, that two and two make four. They had knelt side by side in the little primitive church at Laragne, their little souls overburdened with emotion and religious fervour, when they made their first communion: Fluerette in a beautiful white dress, with a wealth of white roses on her fair hair, and a long tulle veil that descended right down to her feet; and Amédé in an exquisite cloth coat with brass buttons, a silk waistcoat, buckled shoes and a white ribbon sash on his left arm.

27

And when Amédé had been old enough to be entrusted with his father's errands over at Serres, a couple of leagues away, Fluerette had climbed behind him on the saddle, and with her arms round his waist, so as to keep herself steady, they had ridden together along the winding road white with dust, Ginette, the good old mare, ambling very leisurely as if she knew that her riders were in no hurry to get anywhere that day.

And now Fluerette was eighteen and Amédé twenty, and her hair was like ripe corn, and her eyes as blue as the sky on a midsummer morn, whilst her mouth was dewy and fragrant as a rose in June. No wonder that poor Amédé felt as if his feet were of lead and his neck too big for his cravat, and when presently she asked him to fill a vase with water out of the carafe so that she could place the beautiful flowers in it, is it a wonder that he spilt the water all over the floor, seeing that his clumsy hands met her dainty fingers around the neck of the carafe?

The good Hector pretended to be very angry with his son for his clumsiness.

"*Voyez-moi cet imbécile!*" he said in that gruff voice of his which had become a habit with him, because he had to use it all day in order to ward off the naughty village urchins who tried to steal the apples out of his shop.

"Mam'zelle Fluerette, why don't you box his ears?"

Which, of course, was a very funny proposition that caused Fleurette and Amédé to laugh immoderately first and then to whisper and to chaff whilst they mopped the water off the tiled floor. And the good Hector turned once more to Bibi, and shaking his powerful first at nothing in particular, he brought it down with a crash upon the table.

"And now those *gredins*, those limbs of Satan are taking him away for cannon-fodder! Ah! the devils! the pigs! the pig-devils!"

Bibi looked up inquiringly.

"Taking him away, are they?" he asked dryly. Then he added with an indifferent shrug of the shoulders: "Amédé is twenty, isn't he?"

"What's that to do with their dragging him away from me, when I want him to help in the shop?" Hector retorted with what he felt was unanswerable logic.

"What would be the good of keeping shop, my good Hector," Bibi rejoined simply, "if France was invaded by foreigners as she is already ruined by traitors?"

"Well! And isn't she ruined now by all those devils up in Paris who can think of nothing better than war or murder?" growled Hector Colombe, heedless of the quick gesture of warning which Bibi had given him.

Adèle, the girl from the village who gave old Louise a hand about the house when Bibi was at home, had just come in from the kitchen with a pile of plates and dishes which she proceeded to range upon the dresser. Hector shrugged his big shoulders. Whoever would think of taking notice of Adèle? A wench who got five *sous* a day for scrubbing floors! An undersized, plain-faced creature with flat feet and red elbows. Bah!

But Bibi still put up a warning finger:

"Little pitchers have long ears," he said in a whisper.

"Oh! I know, I know," Hector rejoined gruffly. "It is the fashion these days for us all to spy upon one another. A pretty pass they have brought us to," he added, "your friends in Paris."

To this Bibi made no reply. No doubt he knew that it was impossible to argue with Hector, once the worthy *épicier* was in one of his moods. Adèle had finished her task and glided out of the room, silent, noiseless, furtive as a little rat, which she vaguely resembled with small, keen eyes, and pointed nose and chin. In a corner of the room, by the window, still busy with those flowers which seemingly would not set primly in the vase, Fluerette and Amédé were talking under their breath.

"I'm going away, Mam'zelle Fluerette," said he.

"Going away, M'sieu' Amédé? Whither? When?"

"They want me in the army."

"What for?" she asked naively.

"To fight against the English."

"But you won't go, will you, M'sieu' Amédé?"

"I must, Mam'zelle Fluerette."

"Oh, but what shall I—I mean, what will M'sieu' Colombe do? You must remain here, to help him in the shop." And fight against it as she would, there was an uncomfortable little lump in her throat when she pictured how terribly lost M'sieu' Colombe would be without his son.

"Father is very angry," Amédé said rather hoarsely, because he too had an uncomfortable lump in his throat now. "But it seems there's nothing to be done. I have to go."

"When?" Fluerette murmured, so softly, so softly, that only a lover's

29

ears could possibly have caught the whisper.

"I have to present myself tomorrow," Amédé replied, "before *M'sieu' le Commissaire de Police* at Serres."

"Tomorrow? And I have been so happy today!"

The cry came from an overburdened little heart, brought face to face with its first sorrow. Fluerette no longer attempted to keep back her tears, and Amédé, not quite sure whether he should cry because he was going away or dance with joy because it was his going away that was making Fluerette cry, but in time by wiping his face which was streaming with perspiration and tears.

"I wish I could at least have seen those children wedded," the worthy *épicier* muttered in the interval of blowing his nose with a noise like a cloudburst. "At least," he added with the good round oath which he reserved for occasions such as these, "before they take my Amédé away."

Bibi on the other hand appeared to be more philosophical.

"We must wait for better times," he said, "and anyhow Fluerette is too young to marry."

Chapter 5

Parting is not such sweet sorrow as the greatest of all poets would have us believe. At any rate Fleurette did not find it at all sweet, on this her eighteenth birthday, which should have been a very happy one.

It was bad enough saying *"adieu"* to Bibi. But Fleurette was accustomed to that. Of late Bibi had been so often and so long absent from home: sometimes weeks—nay! months—would elapse, and there would be no Bibi to fondle Fleurette and bring life and animation within those white-washed walls that held all that was dearest to her in the world. It was undoubtedly heart-rending to bid Bibi *adieu*: but in a way, one knew that the darling would come back to Lou Mas as soon as he was able, come for one of those surprise visits that made Fleurette as gay as a linnet all the while they lasted. But to say goodbye to Amédé was a different matter. He was going into the army. He was going to fight the English. *Le Bon Dieu* alone knew if Amédé would ever come back. Perhaps he would be killed. Perhaps—oh! perhaps—

Never in her life had Fleurette been so sad.

And now the last of the goodbyes had been said. Bibi, accompanied by M'sieu' Colombe and Amédé, had walked away in the direction of the village, where he would pick up his horse, and start along the main road that led to Serres and thence to Paris.

Fleurette remained on the bridge for some time, shading her eyes against the sun, because they ached so from all the tears which she had shed. The three men had become mere specks, 'way down the road: old Louise had gone back to her kitchen with Adèle, only Fleurette remained standing on the bridge alone. Tears were still running down her cheeks, whilst with aching eyes she strove to catch a last sight of Bibi as he and his two companions disappeared round the bend of the road. Or was it Amédé she was trying to see?

The afternoon sun had spread a mantle of gold over the snowy crests of Pelvoux: on the sapphire sky myriads of tiny clouds seemed to hold hearts of living flame in their fleecy bosoms. The wavy ribbon of the Buëche was like a giant mirror that reflected a whole gamut of glowing tints, blue and gold, and purple, whilst on the winding road, the infinitesimal atoms of dust seemed like low-lying clouds of powdered topaz. Suddenly in the direction of Sisteron those clouds rose, more dense: something more solid than powdered topaz, animated the distance: grew gradually more tangible and then became definite. Fleurette now could easily distinguish ten or a dozen men coming this way. They all wore red caps on their heads. Ahead of them came a man on horseback. He wore a tricorn hat, adorned with a tricolour cockade, and the sun drew sparks of flame from the steel bit in his horse's mouth and from the brass bosses and buckles on the harness.

Now Fleurette could hear the dull stamping of hoofs on the dusty road, and the tramping of heavy, weary footsteps: and she watched, fascinated, these men coming along.

All at once the rider put his horse to a trot, and the next moment he reined in on the bridge. He put out his hand and cried a sharp: "*Halte!*" whereupon the other men all came to a halt. Fleurette stood there wondering what all this meant. Vaguely she guessed that these men must be soldiers, though, of a truth, with the exception of the one on horseback and who appeared to be their officer, there was very little that was soldierly about them. Their red caps were of worsted and adorned with what had once been a tricolour cockade but was now so covered with dust that the colours were well-nigh indistinguishable. The men's coats, too, once blue in colour and fitted with brass buttons, were torn and faded, with several buttons missing: their breeches were stained with mud, they had no stocking inside their shoes, and it would have been impossible to say definitely whether their shirts had been of a drabby grey when they were new, or whether they had become so under stress of wear and dirt. Fleurette's recollection flew back to the smart soldiers she used to see when she was a tiny tot and Bibi took her to Serres or Sisteron on fête days when the military band would march past in their beautiful clothes all glittering with brass buttons, and their boots polished up so that you could almost see yourself in them.

But there! everyone knew that these were terribly hard times and that new clothes were very, very dear: So Fleurette supposed that the poor soldiers had to wear out their old ones just like everybody else. And her sensitive little heart gave an extra throb or two, for she had suddenly remembered that M'sieu' Amédé would also be a soldier very soon, wearing a shabby coat, and perhaps no stockings inside his shoes. Still thinking of M'sieu' Amédé, she was very polite to the man on horseback, although he was unnecessarily abrupt with her, asking her gruffly whether Citizen Armand was within.

Fleurette said "No!" quite gently, and then, choosing to ignore the coarse manner in which the man uttered a very ugly oath, she went on: "Father has been gone a quarter of an hour and more, and if you—"

"Citizen Armand, I asked for," the officer broke in roughly, "not our father."

"Father's name is Armand," Fleurette said, still speaking very politely. "I thought you were asking for him."

The horseman, she thought, realising his mistake, should have excused himself for speaking so rudely: but he did nothing of the sort. He just shrugged his soldiers and said in a very curious way, which sounded almost like a sneer:

"Oh! is that how it is? You are Citizen Armand's daughter, are you?"

"Yes! *M'sieu' l'officier.*"

"Call me citizen lieutenant," the man retorted roughly. "Hasn't your father taught you to speak like a good patriot?"

Fleurette would not have admitted for the world that she was half-afraid of this unkempt, unshaved officer with the gruff voice, but she felt intimidated, shy, ill at ease. She would have given worlds to have someone friendly beside her, old Louise, or even Adèle.

"Shall I call Ma'ame Louise," she suggested, "to speak with her?"

"No," the man replied curtly, "what's the use if your father isn't there? Which way did he go?"

"To the village first, M'sieu'—I mean citizen, to pick up his horse which he always leaves at M'sieu' Colombe's stables. He is going to Paris afterwards."

"How far is it to the village?"

"Less than a quarter of a league—er—citizen."

"And the house," the officer asked again, "where the *ci-devant* Frontenacs live, is that far?"

"About half a league by the road from here," Fleurette replied, "the other side of the village. There is a short cut behind this house, past the mill, but—"

The man, however, was no longer listening to what she said. He muttered something that sounded very like an oath, and then turned to the soldiers: "*Allons! Marche!*" he commanded sharply. The men appeared terribly dusty and tired and hardly made a movement to obey: at the first call of "*Halte*", some of them had thrown themselves down by the edge of the road and stretched out full length on the heaps of hard stones pile up there; others had wandered down the slope by the bridge, and lying flat on the ground were slaking their thirst in the cool, clear water of the stream. Fleurette was very sorry for them.

"May they wait a moment, *M'sieu' le*—I mean, citizen lieutenant," she pleaded. "I'll get them something to drink. We haven't much, but I know Louise won't—"

But the officer took no further notice either of her or of the men. Having given his order to march, he had readjusted the reins in his hands, and struck his spurs somewhat viciously into his horse's flanks. The horse reared and plunged for a moment, then started off at a sharp trot, clouds of dust flying out from under its hoofs.

The men made an effort to rise. Fleurette put up a finger and smiled at them all.

"Wait one minute," she said, and ran quickly back into the house.

There was the best part of a bottle left of that good red wine: Bibi had not touched it again after he broke the stem of his glass. Fleurette had picked up the bottle and taken a tin mug from the dresser and was about to start out again before Louise thought of asking her what she was up to.

"There are some poor, tired soldiers outside on the bridge," Fleurette replied, "I want to take them something to drink. There's not much of it, and twelve of them to share it, but it will be better than nothing, and perhaps *le bon Dieu* will make a miracle and make it be enough. They seemed so thirsty, poor dears."

"Let Adèle go," Louise said curtly. "I don't like you speaking with those vagabonds."

And while Adèle ran out, as she was bid, with mug and bottle,

Louise continued to mutter half under her breath:

"I can't abide these *sans-culottes*. Brigands the lot of them. What are they doing in the neighbourhood, I'd like to know. Up to no good you may depend. Let Adèle talk to them. It is not fit for a well-brought-up wench like you to be seen in such company."

Fleurette did not pay much attention to old Louise's mutterings. There was plenty to do in the house with washing up and tidying things away. And it was Louise's habit to grumble at anything that was in any way unusual: a wet day in August, or a mild one in December, a *calèche* on the road, a horseman, a soldier, or a letter for Bibi. She was always called "old Louise" although, in truth, she had scarce reached middle age; but her skin was dry and rough like the soil of her native Dauphiné, her face and hands were prematurely wrinkled, and her voice had become harsh of late, probably for want of use, like a piece of mechanism that has stood still and begun to grind for want of a lubricant. In Armand's house, when he was absent, she ruled supreme. Fleurette never dreamed of disobeying, and Armand's only peremptory orders to Louise were never to mention politics or current events to the child.

Louise had nursed Fleurette at her breast when Fleurette's mother died in child-bed, and she had left her own baby in the care of her sister, already a widow and childless. Considerations of money had prompted her at the time, for Monsieur Armand, as he was then, had made her liberal offers: afterwards, it was too late to regret. Her own daughter, Adèle, born of an unknown father who loved and rode away, had been brought up to a life of drudgery by her aunt, who sent the girl out to earn her own living as soon as she could toddle, whilst Fleurette was brought up to have everything she wanted; petted and idolised by a father plentifully supplied with money. Fleurette and Adèle were foster-sisters, but with destinies as wide apart as the peaks of Pelvoux.

But Louise never spoke one bitter word when she saw Adèle with toil-worn hands scrubbing the kitchen floor on which Fleurette trod with dainty, high-heeled shoes. Perhaps she loved her foster-child more than she did her own; perhaps it was only the same considerations of money that had already guided her conduct before, that prompted her later to indulgence towards the rich mans' daughter, whilst reserving her pent-up acrimony for the household drudge. No one knew what Louise's feelings were toward Adèle—Adèle herself least of all. The girl was silent, reserved, self-contained, very conscientious in her work, but not very responsive to the many kindnesses shown her by M'sieu' Armand or Mam'zelle Fleurette. She still lived with her aunt who had brought her up, and she appeared to lay no claim to her mother's affection: she had earned her own living ever since she was ten years of age, and now, at eighteen, she looked more like a woman than a girl: her little face was all pinched up, the lips thin, the eyes either sharp as needless or expressionless like those of a rodent. She hardly ever spoke and no one had ever seen her smile.

Old Louise's mutterings presently turned toward Adèle's prolonged absence:

"What is the girl about now, I should like to know? She is not a gossip as a rule."

She went on with her washing up for a moment or two longer, and then said sharply:

"Run along, Fleurette, and see what the wench is doing. Lazy baggage, with all the work there's still to do."

Fleurette ran out at once. She too wondered why Adèle was such a long time. And there, sure enough, standing on the bridge, was Adèle talking to the soldiers. The officer was already out of sight. Adèle talking! and Fleurette even thought that she heard her giggle. Incredible! The soldiers were all laughing, and one of them was in the act of drinking the last drop out of the tin mug.

Fleurette stood for a moment on the doorstep, vaguely wondering what in the world had come over Adèle, when a rather curious incident occurred: the soldiers were all laughing, jesting apparently with the girl, and one of them, with head tilted back, was draining the last drop out of the tin mug. Fleurette was on the point of calling to Adèle when her attention was arrested by the appearance of an old man carrying what looked like a load of faggots tied up in coarse sacking. He seemed to have climbed the slopes on the opposite side of the road; at any rate there he was, all of a sudden, immediately behind the group of soldiers.

He appeared to be drunk, for he staggered as he walked and leaned heavily on a stout gnarled stick. Fleurette could not have told you exactly how it all happened, but all of a sudden Adèle's giggling and the soldiers' jests were interrupted by the old faggot-carrier tumbling down clumsily, right between them all.

Adèle screamed. The soldiers swore, and one of them went to the length of giving the old man a savage kick, whilst two others incontinently picked him up between them and flung him over the parapet of the bridge. Fleurette gave a cry of dismay and ran to the poor man's assistance. She felt hot with indignation at such wanton brutality. How right, she thought as she ran, had old Louise's estimate been of these soldiers—little better than brigands they were, and cruel to boot. The poor faggot-carrier, for such he seemed to be, was lying half in and half out of the stream: the grass and sloping ground had somewhat broken his fall, but nevertheless there he lay, motionless and groaning piteously. Fleurette called peremptorily to Adèle to come and help her hoist up the poor man on his legs again. He was very dirty, dressed in nothing but rags, his feet swathed in coarse bass matting; he was stockingless, shirtless and hatless; but he appeared to be powerfully built and Fleurette marvelled how he could have allowed himself to be thus maltreated without a struggle. No doubt he was drunk or crippled with rheumatism.

Up on the bridge the soldiers were preparing to start once more on their way. They took no more notice of their unfortunate victim nor of Adèle; but Fleurette looking up felt that their last glance was for her; some of them were regarding her with a leer, others with more pronounced malevolence. She distinctly saw one man nudge his neighbour and point a finger at her: whereat both of them gave a mocking laugh.

She felt hurt and indignant: in her sheltered life she had never met with malevolence before. However, for the moment, her first care was for the poor faggot-carrier. Adèle had come to her assistance, and together the two girls succeeded in getting the old man on his legs again. He appeared more scared than hurt, and with his big, toil-stained hands, he felt himself all over to see, perhaps, if any bones were broken; and all the while he kept on murmuring rather pathetically: "*Nom de nom, de nom de Dieu!*" as if surprised that such a tragic adventure should have happened to him.

Fleurette asked him if he were hurt, and he replied: "No, *Mam'zelle*, that is citizeness," and he added: "Ah, I shall never get used to these new ways. I am too old."

"Can you get on your way now?" Fleurette asked.

"Yes! yes, *Mam'zelle*, that is citizeness. But," he went on piteously, "I am so hungry. I come from over Mison way and I have not had a bite since seven o'clock this morning."

This naturally stirred Fleurette's kind, compassionate heart. She told Adèle to run into the house and ask Louise for a hunk of bread. Adèle, silent and self-contained once more, obeyed without comment. The incident was closed as far as Fleurette was concerned. Her thoughts flew back to Amédé and to his last day and evening which he would be spending in his cosy home. She wished she had been bold enough to ask him to come and bid her a last *adieu* tomorrow morning before he went away to fight the English.

And while she stood there gazing out over the valley where the metal cross on the church steeple of Laragne glistened like gold in the sunlight, a strange voice—soft yet firm—suddenly struck her ear from somewhere close behind her.

"Papers and valuables are behind the panel in *Madame's* room."

She swung round terrified, so terrified that the cry she was about to utter died away in her throat. She looked about her, scared, shivering with that nameless dread which assails every mortal in face of the supernatural. And yet everything seemed as peaceful as before: the little mill stream splashed and gurgled with its soft, persistent sound; in the old walnut tree a thrush was calling to its mate and the old faggot-carrier was busy tying up his faggots into the sacking again.

Fleurette's eyes rested for an instant anxiously upon him. She expected to see him raise his head, to look about him, to appear scared as she was herself; but he gave no sign of having heard anything of that mysterious voice, fresh and compelling like a command from heaven. Oh no! Fleurette could not have screamed. She was too panic-stricken just at first to utter a sound. And yet nothing had really happened to alarm the most timorous. Only those few words spoken by an unseen tongue. What did they mean? What could they mean? They were simple and commonplace enough: Fleurette repeated them to herself mechanically:

"Papers and valuables are behind the panel in *Madame's* room."

What did it mean? What papers? what valuables? and why should the mysterious speaker have wished her to know that they were behind the panel in *Madame's* room? *Madame* was, of course, Madame de Frontenacs over at the *château*, and all of a sudden Fleurette remembered that the mounted soldier had asked her the way to the *château*. Gradually she was feeling less scared. Less scared but more excited. She looked round at the statue of St. Antoine, at whose feet she had this morning placed a fresh bunch of forget-me-nots. Somehow, she associated the mysterious voice with St. Antoine. Perhaps *Madame* had lost some valuable papers, and the kind saint had chosen this means of letting her know where her treasure was. Fleurette made the sign of the cross on her bosom; she remembered the story of Jeanne d'Arc which *M. le Curé* had used to tell her, of how the humble shepherdess of Domrémy had been compelled by heavenly voices to go forth and deliver France from her enemies and never rest until she had seen the king crowned in his cathedral of Rheims.

Fleurette felt something of that same fervour which had animated Jeanne d'Arc. She felt that she must go forth and tell *Madame* about the valuables and the papers. The evening was warm and she would not need her shawl. She could go just as she was as far as the *château* and be back before the twilight had faded into night. Adèle in the meanwhile appeared at the front door, she had her shawl over her head, and a hunk of bread in her hand. Then only did Fleurette remember the old faggot-carrier. She turned in order to bid him "Godspeed." He stood there quite motionless, leaning upon his stick, bending under the weight of his load of faggots which he had hoisted upon his back. His lank hair hung over his wrinkled forehead and half concealed his eyes. But suddenly through the veil of lank grey hair Fleurette met the mans' glance fixed upon her; and her heart gave a queer jump. Those were not the eyes of a decrepit old man; they were young and clear and bright: of a luminous grey-blue, with heavy lids that could not wholly conceal the humorous twinkle in the eyes, nor yet the kindly, searching glance which was fixed on Fleurette.

This was the moment when she really would have screamed. The sense of something ununderstandable and unreal was more than she could bear, she would have screamed, but those twinkly, searching eyes held her, and at the same time seemed to reassure her, to tell her not to be afraid. She felt as if she were in a dream: unable to do anything, only to stare and stare at the old faggot-carrier, while gradually all her terrors seemed to fall away from her, and she was filled with a sense of courage and of determination.

The whole incident, the voice, the glance, her terror and reassurance had lasted less than five seconds. Already Adèle was close by. She was bringing the bread for the poor, half-starved man, and Fleurette now watched him, fascinated, as he took the bread with a humble: "*Merci, Mam'zelle*," and started at once on it, like a man who has not tasted food all day. He was just a decrepit old man, bent with rheumatism, dirty, unkempt, insecure on his tottering limbs. He even raised his eyes once, and once more looked at her; but the glance was dim like that of an old man; there was no twinkle in the eyes, only the weariness of poverty and old age.

And Fleurette felt that she had dreamed it all: the voice, the glance, the message from St. Antoine, just as her terrors had faded from her, so now her excitement vanished too. It must all have been a dream. It *was* a dream! Perhaps old Louise, who was versed in all kinds of dreamlore, would know of an explanation for the whole mysterious occurrence. Feeling very tired all of a sudden—for she felt the reaction after the tenseness of the last few moments, she went back into the house. In the doorway she turned to have a last look at the old faggot-carrier; leaning heavily on his stick, he was making his way along the bank of the stream. The last she saw of him was his big bundle done up in sacking and his legs bending beneath the weight.

Adèle wrapped in her shawl had gone the other way. She was already up on the bridge. With a little sigh of disappointment Fleurette went into the house. It had been such an exciting dream!

But she did not speak about it to old Louise; she just went quietly about the house, doing one or two little bits of work that Adèle had left undone.

The slowly sinking sun had turned the gold on Pelvoux's snowy crest to a brilliant rose, when Fleurette suddenly announced to Louise that she was going over to the *château*. She often went there, and at all hours of the day.

"So long as you are home before dark," was Louise's only remark. "I don't like those down-at-heel soldiers being about."

Fleurette promised that she would not be late. She picked up her beautiful new shawl and wrapped it around her shoulders. The *château* was not far; over by the mountain track, it was not more than a quarter of a league at most. Swiftly Fleurette ran out of the house and then along the edge of the stream—the same way that the old faggot-carrier had gone an hour so ago.

And now the mantle of twilight was falling over the valley; the jade-coloured sky held myriads of tiny, fleecy clouds of a brilliant, glowing crimson, which one by one faded into grey along the snow of Pelvoux reflected the glory of the sinking sun, and in the old walnut-tree the thrush's song was stilled.

Chapter 6

The place was always called *le château* for want of a more appropriate name. As a matter of fact, it was just a large, rumbling roomy farmhouse with stables and stable-yards and sheds and outbuildings, all built in a mass and at different times as necessity demanded, in the midst of a really fine park, shady with century old trees and fragrant with acacias and roses. Here for many generations the de Frontenacs, father and son, had lived, toiled, and died, farming their land, honouring their king and otherwise not troubling their heads over much with politics or with art or literature. They were good, kindly, honest folk, all of them, and if the light of their intellect burned somewhat dim, that of their charity was always kept fed and bright.

They belonged to that sturdy stock which had given France one of her most valiant sons in Louis de Frontenac, the man who had made Eastern Canada a jewel worthy of the crown of France. The jewel had been lost since then, irretrievably lost to the English, and the crown of France been dragged in the mire of a bloody revolution, its glory forever overshadowed by the unforgivable crime of a purposeless regicide: but the present holder of the ancient name and owner of the lands had kept himself aloof from the awful dissension that raged in the big cities; he had remained in his heart loyal to his martyred king, and though shorn of most of his wealth, deprived of a great deal of his inheritance, perpetually threatened with confiscation or attainder, he continued to lead the simple life, hoping for better things, detached as far as he was able from the turmoil that was ruining his country and shaming her in the eyes of the world.

At all seasons of the year, and in all weathers, he could be seen out on his farm, directing the work in fields or stables, clad in rough boots and breeches, abrupt of speech, but kindly in deeds, beloved by some, envied by others, hated only by those few who see in every noble life a reproach to their own.

His wife was the daughter of an admiral in the late king's navy, who had thought it prudent to serve the Republic, as he had served his king, with commendable detachment from his country's politics. Though brought up in the midst of the gaieties and luxuries of Paris, Anne de Grandville had been quite content to follow the husband of her choice to the lonely house in the Dauphiné, and to fall in with his bucolic ways: she donned a cotton kirtle and linen apron as readily as she had donned silken panniers in the past, and took as much pride in her cooking now as she had done once in her proficiency in the dance.

At one time, Charles de Frontenac had sorely grieved because he had no son to whom he could bequeath his glorious name and fine inheritance, but now he was glad. With France handed over to the control of assassins, bandits, and regicides, the name of Frontenac might, he opined, just as well die out. What was the use of toiling to improve land which tomorrow might be wrested from its rightful owners: what was the use of saving money which would probably on the morrow fall into the hands of brigands?

"Lay not up for yourselves treasures on this earth where rust and moth doth corrupt and where thieves break through and steal!" had never been so wise an admonition as it was today. All that Charles de Frontenac hoped to do was to put by a sufficient competence to keep his wife and invalid daughter in comfort once he was under the ground. That daughter was the apple of his eye. Bereft of position and most of his wealth, all his thoughts and hopes were centred on this delicate being who seemed like the one ray of sunshine amidst thunder-clouds of disappointment and treachery.

Rose de Frontenac had been a cripple from birth, and it was her delicacy and her helplessness that had so endeared her to her father. He was a man resplendent with vigour and of herculean strength: one of those bull-necked men who could have taken his place in an ox-team and not proved a weakling. His hands were rough, his fist as hard as a hammer. His clothes smelt of damp earth and of manure; the descendent of a long line of aristocrats, Charles de Frontenac, was above all a son of the soil. To him his pale-faced, fragile daughter seemed like a being from another world; he hardly dared touch her cheek with his thick, clumsy fingers, nor dared he approach her save after copious ablutions and sprays of scent. His heart was as big as his body. He adored his daughter, he loved his wife, he beamed with fondness for Fleurette: Fleurette who was as gay as a linnet, who could always bring a smile to the pale lips of his wan, white Rose: Fleurette, who could sing like a lark, prattle like a young sparrow and whose corn-coloured hair smelt of wild thyme and of youth.

Chapter 7

Fleurette had walked very fast. She was still tremendously excited and would have ran all the way, only that the road for the most part led sharply uphill and that her heart was beating and pumping wildly with agitation.

Strangely enough the gates of the park were wide open, which was very unusual, as they were always kept closed for fear of the footpads and vagabonds. Old Pierre, who was in charge of the gate, was nowhere to be seen. Fleurette ran along the sanded avenue which, bordered by *bosquets* of acacia and elder, led in sharp curves up to the house. Twilight was slowly fading into evening, but even through the gathering darkness Fleurette noticed that the avenue, usually so beautifully raked and tidy, was all trampled and knocked about as if by the weight of many heavy feet. A minute later the main block of the *château* stood out before her, like a solid mass silhouetted against a jade-coloured sky. Just above the pointed roof of the turret at the furthest angle above the *façade*, a star shone with a cold, silvery radiance.

The entrance into the main building was under a broad archway which intersected the *façade* and led into the great farmyard and to the sheds and farm-buildings. Fleurette felt vaguely conscious that something unusual had occurred at the *château*; though the place looked peaceful enough, it appeared strangely deserted at this hour, when usually men and maids were still about their work. She slipped quickly under the archway, and turning sharply to the left, she came to the great paved hall where servants and farm hands sat at meals.

She found the place in a strange state of confusion: the men—they were all old men these days, as all the young ones had had to go and join the army and fight the English—the men were standing about in groups, talking and gesticulating with their arms, after the manner of the people of Dauphiné, who are glib of speech and free with their gestures; the maids were gathered together in the dark corner of the room, holding their aprons to their eyes. The oil lamp which hung from the whitewashed ceiling had not yet been lit: only one or two tallow-candles on the table guttered in their pewter scones.

Old Mathieu, who was the acknowledged father of the staff and who was affectionately called Papa by the maids, was the first to spy Fleurette, who stood disconcerted in the doorway.

"Ah! Mam'zelle Fleurette! Mam'zelle Fleurette!" he exclaimed and lifted his hands and cast up his eyes with an expression of woe: "*Quel malheur! Mon Dieu, quel malheur!*"

He had on his bottle-green coat, his buckled shoes, and the white cotton gloves which he wore when he served the family at meals upstairs. They had just finished dinner, it seems, when the awful calamity occurred.

"But what is it, papa?" Fleurette asked, feeling quite ready to cry in sympathy. "What has happened?"

"The soldiers, *Mam'zelle!*" Papa replied, and a fresh groan went the round of men and women alike, and one or two of the girls sobbed aloud.

Now as far as Fleurette was concerned, as recently as this very morning, the inner meaning of these words "the soldiers!" would not perhaps have had much significance. In her own little home, by Bibi's strict orders, politics and social questions were never discussed. Fleurette was not supposed to know anything of the conflicts that were raging in the great cities, in the name of liberty and of fraternity. The horrors of summary arrests, of perquisitions, of sentences without trial, of wholesale executions, of hatred and revenge and lust were supposed to be beyond her ken; and knowing Bibi's abhorrence of those subjects being broached, she kept her counsels and her knowledge to herself.

But Fleurette was not brainless, and she had a large heart. With her brain she had noted many things which were wilfully kept away from her, and her kind heart had often been filled with pity at many of the tales which she had heard in the village, tales of suffering under this new kind of tyranny wielded, it seems, in the name of liberty and of the brotherhood of man. She had heard many things and had forgotten nothing; but somehow until this morning these things had seemed remote, like the tales of ogres and demons which are told to frighten children. She had not disbelieved them, but vaguely she felt that nothing of the sort could possibly happen to people whom she knew and loved.

But since this morning many things had occurred which had widened her range of vision. Amédé, who did not want to go away, was being dragged from his home in order to be made into a soldier and to fight the English. She had actually seen some of those soldiers, ragged, uncouth and unkempt, with their officer, like a great bully, speaking to her, as if she were a mere slut out of the streets. He had jeered when she told him that she was Citizen Armand's daughter, and the soldiers had nudged one another and seemed to mock her when she met their glance. Then again, she had heard the mysterious voices and seen something in the person of a decrepit old faggot-carrier that had thrilled and puzzled her. All these things had worked a subtle change in Fleurette. The tales of ogres and demons no longer appeared quite so remote. The fact that there were evil and sorrow in the world had in a vague kind of way been brought home to her, and also that the spectre of death and misery of which she had only heard was actually lurking in this peaceful corner of Dauphiné and had already knocked at this very door.

"The soldiers!" meant something to her now.

"What happened?" she asked, and a dozen tongues were ready to embark on the telling of the tragic event. It was just after dinner. *Madame* and *Mademoiselle* had retired to the *boudoir*, as usual, and *mon-*

43

sieur was sipping his wine in the dining room, when the great bell at the gate clanged loudly. Pierre, who was still at work in the stables, ran to open the gate: he was almost knocked down by two men on horseback who, without a word or question, rode past him along the avenue up to the house followed by a dozen men or more in tattered uniforms and wearing dirty read caps on their heads. The sound of horses and of men stamping the ground brought some of the maids and farmhands out into the yard. The soldiers had come to a halt under the archway, the two riders then dismounted and ordered André to take their horses round to the stables. André, of course, did not dare disobey. Then, as the entrance door was closed, one of the soldiers knocked loudly against it with the butt-end of his musket, whilst one of those who had been on horseback and who appeared to be in authority called out summarily:

"Open in the name of the Republic!"

Old Mathieu, who was upstairs clearing away the dinner things, terribly scared, ran down to open the door. Again, without a word or question, the soldiers pushed past him until they came to the vestibule where they demanded to know where were the *ci-devant* Frontenacs. Old Mathieu here paused in his narrative and once more threw up his hands and cast up his eyes in horror.

"*Ci-devant, mam'zelle!*" he exclaimed. "I ask you! Just as those devils up in Paris talked of our poor martyred king and queen!"

Of course, he tried to stop the brigands from going up to see *Madame* like that, in their dusty shoes and dirty clothes. But what could he do alone among so many? Ah! if only Baptiste and Jean, Achille and Henri had been there, as in the good old days, fine sturdy fellows of the Dauphiné: they would soon have got the better of these down-at-heel bandits, and if it was a case of protecting *Madame* and *Mademoiselle*, why! there would have been some broken heads, and the soldiers of the Republic would have sung another song than they were singing now, the muckworms! But there! Henri and André and the lot of the young ones had all been taken for cannon-fodder, to fight against the English, and there were only a few fogies left now like he—Mathieu—and the women.

Anyway, poor old papa was helpless. All he could do was to precede those hell-hounds upstairs, so that he might at least warn *Monsieur* of what was coming. But even this they would not let him do; as soon as he had reached the upstairs landing, the same man who had ordered him to open the front door in the name of the Republic, and who wore a tricolour sash around his middle, this same man grabbed him by the shoulder and thrust him aside as if he were a bundle of faggots. And without more ado, he just walked into the dining room where *Monsieur* was still quietly sipping his last glass of wine.

From seeing *Monsieur* sitting there, the beautiful long-stemmed wine glass in his hand, his face quite serene, you would have thought that he had heard nothing of the turmoil on the stairs. But he had heard everything, the tramping of feet, the rough voices, the curt command to open in the name of the Republic. He knew what was coming. Perhaps he had expected it long ago. It was well to be prepared for anything these days. Anyway, there he sat, glass in hand, his elbow resting on the table, where Mathieu had but a few minutes ago been engaged in clearing away the dessert. At the rude entry made by all those ragamuffins into his beautifully ordered dining room, he just turned his head and looked at the men.

"In the name of the Republic," the man with the sash said curtly. *Monsieur* put his glass down and rose slowly to his feet.

"What is it you want?" he asked quietly.

"The rest of the family, first of all," the man with the sash replied. "I want you all here together."

"Madame de Frontenac and my daughter Rose are not at home," said *Monsieur*, still speaking very quietly.

"That's a lie," the other retorted. "They were at meal here with you."

And with careless finger he pointed to the serviettes and plates which still littered the table. *Monsieur* did not wince under the insult; nor was the saying of such a brigand an insult to so high-minded a gentleman as *Monsieur*. All he said was:

"That is so. Madame and Mlle. de Frontenac were at dinner with me, until half an hour ago when they left the house together."

"Whither did they go?"

"That I do not know."

"Which is another lie."

"If I did know," *Monsieur* rejoined imperturbably, "I would not tell you."

"We'll soon see about that," the man with the sash said grimly. He then turned to the soldier who appeared to be in command over the others: "*Allons!* citizen lieutenant," he said curtly, "the rest is your business. The two women have got to be found. That's the first thing, after that we shall see."

The officer then ordered two of his men to stand on guard over *Monsieur*, and since then the tramp, tramp of the soldiers' feet had resounded throughout the *château*. Upstairs they went, and downstairs; in *Madame's* room and in *Mademoiselle's*, in the kitchen, the stables, the offices. They interrogated the men, they bullied the women; they turned everything topsy-turvy; they raked about in the hay and the straw of the stables, they scoured the park, they glued their ugly, dirty noses to the sanded paths, trying to find the imprint of footsteps. But neither of *Madame* or *Mademoiselle* had they yet found a trace. They were still at it, raking and scouring and searching. In the intervals they tried to browbeat *Monsieur*, threatening him with summary shooting one moment, which only made him laugh and shrug his shoulders, and promising immunity for his women-folk if he would say where they could be found. But these promises only made *Monsieur* laugh and again shrug his shoulders.

"Immunity?" he said. "They have that already, thank God! for they are beyond your reach now. If they were not, do you think I would trust to your promises?"

Old Mathieu paused. The story had neared its end:—this tale of woe and anxiety and horror, such as the worthy old man had never thought to see. The others had not much to say; the maids were still crying, with excitement rather than grief, and the old men stared open-mouthed, or sagely nodded their heads. "Then," Fleurette put in at last, "*Madame* and *Mademoiselle* have gone. Really—really gone?"

Mathieu nodded with another sigh, half of perplexity, half of woe.

"But whither?" Fleurette insisted. "How? Why?"

"God alone knows, *Mam'zelle*," papa averred. "He has spirited *Madame* and *Mademoiselle* away to save them from these brigands."

"Did anybody see them go?"

Men and maids shook their heads. No one had seen *Madame* or *Mademoiselle* go. Old Mathieu was the last to have seen the ladies. He had just begun to clear the table, when they rose, and, as was their custom, went through to the *boudoir*. Mathieu had opened the door for them. And now he came to think of it, the ladies had each kissed *Monsieur* very tenderly before they went out of the room. Yes! the kiss had seemed like a farewell. Mathieu shook his head dolefully: he remembered it now but hadn't thought anything about it at the moment. *Monsieur* certainly appeared more thoughtful. Usually, while he drank his last glass of wine and Mathieu was engaged in washing the silver in the large copper bowl which he always brought into the room for that purpose, *Monsieur* would chat with him, talk over the gossip of the day. But tonight, he had been unusually silent. Yes! Mathieu now remembered quite distinctly about the kiss, and about *Monsieur* being so silent. But he certainly had noticed nothing else unusual, until the moment when those brigands banged at the door and demanded admittance in the name of their godless Republic.

Mathieu was on the stairs at that moment, so he did not know how *Monsieur* had looked when he heard all the tramping and the noise. But *Madame* and *Mademoiselle* were gone, of that there could be no doubt. The brigands had searched for them, like so many dogs digging for a bone, and not a trace was there of the two ladies, for the *bon Dieu*, no doubt, had made them invisible.

Of old Mathieu and the staff, the officer in command took no notice, after he had summarily ordered them to muster up in the hall; he had counted up the indoor servants and the farmhands; those who had their homes outside the precincts of the *château*, he ordered roughly out of the place.

"Get back to your homes!" he had said to them, after he had inspected and questioned them; "and stay there quietly, if you value your lives."

So, there were only half a dozen old men, the four girls and the staff's cook left in the *château*. All of them were scared, and as Mam'zelle Fleurette could see, they just stood about and talked and talked while the girls did nothing but cry. He—Mathieu—could do nothing with any of them. The work of the house ought to be carried on; none of them had had any supper yet. But there! young and old, they were, all of them, too much upset to work or to eat; and the *tramp-tramp*, upstairs and downstairs was nerve-shattering to everybody.

Fleurette listened to the amazing story until the end. As Mathieu said, there was the ceaseless tramping of feet still going on. They—those horrible soldiers of the Republic, unworthy to be called Frenchmen—were still searching for *Madame* and *Mademoiselle* in order to drag them to Orange where the awful guillotine had been at work these months past; or perhaps even to Paris—that den of horrors beside which the stories of demons and ogres were but trivial tales.

Madame and *Mademoiselle*! who never in their lives had done harm to anyone: but rather spent every hour of the day planning and executing kind deeds! And *Mademoiselle!* so delicate and frail that even her father, who idolised her, hardly dared touch her. And now these men, these rough and uncouth soldiers, with their harsh voices and bullying ways, to think of their approaching *Mademoiselle*, pushing her, dragging her, it made Fleurette's blood boil even to think of such a possibility. No wonder that the *bon Dieu* made them invisible to the eyes of all those bandits.

Tramp! tramp! tramp! and now a loud banging as if pieces of furniture, chairs, tables were being overturned, and then a crash, as of broken china!

"Holy Virgin!" Papa Mathieu exclaimed with a loud groan; "to think of *Madame's* beautiful things! Those brigands are furious at not finding *Madame* and *Mademoiselle* and are venting their wrath on inanimate things."

It was these words of old Mathieu that sent Fleurette's thoughts flying in another direction—back to the early afternoon of this memorable day—back to the first visit of these awful soldiers, and to the faggot-carrier with his bundle tied up in sacking. From thence to the voice! The mysterious voice that had told her where valuables and papers were to be found. It was such a flash of recollection that her whole face became transfigured; anxiety and superstitious awe gave place to that same fervour which had animated her when she met the eyes of the faggot-carrier: eyes that conveyed a message, which at last she was beginning to understand.

"Papa!" she cried impulsively.

"Yes, *Mam'zelle?*" Mathieu asked with another sigh.

"Did anything else happen—I mean anything unusual?—did *Madame*—or *Monsieur*—receive a letter? a message? or—or did any other stranger come to the *château* this afternoon?"

"Oh, think, Papa Mathieu, think," she implored with tears of agitation choking her voice. "I cannot tell you how important it is. Try to remember—was there anything?—anybody?—"

Papa persistently shook his head, until Pierre, who was the gate keeper, reminded him that *Monsieur* had gone down the avenue as far as the gate, just ten minutes before dinner was served.

"There's nothing very unusual in that," Mathieu retorted. "*Monsieur* is often out just before dinner is served."

"Yes!" Pierre insisted. "But what did he do this evening? He walked straight to the gate, which I had closed half an hour before. I saw him. He walked straight to the gate, he did, and you know the old acacia tree just the other side? Well! *Monsieur* put his foot on a bar of the gate and reached over to the forked branch of the old tree. I saw him quite plainly, I tell you. And when he walked back to the house he had a piece of paper in his hand with some writing on it, which he was reading. And I think, papa," Pierre concluded triumphantly, "you'll have to admit that there was something unusual in that."

But Mathieu, with the obstinacy of old age and long service, would not admit it, even now.

"*Monsieur*," he said, "met the mail-carrier at the gate, he often comes at this hour. He gave *Monsieur* a letter. *Monsieur* often gets letters— "

But here André interposed. Old André—they were all of them old— worked in the stables, and it was he who had taken the two horses from the soldiers when ordered to do so and walked them around to the stables. It was then that he noticed two beggars hanging about in the yard: a man and a woman. He had peremptorily ordered them off the premises.

"Beggars!" Fleurette exclaimed eagerly. "What were they like?"

André said that as the sun was in his eyes he couldn't see them very well. There was a man and a woman. He was busy with the horses and upset by the arrival of all these brigands. The woman he couldn't see at all because of the shawl which covered her head, but he recollected that the man was a big fellow, bent nearly double under a huge bundle tied up in sacking.

"When I spoke to him," André went on, "he mumbled something or other, but I just told him to clear out, he and his woman; we'd enough of vagabonds, I said, in the place with all these soldiers."

"And did he go?" Fleurette asked.

"Yes! I must admit he went off quite quietly after that. I did not think he meant any evil, because when he first caught sight of me he did not attempt to hide or to run away."

"If he had," André went on after a moment or two, "I would have been after him pretty quickly, and wanted to know what was in that big bundle."

He paused, a look of perplexity and of shamefacedness came over his wrinkled old face while he thoughtfully scratched his head: "Now I think of it," he said, "I ought to have inspected that bundle. It looked mighty heavy for faggots or for rags. Perhaps he had been up to no good after all—and directly after I lost sight of him and his woman I saw a whole lot of faggots lying in a heap close by the stable door."

The other old men and the maids had gathered closer round André and Fleurette. His was the first they had heard of the old vagabond and his woman, and the bundle which appeared so heavy.

"You certainly ought to have inspected that bundle, André,"

Mathieu said sententiously. He felt that there was a chance of recapturing his dignity which seemed to have been slightly impaired through his argument with Pierre. He could reassert his authority at any rate by rebuking André. "It looks," he went on, "as if the old vagabond had brought a lot of faggots with him, then turned them out of the sacking and replaced them by God knows what valuables he may have stolen."

"I was so upset, you understand, papa!" André murmured ruefully.

"We were all of us upset, as you call it, André," papa rebuked sternly, "but that is no excuse for neglect of duty."

"Don't scold André, papa," Fleurette broke in excitedly. "My belief is that the old vagabond, as you call him, was a messenger from the Holy Virgin, sent on purpose to get *Madame* and *Mademoiselle* safely out of the way."

"Oh, *Mam'zelle!*"

"From the Holy Virgin!"

"*Sainte Marie, mère de Dieu, priez pour nous!*" came in chorus from the maids. Even the cook, an elderly woman, jealous of her own dignity, was unable to conceal her excitement. The old men shook their heads, looked wise and sceptical.

"What makes you say that, Mam'zelle Fleurette?" Mathieu asked in an awed whisper.

But Fleurette was silent now. Already she had repented of having said so much. Discretion would have been so much wiser. That was the worst of her: she always allowed her tongue to run away with her. She looked eagerly from one anxious face to the other: well she knew that the little she had said would be talked over and commented on and be made the subject of gossip until it reached the village and possibly even Serres and Sisteron; and God only knew what harm this might do to *Madame* and *Mademoiselle*. She bit the tip of her tongue hard just to punish it for having wagged too freely, and seized with a sudden impulse, which she found irresistible, she snatched up a candle from the table and incontinently turned and fled out of the hall, leaving the others to gape and stare after her, to scratch their heads, and to conjecture.

Aye! and to gossip, too.

Chapter 8

Perquisitions in those days of Liberty, Fraternity and Equality were perhaps among the minor horrors that befell innocent and guilty alike,

at the behest of tyrants more implacable than the Inquisitors of Medi-
aeval Spain, more cruel than the Borgias: but they were terrible none-
theless. A perquisition meant, in most cases, the destruction of every
household treasure, every family relic cherished through the generations, it meant the wanton smashing of furniture and mirrors, the
ripping up of valuable tapestries and of mattresses, the defacement of
priceless pictures, it meant prying, hostile eyes thrust into receptacles,
however secret, into private papers and even letters. Nothing was sacred to men deputed to insult and to offend, just as much as to search.

When Fleurette reached that part of the house which was occupied by the family, she was confronted by the wildest, the most
heart-stirring confusion. The carpets had been torn off the floors, the
furniture for the most part lay in broken heaps about the room, mirrors and pictures had been dragged off the walls, broken crockery
and glass were scattered everywhere, intermingled with horsehair and
other stuffing out of chairs and mattresses, whilst all the walls, the
doors, the window-frames bore traces of rude handling with bayonet
or the heel of a boot.

Fleurette, wide-eyed and appalled, ran from room to room; the
uttering tallow-candle which she held threw flickering lights and grotesque shadows on the scattered objects about her, made them seem
more weird, like the appurtenances of an abode of ghosts. Here in the
pretty *boudoir Mademoiselle's* embroidery frame lay smashed to tinder
wood with threads of the work still hanging to it, bits of rags, pathetic
in their look of abandonment and desolation. There in the withdrawing room, the beautiful satin-wood spinet with its painted panels and
exquisite marquetry was lying on its side, its body gaping like a gigantic wound, the strings emitting a final vibration like the last song of a
dying swan.

From the direction of the dining room came the incessant murmur
of voices, but throughout the rest of the apartments, in the midst of
all the wreckage, a silence reigned as of the grave. The place now was
completely deserted. It seemed almost as if some terrible tornado had
swept through these living-rooms; some implacable forces of nature
rather than the hatred and cupidity of men. An earthquake could not
have been more devastating, a fire more destructive.

And now in the midst of it all Fleurette came to a standstill, candle
in hand: her breath came and went in quick short gasps, and her heart
was beating furiously. The silence in this semi-darkness with those
long, ghost-like shadows seemed to oppress her; the broken bits of

beautiful things which she had known and loved ever since she remembered anything, gave her an awful feeling of desolation and a kind of foreboding of things, still worse, to come. It was instinct which had brought her to a halt here in this one room amongst the others. It was always known as *Madame's* room, for here *Madame* would always sit when she gave her orders to various members of the household, here that she would look through the household accounts whilst Fleurette and Rose, when they were still children, would sit in a corner of the sofa by the huge hearth, hand in hand, with a picture book on their knees, silent like a pair of tiny white mice, waiting until *Madame* had finished her, because then they would all go into the garden to gather flowers for the rooms, and fruit for desert, or perhaps go down into the kitchen and learn how to dress a chicken for the table, or how best to mix a salad.

And Fleurette stood for a moment or two quite still, holding the candle high above her head, contemplating this wreckage. Then, having found a safe place in which to deposit the candle, she carefully closed the door which gave, like several others, on a long corridor that led to the main staircase at one end and to the service stairs at the other. The time had come to cease contemplation, to drive away superstitious fears and to act. Closing her eyes, Fleurette strove first of all to recapture pictures of long ago, to recreate the scenes enacted in this room, before this awful calamity had fallen on these people whom she loved so dearly. Memory was not rebellious. She could see the whole picture just as it had impressed itself on the tablets of her mind when she used to sit here as a child. There by the window *Madame's* desk used to stand.

It was lying on its side now, the drawers wrenched open, the handles broken, papers, pen and sand scattered about; the ink had run out and stained the beautiful old Aubusson carpet. But there, *Madame* used to sit. Fleurette could almost see her now, at the desk. Her big household books were open before her. Writing, calculating, and putting her money by in a leather bag. And presently she would rise, pick up her bag and books and carry them across the room to a spot close to the wall, the other side of the hearth. Here she would come to a standstill, and putting her beautiful hand somewhere against the wall, she would turn to the girls—they were mere children then—and smile at them in a mysterious way; and they would say solemnly "Open *Sesame!*" just as they had heard in the tale of Ali Baba and the forty robbers, which Monsieur de Frontenac had often told them. As soon as they had said the magic words the wall would open like the entrance of the robbers' cave in the tale of Ali Baba, disclosing a recess into which *Madame* would put her books and her bag of money. Then she would once more turn and give a sign to the children and they would say: "Close Sesame!" and the mysterious door would swing to again and no trace be left of the recess which lay hidden somewhere behind the panelled wall.

The whole picture stood out before Fleurette's mental vision in every detail; the exact spot where *Madame* used to stand, the way she put out her hand and touched the panelled wall. Carefully picking her way through the maze of broken furniture, Fleurette came to a halt on the very spot where she had so often seen *Madame* standing, with her books and money-bag in her arms. She put out her hand and touched the panel as *Madame* had done: all over the carved panels she put her hand, touching and pressing each bit of carving in its turn. Her heart was still beating wildly, but not in any way with fear. In fact, she was surprised at herself for not being afraid. It was just the excitement of this wonderful adventure! She, Fleurette, who had seen nothing of the world beyond her own village of Laragne and an occasional glimpse at Sisteron, suddenly found herself guiding the destinies of people whom she loved—the messenger sent by the *bon Dieu* to help them in their need. There is no young human creature living who would not respond, heart and soul, to such a call, and Fleurette was of the South, a child of that romantic land of Dauphiné which had given so many of her heroic sons to strive and work for France.

And suddenly, as Fleurette pressed her finger on every piece of carved relief, one by one, she felt the centre of a dog-rose yield to the pressure. Softly, noiselessly, the panel swung outwards, and there in the recess were the familiar household books and the money-bag. Beside them lay a leather wallet and a small casket fitted with a brass lock. Without any hesitation Fleurette took the bag, the wallet and the casket, leaving the books where they were. Never for a moment did the thought occur to her that she might be discovered in what would be a highly compromising position. She was too simple-minded, too innately honest to think that she might be suspected of theft.

Having stowed the wallet and the bag in the wide pockets of her kirtle and hidden the casket beneath her shawl, Fleurette picked her way back across the room. She left the mysterious recess open because she did not know how to close it and did not want to waste any time trying to find out. She found her way to the door and opened it, then she blew out the candle and finally peeped out into the corridor.

It was deserted. The lingering evening light, pale and ghostlike, came creeping in through the row of tall arched windows facing her. As everywhere else in the *château*, the corridor bore the melancholy traces of the soldiers' passage. It was the same devastation. The same wanton destruction was only too apparent in the torn carpet and the fragments of glass and broken sconces that littered the floor. Fleurette, turning her back on the direction of the main staircase, made her way to the back stairs which wound in a close spiral down to the service door.

Fleurette descended with quick, furtive steps, until, past the first curve of the spiral, the stairs were in total darkness. But she would have found her way all about the *château* blindfold, so well did she know its every nook and cranny. She came to the door and fumbled for the bolts. She had drawn one and taken off the chain, when she heard a measured tramp on the other side of the door. Steps were coming this way along the flagged path; a moment or two later they came to a halt close to the door. Fleurette hardly daring to breathe, listened. A voice said: "Did you go in there?"

"No, citizen," replied another, "not by this door. The bolts are fastened on the inside."

Something else was said which Fleurette did not catch, and the steps receded in the direction of the front of the house. She waited a minute or two longer, breathless and motionless, until she heard what she thought was the tramp of feet in the corridor above her. The soldiers had apparently been ordered to come round again, perhaps they would be coming down those stairs. To hesitate now might prove fatal. Fumbling once more in the gloom, Fleurette found the last bolt and drew it, and the next moment was out in the open. The back door gave on the yard. On the right were the stables, and facing the door, the riding school and one or two sheds; on the left the kitchens and the servants' quarters. In this direction too was the great archway and the main entrance into the house. Past the archway was the park and the avenue leading to the big gates.

After a moment's reflection Fleurette decided to avoid these main approaches: there was another way across the park, past the stable gate. Hugging the casket closely under her shawl, Fleurette set out in the direction of the stables. There was no one about and she felt comparatively safe. Night was now rapidly drawing in, and she fortunately had on a dark kirtle and dark worsted stockings. The air was very still and the waning moon not yet risen in the east. From far away came the sound of the bell of Laragne church. It struck eight. Fleurette felt a pang of anxiety. She had promised to be home before dark and Louise would be anxious and cross: and there was still something she wanted to do before she went home. Now she was past the stable door where, in a heap, just as old André had said, there lay a pile of faggots. The sight of them gave Fleurette a happy thrill. Was she not obeying the dictates of the mysterious voice which had spoken to her through the medium of the old faggot-carrier?

The next moment, a firm step resounded on the flagstones of the stables, and a second later a man appeared under the lintel of the door.

"Fleurette! what in God's name are you doing here?"

Smothering a startled cry, Fleurette turned and found herself face to face with her father. He was standing at the stable door; his hands were clasped behind his back, and he had a tricolour sash round his waist. Now women, young girls, especially, those born and bred in outlying country districts, are credited with being stupid, silly in their fears, timorous like hens; and so, no doubt would Fleurette have been in ordinary circumstances. She may not have been either clever or brave originally; she would perhaps have behaved in a silly, timorous fashion but for this one fact, that she knew something terrible was happening to the Frontenacs whom she loved, and that she had been deputed by the *bon Dieu*, or merely by a human friend, to do something important for them. In order to do this, she must keep her head; and trust any woman to keep her head if one she loves is in peril.

"What are you doing here, Fleurette?" Bibi reiterated rather sternly.

And Fleurette, with a well-simulated nervous little laugh, retorted lightly:

"Why, Bibi *chéri*, I might retaliate! What are you doing here? I thought you were on your way to Paris."

"What are you doing here, Fleurette?" Bibi said once more, and Fleurette thought that his voice had never sounded so harsh before.

"But, Bibi," Fleurette said simply, "I often come to see *Madame* and *Mademoiselle*. And after you left this afternoon I felt so lonely and sad, I thought I might seek Mademoiselle Rose for company."

"And have you seen her?"

"No. They told me *Madame* and *Mademoiselle* had gone."

"Who told you?"

"Papa Mathieu."

"What else did he tell you?"

55

"Only that there were soldiers come to the *château*, and that I'd better go home again—and so I'm going."

"He didn't tell you anything else?"

"No," Fleurette replied innocently. "Was there anything else to say?"

"No—er—no," Bibi rejoined. "Of course not. But Fleurette—"

"Yes, Bibi darling?"

"How often must I tell you that you must not talk of "*Madame*" and "*Mademoiselle*"? There are no *Madames* and *Mademoiselles* now; we are, all of us equally, citizens of France."

"Yes, Bibi," Fleurette rejoined demurely. "And I really, really am very careful when strangers are about. It doesn't matter what I say before you, does it, *chéri* Bibi?"

"No, no," Bibi muttered, seemingly without much conviction, and Fleurette then went on quickly:

"I must run home now, *chéri* Bibi, or Louise will be getting anxious. You are coming too, aren't you? Louise will get you such a lovely supper and then—"

"No, my little one," Bibi said. "I can't. Not tonight. I must be in Orange tomorrow."

"But Bibi—"

"Run along, child," Bibi broke in almost fiercely. "It's a dark night, and there are always vagabonds about."

"Ah well then, goodnight, Bibi," Fleurette murmured meekly.

And suddenly Bibi put out his hand and grasped Fleurette by the wrist.

"Are you not going to kiss me, Fleurette?" he asked with oh! such a tone of sadness now in his voice.

It was a terrible moment. What a mercy that the darling had seized her left wrist, rather than her right, because with her right hand Fleurette was hugging the small casket under her shawl. There were also the wallet and the moneybag in the pocket of her kirtle: oh! if Bibi should knock against them! Fortunately, it was dark, and he could not see the bulge under her shawl. But, of course, she could not part from Bibi *chéri* without giving him a farewell kiss. He seemed sad and unhappy, and there was something about his whole manner that Fleurette did not understand.

At first, when he startled her by suddenly appearing at the stable door, she had not even tried to conjecture what he was doing here; she was too deeply absorbed in her own adventure for the moment to

56

do more than vaguely wonder what part Bibi was playing in the tragic events that had wrought such desolation at the *château*. Bibi *chéri*, who worshipped his little Fleurette, who was always so kind, so gentle, a slave to every one of her whims; he must have been dragged into this horrible affair, was perhaps an innocent tool of those cruel people in Paris, who monopolised his time and kept him away from his home.

Indeed, she had no mistrust in him whatever; but her trust in him did not go to the length of telling him about the casket, or the mysterious voice of the faggot-carrier; those were her own secrets, secrets too which concerned the Frontenacs for whom Bibi had never evinced a very great affection and had even tried to dissuade Fleurette from having too much intercourse with them. It was in fact her love for *Madame* and *Monsieur*, and for Mademoiselle Rose, and Bibi's strange dislike of them, which had brought the only clouds in the sunshine of their affection.

But of this Fleurette was not thinking at the moment, her one thought was of her secret and how best to guard it. All the same she would not have denied Bibi *chéri* the kiss he asked for. She must take the risk, that was all, and once again trust to her wits. She allowed him to put his arms round her neck and held up her fresh young face for his kiss: she held the casket so carefully that he did not feel its sharp angles. All was well, for now she was free from his embrace, but still he had hold of her left hand, and drew her close to him.

"Fleurette, my little one," he said earnestly.

"Yes, Bibi."

"Do you know where the two Frontenac women have gone to?"

"No, Bibi, I do not," Fleurette was able to reply in all truthfulness, and looked her father straight in the eyes. "They were gone before I came."

"It is for their good that I ask you."

"I am sure it is, Bibi, but really, really I do not know."

Bibi gave a quick, impatient sigh.

"Ah, well! goodbye, my Fleurette."

"Goodnight, Bibi."

At last she was free. With her left hand she blew a last kiss to Bibi, and then quickly sped across the yard. Her heart felt heavy and there was an uncomfortable lump in her throat. For the first time she had been brought face to face with the realities of life. Hitherto she had lived in a kind of fairyland in which she was the carefully tended and guarded queen, and Bibi the acknowledged king as well as slave.

Everything in the world was perfect, and lovely, and wonderful; the men and women in it—not only Bibi, but Louise, and M. Duflos the butcher, and M. Colombe the grocer, and—and M. Amédé—they were all kind and generous and gentle. But now cruelty and spite had come within her ken. An ugly ghoul called "hatred" had passed by hand in hand with his ugly brother "mistrust" and the latter had whispered something in her ear just now, which had caused her to shrink within herself when Bibi had kissed her, and to turn from him and to run away with a strange sense of relief.

She did not look back as she sped across the yard, and when she came to the small postern gate she was thankful to find it on the latch, so that she could slip out unseen.

Chapter 9

Fleurette was too young, too ignorant for self-analysis. She could not have told you what had made her act in the way she did, nor what had caused her so to mistrust Bibi as not to share her precious secret with him. All she knew was that she had had a wild desire to get away from him.

A cart-track led from the postern gate across a couple of fields where it joined the main road; one or two isolated farm buildings belonging to M. de Frontenac, and the open fields on both sides, made the track fairly safe from foot-pads. The main road too which led through the village would be safer after dark, than the short cut over the mountains. Fleurette hastened along, hugging her treasures, hoping that she would not fall in with the soldiers on their return from the *château*.

The weather had not fulfilled the promise made by the beauty of the sunset: heavy clouds hung over the sky; only one or two streaks of pale lemon-coloured light, like great gashes through the leaden clouds, still lingered in the West. Through the gloom farm-sheds and isolated trees loomed out like great immobile giants, and, on the right, the dense mass of the avenue of acacias and elder and the great gates of the *château*.

Fleurette was already well on her way along the high-road and in sight of the first house of the village, the cottage where Adèle lived with her aunt, the widow Tronchet, when she heard the all too familiar sound behind her of the heavy tramping of feet and of horses' hoofs raising the dust of the road. The night was so still that the sounds reached her ears distinctly. She heard the lieutenant's harsh voice giving a brief word of command: the creaking of the château gates, as they swung upon their hinges. Just then Roy, *Monsieur's* dog, set up a dismal howl, and from one of the tall poplar-trees that bordered the road an owl gave a hoot and fluttered out into the night.

Fleurette broke out into a run. She knew that she could ask for shelter in the widow Tronchet's cottage and wait there until the soldiers had gone by. Perhaps Adèle would walk home with her after that. Fortunately, she could already perceive the light glimmering in one of the tiny windows, and just at the moment Adèle came out of the front door, probably to see for herself what the unusual sounds were about.

She was mightily surprised to see Fleurette come running along.

"They are the same soldiers, Adèle," Fleurette explained breathlessly, as she followed her foster-sister into the cottage, "who were at Lou Mas this afternoon. Close the door, do, and I'll tell you all about them."

The widow Tronchet came out of her kitchen and looked disapprovingly at Fleurette. She did not like the girl and discouraged all intercourse between her and Adèle. She was a thrifty, hard-featured, hard-hearted peasant—older than her sister Louise by a couple of years—who had exacted every ounce of work and obedience from Adèle in payment for the shelter of her roof and for her daily bread. She had never forgiven her sister for leaving Adèle on her hands, though the girl had always worked her fingers to the bone, grudgingly no doubt, but diligently, in order to bring additional comfort into the cottage. But it was a poor, ill-furnished cottage, wherein food was none too plentiful, and beds hard, whereas Louise at Lou Mas lived in the lap of luxury; and envy had fostered dislike until it had almost become hatred.

She listened, with a frown on her hard, wrinkled face, to Fleurette's breathless tale of what had happened at the *château*. It would be the gossip of the village by tomorrow, that the soldiers of the Republic had arrested *Monsieur*, and that *Madame* and *Mademoiselle* had fled no one knew whither.

"Oh,' Ma'ame Tronchet," Fleurette concluded, her fresh voice hoarse with sobs, "dear Ma'ame Tronchet, you don't think they're really going to harm *Monsieur*, do you?"

The widow Tronchet shrugged her shoulders and gave a short, harsh laugh.

"I'm not thinking about it at all one way or the other," she said drily. "What difference does it make to us poor people," she went on, grumbling, while she busied herself about the room, "what happens to all those *aristos?* They never cared what happened to us."

For the moment Fleurette could do no more than stare at the widow Tronchet, in horror. Never had she heard anyone say anything so wicked. She was quite ready to defend *Monsieur* and *Madame* against any accusation of hard-heartedness and would have done so at risk of offending the disagreeable, ill-natured old woman, but for the moment her attention, as well as that of Adèle's, was riveted on the sounds outside. The soldiers had just come round the bend of the road; they were quite close to the cottage already, with the two horsemen walking their mounts in the van.

"They are going on to Serres," Fleurette whispered. In her heart she was wondering what Bibi was going to do. He was evidently not going to Orange, as he had said he would. Would he spend the night at Lou Mas after all? If he did, was there any danger of Fleurette's secret leaking out? Of Bibi *chéri* finding out something about the casket and the precious wallet? Fleurette was still hugging the casket, she could see the widow Tronchet's hard, steely eyes, gazing curiously at the bulge underneath her shawl, and then at the fullness in her kirtle where the wallet and the money-bag lay hidden in the pockets: Fleurette felt the blood rush up to her cheeks, and then had the mortification of seeing Adèle's pinched-up little face break into a smile. Of what were those two women thinking? Surely not that she, Fleurette, had been stealing. Their faces were so inscrutable: the older woman's hard and set, and Adèle's rat-like and furtive, as if determined to conceal her thoughts.

The next moment they all heard the horsemen go by. Adèle ran to the door and peered out into the night. Over her shoulder she said to Fleurette:

"There's your father riding with the soldiers. Shall I shout to him and tell him you are here?"

Instinctively Fleurette shook her head, and with that same inscrutable smile still on her face, Adèle deliberately closed the door again.

"They've got *Monsieur* walking between them," she commented drily.

"It would have been better," the widow said acidly to Fleurette, "for Citizen Armand to know that you are here. It won't be safe for women to be alone on the high-road this night, I am thinking."

Then, as Fleurette remained silent, debating within herself what she had best do, the old woman went on curtly: "The sooner you get home now, my girl, the better. Adèle has got to put in an hour's work at Citizen Colombe's up at the village: it is miserable pay enough," she continued muttering to herself, "and a shame that one girl should have to work so hard, whilst another lives a pampered life of luxury. But anyway," she concluded abruptly, "I can't be wasting any lamp-oil on you."

"No—no—of course not, Ma'ame Tronchet," Fleurette stammered. But the widow, still muttering under her breath, was paying no more attention to her. She had climbed on to a chair and reaching up to the lamp that hung from the ceiling, she turned out the light. The room was now in darkness except for the light that came in through the open kitchen door. The widow with a curt: "Don't be late, Adèle," went off into the kitchen, and a moment or two later could be heard busy with her pots and pans.

Adèle had picked up her shawl, and equally unceremoniously gone as far as the door, when Fleurette called her shyly back.

"Adèle!"

The girl turned without speaking, her hand on the door which she was holding open.

"If you are going to M'sieur Colombe, could you—" Fleurette stammered, "I mean, would you tell Monsieur Amédé, that—that I am here, and perhaps—"

"Why don't you come along with me?" Adèle retorted drily, "and tell him what you want."

Of course, Fleurette could not tell her that she did not want Monsieur and Madame Colombe to know that she had something important to say to M'sieu' Amédé. So, all she said was: "Oh, Adèle, please!"

Adèle retorted with a shrug of the shoulders and an ugly little sneer:

"You don't want his papa and mama to know, I suppose."

Fleurette whispered: "No!"

"Very well!" was all that Adèle said in reply. "I'll tell him."

And in her usual, furtive, noiseless way she went out of the house, closing the door behind her.

Chapter 10

Fleurette remained in darkness, silent, motionless as a little mouse, listening for the well-known footstep which in a few minutes, she knew, would be at the door. It had perhaps been a rash thing thus to give herself away to Adèle, but the girl was uncommunicative and had never been known to gossip. Between two risks Fleurette had chosen the lesser one. If Bibi—as she feared—was going back to Lou Mas, there would be no chance whatever of keeping the secret of *Madame's* casket and valuables from him, and what Bibi's attitude would be towards them, Fleurette could not guess. It was the great Unknown. For *Madame's* sake and *Mademoiselle's* she would not risk it.

Like an inspiration the thought of M'sieur Amédé had occurred to her; of Amédé who, when she was a little girl and he a growing lad, would always take the blame on himself and know how to shield her when they had got into mischief together. She felt now, especially since this afternoon, that she could trust Amédé in a way that she had never trusted anyone else. Not even Bibi. Unfortunately, Adèle had to be made a part confidant of the purpose: but after all what did Adèle know? She couldn't know anything about the casket and *Madame's* valuables: and if she did sneer, or even talk to her aunt about this message sent to M'sieu' Amédé through her, well! Fleurette was prepared to face the gossip—as long as her secret was safe.

She was counting the minutes—the seconds—Five minutes for Adèle to go to the Rue Haute: three and a half for Amédé to run along here—she did not doubt that he would run. Then there would be the intervening time whilst Adèle sought for an opportunity to speak to him alone. But oh! how Time dragged on leaden-footed! Nearly fifteen minutes must have gone by since Adèle went away. The widow Tronchet was still busy in the kitchen, rattling her pots and pans: but any moment she might finish and perhaps come in here and find Fleurette still waiting. Then there would be more acrimonious remarks, questions, arguments—Had Fleurette known anything about nerves, she would have said that hers were irritated to snapping-point; but there was little talk of nerves in that year, 1794, and none in this remote corner of Dauphiné.

Fleurette found it very difficult even to sit still. Would Amédé never come! All sorts of possibilities occurred to her, bringing her to the point of screaming with impatience. Perhaps he was from home or working in the shop under his father's eye. Perhaps the soldiers had called at the *épicerie* and taken him away, and Fleurette would never see him again—Oh! if only time would stand still until Amédé came!

Then at last, when she was on the point of bursting into tears with disappointment, she heard the quick, familiar step. Amédé!!! As noiselessly as possible she opened the door and slipped out. There, sure enough, was Amédé coming along. Though it was very dark now,

Fleurette knew it was he because of the sound of his footsteps. Hearing hers, he came to a halt, and she ran up to him, breathless with excitement. All at once the enormity of what she had done struck terror in her heart. She, Fleurette, whose reputation had stood hitherto above all gossip, who for three years in succession had been crowned Queen of the month of May, an honour only accorded to girls of spotless character, she had actually given an assignation to a young man—at night—far from her home and his!

And with the horror of what she had done came an intense shyness. What would M'seur Amédé himself think of her? Indeed, she had to evoke all her fondness for *Madame* and all her fears for *Mademoiselle* before she could summon enough courage to approach him, and to place a timid little hand upon his arm. She felt it trembling at her touch, and through the silence of the night came an answering timid sigh and whisper:

"Mam'zelle Fleurette! What can I do in your service?"

His timidity gave her courage. Gently she led him to the edge of the road where the tall poplar-trees cast long, impenetrable shadows.

"M'sieur Amédé," Fleurette began, whispering low so that chance eavesdroppers might not hear: "I don't know what you'll think of me. I know I have done something which everyone in the village would call reprehensible. I sent for you in secret because—because, M'sieur Amédé, there is no one in the world I can trust, as I do trust you."

This time there came no sigh on the part of the young peasant, only a quick intaking of the breath, as if he had suddenly been dazzled by a wonderful light. His hard, rough hand crept up shyly and fastened over the soft, quivering one that lay upon his sleeve just like a frightened bird. But he was a man of few words, and therefore said nothing: and Fleurette, encouraged by the pressure of that rough hand, went on more glibly.

"It is about *Monsieur, Madame* and *Mademoiselle,*" she said, "up at the *château*. Soldiers have visited the place and they have broken the furniture and torn the beautiful carpets and the curtains: why, I know not. They have also called *Monsieur, Madame* and *Mademoiselle* traitors and aristos, and they have seized *Monsieur* and dragged him away from him home. By a miracle, M'sieur Amédé, a miracle wrought by the *bon Dieu* himself, *Madame* and *Mademoiselle* were able to escape out of the *château* before those awful soldiers came. I know that they are safe, but—"

"How do you know that, Mam'zelle Fleurette?" Amédé asked also in a whisper.

"Because, M'sieur Amédé," she replied, "there is a mysterious personage working for the safety of *Madame* and *Mademoiselle*, under the direct guidance of the good God. I feel quite sure that *Monsieur* will also presently be saved through him."

"A mysterious personage, Mam'zelle Fleurette?"

"Yes, a direct messenger from Heaven. He has come down to earth in the guise of an old faggot-carrier. He looks old and decrepit and toil-worn, but when he speaks his voice is like that of an archangel, and if he looks at you his eyes give you the strength of giants and celestial joy."

"But, Mam'zelle Fleurette—"

"His voice spoke to me this afternoon, M'sieu' Amédé. All it said to me was that papers and valuables were behind the panel in *Madame's* room. At that time, I knew nothing about the soldiers. I had seen them but did not know that they were going to the *château* to arrest *Monsieur* and *Madame* and Mademoiselle Rose. Nevertheless, when that voice spoke to me, I felt I must go over to the *château* as quickly as may be."

"Why did you not send for me then, Mam'zelle Fleurette?"

"I seemed to be in a hurry, impelled to run along as fast as I could. So, I went by the mountain track. When I arrived at the *château*, the soldiers had been there some time. They had turned the place topsy-turvy, scared the servants and smashed and torn up everything, leaving nothing but the walls intact. It seemed as if a great tempest had swept by and wrecked everything. *Monsieur* was under arrest and *Madame* and *Mademoiselle* had gone. No one knew whither. Then suddenly I remembered that mysterious voice: I found my way to *Madame's* room, and I found the panel, behind which *Madame* used to hide her household books and her money. I had often watched her doing this when I was a child. I tried to remember how to make the panel work and the good God helped me. And behind the panel I found *Madame's* papers and her money, and a small box which, I am sure, has precious things in it, or it would not have been there."

"Then what did you do, Mam'zelle Fleurette?" Amédé gasped under his breath, his none too sharp wits slowly taking in the details of the amazing adventure.

"I just took the wallet, M'sieu' Amédé," she replied simply, "and the money-bag, and the box. And here they are."

She tapped the pockets of her kirtle and made him feel the bulge underneath her shawl.

"Oh, *mon Dieu!*" he exclaimed fervently.

And then she told him about Bibi, and how frightened she was lest when she returned to Lou Mas she should find him there. Bibi's sympathies seemed to be all with the soldiers, she explained, and he would for certain make her give up *Madame's* papers and valuables to the lieutenant.

"That is why," she concluded with a return to her first timidity, "I wished to speak with you, dear M'sieu' Amédé."

"The Eternal Eve!" It was the first time Fleurette had used an endearing word when speaking to Amédé. Born and bred in this remote corner of Dauphiné, unsophisticated, untutored in the ways of *coquetry* and cajolery, she knew nevertheless, true daughter of the first mother that she was, that after this he would be mere wax in her hands.

He was!

All that he wanted to know was what he could do for her. Had she asked him to throw himself into the Buëche, he would have done it: but all that she wanted was for him to put her treasures in a safe place, until such time as *Madame* required them.

"If Bibi knew what I was doing, M'sieu' Amédé," she pleaded, "he would order me to give up *Madame's* property. But I know that the *bon Dieu* meant me to take charge of it, or why," she argued *naïvely*, "should He have sent His messenger to me?"

Of course, Amédé was only too ready to share the burden of this wonderful secret with Fleurette.

It was wonderful to share anything with this loveliest being in all the world; and the thought that she trusted him more even than her father, was sending him well-nigh crazy with joy.

"I'll tell you what I'll do, Mam'zelle Fleurette," he said: "There's an old tool-shed at the back of our house where all sorts of rubbish are kept. It is an absolute litter now, and the back of it has not been cleared or interfered with for years. But I know of a convenient hole in the flooring, hidden well away in a corner. I'll put these things there. They'll be quite safe—Mam'zelle Fleurette, you'll know where to find them after I've gone away, if you want them."

"After you've gone away?"

For the moment she had forgotten. Of course, he was going! How could she forget? He was going to join the army—to fight the English—! Perhaps he was never coming back—oh! How could she—how could she forget?

Amédé after the long speech which he had delivered in a whisper—his longest speech on record—had remained silent. The tone of anguish in Fleurette's voice, just now when he recalled the fact that he was going away, had given him an immense thrill of joy. Altogether poor Amédé felt so happy that he was almost ashamed. The night was so beautifully still: the wind had gone down, and slowly the great clouds that had obscured the sky since sunset were rolling away over the valley. Already overhead a patch of translucent indigo appeared, ever-widening, and revealing one by one the scintillating worlds that are beyond man's ken. Amédé did not want to speak; he wanted it less than he had ever done before. He just wanted to stand there beside this exquisite creature, wrapped in the silence of the night, feeling her nearness, hearing the gentle murmur of her breath come and go through her perfect mouth. She had extracted the casket from under her shawl and given it to him to hold, and she also gave him the wallet and the money-bag; and as she did this, her little hand, so soft and so warm, came in contact with his now and then—quite often—and poor Amédé was on the point of swooning with delight.

"I do trust you, M'sieu' Amédé," she whispered in the end: "and you'll do this for *Madame's* sake, will you not? and also for *Mademoiselle's*. And also," she added softly, "for mine."

"Oh! Mam'zelle Fleurette," Amédé sighed. What he had wished to say was: "I would die for you, beloved of my heart: at a word from you I would lay down my life or barter my soul." But Amédé had no command of words and was now cursing himself for being a clumsy fool. He stowed away the wallet and the bag into the pockets of his breeches and tucked the casket underneath his blouse.

"And now I must go home, dear Monsieur Amédé," Fleurette said. "As it is, I am afraid Bibi will be anxious."

Her hand was on his arm: and with a sudden impulse he stooped and pressed his lips against that exquisite little hand. Fortunately, they were still standing in the shadows cast by the poplar-trees, or Amédé must have seen the blush that rose to Fleurette's cheeks when she felt the delicious thrill of that timid kiss. A soft breeze stirred the branches above their heads, and through the quivering leaves there came a sigh that was like an echo of their own. And above the crests of Pelvoux the waning moon suddenly rent the last clouds that veiled her mystery and flooded the snowy immensities with a shower of gold. Slowly the shades of night yielded to the magic, and the high-road glistened like a silvery ribbon winding, snake-like, toward Laragne.

Fleurette gave a sudden start of alarm.

"What is it, Mam'zelle Fleurette," Amédé asked.

"Someone," she said. "I saw someone move there—furtively—among the shadows."

He turned to look. A small figure wrapped in a shawl had just gone past on the other side of the road.

"It is only Adèle," he said carelessly. "She is going home."

Not altogether reassured, Fleurette peered into the shadows. She did not think that it was Adèle whom she had seen, or, if it was Adèle, there was someone else lurking in the shadows, she felt sure: and though she was not altogether frightened, she felt herself trembling, and her knees giving way under her. No doubt it was in order to save herself from falling that she had leaned more heavily against Amédé's arm. Certain it is that he put that arm round her, only in order to support her; but the contact of that warm, quivering young body against his breast sent the last shred of his self-control flying away on the evening breeze.

The high-road was bathed in honey-coloured light, but these two were standing in the deep shadow cast by the poplar-trees; and the darkness wrapped them round as in a velvety, downy blanket. His arm tightened round her shoulders, pressed her closer and closer to his breast, held her there so closely that she could scarcely breathe.

It was only in order to get her breath that she raised her face to his; far be it from me to suggest that it was for any other motive; but this proved the final undoing of poor M'sieu' Amédé; for the next moment his lips were fastened hungrily on hers, and her sweet young soul went out to him, in a first, a most delicious kiss.

Chapter 11

It all seemed like a lovely dream after that: this walking together arm in arm down the high-road with the waning moon throwing great patches of silvery light to guide them on their way.

They went through the village, not caring whom they met. They belonged to each other now; that wonderful kiss was a bond between them that only death could sever. That was how they felt; supremely, marvellously happy, thrilled with his new delight, this undreamed joy: and with it all a cloud of measureless sorrow at the impending fare-well. The magic words had been spoken: "You love me, Fleurette?" The eternal question to which the only answer is a sigh. No, they did not care whom they met. They could laugh at gossip now: from this night they were tokened to one another, and only *M. le Curé's* blessing could make their happiness more complete.

As a matter of fact, they met no one, for they avoided the main street of the village and made their way to Lou Mas along narrow by-paths that meandered through orchards of almond-trees heavy with blossom. For the most part they were silent. Fleurette's little hand rested on Amédé's arm. Now and then he gave that hand a quick, excited squeeze and this relieved his feelings for the time being. Under his other arm he hugged the casket, the precious treasure that had been the mute but main spring of his happiness. It represented Fleurette's trust in him: that priceless guerdon he would not have bartered for a kingdom.

"You will not part with *Madame's* valuables, will you, Amédé?" she had enjoined him most solemnly. "Not to anyone?"

"Never, Fleurette," he had replied solemnly. "On my soul!"

When they were within sight of Lou Mas, they decided that it would be best for him to turn back. She, Fleurette, was quite safe now, and of course old Louise would be waiting for her—and perhaps Bibi. She was not going to make a secret of her walk home with Amédé. Indeed, she wished it proclaimed from the house-tops that they were tokened to one another, and that they would be married as soon as this horrible war was over. There was to be no secret about it, and Fleurette knew well enough that neither Bibi nor M'sieu' Colombe would object; but because of *Madame's* valuables, she did not want Amédé to come to Lou Mas until tomorrow. And so that first wonderful kiss found its successor in another—one that was perhaps even more delicious, because it was more poignant—the precursor of the last farewell.

Fleurette found Louise anxiously waiting for her. Bibi had not returned and the old woman knew nothing, of course, of the tragic events that had occurred at the *château*. Fleurette told her what had happened, and while she was speaking Bibi came in. He looked tired and anxious, but Fleurette thought it prudent not to appear to notice anything unusual about him. He made no reference to the events at Frontenac, and when nine o'clock came he kissed Fleurette as tenderly, as unconcernedly as usual. Nine o'clock! What a lifetime, as far as Fleurette was concerned, had been crowded into this past hour!

She went to bed as in a dream, partly made up of sorrow and partly of great joy: even the excitement of her adventure at the *château* was lost in the immensity of that joy. Fleurette fell asleep with her cheek against the hand on which Amédé had planted that first timid kiss.

When she came down in the early morning Bibi had already gone.

Chapter 12

The soldiers of the Republic together with their officer had spent half the night at Laragne in the tavern kept by the Père Gramme, drinking and jesting with the drabs of the village. Each man had a tale to tell of his own prowess at the *château*, and how but for him, the *ci-devant* Frontenac would have slipped through the fingers of justice as readily as the two women had gone.

They were very proud of their prisoner, who sat lonely and silent in a corner of the low-raftered room, foul with the odour of sour wine and perspiring humanity. Monsieur de Frontenac—the *ci-devant* as he was curtly termed—was apparently taking his misfortune calmly; neither threats nor vain promises caused him to depart from his attitude of quiet philosophy. The soldiers had, of course, made up their minds that he knew well enough where his wife and daughter were in hiding, but they had also realised by now that it was not in their power to force him to divulge what he knew.

The lieutenant—a man who had begun life as a notary's clerk, and therefore had some education—was content to shrug his shoulders and to declare that the citizens of the nearest Committee of Public Safety had plenty of means at their disposal for making an obdurate prisoner speak. He recalled that at the trial of the Widow Capet she had been forced into admissions which, before that, she would sooner have died than make. Mocking glances, jeers and insults were thereupon cast on the prisoner who remained as unconcerned, as serene as before.

The lieutenant had commandeered billets for his men in the better houses of the village, and just before midnight the party broke up. The prisoner was then conducted to the small, local *poste de gendarmerie* and there incarcerated in the cell usually occupied by vagabonds and cattle-thieves. Two or three of the soldiers remained at the *poste* to reinforce the local *gendarmes*, in case some hot-heads in the village meditated a *coup* to wrest the traitor Frontenac from the clutches of justice. The lieutenant himself had selected the house of Citizen Colombe the grocer of the Rue Haute for his night-quarters. To say that the worthy *épicier* did not accord this representative of his country's army a warm welcome, would be to put it mildly. He was furious and showed it as plainly as he dared; but there is in every French peasant a sound vein of common sense, and he knows—none better—when submission to the ruling powers is not only the best policy, but at the same time the most conducive to the preservation of his own dignity.

Ma'ame Colombe—or rather the citizeness—made the lieutenant comfortable and that was all; but at the bottom of her heart she felt that she must do unto him as she would wish her own son to be done by presently, when he too was a soldier in that army which she detested. She fell asleep thinking of Amédé tramping the high-road as these men had done, stockingless, hatless, with unwashed shirt and a dirty worsted cap on his head; and she dreamed all night of him, deprived even of his weekly bath in the big tub, over in the wash-house. That is what she objected to mostly in these men: the dirt. It was wonderful, of course, their fighting for their country, now that all the other countries in the world were attacking France, but Ma'ame Colombe argued to herself that patriotism might just as well be allied to cleanliness. Even the lieutenant, who was after all an officer, and should be setting a good example to his men, would have looked much more imposing if he had washed his face and taken the dust of the road out of his hair.

Great, therefore, was Ma'ame Colombe's astonishment the next morning when she, along with several of her friends, being at the market, saw another detachment of soldiers marching into Laragne from the direction of Sisteron. Only eight of them there were, with one officer and a wagon drawn by two splendid horses; but *nom du ciel!* what a different set of men and horses these were. The men clean as new pins, magnificently dressed in blue coats with white facings and belts, white breeches—all spotless—and black gaiters that reached midway up their thighs.

Beneath their elegant *chapeau-bras*, each adorned with a silk tricolour cockade, they wore their own hair, down to their shoulders, unfettered by the old, ridiculous queue, and each man had successfully cultivated a fierce and magnificent moustache. Everything about them glistened with cleanliness, their boots, their buckles, their muskets; as for the officer, never in all their lives had the good ladies of Laragne seen anyone so magnificent: tall, blond, with a moustache that he could easily have tucked behind his ears, and a little tuft of blond beard at the tip of his chin, he walked with drawn sword at the head of his squad, a superb tricolour sash further enhancing the glory of his attire.

Potatoes and eggs and butter were forgotten, while market-women and customers stood gaping, open mouthed. Never had such beautiful specimens of manhood been seen in Laragne. By the time they reached the Rue Haute all the village had turned out to have a look at them, and heads appeared at every cottage window. The village urchins followed the little squad, intoning the *"Marseillaise"* and giving vent to their excitement by performing miracles of acrobatic evolutions. Even Ma'ame Colombe, who was at the moment selecting a piece of meat for Sunday's dinner, could not help but say to herself that she would not mind Amédé being in the army if he was going to look like that!

At that very moment one of the urchins paused in the midst of a magnificently sketched somersault in order to run down the street and back to the market-place, shouting excitedly:

"Ma'ame Colombe! Ma'ame Colombe! the soldiers are at the *épicerie."*

And so they were! Ma'ame Colombe hastily straightened her cap and snatching up her market basket, ran to the corner of the Rue Haute just in time to see the soldiers with their officer and wagon come to a halt outside her front door. The worthy Hector with his son Amédé, and the old man who helped in the shop, were busy taking down the shutters and displaying the sacks of various kinds of haricots and lentils in tempting array all along the shop front. Ma'ame Colombe heard the magnificent officer give a quick order: *"Halte!"* and *"Attention!"* and the next moment she saw him enter the shop followed by his men, the wagon remaining drawn up a little further down the street. The urchins and gaffers crowded round the doorstep open-mouthed, and Ma'ame Colombe had some difficulty in pushing her way through into her own house.

The officer began by asking Hector Colombe how many soldiers of the Republic were still sleeping under his roof.

"Only the lieutenant and two men, *M'sieu' l'officier*," Hector replied. Whereupon the officer broke in curtly:

"Call me citizen captain. This is the Army of the Revolution and its soldiers are not *aristos* meseems."

Which remark boded no good to Ma'ame Colombe's ears. Clean or dirty they all appeared to be the same type of brigands; overbearing, exacting and merciless! Ah that poor dear Amédé!

The officer then demanded to see the lieutenant and the two soldiers. Amédé offered to call them, but was stopped by a brief command from the captain:

71

"No, not you," he said curtly, "I want you here, the citizeness can go."

Ma'ame Colombe, obedient and vaguely frightened, put down her basket and went upstairs to fetch the lieutenant and the two men, who were still in bed. But although she had only been gone a couple of minutes, her sense of fear took on a more tangible form when she came down again, for she found all the drawers of the counter open, and much of their contents scattered about the floor. Some of the soldiers were busy ferreting about, behind and under the counter. The officer stood in the middle of the shop talking with Hector, who looked both choleric and sullen; in the doorway, the crowd of gaffers were being kept back by two of the soldiers, who were using the butts of their muskets when some venturesome urchin tried to cross the threshold. But what filled poor Ma'ame Colombe's heart with dismay was the sight of Amédé sitting in the parlour behind the shop, with two other soldiers obviously on guard over him.

Her instinct prompted her to run first of all to her husband with a quick whispered: "Hector, what does this mean?"

But the magnificent officer brusquely thrust himself between her and Hector and said gruffly: "It means, citizeness, that not only treason, but also theft has been traced to this house, and that it is lucky for you that news of it reached the Committee of Sisteron in time, else," he added grimly, "it had been worse for you and your family."

"Treason and theft?" Ma'ame Colombe exclaimed in hot indignation. "You must take it from me, young man, citizen, captain, or whatever you may be, that I'll allow no one to——"

"Hold your tongue, woman," the officer broke in curtly; "you do yourself no good by these protests. Obedience is your wisest course."

"Good or no good," Ma'ame Colombe persisted heatedly, "I won't have the word theft used in connection with this house, and if——"

"Make your wife hold her tongue, citizen," the officer, now addressing Hector once more, broke in curtly, "or I shall have to send her to the *poste* for interfering with a soldier of the Republic in the execution of his duty."

Poor Hector Colombe, whose choler was shrinking in inverse ratio to that of his wife, did his best to pacify the worthy dame.

"It is all a mistake, Angélique," he said gently. "*M'sieu' le Capitaine—pardon!* the citizen captain thinks that Amédé has some papers and valuables belong to *Madame*—I mean, to the Citizeness Frontenac——"

"Are they calling my Amédé a thief, then?" Ma'ame Colombe demanded hotly.

"No! No!" Hector replied, trying to be patient and conciliatory. "Have I not told you that it is all a mistake? Everyone knows there are no thieves in this house; but it seems the authorities think that Amédé may have hidden those valuables *pour le bon motif.*"

"If he had," the mother retorted obstinately, "he would say so. Let me just ask him—"

Hector had hold of her hand, but she wrenched it free, and before any of the soldiers could bar the way, she had run into the back parlour, shouting:

"Amédé, my little one, have you told those soldiers that you know nothing of *Madame's* valuables? Why, *nom de Dieu!*" she went on, hands on hips, defiant and aggressive like the true female defending its young, "look at the innocent. Is that the face of a thief?"

She pointed at Amédé, who, however, remained strangely silent.

"*Voyons, mon petit,* tell them!" Angélique Colombe went on with perhaps a shade less assurance than she had displayed at first. The next moment, however, the captain had seized her unceremoniously by the arm, and dragged her back into the front shop. Here he gave her arm a good shake.

"Did I not order you to hold your tongue?" he demanded roughly.

Cowed, in spite of herself, not so much by the officer's tone of command as by Amédé's silence, Ma'ame Colombe did, in effect, hold her tongue. A sense of disaster as well as of shame had suddenly descended upon her. Her ample bosom heaving, she sank into a chair, and threw her apron over her head. She was not crying, but she felt the need of shutting out from her vision the picture of Amédé looking so confused and sullen, of Hector looking as perplexed as she was herself, as well as of that magnificent officer with his fine clothes and his tricolour sash.

But chiefly she wanted for the moment to lose sight of that crowd of gaffers and urchins and neighbours, all staring at her, with that unexplainable feeling, not exactly of contentment for her misfortune, but which can only be expressed by that untranslatable word *Schadenfreude.* Thus, shut out from the rest of her little world, the poor woman slowly rocked herself backwards and forwards, murmuring inaudible words under cover of her apron, until she heard the captain's voice saying abruptly:

"Were you the officer in charge of detachment number ninety-seven?"

Curiosity got the better of sorrow, and Ma'ame Colombe peeped round the edge of her apron. The picture which she saw made her drop her apron altogether. The lieutenant who, the night before, had been so overbearing and so hilarious, stood before his superior officer now, a humble, dejected figure, dreading reprimand, like a schoolboy fearing the cane.

"I am in charge of the detachment ninety-seven—yes, citizen captain," he replied haltingly.

What a contrast these two! Ma'ame Colombe, in spite of her anxiety, her indignation and what not, could not help but compare. Woman-like, she had an eye for the handsome male, and what more gorgeous than this captain of the Republican, or revolutionary army, as he apparently liked to style his men, with his braided jacket and superb tricolour sash, with his blond hair and fierce *moustachios?* He poked his tufted chin out at the bedraggled-looking lieutenant before him, looked down with obvious contempt at the latter's ragged coat and mud-stained breeches. But he made no remark on the want of cleanliness and decency, as Ma'ame Colombe expected him to do.

"Where do you come from?" he demanded.

"From Orange, citizen captain."

"What is your objective?"

"After this, Serres, citizen captain, and then Valence."

"And your orders are to arrest on the way every person suspected of treason against the Republic?

"Yes, citizen."

"And how have you obeyed these orders, citizen lieutenant?" the captain demanded sternly.

"I have done my best, citizen captain," the other replied with an attempt at bluster; "at Vaison—"

"I am not talking of Vaison, which you know quite well, citizen lieutenant. I wish to know how you obeyed the orders given to you to arrest the *ci-devant* Frontenac, his wife and daughter?"

"Citizen—"

"Have you done it, citizen lieutenant?" the officer thundered, and all of the bluster went out of the subaltern as he stammered meekly:

"When we reached the house of the *ci-devant* Frontenac, the two women had gone."

"Gone?" and the captain's voice boomed through the low-raftered room like a distant roll of cannon. "Gone? Whither?"

"Gone, citizen captain," the lieutenant murmured under his breath:

74

"spirited away. The devil alone knows how."

"Which means that there is a traitor among you."

"Citizen captain—" the other protested.

"A traitor I say. You had secret orders, and yet the women were warned!" And once more the officer's glance flashed down with scorn on his unfortunate subordinate. His blond hair seemed to bristle with wrath; his *moustachios* stood out like spikes: he looked a veritable god of vengeance and of wrath.

"Whence," he thundered, "is the *ci-devant* Frontenac?"

"At the *commissariat*, citizen captain, guarded by our men," the lieutenant replied.

"And the rest of your detachment?"

"In billets in the village."

"And did you search this house when you entered it?"

"No—that is—no—I did not—that is—" stammered the wretched man.

"Or the other houses where you billeted your men?"

But this time the lieutenant only shook his head in dejected silence.

"Which means that you allowed soldiers of the Republic to sleep under strange roofs without ascertaining whether they were safe. Why, citizen lieutenant, this place might have been swarming with traitors."

"The people here, citizen, are—"

"Enough. You are relieved of your command, and you will proceed now with us to Sisteron where you will render an account of your conduct before the Committee of Public Safety."

Ma'ame Colombe, who had watched the two men closely during this exciting colloquy, saw an ashen hue spread over the lieutenant's face, beneath the thick coating of grime. Though they did not know much in this tucked-away corner of Dauphiné, of what went on in the great cities, they had vaguely heard how great officers of the army had been deprived of their rank and sent to the guillotine for not doing their duty by the Army of the Republic. The crowd at the door had also listened in silence; many a cheek turned pale at sound of that thundering voice which held in its arrogant tone a menace of death.

And now the captain turned to the other two down-at-heels soldiers who stood skulking behind their lieutenant.

"Go," he commanded, "round the billets where your comrades are. Bring them hither. And one of you to the *commissariat* and bring the *ci-devant* here too. And no delay, remember. No gossip on the way as

75

you value your lives. I give you five minutes to have all the men and the prisoner here."

The men went immediately to execute the peremptory order, while the lieutenant remained in the shop looking the picture of humility and dejection. Ma'ame Colombe who had a kindly heart inside her ample bosom, felt almost sorry for the man, so miserable did he look. Indeed, it seemed as if this squad of elegantly clad soldiers sowed anguish and terror in their path.

But the worst was yet to come. Ma'ame Colombe thought that she had probed the last depths of humiliation when she heard that gorgeous officer call her Amédé a thief. To such a pass had this so-called revolution brought the respectable children of France, that they saw themselves bullied and insulted, and held up to shame before their neighbours. What was all that in comparison with the shame of seeing Amédé confronted with the proof that in very truth he was in possession of papers and valuables which were the property of Madame de Frontenac?

It all happened so quickly. Poor Ma'ame Colombe could scarce believe her eyes. All that she saw was two soldiers guided by their sumptuous captain go straight through the back parlour and out by the back door into the yard. What happened out there she did not know, but a minute or two later the three men were standing once more in the parlour, and the captain had in his hand a small box, a thick leather wallet and a bag which obviously contained money.

At sight of these Amédé—her Amédé—had jumped to his feet as if he had been stung; all the blood rushed to his face, and made it crimson with choler, and it looked for the moment as if he would hurl himself on the officer of the Republican Army—which would have meant instant death for him, as the soldiers had already shouldered their muskets. Ma'ame Colombe gave a terrified shriek, whereat Amédé suddenly seemed to realise his position, the flush died out of his poor face, and with eyes downcast he resumed his former silent, constrained attitude.

The captain shrugged his shoulders and with a note of dry sarcasm in his voice he said:

"I see you make no attempt at denial. You are wise, citizen. Try and induce your mother not to shriek and you'll find that everything will turn out for the best."

He did not say this unkindly, and poor Ma'ame Colombe even thought that she detected an indulgent tone in his voice. She rose to her feet and put her podgy hands together, and when the captain re-entered the shop she looked up at him with tearful, entreating eyes.

"He did it with a good motive, *M'sieu' le*—I mean citizen captain. Look at the innocent. He is no thief. I swear he is no thief. I'd like," she went on, turning fiercely round and darting defiant glances on the crowd of gaffers on the doorstep, "I'd like to see the man who dared to say that my Amédé is a thief."

The officer had handed the *pièces de conviction* to one of his men, with orders to put them in the wagon. Then he commanded Amédé to stand up before him.

"Thief or no thief," he said drily, "you are guilty of having acted contrary to the interests of the Republic. You know what that means?"

Amédé made no reply, only hung his head, and twiddled his hot fingers together.

"It means," the officer continued, "that but for one thing, your life would have had to answer for this act of treason."

A groan went round the crowd on whose ears those words had fallen like the toll of a passing bell. But Ma'ame Colombe did not utter a sound. She clung to her Hector and the two old people stood there hand in hand, striving by this loving contact to conquer the icy fear that had gripped their hearts.

"The one thing that will probably save you," the officer resumed after a dramatic pause, "is that the Republic has need of you in her revolutionary army. The enemy is at the gates of France, you are young, healthy, vigorous; it is for you to show your mettle by defending your country. Thus, you will redeem the past. For the moment it is my duty to take you before the Committee of Public Safety, whose final word will dispose of your fate."

He spoke loudly so that all the listeners might hear. Gaffers and urchins and market-women hardly dared to breathe. They felt awed, and could only gaze at one another, as if trying to read each other's thoughts. And while awed whispers still went the round, the down-at-heels soldiers, who had spent the night in the village, came skulking back in groups of two or threes. They pushed their way through the crowd into the shop. One of the last to arrive was M. de Frontenac, closely guarded by two of the men.

And there they all stood now in the shop, a dozen or so of them, beside the sacks of haricots and button-onions and split peas; all of them with the exception of the prisoner, looking dirty and bedraggled, with their worsted caps covered in dust, bits of hay and straw clinging to their coats and to their hair, bare-legged and grimy-faced, the steel of their bayonets dull with sludge, their breeches mud-stained. Such a contrast to their superb officer and his splendidly attired squad. And they could hear the women drawing humiliating comparisons, tittering and pointing fingers of scorn at them, whilst even the drabs, with whom they had drunk and jested the night before, turned contemptuous shoulders upon them now.

And thus, they were mustered before the magnificent captain; all soldiers together, shoulder to shoulder, the down-at-heel and the *grandees*—*aristos* one would have called them, only that they were of the revolutionary army, which set out to exterminate the very last of the aristocracy, the hated tyrants and dissolute brood. And while they stood there, under the eye of the officer, the crowd outside watched them, and instinctively something of the spirit that animated the rest of France, swept like a poisonous sirocco over these worthy villagers of Laragne; same spirit that in the great cities sent old women knitting and gossiping at the foot of the guillotine and that prompted young girls to dip their kerchiefs in the blood of its victims. A poisonous wind like the breath of demons! Some of the men and women had been to Sisteron and heard the hymn of hate, the Carmagnole! "*Ça ira! Ça ira! Les aristos à la lanterne!*" One or two of them began to hum it, stamping their feet to its rhythm.

Gradually the song swelled, one after another they took up the tune, these village men and maids who, unbeknown even to themselves had absorbed some of the insidious poison of hatred and black envy.

"Right! Turn!" the captain commanded, and marking time with their feet, the little squad now over twenty strong, started on its way. Ma'ame Colombe, now loudly moaning, still clung to her boy. He was very brave and tried to reassure and to comfort her. Anyway, he would have had to go today, he argued, his orders were to report himself at Serres, to be drafted into the army. From the officer's attitude it certainly seemed as if nothing more terrifying was to happen to him. The boy was brave enough too not to let his mother know how doubly his heart ached, because he was saying goodbye to his home, and could not say goodbye to Fleurette. His heart was filled with the image of Fleurette, but he would not add to his mother's sorrow by speaking to her of his own. He was just an unsophisticated village lad, knowing little, understanding less. His own life and comfort were nothing to him, beside the sorrow which his mother felt and which, he knew,

78

would bring such countless tears in Fleurette's lovely blue eyes. The father too tried to be brave; the effort to keep back his tears brought the perspiration streaming down his round, kindly face. When the crowd—his friends and neighbours some of them—intoned the revolutionary song, his powerful fist was clenched, but he did not shake it at the singers. His sound common sense had come again to his rescue, and whispered to him that for Amédé's sake, quiet submission was the soundest policy.

While mother and son clung to one another in a last farewell, Hector contrived to approach M. de Frontenac who, alone in the midst of such excitement and such conflicting emotions, had remained perfectly calm. The casual observer, not knowing him, might have thought that the fate of his wife and daughter, his separation from them, and the blow that destiny had dealt to these worthy folk here, whom he had known all his life, had left him completely indifferent. He had spent the night in a prison cell, under the eye of men—the local *gendarmes*—whose welfare and whose families had been his care for years; but seemingly he had slept peacefully.

At any rate his face showed no sign of fatigue, or his eyes of sleeplessness. He had dressed with scrupulous care; his well-worn clothes, the ones he was wearing at dinner when the soldiers made irruption into the *château*, were clean and tidily put on; his cravat neatly tied, his hair smooth. When Hector Colombe approached him, he gripped the worthy *épicier* warmly by the hand.

And now the crowd parted to allow the soldiers to pass. Some of the girls tried to ogle the handsome ones and to leer at the others, but no one attempted to do more than stare in awe and admiration at the magnificent officer. The two prisoners were ordered to mount into the wagon; one of the soldiers took the reins and the next moment the order, "Quick March!" was given.

The crowd broke into an excited "Hurrah!" and the little squad slowly moved off, officer *en tête*, and the wagon in the rear, in the direction of Sisteron. Then one of the villagers once more struck up the *Carmagnole*, and the crowd took it up. "*Ça ira! ça ira!*" they sang gaily, and the men took the girls by the waist and twirled them round in a gay rigadoon. Old men and young girls; for there were no young men in the villages of France these days, when the army claimed them all, they danced and twirled in the wake of the retreating squad, and around them bare-footed urchins somersaulted along in the cloud of dust raised by the horses and wagon.

And that was the picture that Amédé Colombe and Charles de Frontenac, sitting side by side in the wagon, saw gradually receding before their eyes as they were driven away, prisoners from their homes.

Chapter 13

But in Lou Mas nothing was known of the tragic events that were occurring at Laragne. Old Louise and Fleurette were busy with housework, and if Fleurette went about the house, silent and wistful, it was because presently she would have to say the inevitable farewell to Amédé.

It was Adèle who brought the news. Young Colombe had been arrested by soldiers of the revolutionary army, she said, and he and M'sieu' de Frontenac had been taken to Sisteron. A superior officer of the army had come in this morning and relieved the lieutenant of his command. There had been great excitement in Laragne owing to the arrival of this new detachment of soldiers who were as splendid as those of last night had been travel-stained and bedraggled. The whole of the squad, headed by that magnificent officer, had marched away in the direction of Sisteron, the two prisoners sitting in the wagon in the rear.

It was only bit by bit that old Louise succeeded in dragging all this news out of Adèle. The girl's habitual reticence was put to a severe test by all the questions and cross-questions, whilst Fleurette stood by wide-eyed, distraught with the idea of these horrible complications in which her poor Amédé was being involved. But she would not show any emotion before Adèle, she felt vaguely that her foster-sister, never very expansive towards her, had suddenly become almost inimical. So, she waited until Louise had extracted all the news she could out of the taciturn girl, and curtly ordered her back into the kitchen; then as the old woman was about to follow, Fleurette caught her by the hand.

"Louise," she said in a tone of almost desperate entreaty, "dear, kind Louise, I must go to Sisteron—at once."

"To Sisteron?" old Louise exclaimed, frowning. "Heavens alive, what is the child thinking of now?"

"Of M'sieu' Amédé, dear Louise," Fleurette replied. "You heard what Adèle said. They have taken him to Sisteron."

"And what of it?" Louise asked—but she asked for form's sake only, she knew quite well what was going on in Fleurette's head.

"Only this, dear Louise," the girl said with a little note of defiance piercing through her shyness. "We—that is Amédé and I—are

80

tokened to one another."

"Tokened?" the old woman exclaimed with a gasp. "Since when?"

"Since last night."

"And without your father's consent? Well! of all the——"

"*Chéri* Bibi would approve," Fleurette asserted, "if he knew."

Old Louise shrugged her shoulders. She would not trust herself to speak because the child looked so sweet and so innocent, and her pretty blue eyes were so full of tears, that Louise felt an almost unconquerable desire to take hold of her and hug her to her breast. Which act of weakness would have seriously impaired her authority at this critical juncture. She was wondering what to say next—for in truth she more than suspected that the child was right, and that Citizen Armand would not object to those two young things being tokened to one another, when Fleurette broke in gently:

"So, you see, dear, kind Louise, that I must go to Sisteron—now—at once."

"But Holy Virgin, what to do?"

"To see Amédé and comfort him."

"They won't let you see him, child."

"Then I will find *chéri* Bibi," Fleurette retorted calmly. "He has a great deal more authority than you and I credit him with, Louise. He can order whom he likes not only to let me see Amédé, but even to set him free."

"He would be very angry," Louise argued, "to see you wandering about the high-roads alone, while all those soldiers and riff-raff are about."

Fleurette gave a quaint little smile.

"Bibi's anger against me never lasts very long," she said. "Anyway, I will risk it. Louise dear, will you come with me?"

"I?"

"Of course, you said that Bibi would be angry if I roamed about the high-roads alone."

Louise stood squarely in front of Fleurette, looked straight into those blue eyes, which never before had held such a determined glance. Fleurette could not help smiling at the old woman's look of perplexity; she was the typical hen seeing her brood of ducklings take their first plunge in the pond.

"If you won't come with me, Louise dear," the girl said simply, "I shall have to go alone."

"Get along with ye, for an obstinate wench," Louise retorted gruffly. But the next moment she had already changed her tone. "Get on your thick woollen stockings, child," she said, "and your buckled shoes, and your brown cloak, while I put a few things in a basket for our dinner. If we don't hurry, we shan't be in Sisteron before nightfall."

"M'sieu' Duflos will lend us his cart or a horse," Fleurette rejoined gleefully, "but I won't be long, dear, kind Louise."

And swift as a young hare she ran out and then up the outside staircase to her room under the overhanging climbing rose.

A few minutes later the two women started on their way. Fleurette had on her dark kirtle, her thick stockings and buckled shoes; her fair hair was tucked away underneath her frilled mob-cap. She carried her own cloak and Louise's on her arm, whilst Louise tramped beside her, carrying a basket in which she had hastily packed a piece of bread, some cheese, and two hard-boiled eggs. If M'sieu' Duflos, the butcher, would lend them his cart, they would be in Sisteron by mid-day; but in any case, they would be there before dark.

Chapter 14

But M'sieu Duflos had no cart to lend them—that is he had no horse. Didn't Mam'zelle Fleurette and Ma'ame Louise remember? Some of those brigands had been round the week before and requisitioned every horse they could lay their hands on all over the countryside; old nags, mares with foals, butchers' cobs, nothing came amiss to them, nothing was sacred. Oh, those soldiers! Were they not the curse of the country? And what difference there was between the so-called revolutionary army and a pillaging band of pirates, M'sieu' Duflos, the butcher, really couldn't say.

All this he told the two women, to the accompaniment of wide gestures of his powerful arms and much shrugging of his broad shoulders. It was Fleurette who had put the question breathlessly to him, as soon as she had caught sight of him standing on the door of his shop, blocking it with his massive bulk.

"A horse? A cart? Alas! it was impossible! Ah! those brigands! those brigands!"

Fleurette could not conceal her disappointment at first; but she was so brave, so resolute; she was for making an immediate start so as to get to Sisteron before dark. Perhaps they would meet horse and cart belonging to some neighbour luckier than poor M'sieu' Duflos. But Louise, more prudent, saw an opportunity for putting the mad adventure off until the next day. A start in the early morning could then be made, she argued, and horse or no horse, Sisteron might be reached before the sun was low. A good project forsooth. Let Fleurette return with her quietly now to Lou Mas and sleep on it. That was it! sleep on it! If only Fleurette would do that she, Louise, felt quite sure that counsels of prudence would prevail.

M. Duflos sagely nodded his head. Sisteron? He could not conjecture why Mam'zelle Fleurette should wish to go to Sisteron. Without an escort! And on foot! What would Citizen Armand say to it, if he knew?

Up to this point, you perceive, not a word about the exciting events that had convulsed Laragne a little over two hours ago. M'sieu' Duflos, watching Fleurette, marvelled how much the girl knew. She on the other hand was longing to ask questions, whilst dreading to lose time in unnecessary gossip. She looked about her at the familiar objects: the pump, the shop fronts, the *poste de gendarmerie*, on the other side of the square, and in the corner of this Rue Haute where the soldiers must have stood this morning with Amédé, a prisoner amongst them.

Everything for the moment in Laragne appeared calm, not to say commonplace. The women had all gone home to cook the midday dinner; the men were at their work. Every moment she thought that she must see Amédé coming round the corner with his slow swinging steps, looking for her! M'sieu' Duflos and Louise were talking together, not exactly in whispers, but under their breath; the way people talk when the subject is exciting and perhaps awe-inspiring. And suddenly M. Duflos exclaimed with a great, big sigh of compassion:

"If it is not a misery! *Mon Dieu! Mon Dieu!* those poor Colombes!"

His kindly glance turned to Fleurette, and he saw her big blue eyes fixed on him. And as he was a very worthy fellow this M. Duflos, with a daughter of his own, he could not somehow return that glance; there was something in it that reminded him of a young animal in pain. He guessed that she had heard the news about young Colombe, and he knew, as everyone did in Laragne, that Fleurette, over at Lou Mas, and Amédé Colombe were fond of one another, and that they would be tokened as soon as the girl had turned eighteen.

This love-romance had been part of the village life ever since the two children had made mud pies together in the market square with the dust of the road and the water from the fountain, and though Armand, over at Lou Mas had become very queer of late, and no one knew anything about the mysterious business which, of recent years, kept him away from home for months on end, every one remembered the pretty Marseillaise whom nineteen years ago he had brought to Lou Mas as a blushing bride, and no one had forgotten the terrible tragedy of her death when she gave birth to Fleurette. With the kindliness, one might say the indifference, peculiar to the peasant, the neighbours put down Armand's growing moroseness after that terrible event, and his secretive ways, to grief over the death of his young wife; and then after a while, they ceased to trouble about him at all, and almost forgot him as it were.

But Fleurette had grown up among them all, a true child of sunny Dauphiné, in spite of her fair hair and blue eyes. They all loved her because she was so pretty, and though M'sieu' Colombe, the prosperous grocer of the Rue Haute, might at one time have had more ambitious views for his son, he and Ma'ame Colombe soon fell victims to Fleurette's charm, her dainty ways, her quaint little airs, as if she were a lady strayed into this remote village from some great city, and, above all, being natives of the South, and children of France, they succumbed to the fascination of her wealth; for there was no doubt that Armand was rich, and no doubt that he had made a declaration both privately to his friend Colombe and officially before the notary at Sisteron, that he would give his only child a dowry of ten thousand *livres tournois*, the day she married with his consent.

And here was this child now, whom everyone knew and whom everyone loved, turning great, pleading eyes on M'sieu' Duflos until the worthy fellow felt so uncomfortable that he had to clear his throat very noisily and to expectorate on the sanded floor of his shop with a sound like the falling of a shower of hailstones on a tiled roof. He thought that Fleurette knew all the details of this morning's dramatic story.

"*Voyons*, Mam'zelle Fleurette," he said with a rough attempt at consolation. "They won't do anything to Amédé. Really. The boy meant no harm."

All then would have been well if that fool Aristide Sicard, who was M'sieu' Duflos' errand-man, had not put in a word.

"No one," he said, "is going to believe that Amédé Colombe is a thief."

"A thief?" and Fleurette gave a funny little gasp. "Why should they think that Amédé is a thief?"

M'sieu Duflos, the butcher, had given his errand-man a vigorous kick, but the correction came too late. And now Fleurette wanted to know more.

"What is your meaning, M'sieu' Aristide?" she insisted with that funny little air of determination of hers, whilst a frown appeared between her brows.

As M'sieu' Duflos explained to the neighbours afterwards, Fleurette looked as if she might be capable of anything at the moment. He was quite frightened at the expression in her blue eyes. It was too late to undo the mischief that that fool Aristide had done, so the butcher took the matter into his own hands. He had a sound knowledge of human nature, had M'sieu' Duflos, and he prided himself on his tact.

"You see, Mam'zelle Fleurette," he began, "it's this way. Those scurvy knaves—I mean the soldiers of the Republic—were full of choler because they had not found enough to steal at the *château* when they arrested poor M'sieu' de Frontenac. At first, it seems, they thought that *Madame* and *Mademoiselle* had taken their valuables away with them when they ran away; but later on, something must have aroused their suspicions, or else the same kind of fool as Aristide here must have got talking. Anyway, they seem to have got the idea that Amédé Colombe had hidden *Madame's* valuables away somewhere and—"

"*Madame's* valuables!" Fleurette exclaimed, trying to hide something of the excitement which was causing her heart to thump furiously. "They thought that Amédé—?"

"Why, yes!" M'sieu' Duflos replied to her half-formulated query. "And unfortunately—"

"What?"

"Well! They found *Madame's* valuables—"

But the worthy butcher got no further with his story. Without another word and swift as lightning, Fleurette had turned on her heel, and the next moment she was speeding across the market-place in the direction of the Rue Haute, whilst M'sieu' Duflos was left gazing in ludicrous perplexity at old Louise.

"What's the matter with the child?" he queried, and thoughtfully passed his hand through his harsh, bristly hair. "I thought she knew."

Old Louise shrugged her shoulders.

"She only knew that the lad had been arrested," she said, "but she had not heard about *Madame's* valuables being found in the Colombes' cart-shed. I was just able to stop Adèle telling her. She is so fond of M'sieu' Amédé." Louise added with a sigh: "Oh! how I wish her father were here."

M'sieu' Duflos was watching Fleurette's trim little figure speeding across the square and then disappearing round the corner of the Rue

Haute.

"She's run over to the *épicerie*," he commented drily. "The Colombes are fond of her. They'll be able to comfort one another. Come
in and have a *petit verre*, Louise. The child will be back soon."

But Louise would not come in, she did not want to lose sight of
Fleurette, so after thanking the kind butcher for his hospitality, she too
turned to go in the direction of the Rue Haute. But at the last M'sieu'
Duflos had one more word to say to her.

"There's one thing more, Ma'ame Louise," he said, with unwonted
earnestness in his round, prominent eyes. "If I were you I would look
after that wench of yours, Adèle, a bit sharper. No offence, you know,
but people have been talking in the village. She was rather too familiar
with all those draggled-tailed soldiers last night."

Old Louise, with all a peasant's philosophy, shrugged her fat shoulders.

"You may be right, M'sieu' Duflos," she said drily, "but the girl, you
know, is no care of mine. My sister Amèlie looks after her."

After which she gave a friendly nod to the amiable butcher and
made her way up to the Rue Haute as fast as she could, though this
was not really so fast as Fleurette's nimble little feet had carried her.

Chapter 15

There had been no need for words. As soon as Fleurette had entered the shop Ma'ame Colombe had stretched out her arms, and
Fleurette ran to her at once to be enfolded in a great maternal embrace. With her fair hair resting on Ma'ame Colombe's ample bosom,
the child began by having a good cry. She had had none since she
heard the fatal news, for excitement had kept every other emotion in
check. But now with those motherly arms round her, she felt free to
let her sorrow and anxiety have free rein. Ma'ame Colombe's ample
bosom heaving against hers, and the older woman's tears wetting the
top of her fair head, Fleurette looked up, swiftly drying her eyes, and
put on a reassuring smile.

It was difficult to speak at first with all those sobs choking one's
voice; nevertheless, whilst mopping her eyes with her pocket-hand-
kerchief, Fleurette contrived to say:

"You know, Ma'ame Colombe, that it is all right, don't you? About
Amédé, I mean."

"All right, my dear? All right?" the poor woman reiterated and
shook her head with pathetic dubiousness. "How can it be all right,

86

when my Amédé is accused of being a thief? And before the neighbours too!" she added, whilst a deeper tone of crimson than her kitchen-fire had lent to her kind old face, spread over her cheeks.

"That's just it, Ma'ame Colombe," Fleurette continued eagerly. "Presently—tonight I hope—everyone will know that it was not Amédé who took those things."

"Of course, he didn't take them. But you know what village gossip is. If Amédé did not take *Madame's* valuables, they keep on saying, how came they to be in our cart-shed? Oh, *mon Dieu! mon Dieu!*" she moaned, "to think that my Hector and I should live to see such disgrace."

"But, Ma'ame Colombe," Fleurette put in, somewhat impatient with the older woman's lamentations, "I am going to Sisteron tonight to tell the *gendarme* how *Madame's* valuables came to be in your cart-shed, and who it was that stole them."

"You, child? How should you know?"

"Because it was I who took the valuables out of the secret place in *Madame's* room," Fleurette said glibly, "and I gave them to Amédé to take care of, and because it was I who gave them to him he hid them in a corner of the cart-shed."

"Holy Virgin!" was all that Ma'ame Colombe was able to say in response to this amazing story, "the child has taken leave of her senses."

"No, no, Ma'ame Colombe," Fleurette insisted earnestly; "it is just as I have told you. I took the valuables out of *Madame's* room while the soldiers were at the *château*, and I gave them to Amédé to take care of."

"But why?" the poor mother exclaimed, in an agony of bewilderment. "In Heaven's name why?"

"Because—"

And suddenly Fleurette hesitated. A hot flush rose to her cheeks and tears gathered in her eyes. She had felt Ma'ame Colombe's perplexed glance on her, and for the time a stinging doubt gripped her heart and made her physically almost sick. What views would other people—strangers or even friends—take of her amazing story? of the heavenly voice and the mysterious faggot-carrier with the wonderful twinkling eyes? Would they believe her? or would they deride the whole tale? or again, like dear, kind Ma'ame Colombe, would they just feel anxious, perplexed, not wishing to condemn, and yet vaguely wondering what could have induced a girl like Fleurette to go rummaging about among *Madame's* things, and inducing young Amédé to help her to conceal them.

An overpowering impulse prompted her to keep her beloved secret to herself. The sight of Ma'ame Colombe's grief-stricken face almost shook her resolution, but in the end, it was that first impulse which conquered. After all it was only a matter of a few days, hours perhaps, and everything would become crystal-clear. Fleurette's little handkerchief was now like a wet ball in her hot hands; she breathed on it and dabbed her eyes; she straightened her cap and smoothed down her kirtle.

"And so, dear Ma'ame Colombe," she said calmly, "I am just going to Sisteron. Probably I shall find Bibi there; but even if I don't, I shall go up to the Committee of Public Safety, and I shall tell them the whole truth, so that there'll be no question of Amédé going to fight the English with the stain of theft upon his name."

It was impossible to say anything more just then, because Louise had arrived at the épicerie, breathless, but happy to catch sight of Fleurette looking quite calm and reasonable.

"I hope you gave the child a good scolding, Ma'ame Colombe," she said. "The idea of her wanting to trapeze the high-road today when all these ruffianly soldiers are still about."

But Fleurette only smiled. "Neither Ma'ame Colombe, nor anyone else," she said, "could dissuade me from going to see Bibi now."

"Why!" Louise exclaimed pettishly, "this morning it was M'sieu' Amédé you wanted to see."

"I do want to see Amédé," Fleurette rejoined simply, "but I must see Bibi first."

And Louise saw her exchange an understanding glance with Ma'ame Colombe. It was all very bewildering and very terrible. Of course, she was terribly sorry for the Colombes, but, just for the moment, she wished them all at the bottom of the sea. A little feeling of jealousy had crept into her heart when she saw Fleurette clinging to Ma'ame Colombe and whispering words into her ears which she, Louise, could not hear, and this uncomfortable feeling added to her discomfort. What could Ma'ame Colombe be thinking about to encourage Fleurette in her obstinacy? Louise could only suppose that all common sense had been drowned in an ocean of grief for the beloved only son.

Ah! if only Monsieur Armand were here!

And with a last sigh and a none too cordial farewell to Ma'ame Colombe, Louise, dolefully shaking her head, followed Fleurette out of the shop.

Chapter 16

It was long past sunset by the time the two women reached Sisteron. Louise was dog-tired, for the day had been hot and the roads heavy with dust. They had started from Lou Mas one hour before noon, and as they left the first outlying houses of the city behind them, the clock of the tower of Notre Dame was striking eight.

The road between Laragne and Sisteron goes uphill most of the way, but withal, it is a beautiful road, winding through the wide valley of the Buëche, past orchards of grey-green olives and almond-trees laden with blossoms. Once past the confluence of the Méouge with the Buëche, it rises in a gentle gradient and gradually reveals to the eye with magnificent panorama of the Basses Alpes with their rocky crests and wide flanks draped in the sombre cloaks of pinewoods: Mont de la Baume, St. Géniez, Signal de Lure; as beautiful a picture as Nature has to offer for the delectation of travellers, but possessing no powers of fascination over the two women, who tramped along in weariness and with anxious hearts.

The road was lonely. Scarce anyone did they meet on the way; no one, at any rate, to inspire old Louise with alarm. Now and then, perhaps, a group of labourers toiling homewards would cast a bold glance on the pretty wench stepping it resolutely beside her old *duenna*. But after a ribald word or two, or at worst a coarse jest, they would pass on and the two women continued their way unmolested.

But the events of the day, subsequently those of the evening, were but one long string of disappointments. As soon as the first outlying houses of the city came in sight, Fleurette began inquiring pluckily and determinedly.

"Citizen Armand," she would ask, "from Lou Mas, over beyond Laragne?"

"What about him?"

"He is an important personage in Sisteron, how could I find him?"

And because she was gentle and had pretty blue eyes, and because she looked weary and anxious, people would do their best to help her. Some suggested one place, some another; the posting-inn—he might be known there, if he sometimes posted to Paris—or else the *commissariat*. This latter place proved a danger spot. A ferocious-looking *commissaire* very nearly detained the two women on a charge of vagabondage. His ugly leers and unveiled threats nearly sent Louise off her head with terror; Fleurette, however, kept up her courage nobly. The thought of Amédé drove every other terror out of her heart. She had vaguely heard that her father had something to do with a certain Committee of Public Safety. When she told this to the commissaire his manner immediately underwent a complete change; he became almost obsequious, placed himself entirely at the disposal of the citizeness for any inquiries she might wish to make about her illustrious father. Unfortunately, he said, the hour was late; the officers of the Committee of Public Safety situated in the Town Hall were now closed for the night. Citizen Armand had probably found shelter under the roof of a friend. Until tomorrow morning nothing could be done.

One thing, however, appeared clear; the soldier who had created so much stir in Laragne this morning had not come to Sisteron nor was anything known of them. There was, the now servile commissary explained, a detachment of the 87th regiment of the line in garrison in the city and two days ago a squad of the revolutionary army lately formed for the purpose of scouring the country for traitors and aristos had passed through Sisteron and gone on in the direction of Laragne. The *commissaire* had heard something about a family named Frontenac against whom there was a black mark for treason against the Republic, but he did not know anything about the arrest of *Monsieur* or the escape of *Madame* and *Mademoiselle*—whom he persistently referred to as the *ci-devants*—nor did he know anything about the arrest of Amédé Colombe, citizen of Laragne.

It was all very disappointing. Fleurette, trying to be brave, nevertheless felt at times an overwhelming inclination to cry. For one thing she was very tired and being young and healthy she was also hungry. She and Louise had consumed the contents of their provision basket when the day was still young. Now it was getting near bed-time and the goal of her efforts not even within sight. The sullenness and mistrust that seemed to hang over the whole city had the effect of further damping her spirits.

The echo of the terrible doings in Orange, in Toulon, and Lyons had penetrated as far as this hitherto peaceful little town. Tales of summary arrests, of death-sentences without trial, of wholesale massacres were on everybody's lips. Accusations of treason, it seems, were more frequent than daily bread. The women looked harassed, hugged their children to their sides, as they slunk down the ill-lit streets, whilst throwing furtive glances over their shoulders. The men stood about in groups of three or four in the dark angles of the streets of beneath the ill-lit doorways until roughly ordered to go their way by men dressed in nothing but rags, who wore a tricolour sash round their waist and a cockade on their worsted cap.

And so ultimately to Les Amandiers, a quiet little inn off the main streets of the town, that Louise knew of through the drovers from Laragne who frequented the place when they were in Sisteron on market-day. Baptiste Portal, the landlord, suspicious at first, not liking the look of the two unprotected women seeking for lodgings at this hour of the night, was mollified by seeing the colour of Louise's money and the blue of Fleurette's eyes. His temper, it seems, had not yet recovered from the assaults made upon it a couple of days ago by a set of ragamuffins who called themselves soldiers of the Republic, and by their loud-spoken and arrogant lieutenant; but he was willing enough to make the two women welcome, and to give them supper and a bed. Then only did they tell him who they were and what the purpose of their journey: to seek Citizen Armand of Lou Mas, whose daughter Fleurette had matters of the utmost importance to communicate to him.

"*Qu'à ça ne tienne!*" Baptiste Portal exclaimed. "Armand was here but a couple of hours after noon. He was on his way to Orange."

"To Orange!" A cry of terror from Louise; one of excitement from Fleurette. Orange, the tiger's den! How could two unprotected women hope to enter it without being devoured? Orange where the guillotine was at work night and day! where men and women and even children were massacred in droves, where innocent people hardly dared to speak or smile or pray, lest they be seized and thrown into prison, only to be dragged out again to a horrible death.

Orange!

But Fleurette only smiled. What had they to fear seeing Bibi *chéri* would be there? Was not Bibi far, far more powerful than the whole of the revolutionary army? Fleurette had seen him at the *château*, with a great tricolour sash round his waist, giving orders, that the officer in command of the soldiers dared not disobey.

Orange! She was not afraid of Orange! Even if the great Robespierre was in Orange she would not be afraid to go.

After all, what did it mean? Two or three days' journey in the old *coche* which, it seems, left the Place d'Armes two days of the week, at nine o'clock in the morning, and lumbering along through Peipin, and Saint Etienne-les-Orgues, gave one the chance of getting a good

91

bed for the night at Sault, and again at Carpentras, if one was too tired to continue one's journey then.

Orange indeed? Why should one fear Orange, when chance was all in one's favour? As luck would have it, it was the very next day that the *coche* would be starting from the Place d'Armes. All one needed was a few things, a clean pair of stockings, a handkerchief or two, a bit of soap and a towel, which dear, kind Ma'ame Portal was only too ready to lend; these were tied in a bundle and formed the only indispensable luggage which Fleurette and Louise would take with them. Fortunately, Louise had plenty of money in her pocket, being always well supplied by Bibi, and then, of course, in Orange, Bibi would be there and he would provide further as necessity arose.

And thus, it came to pass that among the passenger who took their places in the lumbering old vehicle that morning were two females, one of whom had corn-coloured hair and eyes bluer than forget-me-nots.

Chapter 17

The Hôtel de Ville at Orange still stands, as it did then, in the newly-named Place de la République; and if the tourist of today mounts its steps, enters the building through its central portal, crosses the wide vestibule and finally turns down a long corridor on his right, he will, almost at the end of this, come to a door which bears the legend: "*Travaux Publics.*"

Should he be bold enough to push open the door, he will find himself in a perfectly banal room, with white-washed walls covered with maps and plans that are of no interest to him, a large desk at one end, and a few wooden chairs. There is a thin carpet in the middle of the red-tiled floor and faded green rep curtains temper the glaring light of the afternoon sun. But on this day of May, 1794, there were no curtains to the window, and not even a strip of carpet on the floor. There was no desk either, only a long trestle table covered with a tattered green cloth, behind which, on wooden chairs, sat three men, dressed alike in dark blue coats tightly buttoned across the chest, drab breeches and high-topped boots, and wearing tricolour sashes around their waist.

The one who sat in the centre and who appeared to be in supreme authority rested his elbow on the table, and his chin was supported in his hand. He was gazing intently on a man who stood before him, in the centre of the room, the other side of the table; a man who looked foot-sore and weary and who wore a military uniform all tattered and covered with slime and dust.

The two others also kept their eyes fixed on this man. They were listening with rapt interest to the story which he was relating. Early this morning he and a dozen others also attired in tattered uniforms had come into Orange in a state bordering on collapse. They had made their way to the barracks where the officer in command had mercifully given them food and drink. As soon as they had eaten and drunk, they tried to tell their story; but this was so amazing, not to say incredible, that the officer in command had thought it prudent to send for the superintendent of *gendarmerie*, who in turn had the men conveyed to the Hôtel de Ville, there to be brought before the Representative of the Convention on special mission who sat with the Committee of Public Safety.

And now Lieutenant Godet stood alone to face the Committee; the others had been handed back to the *gendarmerie* to be dealt with later on. The representative on special mission who sat with the two other Members of the Committee at the table covered with the tattered green cloth, had questioned Godet, and he thereupon embarked upon the story of this amazing adventure. He began by relating the events which three days ago had set the quiet little commune of Laragne seething with excitement. He told of the arrival of the squad of soldiers in magnificent uniforms, under the command of an officer more superb than anything that had ever been seen in the countryside before.

He told of the perquisition in the house of Citizen Colombe the grocer, by those magnificent soldiers, of the finding there by them of certain valuables belonging to the *ci-devant* Frontenacs, valuables which he himself had vainly searched for in the *château*, the evening before. He told of the arrest of young Colombe: of the high-handed manner in which the superb officer had relieved him, Godet, of his command, and ordered him and his men, together with the *ci-devant* Frontenac, to join his squad, and to march with him out of Laragne. He had told it all with a wealth of detail, and the members of the Committee had listened in silence and with rapt interest.

But now the man at the table who was the representative on special mission, and who appeared chief in authority, broke in with an exclamation that was almost one of rage.

"And do you mean to tell me, citizen lieutenant," he said in a harsh, rasping voice, "that you could mistake a lot of English spies—

for that is what they were, you may take it from me—that you could mistake them, I say, for soldiers of our army. Where were your eyes?"

Lieutenant Godet gave a shrug which he hoped would pass for unconcern. In reality he felt physically sick; a prey to overwhelming terror. At first, when he and his men had come in sigh of the city, they had felt nothing but relief to see the end of what had been, almost martyrdom. It was only afterwards, when he found himself in this narrow room, with its white-washed walls and its silence, and face to face with those three men, that fear had entered his heart. He felt like an animal in a cage—a mouse looking into the pale, piercing eyes of a cat. He passed his tongue once or twice over his parched lips before he gave reply.

"I was not the only one, citizen," he said sullenly, "who was deceived. The whole commune of Laragne was at the heels of those soldiers. My own men were mustered before the pseudo-captain and heard him give words of command."

"But Englishmen, citizen lieutenant," the man at the table argued; "Englishmen! Their appearance! Their speech!"

"They spoke as you and I would, Citizen Chauvelin," Godet retorted, still sullenly. "As for appearance, one man is like another. I could not be expected to know every officer of our army by sight!"

"But you said they were splendidly dressed!"

"They were. I knew the uniform well enough. Had there been a doubtful button or a galloon wanting I should have spotted it."

"But so clean!" one of the others at the table remarked with a sigh, that might have been of envy, "so magnificent!"

"I knew that there were some *compagnies d'élite,*" the lieutenant rejoined, "attached to certain regiments. How could I guess?"

"It might have been better for you if you had," the man in the centre remarked drily.

Godet's wan face took on a more ashen hue; again, he passed his tongue over his parched lips.

"Haven't we had enough of this?" one of the others at the table now put in impatiently. "We are satisfied that those English spies, or whatever they were, acted with amazing effrontery, which makes me think that perhaps they are a part of that gang that we all know of, and of which Citizen Chauvelin spoke just now. We are also satisfied that Citizen Lieutenant Godet did not show that acumen which an officer in his responsible position should have done. What we want to know now is, what happened after the pseudo-captain of the so-called

33rd division had arrested that young Colombe and marched out of Laragne?"

"And in your interest, citizen lieutenant," the man in the centre rejoined sternly, "I advise you to make a statement that is truthful in every detail."

"Had I wished to tell lies," the soldier retorted sullenly, "I shouldn't be here now. I should have——"

"No matter," the other broke in curtly, "what you would have done. The State desires to know what you did."

"Well!" Lieutenant Godet began after a moment or two during which he appeared to collect his thoughts. "We marched out of Laragne in the direction of Serres. The captain—I still, of course, looked upon his as a captain—had so disposed us that I and my own men were between two squads of his. We were footsore, all of us, because we had had three days' tramping in the dust, one day battling against hard wind, another with long hours spent in scouring the *château* of those traitors Frontenacs; we were also very hungry. Remember that we had been dragged out of our beds in the early morning, and not given a chance of getting a bite or drink before starting on the march. But they, the others, were fresh as if they had just come out of barracks with their bellies full. They marched along at a swinging pace, and it was as much as we could do to keep step with them."

The man's voice became somewhat more steady as he talked. The note of terror which had been so conspicuous in it at first had given place to one of dull resentment. Encouraged by the obvious interest which his story had evoked in his hearers, he resumed more glibly:

"About half a league north of Laragne, a bridle-path branches off the high-road; into this the captain ordered his company to turn, and we continued to plod along through the dust and in the midday heat, till we came to a tumble-down cottage by the roadside; a cottage flanked by a dilapidated shed, and a bit of garden all overgrown with weeds. Here a halt was called, and the prisoners were ordered out of the wagon. A moment or two later a woman appeared at the cottage door, some words were exchanged between her and the captain, and subsequently, when order to march was given, the prisoners marched along with us; the wagon and horses having been left behind at the cottage."

"Didn't you think this very strange, citizen lieutenant?" one of the men at the table asked; "a wagon and horses which you would naturally presume belonged to the State, being thus left at a tumble-down

95

roadside cottage?"

"Whatever I may have thought," the lieutenant replied, "it was not my place to make observations to my superior officer."

"Superior officer!" the man in the centre remarked, with a gesture of contemptuous wrath.

"I think, Citizen Chauvelin," the accused now put in a little more firmly, "that you are unnecessarily hard on me. There was really nothing to indicate——"

But the other broke in with a vicious snarl:

"Nothing to indicate——? Nothing? The eyes of a patriot should be sharp enough to detect a spy or a traitor through any disguise——"

He paused abruptly, and cast a quick, inquisitorial glance at his two colleagues first, then at the soldier before him. Had he detected a trace, a sign, a flicker of the eyelid that betrayed knowledge of his own past? of the times—numberless now—that he too had been hoodwinked by those bold adventurers who called themselves the League of the Scarlet Pimpernel, and by their chief whose prowess in the art of disguise had marked some of the most humiliating hours in Chauvelin's career? Calais, Boulogne, Nantes, Paris; each of those great cities had a record of the Terrorist's discomfiture when brought face to face with that mysterious and elusive Scarlet Pimpernel. Even now, crushed in the hot palm of his hand, he held a scrap of paper which had revealed the author of the plot to which that fool Lieutenant Godet had fallen a victim—just as he, himself, Chauvelin, had done—just like that—and so many times—The penalty for him had always been more humiliation, a further fall from the original high place which he had once occupied in Paris: and with it the knowledge that one day the masters of France would tire of his failures. Ah! he knew that well enough, he knew that they would tire, and then they would crush him as they had crushed others, whose only crime, like his, had been failure.

His only claim to immunity, so far, had been the fact that he alone, of all the members of the National Assembly, of all the members of the Committees, or of the Executive, knew who the Scarlet Pimpernel really was; he had seen him without disguise; he knew him by name, not only him but some of his more important followers; and when some of the ferocious tyrants, who for the time being were the masters of France, did at times loudly demand the suppression of Citizen Chauvelin, for incompetence that amounted to treason, there were always others who pleaded for him because of that knowledge. Many felt that with the death of Chauvelin, the last hope of capturing that band of

English spies would have to be abandoned; and so, they pleaded for his retention and their fellow-tyrants allowed him another few months' grace so that he might accomplish that which they knew was the great purpose of his life. And whenever in the opinion of those bloodthirsty tigers, who held France under their domination, some outlying provincial districts had need of what they called "purging from the pestilence of traitors," whenever wholesale arrests, perquisitions, wholesale death-sentences or brutal massacres were the order of the day, Citizen Chauvelin was sent down with special powers, always in the vain hope that the Scarlet Pimpernel, emboldened by success, would fall into the trap perpetually set for him. The English spy's predilection for *aristos*, his sympathies so quickly aroused when traitors happened to be women or young children, was sure to draw his activities to any region where prisons were full and the guillotine kept busy.

Thus, it was that Citizen Chauvelin had been sent to Orange. The Southern provinces of France had been left far too long to welter in a morass of treason; there were veritable nests of traitors in the *châteaux* and farms of Provence and Dauphiné. The country had to be purged: the traitors extirpated; the magnificent Law of the Suspect be set in motion to do this cleansing process.

Any man who ventured to criticize the government, who complained of taxation or restrictions was a traitor; any man or woman who owned more than they needed for bare subsistence, who refused to pour of their surplus into the lap of patriots, was a traitor, and the country must be purged of them, until the dictatorship of the proletariat was firmly established, until every man, woman and child in the whole of France had been dragged down to the same level of mental and physical wreckage.

There had been a dramatic pause after Chauvelin's outburst of contemptuous wrath; for a minute or two, while the old clock up on the wall ticked away with slow monotony, a strange silence remained hanging over the scene. Whatever the other three men may have known or remembered of the noted Terrorist's past history, they thought it wiser to say nothing. In these days of universal brotherhood and Liberty, every man in France was frightened of his neighbour. The time had come when the lustful tigers, satiated with the blood of those whom they deemed their enemies, had turned, thirsting, for that of their whilom friends. The makers of the Terror had started digging their fangs into each other's throats. The victory now was to the most ferocious. After the Girondins, Danton, he, who had ordered the

97

September massacres, two and a half years ago, had had to yield to a more vengeful, more merciless power than his own.

Chauvelin knew that. The victory today was to the most ferocious. He who would sacrifice friends, brother, sister, child, was the true patriot; the man who stayed his hand in face of a revolting crime that would put a wild beast to the blush, was unworthy the name of citizen of France. Therefore, death to him. Death to the weakling. To the Moderate. This was the era of the Universal Brotherhood of Death.

What chance then had this unfortunate Lieutenant Godet now? brought to justice—save the mark!—before a man who knew that to show weakness was to court death. No wonder that all the swagger and the arrogance which made him but a day or two ago the terror of a lot of peasants at Sisteron or Laragne, was knocked out of him, by a mere glance from those pale, piercing eyes. And he—a mere notary's clerk born and bred in the depth of Dauphiné, and thrust into the army, as a mule is thrust into harness—knew nothing of Paris save from hearsay, and nothing of the men whose word had even sent a king and queen to the scaffold. He knew nothing of Citizen Chauvelin, save that he was a man of power, before whose piercing glance and tricolour sash every man instinctively cringed and trembled. He knew nothing of Chauvelin's tussles with those same English spies who had so effectually led him, Godet, by the nose; nothing of Citizen Chauvelin's past life, very little of the present. He was just a mouse in the power of a cat; allowed a little freedom just now, while he told his tale of failure.

"Continue, citizen lieutenant," Chauvelin now said more calmly. "We are listening."

"Let me see," Godet rejoined vaguely, "where was I?"

"On the bridle-path off the main road," Chauvelin responded with a sneer; "half a league north of Laragne. The wagon and horses presumably belonging to the State left in a tumble-down cottage by the roadside. A thrilling situation forsooth. An ordinary situation you would have us believe. Pray continue. What happened after that?"

"We marched and we marched and we marched," the lieutenant resumed sullenly. "We marched until we were ready to drop. We had had three days of marching and had started in the morning without a bite, hungry! *Nom d'un nom!* how hungry we were! and weak and faint! The hours sped on; we could see the sun mounting the heavens and then start on its descent. The heat was intense, the dust terrible. It filled our eyes, our nostrils, our mouths. The soles of our feet were bleeding, sweat poured down our faces and obscured our vision. We marched and we marched, through two villages, the names of which I do not know; then over mountain passes, across rocky gorges, stepping over streams, climbing the sides of hills, the banks of rivers. I am a stranger in these parts. And I was tired. Tired! I knew not where we were, whither we were going. March! March! March! Ceaselessly. Even had I dared, I would no longer have had the strength to ask questions or to beg for mercy."

And at the recollection of those hours of agony, Lieutenant Godet wiped the perspiration from his streaming brow.

"Well?" Chauvelin queried drily, "and the others, the Englishmen?"

"They marched along at a swinging pace," Godet replied, smothering a savage oath. "Without turning a hair. They kicked up no dust. They did not sweat. They just marched. No doubt their bellies were well filled."

"And the prisoners?"

"They set to with a will. And I make no doubt but they had fed and drunk while they sat in the wagon. At any rate they showed no fatigue."

"How long did you continue on the march?"

"Till one by one we—my comrades and I—fell out by the roadside."

"And those who fell out were left, while the others went on?"

"Yes! We had gone through the second village, and were marching along the edge of a stream, when the first lot of us dropped out. Three of my men. They just rolled down the bank of the stream; and there lay on their stomachs trying to drink. The captain—or whatever he was, curse him!—called "Halt!" and one of his men ran down the bank and had a look at those three poor fellows who lay there striving to slake their hunger as well as their thirst in the cool mountain stream. But, *nom de nom!* They—the miscreants!—had no bowels of compassion. I believe—for in truth I was too tired to see anything clearly—that one of them did leave a hunk of bread by the side of the stream: perhaps he was afraid that those poor fellows would die of inanition and then their death would be upon his conscience."

"Well! And did all the men fall out that way?"

"Yes! We were marching three abreast: and three by three we all fell out. Always beside the stream, for we suffered from thirst as much as from hunger. The stream seemed to draw us, and three of us, as if by common understanding, would just roll down the bank and lie on our stomachs and try to drink. The captain no longer called a halt when that happened. One of his own men would just throw pieces of bread down to the edge of the stream, just as they would to a dog."

"And you were the last to fall out?"

"The very last. I verily believe, when I rolled down the bank and felt the cool stream against my face, that I had died and reached the Elysian fields. A piece of bread was thrown to me, and I fell on it like a starved beast."

"And then what happened?"

"Nothing."

"What do you mean? Nothing?"

"Nothing as far as we were concerned. The bank of the stream, for a length of two kilometres or more, was strewn with our dead—that is not dead, you understand, but fatigued, and only half-conscious with hunger: while those miscreants, those limbs of Satan, marched off without as much as a last look at us! Gaily they marched away singing. Yes, singing, some awful gibberish, in a tongue I did not understand. That is," poor Godet went on ruefully, "when first I had an inkling of the awful truth. That strange tongue gave it away. You understand?"

The others nodded.

"And then, by chance, I put my hand in the back pocket of my tunic and felt that piece of paper."

With finger that quivered slightly, he pointed to Chauvelin's hand; between the clenched claw-like fingers there protruded the corner of a scrap of paper. Chauvelin failed to suppress the exclamation of rage which rose to his lips.

"*Nom de nom!*" he muttered savagely through his teeth, and with his handkerchief he wiped the beads of moisture that had risen to the roots of his hair.

"And so, they marched away," one of the others remarked drily. "In which direction?"

"Straight on," the soldier replied laconically.

"On the way to Nyons, I suppose, and Valreas?"

"I suppose so. I don't know the neighbourhood."

"You do not seem to have known much, Lieutenant Godet," Chauvelin put in with a sneer.

"I come from the other side of the Drac," Godet retorted. "I could not—"

But Chauvelin broke in with an oath:

"Wherever you come from, citizen," he said sternly, "it was your

100

duty to become acquainted with the country through which you were ordered to march your men."

"I had no orders to take them through mountain passes," Godet remarked sullenly. "We came through here a month ago and have kept to the high-road. At Sisteron I had my orders to arrest the *ci-devant* Frontenacs. You, Citizen Chauvelin, must know how conscientiously I did my duty. All the orders you gave me I fulfilled. After Sisteron you ordered me to go to Laragne, and thence to Serres. It was you ordered me to a halt at Laragne for the night."

"All this is beside the point," one of the others broke in roughly. "All we can gather from this confused tale is that all traces of the English spies have completely vanished."

"For the moment," Chauvelin assented drily. "It is for Lieutenant Godet to find those traces again."

He spoke now with extreme bitterness, and the glances which he levelled at Godet were both hostile and threatening. It would be curious to try and follow the mental processes which had given rise to this hostility. Godet, after all said and done, had only failed in the same manner as he himself, Chauvelin, had so often done. He had been hoodwinked by a particularly astute and daring adventurer who was an avowed enemy of France: and if being thus hoodwinked was a crime against the State, then the powerful member of the Committee of Public Safety and the humble lieutenant of infantry were fellow-criminals. This, of course, Godet did not know. Not yet: or he would not have been in such dread of this man with the pale eyes and the talon-like hands. The others he did not fear nearly so much. No doubt they too were cruel and vengeful these days. Strike or the blow will fall on you, was the rule of every man's conduct. Pochart and Danou took their cue from Chauvelin; his was the master-mind, his the more ruthless nature, all they did was to try and show their zeal by saying Amen to every suggestion, every sarcasm, every accusation put forth by their colleague.

In fact, the proceedings by now had developed into a kind of duel between the accused and the principal judge; it was a duel made up of acrimonious accusations on the one hand, and of defence that weakened perceptibly as the accused became more and more confused through ever-increasing terror. The other two only put in a word here and there. They wished to know how the adventure had finally come to an end.

"In a long, weary tramp to Orange," Godet replied; "weary beyond what words can describe, footsore, hungry and thirsty we tramped."

They had to cover three leagues. How they lived through it, they none of them knew. At one or two villages which they encountered, they obtained a little food, and some drink. For the space of a league and a half, he, Godet, and two others got a lift in a farmer's wagon. On the way they asked news of the English spies. They had been seen marching merrily; but soon all traces of them had vanished.

"Had I been the traitor you say I am, Citizen Chauvelin," Godet said in the end, "would I have come into Orange with my tale? I would have tried to run away and to hide. Made my way to Toulons, what? and joined the army there. You would not have found me then; months would have gone by before you heard of my adventure."

"You underestimate the power which is in my hands, citizen lieutenant," was Chauvelin's curt comment. "Only one thing could save you from the consequences of your treachery, and that was to speak the truth and to redeem your crime."

He paused a moment, and then addressing his two colleagues, he said with slow deliberation:

"We all agree, I think, that Citizen Lieutenant Godet has been guilty of gross negligence, which today, when France is threatened by traitors within as well as by her enemies on her frontier, amounts to treason against the State. Silence!" he went on, throwing a stern glance on Godet who had uttered a violent word of protest. "Listen to what hope of indulgence it is in my power to give you. The State against whom you have sinned well grant you the chance of retrieving your crime. We will grant you full powers under the new Law of the Suspect. You shall go into the highways and the byways with full power to seize any man, woman or child, whom you as much as vaguely suspect of complicity in this affair. Do you understand?"

"I think I do," Godet replied dully.

"The State," Pochart put in sagely, "would rather have the English spies than your head, citizen lieutenant."

"The State will have Citizen Godet's head," Chauvelin rejoined drily, "or the English spies. The choice rests with Citizen Godet himself."

There was a moment's pause. The eyes of the soldier were fixed upon the pale, determined face of his ruthless judge. He knew that his life hung upon the decision uttered by those thin, bloodless lips. He was in the grip of a white terror; his teeth were clenched and his tongue clove, hard and dry, against the roof of his mouth. He was terrified, and in his wildly beating heart there was an immense hatred for the man who thus terrorized him. He longed to get at him, to grip him by the throat, to scream out insults into that pale, stern, colourless face. He longed to see that same fear of death which was paralysing him, dim the light of those pale eyes. His own impotence made that hatred more intense. It shone out of his eyes, and Chauvelin meeting them caught the glance like that of an enraged cur, ready to spring. Indifferent, he shrugged his shoulders and the ghost of a sneer curled round his thin lips. He was accustomed to hatred and desire for revenge.

"Citizen lieutenant," he said at last, "you have heard the decision of the committee. It has been found expedient to withhold punishment from you, because it is in your power to serve the State in a way that no other man could do at this moment. You have seen the English spies face to face; you know something of their appearance, something of their mode of speech. Go then into the highways and byways, the men who with you were guilty of negligence shall go with you. It is for you to use the full powers which the Law of the Suspect has placed in your hands. Go scour the country. Yours is the power to seize any man, woman or child whom you suspect of treason to the State, make use of that power in order to track down to their lair the English foxes who have outwitted you. Only let me add a word of warning in your ear. Do not be led by the nose a second time. If you are, no power on earth will save you. The State may forgive incompetence once: the second time it will bear the ugly name of treason."

He had risen to his feet, and just for a moment the muscles of his hand relaxed, and the scrap of paper which he had crushed into a ball rolled upon the table.

His colleague Pochart picked it up and idly opened and smoothed it out: he studied for a moment or two the close writing upon it, then looking inquiringly up at Chauvelin.

"Can you tell us what is written on this paper, citizen?" he asked.

And while he spoke he tossed the paper across to his colleague Danou.

"Is it English?" Danou asked, puzzled.

"Yes," Chauvelin replied curtly.

"It looks like poetry," Pochart remarked.

"Doggerel verses," commented Chauvelin.

"And you can't read it?"

"No!"

"I thought you knew English."

"Not I."

"Strange why a bit of doggerel verse should have been slipped into the pocket of Citizen Godet's tunic," Pochart remarked drily. "And there's your name, Citizen Chauvelin," he added, pointing to the words "*À mon ami* Chauvelin," which preceded the four lines of poetry written in English, a language which, apparently, no one here understood.

But Chauvelin was at the end of his patience. He seized the scrap of paper and tore it savagely into innumerable little pieces.

"Enough of this futility," he said, and brought his clenched fist down with a crash on the table. "The English spies have been facetious, that is all. We do them too much honour by attaching importance to this senseless, childish verse. Lieutenant Godet," he went on, once more addressing the accused, "you are dismissed, under the conditions I told you of just now. When next we meet face to face, you will either be the lucky man who has helped to lay these impudent English adventurers by the heel, or you will stand before me arraigned for treason and preparing for death. Now you can go."

Without another word Godet turned on his heel and went out of the room. Past the guard at the door, he went with head erect, and with a firm step he walked the whole length of the corridor. But there was one moment when in the vestibule he found himself alone. Unwatched. At any rate he thought so. So, he paused and looked over his shoulder in the direction of the room where he had just spent an uncomfortable two hours. He paused and raising his fist, he shook it at the unseen presence of the man who had so terrorised him, and whom he hated because of the terror which he inspired.

"With a bit of luck," he muttered through his teeth, "we shall be even yet, you and I, *mon ami* Chauvelin."

Then once more with a firm step he walked out of the Town Hall.

Chapter 18

It was on the following day that the *coche* from Sisteron was due to arrive at Orange, and Lieutenant Godet, his mind set on the one purpose, to find a clue to his mysterious adventure with the English spies, hied him to the posting-inn which is situated in the Rue de la République.

At noon the *coche*, covered with dust, unloaded its wearied passengers; a farmer and his son come to negotiate a sale of stock; the wife of Citizen Henriot, the lawyer, home from her annual visit to her mother; two or three skilled *artisans* from the country, come to seek their fortune in town, and so on; and finally there descended from the *coche* two women, one of whom carried a small bundle, while the other—well! at sight of the other Citizen Lieutenant Godet uttered such a cry of surprise and of excitement that the crowd around him thought that here was a poor soldier who had taken leave of his senses.

The woman who had caused Lieutenant Godet thus to lose his self-control, was a perfectly self-possessed young woman wrapped in a cloak and hood from beneath which peeped strands of golden curls that vied in colour with the ripe corn of the Dauphiné, and eyes bluer than the sky that spread over Orange on this exquisite midday in May. The older woman who accompanied her appeared travel-stained, weary and cross; not so this beautiful girl, who tripped lightly from the *coche* towards the parlour of the posting-inn and with a little air of triumph and encouragement called gaily to her companion:

"The end of our journey, my Louise! And now to find Bibi!"

Even in these days of advanced democracy which in Orange had of late reached its apogee, the shattering of ancient manners and customs had not got to the stage where a beautiful woman would not command the attention and services of impressionable males, to the exclusion of others less favoured. And thus it came to pass that while the other weary and travel-stained passengers were left to look after themselves and their bits of luggage, and to wait their turn until such time as the servants of the inn were pleased to get them refreshments, the landlord himself, a florid man in shirt sleeves and baize apron, bustled obsequiously around Fleurette and Louise, offering wine bread and advice, polishing the chairs on which they were invited to sit, and generally placing himself and his house at the disposal of this attractive customer.

Fleurette took all these attentions as a matter of course. She was accustomed to being the centre of attraction at Lou Mas or in the house of M'sieu' and Ma'ame Colombe, and although her trust in the good-will of men had received one or two somewhat rude shocks of late, she still retained that self-possession and gentle air of mingled modesty and graciousness which is the attribute of every pretty, unspoilt woman. She asked for a room where she and her companion might tidy their kerchiefs and caps, and use their precious piece of scented soap, and she felt so triumphant and so elated that when she found herself in the privacy of that room she took poor old Louise by the waist and twirled her round and around in a mad dance.

"We are in Orange, Louise darling!" she cried. "We are here! here! here! and in less than an hour we shall have found Bibi will have commanded Amédé to be set free! Just think of it, Louise," she went on more seriously, "four whole days since he was arrested! Poor, poor Amédé, under a horrible accusation of a sin which he never committed! What he must have suffered! What he must have thought of me who knew the truth and did not at once set to work to obtain his freedom."

Gradually her tone became more and more dull, all the excitement died out of it. She saw Amédé in prison, with irons round his wrists and ankles, or else standing before stern judges who condemned him to a terrible punishment, because he held his tongue, and would not accuse the real delinquent, who was none other than she, Fleurette. She sighed, and her eyes now were full of tears, while old Louise, stolidly, and with much grumbling, got some water and proceeded to wash her face and hands and to tidy her dress.

"Come, child," she said drily after a while, "we'll go down now and get something to eat."

She had never ceased to protest against the madness of this adventure, prophesying every kind of calamity for them both: but Fleurette with the quiet obstinacy of the habitually meek had persisted. She had begun by wheedling the money out of Louise, then obtained the passes for places in the *coche*. Once on the way, it would of course have been ridiculous to turn tail and go back, and *Louise*, led unconsciously by a force of will stronger than her own, had found herself meekly acquiescing in all the arrangements which Fleurette made on the way. As a matter of fact, she had not ceased to marvel at the child. Here was this young thing, who had never travelled in a *coche* before, who had never in her life been further than Serres and Sisteron, calmly undertaking a three days' journey, sleeping and eating in strange inns, and arriving at her destination unscathed.

There certainly was a miracle in all this good luck, for old Louise had heard many a tale of what terrible adventures usually befell unprotected females upon the high-roads. What she did not realise was that the miracle merely consisted in the fact that in these outlying corners of beautiful France, in Dauphiné and in Provence, there was still plenty of the good old kindly stock left, some of the chivalry, the warmth of heart, the *bonhomie*, which all the tyranny and the cruelty perpetrated in the great cities had not contrived to kill; and that there was something in Fleurette's beauty, her simplicity as well as her determination, which brought forth that chivalry and *bonhomie* and helped her to win through.

When the two women returned to the parlour, where hot milk and country bread awaited them, they were met by a young soldier, who very politely and deferentially claimed acquaintance with them.

"You would not remember me, citizeness," he said, more particularly addressing Fleurette, "but I and some very weary soldiers under my command are deeply indebted to you for your kindness to us, when, like a good Samaritan, you gave us food and drink, on the bridge near your home. Do you remember?"

He looked very bedraggled and out-at-elbows, but frank and kind. Fleurette raised shy, blue eyes up at his, and gave a little gasp of recognition. She well remembered the soldier. She remembered how sorry she had been for them all, in their shabby clothes and stockingless feet, weary and thirsty, and how she had sent Adèle out to them with food and drink. She also remembered, though she would not remind him of that, that he had been very curt and uncivil with her, had made a sneering remark when she told him that she was Citizen Armand's daughter, and also that the men under his command had been positively cruel to a poor inoffensive old man whom she afterwards befriended.

However, for the moment, she was perhaps conscious of a slight feeling of relief at sight of a familiar face; she had seen nothing but strangers ever since she left Laragne four days ago. So, when the soldier, still speaking quite deferentially, reiterated his: "Do you remember?" she replied simply: "Of course I do, citizen lieutenant." Which goes to prove that Fleurette had learned a great deal in the past three days, and the word "citizen" now came quite glibly to her tongue.

Lieutenant Godet had told her his name, told her that he was a native of Orange and was home on leave for a few days.

"A real piece of luck," he went on lightly, "seeing that perhaps I might be of service to you."

The two women sat down at the table and he helped to wait on them, brought them bread and cheese and a jug of hot milk, and bustled the maid of the inn if the latter appeared to Louise, talked of his own journey, and inquired after her adventures. Louise, despite her innate suspicion of soldiers, gradually unbent to him. The warm food further put her into a good temper, and presently the three of them were conversing in the most amicable manner.

When the meal had been duly paid for, the soldier once more offered his services. Could he pilot the citizenesses through the town?

"Well yes, you can," Louise said resolutely, "we want to find M'sieu' Armand."

"Citizen Armand," Fleurette broke in, "my father. I think you know him, citizen lieutenant."

"Know him?" he exclaimed, "of course I know Armand. Who does not know Citizen Armand in Orange?"

"Then he is here now?" Fleurette cried eagerly.

"Of a surety he is."

"You know where he lodges?"

"Everyone in Orange knows where Citizen Armand lodges."

"Then you can take me to him?"

"At your service, citizeness."

"Now?"

"When you wish."

With a little cry of delight Fleurette gathered up her cloak.

"Let us go," she said simply.

Louise sighing, but stolid, followed meekly. The thought that she would soon relinquish her wayward charge into the keeping of M'sieu' Armand was a comforting one; Fleurette was tripping it gaily beside the soldier, but the latter's dirty clothes and bedraggled appearance still filled old Louise with mistrust.

They crossed the river by the old bridge and then trudged along the dusty streets to a great open place, now called Place de la République. The soldier led the way across the square to a tall stone building, flanked by a square tower, to which a flight of steps gave access. He seemed to know his way about. At the top of the steps a couple of soldiers in somewhat tidier uniforms than his own, were on guard. They stood in what Louise, who had old-fashioned notions as to the behaviour of soldiers on duty, put down as a slouchy and disrespectful attitude. When Lieutenant Godet walked past them they did not salute. This want of respect of the soldier for his officer was another manifestation, it seems, of Equality and Fraternity. Louise, with her nose in the air, sailed past in the wake of Godet and Fleurette.

After crossing a wide vestibule and turning on the right into a long, paved corridor, Lieutenant Godet came to a halt before a door which bore the legend: "Committee of Public Safety, Section III." Beside the door another soldier, also in very shabby uniform, stood leaning upon his bayonet. Fleurette, overawed by the vastness and silence of the place, gazed with vague terror at this man who without uttering a word had put his bayonet athwart the door and held it there, barring the way, motionless as a statue. Lieutenant Godet then spoke to him:

"The citizeness," he said, "is the daughter of Citizen Chauvelin. She desires to speak with him!"

The daughter of Citizen Chauvelin? What did the man mean? Fleurette, puzzled and frowning, pulled him by the sleeve. She was the daughter of Citizen Armand: she'd never heard the name of Chauvelin before. Nevertheless, the soldier on guard lowered his bayonet. Godet pushed open the door and the next moment Fleurette found herself facing a large desk which was covered with papers, and behind which Bibi was sitting, writing. A voice said loudly:

"Citizen Chauvelin, here's your daughter come to see you."

Whereupon Bibi raised his head and looked at her, staring as if he had seen a ghost.

Forgetting everything save the joy of seeing *chéri* Bibi at last, Fleurette gave a glad little cry, ran round the table, and came to halt on her knees beside Bibi's chair, with her arms round his neck.

She felt so glad, so glad that she was ready to cry.

"Bibi," she said softly, whispering in his ear, "*chéri* Bibi, are you not glad to see me?"

Chapter 19

At sight of Fleurette, Chauvelin had stared as if he had seen a ghost. He did not trust his eyes: they were obviously playing him a trick. It was only a second or two later that he realised it was indeed the child, come, Heaven only knew why or how, but here in this awful city where treachery, hatred and cruelty were holding sway under his own command.

Half-dazed, he yielded to the caresses of this one being the whole wide world whom his tigerish heart had ever loved. His arms closed round her beloved form, whose sweet breath as of thyme and violets filled his soul with joy. Then, looking up, he saw Louise standing there: silent, stolid, mutely accusing, and he asked roughly:

"How the hell did you both get here?"

Louise shrugged her shoulders.

"By the *coche*," she said, "from Sisteron."

"I know," he rejoined. "But why did you come?"

"Ask her," Louise replied curtly. "She would come. I could not let her travel alone."

Bibi's two hands were clasped round Fleurette's head, his fingers were buried in her hair: he pressed that dearly-beloved head closer and closer to his breast; joy at sight of her had already given place to terror. What was the child doing here? How and why had she come? He had kept her so completely aloof from real life, that it seemed to him that some awful cataclysm must have occurred over in that peaceful home in Dauphiné, else she were not here.

His pale, restless eyes searched Louise's impassive face:

"Who brought you here?" he reiterated roughly.

"An officer in a draggle-tailed uniform," Louise replied, still speaking curtly, whilst with a glance that was distinctly hostile her eyes swept round the room. "I thought," she added, "that he followed us into the room."

"What was he like?"

She described him as closely as she could, and then added: "I don't remember his name."

She too had heard the name "Chauvelin" spoken by the soldier and for a moment had pondered. Marvelled. In her downright peasant mind vague doubts, doubts that were eighteen years old now, turned to more definite suspicions. She knew well enough that some kind of mystery hung around the personality of Fleurette's father; she knew for instance that he was really a wealthy and high-born gentleman; but eighteen years ago, in the days of the old *régime*, the fact that a high-born gentleman chose to hide a love-romance from the eyes of his equally high-born friends was not an infrequent occurrence.

If at any time during the past eighteen years she had learned that M'sieu' Armand was really a great duke or prince or ambassador, she would have been neither surprised nor suspicious. But Chauvelin!!! For the past three years whenever rumours of cruelty or ruthless persecution of innocent men and women had penetrated to these distant corners of Dauphiné or Provence, the name of Armand Chauvelin had stood out as the protagonist of these terrible tragedies; people spoke of Danton the lion of the revolution, and also of Marat its tiger, of Robespierre and of Chauvelin.

Chauvelin!!!

And he, meeting her glance, understood what went on in her mind. As to this he was indifferent. What Louise thought of him was less than nothing. It was the child that mattered now: the child who clung to him quivering with excitement. The terror in his heart grew in intensity: it gripped him till he felt physically sick. The mad dogs of hatred and cruelty, which he himself had helped to unchain, seemed to be snarling at him and threatening his Fleurette. With a hand that trembled visibly, he stroked the pretty golden hair.

"Now, little one," he said, steadying his voice as much as he could, "are you going to tell me why you've come?"

Fleurette struggled to her feet. Self-possessed she stood before her father and said firmly:

"*Chéri* Bibi, I came in order to right a great wrong. I believe that you are strong and powerful and that you will help me to see justice done. That is why I came to you."

He frowned, more puzzled than before, angered with himself for being so dull-witted, for not making a guess at what had brought the child along. His mind just before she came had been so completely absorbed in the latest adventure of his arch-enemy the Scarlet Pimpernel, that the presence of Fleurette, here and now, had been for him like a sudden stunning blow on the head. He felt dazed and stupid: unable to turn his thoughts into this fresh channel.

"Fleurette, my darling," he pleaded, "try and tell me more clearly. I don't understand. What do you mean by righting a wrong? What wrong?"

"Why," she replied simply, "the arrest of M'sieu' Amédé for a crime which he did not commit.

"You knew M'sieu' Amédé had been arrested?" she insisted.

Yes, he knew that. The mock arrest of young Colombe was one of the tricks played on that fool Godet by those impudent English spies. But what had Fleurette's presence here to do with that?

She was trying to explain.

"Then you know, *chéri* Bibi," she was saying in that sweet, eager way of hers, "that some valuables belonging to *Madame* over at the *château* were found in the shed behind M'sieu' Colombe's shop?"

Yes, he knew that too. But what had she—?

"And that the soldiers accused M'sieu' Amédé of having stolen them?"

A sigh of relief escaped him. He was beginning to understand. Nothing to worry about apparently. Indeed, he might have guessed. The child had come to plead for that young fool Amédé, and—

"And what I had come to tell you, *chéri* Bibi," she went on glibly, "is that it is not Amédé who stole the things belonging to *Madame*."

She paused for a second or two. What she was about to say required courage: and how Bibi would take it she did not know. But Fleurette had come all the way from Lou Mas, had journeyed three days, so that Bibi might right a great wrong, as only he could do, and, once more sinking on her knees beside her father's chair, she added in a clear voice, rendered somewhat shrill with excitement:

"I stole the valuables out of *Madame's* room, *chéri* Bibi."

With a hoarse cry he clapped his hand against her mouth. My God, if someone had heard! The guard outside, or one of these innumerable spies whom he himself had set in motion, and whose ears were trained to penetrate through the most solid walls.

His pale eyes in which now lurked a kind of vague terror, wandered furtively round the room, whilst Louise, equally horrified and frightened, exclaimed almost involuntarily:

"The child is mad, *M'sieu'*, do not listen to her."

Fleurette alone remained self-possessed: she was still on her knees, but at Bibi's rough gesture she had fallen back, steadying herself with one hand against the floor. Slowly, noiselessly, Chauvelin had risen and tiptoed across the room, Louise, wide-eyed and scared, following his every movement. They were furtive like those of a cat on the prowl, and his face was the colour of ashes. He went to the door and abruptly pulled it open. Outside the soldier on guard was quietly chatting with Lieutenant Godet; at sight of Citizen Chauvelin they stood at attention and saluted.

"Go and tell Captain Moisson over at the barracks," Chauvelin said curtly, addressing Godet, "that I shall want to see him here at two o'clock."

"Very good, citizen."

Godet saluted again and turned on his heel. Chauvelin looked at him closely, but his face was expressionless. He watched him for a moment or two, as he, Godet, strode along the corridor. Then he closed the door and went back to his seat behind the table.

He had made an almost superhuman effort to regain his composure. He wanted to hear more and did not want to scare the child. The sight of Godet standing outside the door talking to the man on guard, had made him physically sick, raised that same terror in his heart which his presence and his glance were wont to raise in others. The expression of his face must at one moment have been absolutely terrifying for Fleurette could hardly bear to look at him; but when he sat down again his face was just like a mask, waxen and grey. He turned to her, and rested his elbow on the table, shading his eyes with his long, thin hand. And Fleurette felt how dreadful it must be for him to think that his daughter was a thief.

So, before he had time to ask her any questions she embarked on glib explanations.

"You must not think, *chéri* Bibi," she said, "that I stole those things for a bad motive. I did it because—"

She checked herself, and went on after a second or two:

"You remember, *chéri* Bibi, that evening at the *château* when we met, you and I, by the stable door?"

Yes, he remembered. "But speak softly, child! these walls have ears!"

"I had taken the things out of *Madame's* room then," Fleurette continued, speaking in an agitated whisper, "and hidden them under my shawl." She gave a nervous little laugh: "Oh! I was terrified, I can tell you," she said, "that you would notice."

He had his nerves under control by now. His mind, keen, active, was concentrated on her story, his indomitable will was slowly mastering his terror. What had he to fear? Godet was out of the way, and the child's whispers could not be heard outside these four walls. If only that fool Louise did not look so scared: the sight of her face, open-mouthed and with big, round eyes, got on his nerves. He tried not to look her way. While his glance was fixed on Fleurette he felt that he could think of her, scheme for her and above all protect her—he, so important in the councils of State. So powerful. He could shield her even against the consequences of her own folly.

Of course, he must make light of the whole affair. Oh! above all make light of it. The child was silly, wilful and ignorant, but he would know how to protect her, and how to make her hold her tongue. Louise was a fool, but she was safe and these walls were solid, there was really no cause for this insane terror which had turned him giddy and faint, and at first paralysed his brain.

So, he forced his quaking voice into tones of gentle banter, forced himself to smile, to tweak her cheek and to look gaily, almost incredulously into her eyes.

"*Allons, allons*," he said lightly, "what story is this? My little Fleurette taking things that belong to others? I won't believe it."

"Only *pour le bon motif, chéri Bibi*," she insisted; "because you see the soldiers were at the *château*, and they were ruining and stealing everything they could lay their hands on...And also because—"

Once more she checked herself, loath to give away that one cherished little secret: The mysterious voice at which perhaps Bibi would scoff. But she did tell Bibi how with the precious burden under her

113

shawl she had hurried homewards until, fearing that she would be overtaken by the soldiers on the road, she had sought refuge in the widow Tronchet's cottage. She told him how she had watched him riding past, heading towards Lou Mas, and how she had become scared lest, if he spent the night at home, he would find out what it was that she was keeping so carefully hidden underneath her shawl.

And then she told him how she had thought of M'sieu' Amédé and has asked Adèle to tell him to meet her outside the widow's cottage, and how she had entrusted him with the precious treasure and he had undertaken to hide it in the shed outside his father's shop. But how it came to pass that those other soldiers, who were as magnificently dressed as anything Fleurette had seen in all her life, how they had come to suspect M'sieu' Amédé of the theft, she could not conjecture. All she knew was that M'sieu' Amédé was innocent and that he must be proclaimed innocent at once. At once.

"I stole the things, Bibi," she concluded, "not for a bad motive, I swear, but I did steal them and gave them to M'sieu' Amédé to keep. If anyone is to be punished, then it must be I, not he."

She was sitting on her heels, and looking up boldly, and with a little wilful air at her father. Her dear little hands were resting on her knees. She looked adorable. Chauvelin mutely put out his arms and she snuggled into them, pressing her cheek against his breast with a nervous little gesture, twiddling one of the buttons of his coat.

Old Louise, sitting at the far end of the room, had listened, open-mouthed, wide-eyed, to the tale. Her furrowed face was a mirror of all the different expressions with which Chauvelin regarded her from time to time. Terror and slow reassurance. "If that is all, then I can deal with it!" he seemed to be telling her now, when it was all over, and he knew the worst. He held the child very close to him, and there was a certain nervous terror still lurking in his eyes as he buried his face in the soft waves of her hair.

"Bibi *chéri*," Fleurette insisted, "I must find those who are going to sit in judgement on M'sieu' Amédé. And you will help me find them, won't you? I must tell them the truth. Mustn't I?"

"You shall, child, you shall," he babbled incoherently. He was trying to steady his voice, so as not to let her know how scared he had been.

"When Adèle told us the next morning about the soldiers having found *Madame's* valuables and arrested M'sieu' Amédé, I knew at once that you would help me to put everything right. So, Louise and I just started then and there, as I thought we would find you in Sisteron."

"The child told me nothing," Louise protested in answer to a mute challenge from Chauvelin. "I only thought she wanted to see you in order to plead for young Colombe."

"There is no need," he said steadily, "for me or anyone to plead for him. Amédé Colombe is a free man at this hour."

Fleurette's little cry of rapture gave him a short, sharp pang of jealousy.

"Do you love him so much as all that, little one?" he asked almost involuntarily.

She blushed, and without replying hung her head. For a second or two he debated within himself whether he would tell her the whole truth, then came to the conclusion that on the whole it would be best that she should know. Doubtless she would hear the story, anyhow, from others and so he told it her just as he had had it the day before from Lieutenant Godet. The magnificent soldiers who had come that morning into Laragne were not real soldiers of the revolutionary army, they were a band of English spies whose chief was known throughout France as the Scarlet Pimpernel: a cyncial, impudent adventurer whose business it was to incite French men and women to desert their country in the hour of her greatest need, and who doubtless would incite Amédé Colombe to treachery and desertion. It was that chief, no doubt, who had spied on Fleurette and seen her that night hand over *Madame's* valuables to Amédé Colombe. He had taken this means of obtaining possession of the valuables, as well as of the persons of the *ci-devant* Frontenac and Amédé. Both men and money he would use against France, for the English were great enemies of this glorious revolution, the friends of all the *aristos* and tyrants whom the people were determined to wipe off the face of the earth.

Wide-eyed and dumb, Fleurette listened to him. After the first moment of intense joy, when she heard that Amédé was safe, there had come a sense of exultation that the mysterious voice which had urged her to find *Madame's* valuables had spoken with a purpose and that that purpose was now accomplished. *Monsieur, Madame* and *Mademoiselle* had all been saved by what she believed was a supernatural agency—whatever Bibi might say. No man who was a mere spy and an enemy of France could have accomplished all that this mysterious being had done, from the moment when disguised as a faggot-carrier he had commanded her to look after *Madame's* valuables, until the hour when clad in a magnificent uniform, daring and fearless, he had found such glorious means of saving Amédé and M'sieu de Frontenac too, from prison and perhaps death.

And after the joy and the exultation there had crept into Fleurette's heart a feeling of awe and dread for the father who apparently, she had never really known until this hour. She had only known him as kind, indulgent, loving—loving in a kind of fierce way at times, snarling like a wild cat if she thwarted him—but always indulgent and always secretive. Now he seemed to lay his soul bare before her. His love of France, of that revolution which apparently, he had helped to make. His hatred of those whom he called traitors and enemies of France, the aristocrats, the men who owned land and property, who had ancestors and family pride, and then the English who were the real enemies, who worked against the people, against democracy, and against liberty, who had harboured every traitor that plotted against France. Bibi hated them all and Fleurette felt awed and chilled thus to hear him speak. He, who was so gentle with her always, now spoke as if he approved of all the cruelty perpetrated against those who did not think as he did, and whom he hated with such passionate intensity.

Instinctively, and she hoped imperceptibly, she recoiled from him when he once more tried to clasp her in his arms. This man with the pale eyes and the cruel sneer was not the Bibi she loved. He was just a man whom she feared.

All she wanted now was to get away, to get back to Lou Mas. Since Amédé was safe, why should she stay any more in this awful place where even Bibi seemed like a stranger?

Louise now was standing near her, and Bibi was giving Louise some peremptory orders:

"You will go back now to the Chat Noir," he said, "the inn where you were this morning. There you will wait quietly until I come to fetch you. We will get on the way as early as we can, so as to get to Vaison before dark."

"Vaison?" Louise asked, perplexed. "But the *coche*—"

"We are not travelling by the public *coche*," Bibi broke in impatiently. "My private *calèche* will take us as far as Lou Mas, and I'll not leave you till I've seen you safely home."

"A *calèche!*" Louise exclaimed. "Holy Virgin!"

"Silence, woman," Bibi cried with an oath. "There is no Holy Virgin now."

Well! of course, Bibi had said that sort of thing before now, but never in such a rough, almost savage tone. Slowly Fleurette struggled to her feet. All of a sudden, she was feeling very, very tired. For four whole days excitement and anxiety had kept her up; but now excitement had died down and dull reaction had set in. A sense of unreality came over her: the voice of Bibi giving all sorts of instructions to Louise came to her muffled as if through a thick veil. All that she knew—and this was comforting—was that soon they would all be starting for home: not in a crowded, jostling old *coche*, but in a *calèche*. What a wonderful man Bibi was: so grand and powerful and rich, that he had a *calèche* of his own and could come and go as he pleased. She remembered how deferential the soldiers had been to him that night at the *château*, and even now her eyes fastened on the beautiful tricolour sash which he wore, the visible sign of his influence and power.

When Bibi finally took her in his arms and kissed her as affectionately, as tenderly as was his wont, she swayed a little when he released her and the things in the room started to go round and round before her eyes. Louise put her strong arm round her and Fleurette heard her say: "Leave her to me, she'll be all right!" She felt herself being led out of the room, past the sentry at the door, and then along a corridor.

When she felt the soft, spring air strike her in the face she felt revived and walked steadily beside Louise as far as the inn.

Chapter 20

Bibi's orders to Louise had been to go back to the inn and there to wait until he came in his *calèche* to take them home to Lous Mas. And the two women, ready for the journey home, so tired that only excitement kept them from breaking down, waited for him patiently in the parlour downstairs.

The travellers who had arrived in the early morning by the old *coche*, had all disappeared by now, some had found accommodation at the Chat Noir, others had gone to their homes or to friends in the city; the hour for dinner was not yet, and the personnel of the inn was busy in the kitchen.

The place was deserted and silent; the room itself, hot and stuffy. The air was heavy with the mingled odour of dust, sale grease and boiled food. Up on the wall a large white-faced clock tricked with noisy monotony, and against the small window-pane a lazy fly kept up an intermittent buzz. Now and again from a remote part of the house came the sound of a human voice or the barking of a dog, or the rattling of pots and pans.

Louise, sitting in a large, old-fashioned armchair by the side of the great heart, had closed her eyes. The monotonous ticking of the clock, the buzzing of the fly, the heat and the silence lulled her to sleep. Fleurette, on a straight-backed chair, sat wide awake, unable to keep her eyes closed even for a few minutes, although they ached terribly and she was very, very tired. But there was so much to keep her brain busy. In the past four days, more exiting events had been crowded into her life than in all the eighteen years that law behind her. And round and round they went—these events—beginning with the first sight of the squad of soldiers marching down the high road and coming to a halt on the bridge, until the happy moment when Bibi had assured her that M'sieu Amédé was safe and free, under the protection of that mysterious personage whom Bibi called an impudent spy and enemy of France but whom she, Fleurette, believed to be an agent of the *bon Dieu* Himself.

It seemed a part of her confused thoughts, presently, when she saw the door of the parlour slowly open and the kind soldier who had conducted her to Bibi standing in the doorway. He cast a quick glance all over the room, and as Fleurette was obviously on the point of uttering a cry of surprise, he put up a warning finger to his lips and then beckoned her to come.

She rose, eager as well as mystified, and once more he made a gesture of warning, pointing to Louise and then raising a finger to his lips. A warning it was to make no noise, and not to waken Louise. Fleurette tiptoed across the room to him.

"Your father sent me round," he said in a whisper. He beckoned her to come outside. She cast a last look at Louise who was obviously peacefully asleep, and then slipped out past him into the street.

"There is something your father forgot to say to you," the soldier sad as soon as she had closed the door behind Fleurette. "But he told me not to bring the old woman along, and so as she was asleep—"

"But if she wakes and finds me gone—?" Fleurette rejoined and turned to go back to the inn. "I must just tell her—"

Immediately he seized hold of her hand.

"Your father," he said, "told me to bring you along as quickly as I could. You know how impatient he is. It is but a step to the Hôtel de Ville. We'll be there and back before the old woman wakes."

No one knew better than Fleurette how impatient Bibi could be. If he said anything, it had to be done at once. At once. So, without further protest, she followed the kind soldier down the narrow street. A few minutes later she was back in the Hôtel de Ville, outside the door which bore the legend: "Committee of Public Safety, Section III." The same soldier in the shabby uniform was lounging, bayonet in hand, outside the door, but at sight of Lieutenant Godet he stood up at attention and made no attempt this time to bar the way. Godet pushed the door open and at a sign from him Fleurette stepped into the room. Of course, she expected to see Bibi sitting as before behind the table, alone, busy writing.

Bibi certainly was there, she saw that at a glance, also that at sight of her he jumped to his feet with an expression on his face, far, far more terrible than when she had told him that it was she who had stolen *Madame's* valuables. But Bibi was not alone. To right and left of him two men were sitting dressed very much like he was himself and wearing the same kind of tricolour sash round their waist. There was a moment of tense silence while Fleurette, a little scared, but not really frightened, stepped further into the room.

She could not take her eyes off Bibi, whose dear face had become the colour of lead. He raised his hand and passed it across his forehead. He seemed as if he wanted to speak yet could not articulate a sound. After a second or two he looked down first at the man on his right, and then at the one on his left, then back again at her, and over her head at Lieutenant Godet.

It was Fleurette who first broke the silence.

"What is it, father?" she said. "You sent for me?"

She did not call him Bibi just then; he seemed so very, very unlike Bibi.

But all he said was:

"What—is the meaning of—of this?" and the words seemed to come through his lips with a terrible effort.

"It means, Citizen Chauvelin, that I am trying to do my duty, and redeeming my faults of negligence and incompetence, for which you passed such severe strictures on me yesterday."

The voice was that of Lieutenant Godet. Fleurette could not see him because he stood immediately behind her, but she recognised the voice, even though it was no longer amiable and almost servile as it had been earlier in the day. It had, in fact, the same tone in it which Fleurette had so deeply resented that day upon the bridge when first she had told him that she was Citizen Armand's daughter.

"You ordered me," Godet went on deliberately, "to go into the highways and the by-ways, and you gave me full power to arrest any man, woman or child whom I suspected of connivance with the enemies of France. This I have done. I have cause to suspect this woman of such connivance, and in accordance with your instructions I have brought her before you on a charge of treason."

Whereupon the man sitting on the right of Bibi nodded approvingly and said:

"If indeed you have cause to suspect this woman, citizen lieutenant, you did well to arrest her."

And the man on Bibi's left asked: "Who is this woman, citizen lieutenant?"

Then only did Bibi appear to find his voice, and it came through his lips just as if someone held him by the throat and were trying to choke him before he had time to speak.

"My daughter," was all he said.

As a matter of fact, Fleurette did not understand that something terrible had occurred, she could see well enough, but for the moment the fact that she was in any way involved had not reached her inner consciousness. She did not realise that when Lieutenant Godet spoke of having arrested a woman, he was referring to her. Thinking that she was probably in the way amongst these seriously and busy men, she asked timidly:

"Shall I go, father?" whereat the man on the left gave a short, dry laugh.

"Not just yet, citizeness," he said, "we shall have to ask you one or two questions before we let you go."

"Citizen Pochart," Bibi now rejoined somewhat more steadily, "there is obviously some grave error here on the part of the citizen lieutenant and—"

"Grave error," Pochart broke in with a sneer. "We have heard nothing in the way of witnesses or details of the accusation so far, so why should you think there is an error, Citizen Chauvelin?"

Fleurette could see the struggle on Bibi's face; she could see the great drops of moisture on his face, the swollen veins upon his temples; she saw his hands clenched one against the other, and how he passed his tongue once or twice over his lips. "The citizen lieutenant," he said with a marvellous assumption of calm, "has shown too much zeal. My daughter is as good a patriot as I am myself—"

"How do you know that, Citizen Chauvelin?" the other man asked, the one on the right of Bibi.

"Because she has led a modest and a sheltered life, Citizen Danou," Bibi replied firmly. "Knowing nothing of town life, nothing of intrigues or plots against the State."

"It is impossible," Pochart put in sententiously, "for any man to know what goes on in a woman's head. The soundest patriot may have a traitor for a wife—or else a daughter."

Bibi was obviously making a superhuman effort to control himself. No one knew better than Fleurette how violent could be his temper when he was thwarted, and here were these two men, not to mention Lieutenant Godet, taunting and contradicting him, and she could see the veins swelling upon his temples and his hands clenched until the knuckles shone like polished ivory under the skin.

"My daughter is not a traitor, Citizen Pochart," he said loudly and firmly.

"Lieutenant Godet says she is," Pochart retorted dryly.

"I challenge him to prove it."

"You forget, Citizen Chauvelin," Danou put in suavely, "that it is not for the citizen lieutenant to prove this woman guilty; rather it is for her to prove her innocence."

"The Law of the Suspect," Pochart added, "has been framed expressly to meet such cases as these."

The Law of the Suspect! Ye gods! He himself, Chauvelin, had in the National Assembly voted for its adoption.

"Are we not ordered instantly to arrest all persons who by their actions, their speaking, their writing or their connections have become suspect?" This from Danou who spoke slowly, unctuously, without a trace of spite or anger in his voice. And Pochart, more rough of tone, but equally conciliatory added:

"The Law tells us that if suspect of nothing else, a man, or a woman, or even a child, may be 'suspect of being suspect'. Is that not so, Citizen Chauvelin? Methinks you yourself had something to do with the framing of that law."

"It was aimed at traitors—"

"No! No! at the suspect—"

"My daughter—"

"*Ah, ça,* Citizen Chauvelin," here interposed Pochart with an expressive oath, "are you by any chance on the side of the traitors? What has the State to do with the fact that this woman is your daughter? A patriot has no relatives these days. He is a son of the State, a child of France, what? Her enemies are his enemies, his hatred of traitors should override every other sentiment."

"A patriot has no sentiment," Danou echoed suavely.

Chauvelin now looked like an animal at bay. Caught in net turning round and round, wildly, impotently; seeking an egress and only succeeding in getting more and more firmly enmeshed. But he kept himself under control nevertheless. He felt the eyes of those three men probing his soul. Exulting over his misery. Hatred all around him. Cruelty. Godet openly hostile, vengeful, with a grievance for his own humiliation; ready to hit back, to demand humiliation for humiliation, and terror for terror. Revenge! My God! who but a fiend could dream of such revenge. And the other two; that fool Danou and that brute Pochart! No actual hostility about them. Only envy: a mad desire to save their own skins, to purchase notoriety, advancement at any price—even at the price of innocent blood.

And as a wild beast turning and turning in the trap will pause from time to time and glare out into the open, which means all its life has stood for until now, so did Chauvelin, with soul enmeshed in vengeance and envy, pause a moment in his mad struggle for freedom. He paused and with wildly dilated eyes gazed upon a swift, accusing vision of all the innocent blood he himself had helped to shed. Those clenched hands of his, on which his gaze for one instant rested, fascinated, how many times had they signed the decree which had deprived a father of his son, a wife of her husband, a lover of his mistress. And through the meshes that tightened round him now, Chauvelin gazing into space saw before his eyes the awful word "Retribution" written in letters of fire and blood.

And seeing the writing on the wall, he felt an immense rage against these men who dared to taunt him, who dared to hit at him, through the one vulnerable spot in his armour of callousness and cruelty. How dared they stand up to him, these miserable creatures whose existence was of less account than that of a buzzing fly? And throwing back his head he gazed upon them all, one after the other, meeting their sneering glance with a bold challenge. How dared they defy him? Him, Chauvelin? The trusted friend of Robespierre, one of the makers of this glorious revolution; one of its most firm props? Now a representative of the National Convention on special mission? There stood the child, his daughter, his little Fleurette, silent, wide-eyed, obviously not fully aware of the terrible position in which she stood: and they dared to hit at her, to accuse her, without rhyme or reason, just in order to hit at him through her.

It was Godet, of course, that vile, incompetent brute: savage and cruel like the fool he was: vengeful for the bad half-hour he had been made to spend in this very room. He must have heard something of what the child had said. At one moment her sweet voice had risen to shrill tones. Oh! what a senseless, mad confession! and he had seized upon it so that he might hit back: have his revenge. But he could prove nothing. It would be one man's word against another, and he, Chauvelin, representative on special mission, with the ear of all the great men up in Paris, would see to it, that his word carried all the weight. He would deny everything, swear that Godet lied. His was the power, he was more influential, more unscrupulous than most.

If only the child held her tongue! She would if she was assured that her Amédé was in no danger. How thankful he, Chauvelin, was that he had told her the truth this morning. He couldn't bear to look at her just at this moment, she looking so innocent, so unconscious of danger, but nevertheless he tried to convey to her with eyes and lips the warning to hold her tongue. Chauvelin had been silent for quite a little while; the others thought they had cowed him. In their hearts Pochart and Danou were not a little afraid of him.

A representative on special mission had unlimited power and this Chauvelin was always a crouching beast, ready to snarl and to spring, and they knew well enough how influential he was. But here was a double chance to show their zeal, and to get even with the man whom they had always feared. As for Godet, he had obviously staked everything on this throw. His life was anyhow forfeit; Chauvelin's threats yesterday had left him no loophole for hope. But here was revenge to his hand, and at worst a powerful lever wherewith to force his enemy's hand.

Chauvelin's mind had been so busily at work that for a while he lost consciousness of these men. After his rage against them he forgot their very presence. Nothing mattered—no one—except the child, and his own power to save her. Through that semi—consciousness he heard only vague words. Snatches of phrases that passed rapidly between those two men and Godet. "Proofs—" "Witnesses—" And then Danou's voice, soft and unctuous as usual:

"Of course, the more solid your proofs—"

And Pochart's, rough and determined:

"Why should we not hear that witness now?"

Godet replied lightly: "I have her here. Perhaps it would be best."

It seemed as if they were determined to ignore him, Chauvelin; to shut him out of their counsels. He was so silent, so self-absorbed; they thought that he was cowed, and dared not raise his voice in defence of

123

his daughter. They were all alike these men—these masters of France as they liked to be called—overbearing, arrogant, always menacing, until you hit back, when all the starch would go out of them, and they would cringe, or else become surly and defiant like any *aristo*.

"Go and fetch your witness, citizen lieutenant," Pochart said in the end.

Then Chauvelin woke, like a tiger out of his sleep.

"What?" he queried abruptly, "what is this?"

"A witness, citizen representative," came in unctuous tones from Danou. "It will be more satisfactory in this case—the Law does not demand witnesses—suspicion is enough—but—"

"Out of deference to your position, citizen," Pochart broke in with a short laugh. "Go and fetch your witness, Citizen Godet," he added dryly. Chauvelin brought his clenched fist down with a crash on the table. "I'll not allow you—" he began in thundering accents, and met Danou's sneering, inquiring gaze.

"Allow what, citizen representative?" Pochart asked roughly.

"Refuse to hear witnesses? On what grounds?" Danou put in in smooth, velvety accents.

Godet said nothing. It was not for him to speak; but he met Chauvelin's' glance just then, and almost drained his cup of revenge to its dreg.

"No one," now put in Pochart significantly, "has more respect for family ties than I have. But I am first of all a patriot, and then only a family man. I happen to be a single man, but if I were married and discovered my wife to be a traitor to the State, and an enemy of the people, I would with my own hand adjust the guillotine which would end such a worthless and miserable life."

"Now you, Citizen Chauvelin," Danou said, taking up his colleague's point, "are doing your daughter no good by trying to shield her from punishment if she be guilty."

"You would not dare—"

"Dare what, Citizen Chauvelin? Act up to the principles which you yourself have helped to promulgate in France? Indeed, we dare! We dare strike at the enemies of the State whoever they may be. That woman," he added, indicating Fleurette, "is suspect; the Law of the Suspect gives our Committee power to arrest her. If she be proved innocent, she shall go free. If she be guilty, you, by defending her, cannot save her and do but condemn yourself."

And that was true! No one knew it better than Chauvelin, who

124

but a few weeks ago in Paris had helped Merlin and Douai to frame that abominable Law. The heavy hand of Retribution was indeed upon him. The voice of the innocent had cried out for Vengeance before the Lord and Nemesis, hourglass in hand, had stalked him now at last. All that was left him at this moment, out of all that arrogance which had imposed his personality upon the masters of France, made them forget his failures and fear him even in the hour of humiliation, was just a shred of pride, which enabled him to hide his misery and his despair behind a mask of impassiveness. He even succeeded in hiding his hatred and contempt of these three curs who were yapping at his heels.

And when Pochart for the third time reiterated his order to Godet to go and fetch his witness, Chauvelin made no further protest. He rose from the table and went round to where Fleurette was standing, silent, bewildered, with great tears, like those of a frightened child, running down her cheeks. He held his hands tightly clenched behind his back, to prevent himself from seizing her in his arms and raining kisses upon her golden hair, letting those sneering men see how terribly he had been hit and how he suffered. Godet had gone out of the room to fetch the witness—what witness? and the other two were sitting at the table, whispering together. Chauvelin through compressed lips murmured in Fleurette's ears:

"Try not to be frightened, little one! Don't let them see you are frightened. They dare not do anything to you."

"I am not frightened, *chéri* Bibi," she replied, smiling at him through her tears.

"And you will hold your tongue, Fleurette," he urged under his breath, "about what you told me this morning. Swear to me that you will."

"If M'sieu Amédé is safe—"

"I swear to you on my soul, that we do not even know where he is."

"In that case, Bibi *chéri*—"

Quick footsteps outside the door. A challenge from the man on guard. The opening of the door. Then Godet's voice saying loudly:

"The witness, citizens."

Chauvelin looked up and saw beside Godet woman with a shawl wrapped round her head; she came forward boldly, then threw back her shawl. Chauvelin uttered a savage oath, whilst Fleurette gasped in amazement:

"Adèle!" she cried.

125

Chapter 21

It seemed almost the worst moment of this awful day to see Adèle—Adèle!—standing there, like some sly and furtive rodent, snapping at the hand that had fed and tended it. The lessons taught by all these makers of a revolution which was going to be a millennium for the people, and inaugurate an era of brotherly love, had been well learnt by all those who had nothing to lose and everything to gain by venality, by treachery and the blackest of ingratitude. And Chauvelin himself had been headmaster in that school, where this wretched little bastard had learned how to hate; she was the personification of that proletariat which he had striven to exalt, of the low, mean mind that never tries to rise and only strives to drag down others to the level of its own crass ignorance.

Adèle was only a product of that levelling process which was going to make of mankind one great family, full of love for one another, of pity for the weak and contempt of the strong, and which had only succeeded in arousing a universal hatred in every breast and envy of everything that was lofty and pure. The levelling process according to its early protagonists—idealists for the most part—was destined to eliminate all tyranny and to protect those who were too weak to protect themselves; but all it had succeeded in doing was to substitute one tyranny for another; it had not levelled the classes, made one man as good as another; what it had done was to hurl down from his self-imposed altitude of nobility or of virtue every man who was unwilling to step down of his own accord. It had set every beggar on horseback who was a beggar by nature and kept him there by virtue of ruthlessness and of cruelty.

None but a fellow-beggar, more ruthless perhaps, and more cruel, could unseat him. Death was the only real leveller, and this glorious revolution had become a fraternity of death. The Republic of France must march to Liberty over corpses, one of its makers had said, and another added sententiously that no traitor failed to return; except the dead. Terror reigned now everywhere, marching hand in hand with its hand-maiden the guillotine.

The time was no longer far distant when this titanic battle between all these beggars on horseback would reach its fiercest struggle ere it ended in a gigantic cataclysm, and when the gorge of all these tigers would rise at last in face of the daily hecatombs which had made a graveyard of the fair lands of France. But that time was not yet. Men like Chauvelin had seen visions of Retribution like fiery Fata Morgana pointing to the inevitable hour, but the Godets, the Danous, the Pocharts and the Adèles knew not the signs of the times. They had learnt their lesson and were applying it for their own advancement and above all for their own safety, destroying all that was destructible, taking Earth and Heaven to witness that they whose lives had been nought but misery and hunger would henceforth sweep off the face of the earth all those who had only known ease and comfort, who had practised virtue, and never known despair.

And Adèle whose hatred of Fleurette had thriven all these years as in a forcing-house, had learnt her lesson well. Fleurette to her meant tyranny, the tyranny of riches over her poverty, of good food over her empty stomach, of neat kirtle over her rags. Poverty and Hunger had enchained her to Fleurette's wheel, had forced her to wash dishes, to scrub floors, to sleep on a straw pallet. But now her turn had come. Her very misery had put it in her power to drag Fleurette down to her own level. She had imbibed the principles of this glorious revolution until she felt herself to be one of its prophets. She had spied on Fleurette and denounced her because she had seen at last a way to satisfy her hatred and to lull her envy to rest.

She had plenty to say when questioned by Pochart and Danou; proud of the fact that for over two years now she had supplied the Sisteron section of the Committee of Public Safety with information about the district. She had known the *ci-devant* Frontenacs and it was—she was proud to state—chiefly owing to her that they came to be suspected of treason. They used to turn one of their rooms into a chapel on Sundays and a *ci-devant* priest, who was not Constitutional, performed there, rites and ceremonies with wafer and cup which had long since been decreed treasonable against the State.

Adèle had been forced by the *ci-devant* Frontenac women to be present at these treasonable practices; she had even been made to scrub the floor of that temple of superstition and to remove the dust from the so-called altar. Her patriotic soul had risen in revolt and she had journeyed to Sisteron one day when she was free and placed the matter before the Committee of Public Safety who had commended her for her zeal.

"Adèle!" Fleurette exclaimed involuntarily. "How could you? Indeed, *le bon Dieu* will punish you for this."

At which remark everybody laughed—except Chauvelin, who smothered a groan. Oh! the child! the senseless, foolish, adorable child!

She seemed wilfully to run her darling head into the noose. Adèle turned a sneering glance on Fleurette.

"I'll chance a punishment from your *bon Dieu*," she said flippantly, "for the joy of seeing you punished by the Revolutionary Tribunal."

And strange to say Chauvelin did not strike her, though she stood quite near him, with only the width of the table between her and his avenging hand. But he did not strike her, even though his muscles ached with the desire to strike her on the mouth. It was pride that held him back. How those men would have laughed to see him lose his self-control with this wench who was only emitting principles that he indirectly had taught her. Retribution! Nemesis at every turn.

And now Adèle embarked upon her main story. Her spying on Fleurette. Long, long had she suspected her, with her airs of virtue and bunches of forget-me-nots in front of a statue representing a *ci-devant* saint. "*Saint Antoine de Padoue priez pour nous!*" every time she placed a fresh bunch of flowers before that statue. Bah! such superstition made a patriot's gorge rise with disgust. But Adèle had said nothing. Not for a long time. She knew that Citizen Chauvelin—he was known as Armand over at Laragne—was a great patriot and an intimate friend of Citizen Robespierre over in Paris. So Adèle decided to bide her time, and she did. Until that evening when at last the Frontenacs were arrested and the *château* ransacked. That night Adèle had had her suspicions aroused by Fleurette's strange airs of mystery, her desire to meet Citizen Colombe alone on a dark night. Fleurette had always been such a Sainte Nitouche that Adèle guessed that something serious was in the wind.

Like a zealous patriot she had watched, and she had seen Fleurette hand over a casket and a wallet to the young Colombe. She had heard the two talk over the question of hiding these things in a shed behind Citizen Colombe's shop, and finally seen them locked in each other's arms, which confirmed her in the idea that Fleurette, with all her appearances of virtue, was a woman guilty of moral turpitude.

And still Chauvelin did not strike her on the mouth. He fell to wondering what crime he had committed that was heinous enough to deserve this punishment of impotence.

The others listened for the most part in silence. Only occasionally did one or the other break into a chuckle. *Nom de nom*, what an event! Representative Chauvelin! the man of almost arrogant integrity, sent to Orange to spy and report on the workings of the Committee of Public Safety, one of the makers of the Terror, a man whose every glance was a menace, and every word a threat of death! When Adele had finished speaking, Pochart winked across at Danou. Here was a find that would exalt them both, bring their names to the notice of the great men over in Paris. All sorts of possibilities of reward and advancement loomed largely before them. And Pochart rubbed his large, coarse hands contentedly together and Danou poured himself out a glass of water and drank it down. All these possibilities had made him thirsty.

Fleurette too was silent. For the first time in her life she had come in contact with human passions of which hitherto she had not even dreamed. Adèle, the little maid of all work, with the coarse hands, the red elbows and narrow rat-like face, who wore Fleurette's cast-off clothes and worn-out shoes, had suddenly become an un-understand-able and terrifying enigma. Fleurette felt as if she could not utter a sound, that any word of protest which she might raise would choke her. The girl's words, her bitter accusations, spoken in an even mono-tone, gave her a feeling as of an icy-cold grip upon her heart. Sur-rounded from her cradle onwards with love and care, this first glimpse of spite and hatred paralysed her. Only when Adèle spoke of M'sieur Amédé and of that kiss which had tokened him to Fleurette, that deli-cious kiss under the almond-trees, only then did a hot blush rise to her cheeks, and tears of shame gather in her eyes.

Beyond that she felt like an automaton, while these four creatures who hated her and who hated Bibi were discussing her fate. Bibi was strangely silent and motionless although from time to time the others referred a question or two to him in which case he replied in mono-syllables. There was much talk of "detention" and of "revolutionary tribunal." Of course, Fleurette did not understand what these meant. Since Bibi appeared so indifferent, she supposed that nothing very serious was going to happen to her.

Presently Adèle and Godet were dismissed. Adèle swept past her with her shawl once more over her head hiding the expression of her face. Her eyes did not meet Fleurette's as she glided past like a little rat seeking its burrow. Perhaps she was ashamed. Godet was ordered to send two men along—they would be wanted to take the *citoyenne* to the house of detention. Godet gave the salute and followed Adèle out of the room.

Fleurette's feet were aching. She had been standing quite still for over half an hour and was longing to sit down. Bibi's eyes were upon her now, and his long thin hands were fidgeting nervously with a paper-knife. At one time he clutched it so tightly, and half raised it, as if he meant to strike one or the other of his colleagues. Fleurette tired and a little dizzy, only caught snatches of their conversation. At one time, Bibi said very quietly:

"You are very bold, Citizen Danou, to measure your influence against mine."

And the man on Bibi's left retorted very suavely:

"If I have transgressed, citizen representative, I'll answer for it."

"You will," Bibi rejoined, and his words came through his thin, compressed lips, harsh and dry like blows from a wooden mallet against a metal plate. "And with your head, probably."

"Is that a threat, Citizen Chauvelin?" the other asked with a sneer.

"You may take it so if you wish."

The man on Chauvelin's right, Citizen Pochart, had in the meanwhile been writing assiduously on a large piece of paper. Now he pushed the paper in front of Chauvelin and said curtly:

"Will you sign this, citizen representative"

"What is it?" Chauvelin asked.

"Order for the provisional arrest of one Fleur Chauvelin, suspect of treasonable connections with the enemies of France, pending her appearance before the Revolutionary Tribunal."

Chauvelin raised the paper and read it through carefully. His hand that held the paper was perfectly steady.

"Your signature," Pochart went on, and held out the quill pen invitingly toward Chauvelin, "as Representative of the National Convention on special mission is necessary on this order."

"You may take that as a threat too, Citizen Chauvelin," Danou added with a sly wink directed at his colleague Pochart, "for if you do not sign, there's others that will, and sign one too that will be even more unpleasant for you."

Chauvelin took the pen, and the two men, Pochart and Danou, sprawling over the table, had the satisfaction of seeing him sign the order for the arrest of his own child—her death probably. Not the first time either that something of the sort had occurred, that a man put his seal on the death-warrant of his kith or kin. Had not Philippe d'Orléans voted for the death of his cousin the king? Chauvelin signed with a steady hand, his lips tightly pressed one against the other. They should not see, these fiends, what torture he was enduring; they should not see that at this moment he felt just like a brute beast writhing in agony. Not that he had abandoned hope with regard to Fleurette. He felt confident that he could turn the order into a mere scrap of paper presently and see those two snarling dogs fawning at his feet once more, kicked with the toe of his boot and howling in vain for mercy.

It was only from humiliation that, conscious of his power, he had decided that silence and outward acquiescence were his best policy. He had certain cards up his sleeve which the others wot not of, but he could only play them if he succeeded in lulling them into a sense of security by his obvious indifference. Fortunately, his reputation stood him in good stead. He was known by his enemies to be so ruthless and so unscrupulous—such an ardent patriot, declared his friends—that his indifference now where his own daughter was concerned, did not even astonish Pochart and Danou. It was just like Citizen Chauvelin to send his own daughter to the guillotine. And this estimate of his character helped him to play the *rôle* that would mean life to Fleurette.

So, there he sat for a few minutes, perfectly impassive, his face a mask, his hand perfectly steady, perusing the paper, and then deliberately drawing his pen through one of the words and substituting another.

"We'll say the house of Caristie," he said drily, "the other is already full."

Pochart shrugged his shoulders. Why not concede this point? It was so fine to have the citizen representative under one's thumb. What matter if his daughter was thrust into one prison rather than another?

"Is the guard there?" Danou asked. "We have plenty of business to see to. This one has lasted quite long enough."

"There is still that report from Avignon to look through," Pochart added. "It will need your attention, citizen representative."

"I'll be with you in one moment," Chauvelin replied calmly.

He rose and went to the door. Opened it. Yes! there was the guard sent hither by Godet, two men to escort his Fleurette to the house of Caristie the architect, now transformed into a house of detention. Chauvelin did not even wince at sight of them. He closed the door quietly and then approached Fleurette. He took hold of her hand and drew her to the furthest corner of the room, out of earshot.

"You are not frightened, little one?" he whispered to her.

"No, Bibi *chéri*," she replied simply. "If you tell me not to be."

"There is nothing to be frightened at, Fleurette. These brutes wish you ill; but—"

"Why should they?"

"But I can protect you."

"I know you can, *chéri* Bibi."

"And you won't see that wretch Adèle again."

"I wonder why she hates me! I thought we were friends."

"There are no friends these days, little one," he said almost involuntarily. "Only enemies or the indifferent—They are the least dangerous."

"There are those whom we love."

"You are thinking of Amédé?"

"And of you, *chéri* Bibi."

"You believed me, didn't you, little one when I told you that young Colombe is safely out of harm's way?"

"Yes," she said, "I believed you."

"Then you will hold your tongue about—about what you know?"

"I promise you, *chéri* Bibi. But I won't allow Amédé to suffer for what I did," she added with that determined little air of hers, which Chauvelin had learned to dread.

"He won't. He can't," he declared whilst an exclamation of impatience at her obstinacy almost escaped him. "Have I not told you—"

"We are waiting, Citizen Chauvelin," Danou's unctuous voice broke in at this point. "As you are near the door, perhaps you will call the guard."

He did. And stood silently by, while Fleurette was ordered to follow the men. She obeyed, after a last, smiling glance at Bibi. No! she was not frightened; she felt sure that he could protect her, and so long as M'sieur Amédé was safe—

The last words she said before she finally passed through the door were:

"Poor old Louise! You'll tell her, won't you, Bibi, not to fret for me? and tell her to send me my crochet work if she can. I shall have plenty of time on my hands to get on with it."

Chapter 22

At four o'clock that afternoon the President of the Revolutionary Tribunal sitting at Orange received a summons to accompany Citizen Chauvelin, Representative of the National Convention on special mission, to Paris, there to present his last reports of the cases tried by him since the beginning of the year.

Public Prosecutor Isnard received the same summons; he hastened all in a flurry to the Hôtel de Ville to find Citizen Chauvelin.

"What does it all mean, citizen?" he asked.

Chauvelin shrugged his shoulders.

"I know not," he replied. "The summons came by courier an hour ago. I have my *calèche* here. We could start at daybreak tomorrow and be in Valence before dark. The next day should see us in Lyons, and the middle of next week in Paris."

"Can you not conjecture—?"

Once more Chauvelin shrugged.

"One never knows," he said. "There must have come some denunciation. You and the President have your enemies, no doubt, as everyone else."

Public Prosecutor Isnard's flabby cheeks were the colour of lead.

"I have always done my duty," he stammered.

"No doubt, no doubt," Chauvelin responded lightly.

"You'll be able to justify yourself, I feel sure, citizen. But you know what these summons are. Impossible to argue—or to disobey."

"Yes, I know that. But the business here—"

"What of it?"

"Our prisons are full. A batch of twenty at least should be tried every day. I have forty or fifty indictments ready now and we can keep the guillotine busy for at least a week. All that business will be at a standstill."

"You will have to work twice as hard on your return, citizen," Chauvelin retorted drily.

The arrival of the President of the Tribunal put a temporary stop to the colloquy. He too was flurried and not a little scared. He knew about these summonses that would come from time to time from Paris without any warning. They meant reprimands of a certainty. Perhaps worse. One never knows with leaders of the government over there. One moment they would shout: "Strike! Strike!" at the top of their voices, "let not the guillotine be idle!" They would frame laws to expedite the extermination of all the traitors and suspected traitors. The next, they would draw back, accuse you of over-zeal, over-cruelty, what not? See how Carrier had suffered! He had been sent to Nantes to purge the city of *aristos* and *bourgeois* and *calotins*; he had done his best; invented a new way of disposing of ninety priests all at once by the mere unmooring of a flat-bottomed craft, laden with those traitors, and on a given signal opening all the hatches and sinking the whole craft with her cargo.

Well! Carrier had done that. He had effectually purged Nantes of traitors. Nevertheless, he was summoned to Paris, and his head rolled into the basket on the Place de la République, just as if he had been an *aristo*. Look at Danton, and at—but why recall it all? Anyhow, what a week of desperate anxiety this would be until Paris was reached. President Legrange had thoughts of flight, of taking refuge in the mountains as others had done. But Public Prosecutor Isnard dissuaded him. What was the good of running away? One always got caught, and then it would of a certainty be the guillotine. Chauvelin too was for immediate obedience.

"I too am summoned," he said. "We are all in the same boat. As for the business here, it will have to wait until our return."

Public Prosecutor Isnard could not suppress a taunt.

"There's your daughter, Citizen Chauvelin," he said. "We were going to make quick work of her. I had her indictment all ready. In fact, the chief witness—a wench who looks like an anaemic rat—was in my study when your summons came."

"I know, I know," Chauvelin said with perfect indifference. "Well! all that can wait till our return."

After which he added lightly: "At daybreak, citizens, my *calèche* will be ready outside the Chat Noir. I await you then and advise you to eat a good breakfast. Our first stop will be at Montélimar, where we can get relays. In the meanwhile, I bid you *adieu*. I still have much work to see to before the close of day."

For the first time this day Chauvelin heaved a genuine sigh of satisfaction when the two men had departed. His first manoeuvre had succeeded admirably. With the President of the Tribunal and the Public Prosecutor out of the way, the business of the State would be at a standstill in Orange and he would have at least three weeks of freedom before him in which to act. He had planned this summons and intended to accompany the two men as far as Lyons. There he would find some pretext for sending them on their way without him, whilst he returned in secret to Orange. That was his plan, a risky one at best; but in less than three weeks he would either have found a way of getting Fleurette out of the clutches of these fiends, or he and she would both be dead. Strangely enough at this moment he fell to wondering what his arch-enemy, the Scarlet Pimpernel, would do under the circumstances and he longed for the possession of that same imaginative brain, that marvellous resource and unbounded pluck which had foiled him, Chauvelin, at every turn.

The Scarlet Pimpernel! If that bold adventurer were to know that his bitterest foe was now probing the lowest depths of sorrow, that this cruel Nemesis had overtaken him at last, how he would exult, how jeer at his enemy. And of the many pin-pricks which Chauvelin had had to endure today, he felt that none could hurt him so deeply as the thought that the Scarlet Pimpernel might hear of his trouble and hold jubilee over his soul agony.

Chapter 23

That first night the party slept at Valence in the Maison de Têtes, the quaint old house with its unique façade which stands to this day in the Grand' Rue, and which in that year of grace 1794 had been requisitioned by the Drôme section of the Committee of Public Safety for its offices. A *concierge* with wife and family were in charge of the house and there were two or three additional rooms in it which were often placed at the disposal of any official personage who happened to be passing through Valence. Chauvelin had often stayed there on his way through to Paris and was a familiar figure to the *concierge* and his family; there was no difficulty whatever in finding accommodation for himself and his two friends in the Maison des Têtes for the night. *Calèche* and horses, together with driver and postilion, were put up in the stables at the back of the house.

Night had overtaken the party when some five kilometres outside Valence, and this last part of the way had to be done at walking pace. Thus, it was nearly ten o'clock before the *calèche* drew up in the Grand' Rue outside the Maison des Têtes, and the *concierge*, hurrying to greet the unexpected and important guest, had regretfully to inform him that neither the President nor any of the officials were here to welcome him as they had already gone to their respective homes. But the rooms were there, quite ready, at the disposal of Citizen Chauvelin and his friends, and supper would be got immediately for them. The three travellers stepping out of the *calèche* were more than thankful to find shelter and food at this hour. Already at sunset the sky had been threatening; great banks of cloud came rolling up from the south-west, driven by tearing gusts of wind; by night-time a few heavy drops were falling, presaging the coming storm. No sooner were the travellers installed in the dining-hall in front of an excellent supper, than the storm broke in all its fury.

It was accompanied by torrential rain and a tearing wind. Such wild weather during the month of May was almost unparalleled in the valley of the Rhône, so the *concierge* hastened to explain to the two strangers who accompanied Chauvelin. The night was very dark too, the very weather in fact for foot-pads and malefactors who, alas! infested the countryside more than ever now.

"What would you do?" the man added with a shrug, "so many are starving these days; they get their existence as best they can. Honesty is no longer the best policy."

And then he caught Citizen Chauvelin's eye, and nervously clearing his throat, began to talk of something else. It was not prudent to grumble at anything, to make any remark that might be constructed into criticism of the present tyrants of France.

Supper drew to an end, mostly in silence. Chauvelin was never of a loquacious turn of mind, and neither of the other two were in a mood to talk. After a curt goodnight the latter returned to the room which had been assigned to them. Chauvelin before doing the same gave orders to his driver and postilion to have the *calèche* at the door by seven o'clock on the following morning. Then he too went to bed, there to toss ceaselessly through the endless hours of wakefulness, his mind tortured with thoughts of his darling Fleurette, wondering how she would bear this first night in prison, the propinquity, the want of privacy, the lewd talk, perhaps, or coarse jests of some of her room-mates. It was only in the early dawn that, wearied at last in body and mind, he was able to close his eyes and snatch an hour or two's sleep.

When the *concierge* brought him a steaming mug of wine in the early morning, his first inquiry was after the *calèche*. Was it being got ready?

Yes! the *concierge* had seen the driver and postilion at work this hour past. Everything would doubtless be ready for a start by seven o'clock. It was now half-past six. Chauvelin drank the hot wine eagerly; his sleepless night and all his anxiety had produced a racking headache and a state of mental inertia difficult to combat. Slightly refreshed by the drink, he proceeded to dress. While he did so he heard a great clatter of horses; hoofs striking the cobblestones, a good deal of shouting and rattling of wheels. His windows gave on the Grand' Rue and looking out he expected presently to see the *calèche* being driven round from the stable-yard at the back. But nothing came. He felt nervy and impatient, hoping that nothing would go wrong. Angered too with himself for feeling so flat on this very morning when he would need all his brain-power to carry his scheme successfully to the end.

He intended journeying with the two men as far as Lyons, and there to invent a pretext for separating from them, sending them on to Paris by the stagecoach, and then returning quietly and secretly to Orange alone. Already he was fully dressed and ready to go downstairs. He heard the clock in the tower of St. Apollinaire, striking seven. A minute or two later the *concierge*, wide-eyed and babbling incoherently, came bursting into the room.

"Citizen! Citizen! *Nom de nom, quel malheur!*" These ejaculations were followed by a string of lamentations, and a confused narrative of some untoward event out of which the only intelligible words that struck clearly on Chauvelin's ears were: "*Calèche*," and "cursed malefactors!" His questions remained unanswered; the man continuing to lament and to curse alternately.

Finally bereft of all patience, Chauvelin seized him by the shoulder and shook him vigorously.

"If you don't speak clearly, man," he said roughly, "I'll lay my stick across your shoulders."

The man fell on his knees and swore it was not his fault.

"I could not be in two places at once, citizen," he lamented. "I was looking after your two friends and my wife—"

Chauvelin raised his stick. "What is it that was not your fault?" he shouted at the top of his voice.

"That your *calèche* has been stolen, citizen!"

"What?"

"It is those cursed brigands! They have infested the town these past— "

The words died in his throat in a loud cry of pain. Chauvelin had brought his stick crashing upon his back.

"It was not my fault, citizen," he reiterated protesting. "I could not be in two places at once—"

But Chauvelin no longer stayed to listen. Picking up his hat and coat, he hastened downstairs, to be met in the corridor by the *concierge's* wife and two sons all incoherent and lamenting. The whole house by now was astir. Public Prosecutor Isnard came clattering down the stairs followed by President Legrange, both in more or less hastily completed *toilette*. And thus, the whole party with Chauvelin *en tête* proceeded at full speed to the stable yard, where the yawning coach-house and empty stalls told their mute tale. Of *calèche*, horses, driver or postilion not a sign. The stable-man, an old fellow, and his aid, a very young lad, were busy at the moment telling the amazing story to a small crowd of gaffers and market-women who had pushed their way into the yard from the back and were listening, open-mouthed, to a tale of turpitude and effrontery, unparalleled in the annals of Valence.

At sight of Chauvelin and his tricolour sash, the crowd of gaffers and women respectfully made way for him, and he, seizing the old stableman by the shoulder, commanded him to tell him clearly and briefly just what had happened. Thus, it was that at last he was put in possession of the facts that touched him so nearly. It seems that his own driver and postilion, up betimes, had got the *calèche* and horses quite ready and standing in the middle of the yard. They had in fact just put the horses to, and the postilion and driver were standing by the *calèche* door drinking a last mug of wine, when the from the narrow lane which connects the yard with the rue Latour at the back, a band composed of four ruffians came rushing in. Before he, the stableman, could as much as wink an eyelid, three of these ruffians had seized the driver and postilion round their middle and thrust them into the *calèche*, followed them in, banged the coach door to, whilst the fourth climbed up to the box with the rapidity of a monkey, gathered up the reins and drove away.

In the meanwhile, the lad who had been at work in the stables and heard the clatter came running out. Stableman and lad then ran to the lane and out into the rue Latour, only to see the *calèche* rattling away at breakneck speed. They shouted and strained their lungs to attract the notice of passers-by, and they did attract their attention, but before they could explain what had happened, the *calèche* was well out of sight. The lad ran as fast as he could to the nearest *poste de gendarmerie,* but before the *gendarmes* could get to horse, no doubt those ruffians would have got well away with their booty.

That was in substance the story to which Chauvelin had to listen, and through which he was forced to keep his temper in check. As soon as the stable-man had finished speaking, the lad had put in his own comments, whilst the gaffers and gossips started arguing, talking, conjecturing, giving advice, suggesting, lamenting. Oh! above all lamenting! That the high roads were not safe, everyone knew that to his cost. Masked highway robbers held up coaches, attacked pedestrians, robbed and pillaged the countryside. That the streets of Valence were not safe, was alas! only too true.

The *gendarmerie* was either incompetent or venal, and lucky the man who possessed nothing that could be taken from him. But this outrage today in broad daylight surpassed anything that had been seen or heard before. A *calèche* and pair, *pardieu!* was not like a purse that could be hidden in one's waistcoat pocket. And so on, and so on, while

Chauvelin, still silent and curbing his impatience, went back into the house, followed by his crestfallen friends and by the staff of the Maison de Têtes still lamenting and protesting their innocence and withal beginning to feel doubtful as to what the consequences might be to themselves of this untoward adventure.

The stable-lad was then sent back to the *poste de gendarmerie*, with orders from Citizen Representative Chauvelin that the chief officer in charge present himself immediately at the Maison des Têtes. Whilst waiting for this officer, Chauvelin, sitting in the small parlour, had a few moments' peace in which to co-ordinate his thoughts. The inertia which had weighed upon his spirits the first thing in the morning had been suddenly dissipated. Already his keen, imaginative brain had seized upon this catastrophe, and planned how to turn it to the furtherance of his scheme. And while his friends, no whit less voluble or more coherent than the *concierge* or his kind, were loudly lamenting: "What a misfortune, citizens! What bad luck!" and throwing up their arms in utter helplessness, Chauvelin broke in impatiently upon their wailings:

"We must make the best of it, citizens," he said, "I shall certainly be held up here a day or two, on this stupid business, but it certainly need not detain you. The stage-coach leaves for Lyons at half-past eight if I mistake not. As soon as my *calèche* is recovered, which I doubt not it will be in a couple of days, I'll follow you on. You in the meanwhile can proceed to Paris all the way by stage-coach. It will be perhaps not quite as comfortable as my *calèche*, but it will serve."

They demurred a little. The stagecoach would certainly not be as comfortable as Citizen Chauvelin's luxurious *calèche*, and perhaps a day or two's delay would not be very serious.

"It would be fatal," Chauvelin said emphatically. Orders from Paris such as they had received must be obeyed in the least possible delay, a couple of days idling in Valence, when a stage-coach was available, would certainly be put down to pusillanimity and want of zeal.

He could be eloquent when he liked, could Citizen Chauvelin, and on this occasion he was determined to gain his point—to send these two packing, post-haste, off to Paris, and leave himself free to return to Orange immediately. As to what would happen presently, when those two arrived in Paris and found that they had been hoaxed, that they had not been sent for, and would have to return biting the dust and chewing the cud of their wrath, as to that in truth, Chauvelin had not given a thought. To save his Fleurette, to get her away out of the country at the cost of his own life it need be, was all he thought about, and while the business of trying and condemning prisoners was at a standstill through the absence of these two men, there was a hundred to one chance that he could accomplish his purpose.

Therefore, he put forth all his powers of persuasion—and they were great. He drew lurid pictures of what happened to those who were thought to be guilty of dilatoriness or want of zeal. So much so that he reduced President Legrange and Public Prosecutor Isnard—at no time very valiant heroes—to a state of abject fear, and half an hour later had the satisfaction of bidding them *au revoir*, in the yard of the posting-inn, they having found seats in the stage-coach to Lyons.

As soon as he had seen the last of them, he made haste to requisition a chaise and the only horses to be had in Valence, to take him forthwith to Orange.

As for his own *calèche*, he wished the foot-pads joy in its possession and cared less than nothing what became of his driver or his postilion.

Chapter 24

Could Citizen Chauvelin have seen his *calèche* and horses a couple of hours later on the road, he would perhaps not have been quite so complacent as to its fate. After rattling over the cobble-stones of Valence and tearing down the high road at maddening speed, it slackened a little for the hill, and worked its way slowly up through the small township of Livron. A quarter of a league or so further, it turned off at the cross-roads in the direction of Cest and after another half-hour came to a halt at that small cottage which still nestles to this day, with its tumble-down roof and vine-covered arbour, beside the celebrated Roman ruins at the foot of the hill, not far from the banks of the Drôme.

Three ruffians, grimy from the roots of their hair to their down-at-heel shoes, jumped out of the *calèche*, dragging after them in the open the driver and postilion lately in the employ of Citizen Chauvelin, Representative of the National Convention on special mission. Whilst thus journeying between Valence and Livron these two poor wretches had been securely pinioned with ropes, but they were not gagged, and they used the freedom left to their tongues, by uttering oaths and protests which appeared vastly to amuse their captors.

The fourth ruffian—for ruffian he was—despite the fact that he had donned a *bourgeois'* dress, the better to carry out his *coup* and pass unnoticed on the road, had in the meanwhile scrambled down from the box.

"Quite successful so far," he remarked lightly, speaking in English, and rubbing his hands, which were slender and long and firm, contentedly together.

"What shall we do with these?" one of his companions asked, laughing and pointing to the two woebegone prisoners, who had ceased to curse and to protest, chiefly owing to want of breath, but also through astonishment at finding themselves the victims of some kind of foreign brigands whose language they did not understand.

"Poor beggars!" the other said lightly. "We'll place them in front of an excellent breakfast and I'll warrant we need not as much as tie their legs to their chairs. Get them inside, Ffoulkes, will you, and I'll talk to them as soon as Tony and I have seen to the horses."

"You don't think the *gendarmerie* from Valence will be after us, Blakeney, do you?"

"Not they," Sir Percy replied. "They are very short of horses in these parts, and the best will, I doubt not, be requisitioned by my friend M. Chambertin for his own use. I wonder now," he added musing, "what he is after, taking those two ruffians with him to Paris; and whether his errand is sufficiently urgent to cause him to travel in the stage-coach, now that we have borrowed his *calèche*—"

He paused, slightly frowning, evidently a little puzzled.

"I wonder," he added, "if our friend in there can throw some light upon the matter."

After which Sir Percy Blakeney and Lord Anthony Dewhurst took the steaming horses out of the shafts, relieved them of their harness and gave them a good rub down, a drink and a feed, while Sir Andrew Ffoulkes and Lord Hastings went into the cottage and busied themselves with their prisoners.

My Lord Stowmaries was for the moment in charge of this untenanted cottage, which was a stronghold as well as a rallying place of the League of the Scarlet Pimpernel, as it lay perdu, off both the main and the secondary roads. He it was who had prepared food for his chief and his comrades with the assistance of one Amédé Colombe. The cottage consisted of four rooms; insecurely sheltered against the weather by a cracked roof, and against damp by broken floors. There were a few very rare pieces of furniture in the place, abandoned there by the late owner and his family, worthy farmers whom the League of the Scarlet Pimpernel had conveyed safely out of France when their loyal adherence to their exiled *seigneurs* had brought them under the ban of the Revolutionary Government.

In one of the rooms the two prisoners were busy for the moment pinching one another to see if they were really awake. After thinking that they were within sight of death at the hands of a band of malefactors, they found themselves sitting at a table in front of an excellent plate of soup, some bread and cheese and a very large mug of excellent wine, while the cords round their bodies had been removed. Anyway, a very pleasant dream. Leaving conjecture to take care of itself, they fell to on this welcome repast with a healthy appetite. The door which gave on the larger room had been left open, and through it the two men could see the band of malefactors falling to, just like themselves, in front of an excellent meal, laughing and talking in that same gibberish language which they did not understand.

"They don't look to me much like brigands," the driver remarked presently, speaking with his mouth full, "in spite of their dirty clothes."

"And that tall one," the postilion added thoughtfully, "he seems to be their captain. If you ask me I think he is an *aristo*."

"Or an English spy."

The other shook his head.

"Not he. English spies would have murdered us."

"Then what in the name of hell—"

He got no further, the postilion had gripped him by the arm.

"*Nom de nom!*" the postilion exclaimed; and expressed further amazement by a prolonged whistle. "If that is not Amédé Colombe."

"*Qui çà Amédé Colombe?*" the other asked.

"The son of the grocer over at Laragne. I know, I come from those parts. But what the hell is he doing here?"

Amédé Colombe sitting at the table with his wonderful new friends, caught the sound of his name, and gave an anxious start.

"Do not worry about them, my young friend," Sir Percy Blakeney said reassuringly. "Before they could do you any harm we shall be many leagues out of the way."

At which postilion and driver gazed at one another, more puzzled than ever before. Were the really dreaming, or had they actually heard that foreigner speaking their own language?—and perfectly. The driver was inclined to think that the wine which they had been drinking was potent enough to be the cause of the hallucination. Not that this deterred him from pouring himself out another mugful and drinking it down with much smacking of the lips and sighs of contentment. It was such very excellent wine. Didn't his friend the postilion agree

142

with him? Why of course, and the filing and refilling of the two mugs continued apace and at a great rate.

"They'll be blind in a few moments," Lord Anthony Dewhurst remarked, glancing over his shoulder at the two men.

And he was right in this surmise. In less than a quarter of an hour driver and postilion were blind to the world with arms stretched out across the table, their heads buried in the bend of their elbows, breathing stertorously.

"You are not eating my friend," my Lord Stowmaries remarked to Amédé Colombe, who in truth had been sitting, silent, self-absorbed, neither eating nor drinking.

"Friend, Amédé does not appreciate your cooking, old man," Blakeney put in lightly. "It is fairly bad, I confess. Is it not Monsieur Amédé?"

"It is excellent, milor'," the young man sighed, "but I ask you, how can I eat or drink when I am in such terrible anxiety?"

"We were just going to discuss the best way—and the quickest—of alleviating your anxiety, *mon ami*," Sir Percy rejoined, "all we were waiting for was for these two amiable gentlemen over there to become deaf temporarily as well as blind."

"It is not for myself that I am anxious, milor'," the young man said timidly. He was over shy of these wonderful men, who had led him from adventure to adventure, in a manner that had almost addled his poor brain. His unsophisticated mind was still vibrating with the excitement of the unforgettable hour, when throwing disguise aside these strangers had revealed themselves not as revolutionary soldiers at all, but as mysterious beings, whose actions had appeared to him to savour of the supernatural. It took him a long time to understand the situation.

It seems that his being in possession of Madame de Frontenac's valuables was known to the girl Adèle who was nothing but a spy in the pay of the Committee of Public Safety. She had that night spied upon him and the girl he loved, seen the girl hand over the valuables to him, and revealed the fact to the Committee. Had these mysterious strangers not played the part of revolutionary soldiers and got him, Amédé, safely out of the way, before the real soldiers appeared upon the scene, he would at this moment be languishing in a prison at Sisteron or Orange preparatory to being sent either to the guillotine or for cannon-fodder on the frontier.

All this Amédé understood well enough, he cursed Adèle a thousand times in his heart for being such a snake in the grass. What he could not understand was why these strangers should take an interest in him and in his fate. When to his timid query on that subject their leader laughingly replied: "Sport! *mon ami*, the fun, the excitement nothing more philanthropic, I assure you, just sport!" he understood still less.

No wonder that to him, Amédé Colombe, the whole adventure had come as a manifestation of something supernatural. As for M. de Frontenac, his fellow-sufferer, on the other hand, he had apparently been prepared for that manifestation. It appeared that *Madame* and *Mademoiselle* had already been rescued from peril and taken to a place of safety, where presently M. de Frontenac would be able to join them, always through the instrumentality of these wonder-working strangers. The last thing M. de Frontenac had said to him, Amédé, when he took leave of him a couple of days ago, somewhere in the lonely mountain paths where the party had called a halt, was: "Trust these Englishmen Amédé, trust them with everything you hold dear. Look at me, had I not trusted them with my wife and daughter, I should have seen my dear ones first, and myself afterwards, facing the guillotine at this very hour!"

It was with these words ringing in his ears, that Amédé, sitting now amongst these men to whom he owed his life, had mustered up sufficient courage to reiterate more firmly: "It is not for myself I am anxious, milor'."

"I know that, *mon ami*," Sir Percy replied, "you are thinking of that brave little girl—Fleurette. Isn't that her name?"

"Yes, milor'," Amédé whispered timidly.

"Some of my friends and I are going straightway back to look after her now."

"And you will hurry, milor', you will hurry, will you not? Every day may be fatal for her."

"I think not," Blakeney said in that decisive way of his, which carried so much conviction. "You told me she was the daughter of a man high up in the councils of the revolutionary government."

"One Armand, milor'," Amédé continued. "Little is known of him in the neighbourhood, save that he is a widower and apparently has influence with the government."

"Fleurette is an only child?"

"Yes. She has lived at Lou Mas all her life."

"If her father has influence he can protect her for a time."

"For a time—yes! But—oh milor'!" the poor young man suddenly burst out with passionate vehemence, "if anything were to happen to Fleurette, I would curse you for having saved my life."

Blakeney smiled at the young man's eagerness.

"Listen, friend Amédé," he said lightly, "are you going to trust me and my friends?"

And Amédé, who remembered those last solemn words spoken by M. de Frontenac, looked into those lazy grey eyes, meeting that half earnest, half-humorous glance beneath the heavy lids, replied simply: "Yes, milor'!"

"And you will accord me what my friends accord so ungrudgingly, bless them, implicit obedience?"

Again, Amédé replied simply: "Yes milor'!" And then he added! "What am I to do?"

"For the moment nothing," Sir Percy replied, "but remain here quietly and alone until you hear from me again. Can you do it?"

"If you command."

"You won't mind the loneliness?"

"I shall be thinking of Fleurette and trusting you."

"Come, that's brave!" Sir Percy concluded lightly. "You will find some provisions in the armoire in this room: but apart from that you will find your way every day down to the river, and turning to your right, you will walk along its bank till you come to a derelict shed hidden from view by two old walnut-trees. In a corner of the shed, beneath a pile of leaves, you will find something to comfort you, either a loaf of bread, or a piece of cheese, sometimes a jug of milk or a bottle of wine. Scanty fare probably, but it will suffice to keep the wolf from the door. Those who supply it are poor and risk much to do it. They owe my friends and me a debt which they pay in this fashion. Now are you prepared to live this life of a lonely anchorite while my friends and I return to Laragne and gather news of your Fleurette?"

"If I could only come with you, milor'!" Amédé sighed.

"Tush, man, what were the good of that?" Sir Percy retorted with a slight note of impatience in his pleasant voice. "You would only lead us all—and your Fleurette into trouble."

"But you will bring me news of her soon?" Amédé entreated with tears in his kind, innocent looking eyes.

"Either news of her—or Fleurette herself."

Amédé shook his head. "She would not leave her father," he said dolefully.

"Then she will be safe with him, until better times come along, which will be very soon, friend Amédé, you may take that from me. Another few months—very few—and the dragon's own teeth will be turned against itself. This anarchy cannot endure for ever, because all evil, friend Amédé, is by the grace of God Infinite."

He spoke these last words with unwonted earnestness, and simple Amédé Colombe looked up to him with awe as to a prophet standing there, magnificent in energy and strength, head thrown back, the lazy eyes beneath their heavy lids flashing with unquenchable inner fire. And suddenly he checked himself, laughter chased away earnestness, the eyes twinkled with merriment like those of a care-free schoolboy, rather than a seer.

"La!" he said lightly, "I verily believe we were waxing serious. No cause for that, eh, friend Amédé? My friends and I are off on a gay adventure. To take a message of love from you to a brave little girl who loves you, a shade better methinks, than she loves that mysterious father of hers. Write your love letter, my friend, but be sure and make it brief, and I'll deliver it myself in her own little hands. I saw her, that sweet wench of yours, no woman ever showed more pluck than she did when she went to seek Madame de Frontenac's valuables."

"You saw her, milor'!" Amédé exclaimed wide-eyed. "*Mon Dieu!* is there anything that you do not see?"

"There is, *mon ami*," Sir Percy replied gaily. "I have never seen your pretty Fleurette's mysterious father. He must be a fine man to keep the love of so sweet a daughter. So, write your letter, my friend," he went on, and pointing to an oaken desk at the further end of the room on which were quill-pen, inkpot and sand, "and I promise you that I will deliver it, if only for the pleasure of having a squint at the mysterious owner of Lou Mas. Heigh-ho!" he added with a contented sigh, "but this promises to be fine sport. What say you, Ffoulkes, or you, Tony? We are going to put our heads into the wolf's jaws again, eh? Stow-maries, you, too, and Hastings.

"But we'll do it, and I promise you that the sight of pretty Fleurette will be a fitting compensation for some very unpleasant half hours we may have to go through. Now then, friend Amédé! your love missive, and two of you put the horses to, we'll have to make Montélimar by nightfall! there we'll either abandon the *calèche*, steal a couple of horses and cut across the hills to Sisteron, or keep to the *calèche* and the road as far as the neighbourhood of Orange, where much information can always be gleaned about the district. We'll make no plans now and

146

trust to luck and chance. What?"

Lord Tony then pointed, smiling, to the driver and postilion still fast asleep in the adjoining room.

"What is to happen to those mudlarks?" he asked.

"We'll take them along, of course," Blakeney replied. "So, thrust them into the bottom of the *calèche*, under the seat for choice, and those who sit inside can use them as footstools. Where we leave the *calèche*, there we leave them too, to find their way back to the bosom of their families in due course."

He looked so gay and so full of life and strength, so sure of himself, such pure joy in this new adventure radiated from his entire person, that some of that divine spark in him set Amédé Colombe's blood tingling through his veins. Anxiety, melancholy, doubt fell away from him at a glance from those lazy eyes now twinkling with joy, at sight of that firm mouth, ever softened by a smile; of those long, slender hands, delicate as a woman's, firm as those of a leader of men. Poor Amédé was almost happy at this moment, feeling that he was one with this band of heroes, that just by obedience and self-effacement, he could feel that he was one of them.

In cramped schoolboy hand, he wrote a brief, very brief little line to Fleurette, and told her how he adored her and longed for her nearness. He also told her that whatever else happened he implored her to trust the bearer of this note, who would be the means of bringing her back one day to the shelter of her Amédé's arms.

Less than an hour later he was all alone in the tumble-down cottage that nestled against the ruins of a former, long-since-dead civilisation. The late afternoon was soothing and balmy, the sky of a pale turquoise, clear and translucent, and as Amédé, standing somewhat forlorn at the cottage door, watching the narrow road over which the *calèche* had lumbered a while ago, bearing away his mysterious new friends, the pale crescent of the moon appeared above the snow-capped crest of La Lance, and Amédé, remembering the old superstition, bowed solemnly nine times to the moon.

Chapter 25

What irked Fleurette most in her prison life was the monotony of it: the want of something to do. After she had cleaned out the room which she shared with ten others, and put herself and everything tidy, the day appeared interminably long. She did her crochet work while her supply of thread lasted; old Louise had been allowed to make up a bundle of some clothes for her, and in it she had also put the crochet work and a few hanks of thread, but a few days saw the end of this supply, after which there was nothing with which Fleurette could occupy her fingers. Some of her fellow prisoners had needles, cotton and thimbles, and presently Fleurette, always willing and always smiling, was asked to darn and mend their clothes. She was glad enough to do it, as a means of killing time.

They were a heterogeneous crowd these fellow-prisoners of hers, culled from every social grade from the great lady to the troll out of the street. Misfortune and the precariousness of existence had brought these usually warring elements closely together: friendships sprang up where in the past even a nod of recognition would have been grudged. The Comtesse de Mornas, who belonged to the highest aristocracy of Provence, would take her morning exercise with her arm round the waist of Eugénie Blanc, daughter of a second-hand clothes dealer of Orange.

Hélène de Mornas's husband had been guillotined three months ago on some trumped-up charge or other, and Eugénie Blanc's father, accused of traffic with the enemy—whoever that enemy might be no one knew—had perished in that awful wholesale massacre perpetrated in Orange last month. Sorrow brought these two women together, as it did many others, and when Claire de Châtelard, obviously a woman of evil reputation, sought Fleurette's compassion with a tale of hunger, misery and arrest, that compassion was freely given, and the girl who had led such a sheltered life at Lou Mas, knowing nothing of temptation or of evil, had for daily companion after that, one Claire de Châtelard, the most notorious jade of Orange.

Thus, the first few days went by. In the prison—it is architect Caristie's house with all the furniture turned out of it and the rooms left bare of everything save a few benches, a few paillasses, a table, a wash-hand basin or two—in the prison great puzzlement prevails. Hither-to every day, just before sunset, a captain of the guard with half a dozen men would enter the courtyard and standing there, would in a loud voice read out a list of names. That list was the Roll-call, the decrees of the Revolutionary Tribunal condemning so many to the guillotine on the morrow.

And at all the windows of the house around the courtyard, heads would appear: men and women—yes! and children too—clutching their prison bars and listening. Listening if their name be upon that list. And then a sigh of relief if that name was not called: another day's respite! another day in which to drag this miserable, precarious existence. As for the others, the ones whose names were read out in a loud voice by the captain of the guard, there was nothing for it but to clasp their loved ones, or mayhap only the newly-found friend, in their arms—for the last time. That same night they were transferred to the prison of the Hôtel de Ville, and in the morning the guillotine. Sometimes not that. Just driven like a herd to the slaughter: on the bridge or the Place de la République. And there the guns. And death pell-mell. Like cattle, with ne'er a grave nor a prayer.

That was how it had been before Fleurette's arrival. That cinder-wench Claire de Châtelard told her how it used to be. But Fleurette never saw anything of that. The very day after her arrival was marked by the non-appearance of the captain of the guard with his list. They all wondered, put their heads together, and for an hour or two after the usual time there was whispering, conjecturing going on. Respite for everybody: that was of course what it meant.

But why? Had that awful Revolution really come to an end, as everybody had prophesied it would? Had all those tigers up in Paris really devoured one another, and was there no one left to carry on the infamy? Well! that was perhaps how it was. But no one knew anything. Not the warders. Not the prisoners. Not anybody. Inside these walls wherein news was wont to penetrate with extraordinary precision and rapidity, nothing was known. Nothing. Except that there was no list and that on the morrow the guillotine was idle.

This new departure from regular routine was accepted with the same stoicism as everything else. It was the stoicism of supreme help-lessness, or rather of despair, and it had engendered in all these people, men and women, herded here together on the eve of death, a kind of levity which it is difficult for modern thought to understand. Death was so familiar to them, such a daily companion, that they had ceased to think of him with awe. Familiarity had bred contempt. And derid-ing Death, they turned him into ridicule. Made game of him, defied him to break their spirit.

It was a species of madness born of intense horror and absolute despair. Fleurette at first felt sick and wretched at sight of these peo-ple—proud countesses and high-born *seigneurs*, as well as muckworms and jades—acting the guillotine, as they called it, in the great hall of Architect Caristie's house, which was assigned to them for recreation. She, poor little soul, had never learned to envisage death as anything but awesome for which the Holy Church was at pains to prepare doomed mankind with sacraments and prayers.

The first time she saw them all in their gruesome mummery, she fled affrighted back to the dark, noisome room where she slept, and throwing herself on her miserable paillasse, she sobbed her little heart out with horror and grief, stuffed her fingers into her ears so as not to hear the voices and the laughter that came from the great hall. Here Claire de Châtelard found her an hour later, and I think this was the beginning of their friendship, for the wench found just the right words wherewith to console this ignorant little country mouse.

"Their one recreation," she urged. "They mean no irreverence. Just think of them face to face with death. Always. Deprived of every consolation: mocked, jeered at. This play-acting is only a blind to hide their own misery, the despair which they are too proud to display."

After a while Fleurette dried her tears. But she slept ill that night. Nightmares pursued her. Visions of that mock tribunal, with the mock prosecutor, and the mock culprit. And then the setting up of two chairs and draping them with bits of crimson rags to represent the guillotine. Once or twice she sat up on her hard paillasse, hardly able to smother a scream which would have aroused her room-mates from their sleep. She had seen in retrospect one of the warders, who had helped in the acting of the gruesome play, dressed as Satan with horns and tail and entering the hall with a bound and a whoop. His *rôle* was to snatch the President of the Tribunal and the Prosecutor from their seats and to drag them away with him into everlasting fire, while a weird voice boomed the query: "What hour is it?" and another replied: "Eternity."

Poor little Fleurette! It was her first experience of life. And what an experience! Yet, it had only been one step from Lou Mas with its almond-trees and rippling mill-streams, with Bibi and old Louise, one step from there to this barrack of a house converted into a prison, with all its humiliating propinquities, and all its horrors. Her companions in misfortune were very kind to her. All of them. The men as well as the women. Clair de Châtelard and the Comtesse de Mornas. They all seemed to understand her position, her helplessness, her ignorance. They were so kind! so kind!

They admired her crochet-work, and talked to her of Laragne, or the snows of Pelvoux, or the almond-trees of the Dauphiné. They thanked her and kissed her when she offered to ply her needle for them: to mend their clothes or darn their stockings. Within a few days she became one of themselves. A younger sister in this family of the despairing. Within a week, or mayhap ten days, she had lost her sense of horror at their mummeries, could laugh at the antics of the mock Satan come to carry the mock judges off to hell.

The only thing to which she could not get accustomed was the representation of the guillotine, the inverted chairs and the bits of red rags, the cords, the victim, the basket and the executioner. Oh! that executioner! He was terrible! Especially of late. The *rôle*, like that of Satan, had always been undertaken by one of the warders; rough fellows these, culled from the lowest scum of the city; men who delighted in all the physical and moral torture inflicted on the *aristos* under their charge, who would gloat over the sight of a father torn away from his children and led to the guillotine, who would regale the unfortunate prisoners with tales culled from the *Moniteur* of wholesale executions or brutal massacres.

The idea of acting the part of executioner to the mock representations of the guillotine delighted a certain grim sense of humour which most Southerners possess. There was one man in particular, lately come to replace another who was sick, who threw himself into the gruesome *rôle* with zest. He would strip almost naked for the part, and then cover his face and his large body with a mixture of soot and charcoal and oil so that he looked like a huge negro, with gleaming teeth and long, lank hair, of a pale blond colour speckled with dirt.

Poor Fleurette could not bear to look at him, nor at the mock execution when one or other of her fellow-prisoners would allow himself to be tied to the mock guillotine, amidst the well-acted laughter and jeers of men and women who impersonated the awful rabble that was always to be found around the real guillotine. It was horrible, and Fleurette would run out into the corridor, or back to her miserable paillasse, anywhere where she could shut her ears to that gruesome mockery.

Unfortunately, there came a day when the warder declared that an order had come through, that prisoners must remain together in the hall during the hour of recreation. He said it was so, and there was no one to contradict him. Of all the tyrants that had been set over their fellow-men, these days, none were more dreaded because more autocratic, than prison-warders. As far as prisoners knew, these tyrants' power over them was absolute. In any case they could, if contradicted or thwarted, make it ten thousand times worse than before for those who did not cringe. This order then had to be obeyed and Fleurette, cowering alone in a corner of the hall, kept her eyes tightly shut while

151

the impish scene was being enacted.

Madame de Mornas, aristocrat, dignified, with her arm round Eugénie Blanc's waist, spoke to her very kindly.

"My dear," she said in her gentle, well-bred voice, "if we did not make a mockery of all these horrors we should brood over them, and some of us would go mad."

And Eugénie Blanc, the "old clo" dealer's daughter, added with a shrug: "You dear innocent! You have seen nothing of life as it is. You don't know what it is when memory sets to work and you see things—you see—" She gave a shudder and then a harsh laugh. "This at any rate takes one's mind off memory for a time."

Clair de Châtelard's sympathy was too sincere, though rather more grim: "We've all got to go through the real thing presently; the mockery of it now will make the reality tomorrow more endurable."

"We must practice today," M. de St. Luce, the great scientist said lightly, "our attitude of tomorrow."

That was the general tenor of every one's feelings upon the subject. Fleurette, touched by so much sympathy, tried to smile through her tears, and promised to school herself to the same philosophy. But as soon as all these kindly creatures had left her, in order to join, laughing, in the grim spectacle, she once more closed her eyes and sat in the dark corner, quite still, hoping that no one would notice her. But the laughter at one time was so loud, every one's mood so hilarious, that involuntary she opened her eyes and looked. The mock executioner had just completed his task.

It seems he was complaining that *Madame la Guillotine* was still unsatisfied: she was putting out her arms, ready to embrace another lover. M. de Bollène—a minor poet well known in Provence—was declaiming some verses of his own composition, in praise of that promised embrace. The executioner's coal-black face shone like polished ebony in the flickering light of the tallow candles that guttered in their sconces. Madame de Mornas, almost unrecognisable in ragged kirtle and with a crimson scarf tied round her head, was flourishing her knitting and humming the tune of the *Carmagnole* as an accompaniment to M. de Bollène's verses, whilst Claire de Châtelard sprawled at the foot of the mock guillotine with a red streak across her throat.

And suddenly, to her horror, Fleurette saw the executioner stride towards her corner.

"What?" he cried aloud, "tears? Tears are for *aristos*. To the guillotine with her!" or words to that effect. Fleurette did not rightly understand what he did say, all she knew was that this hideous, horrible man came striding towards her with hands outstretched, and that everyone was laughing or singing or clapping their hands. The next moment she felt that horrible hand upon her shoulder, on her kerchief, her breast. She gave a loud scream and cowered further into the corner thinking the she would faint with terror, until she heard a peremptory voice calling out loudly; "Leave the child alone, man, can't you see she is frightened?"

"Frightened? Of course, she is frightened," the loathsome creature retorted with a laugh. "Did I not say that she was an *aristo?* Let me just call the warder and——"

A woman's voice was raised in protest:

"No, no, don't call the warder. She's done nothing wrong—and he might——"

And Madame de Mornas it was who added:

"You coveted this ring this morning, man, it is yours if you leave the child alone and say nothing to the warder."

How kind people were! How kind! As nothing further seemed to happen, Fleurette ventured to open her eyes: Claire de Châtelard was sitting beside her, trying to comfort her. The gruesome play had apparently come to an end; the prisoners in groups of three or more stood about talking and laughing, preparatory to be driven back to the sleeping-rooms for the night. The black executioner was no longer there.

"He is not a bad man really," Claire de Châtelard said to Fleurette, fondling her hand and smoothing the golden curls that clung to her moist forehead! "only very rough and coarse. Bah! these men!" she went on with a shudder. "The warder is a veritable fiend: a genius in inventing means to punish you if you do not bribe him or give in to him. All my little treasures which I was able to bring here with me, have gone into his rapacious hands. This man is not so bad, he is new to his work, he came a day or two ago to replace one who was ill. But he is only a scavenger. When the warder is dead drunk he takes his place, the rest of the time he does all the dirtiest work in the house. A loathsome creature, what? If he were not so big, we should not be so frightened of him. But he is better than the warder."

Fleurette only listened with half an ear. She still felt bruised and ill after the fright she had had. That horrible black hand touching her breast. It was worse than any nightmare.

She was glad when the bell clanged and the warder accompanied by his new aide—only partially relieved of the soot and the grime of his *rôle*—drove the prisoners like a herd of cattle back into their pens. So many women in one room, so many men in another. He had his list, and with a stout stick in his hand which he flourished as he read out the names, he drove them all in, into their respective night quarters and locked the doors upon them.

Fleurette shared her wretched paillasse with Claire de Châtelard. There was no dressing or undressing in this overcrowded room. No privacy. One just lay down in one's clothes and snatched what rest one could. Oh! the horror of it all to these women, most of them accustomed to dainty homes. Fleurette never knew which moment she dreaded most, that of opening her eyes to another awful day, or trying to close them in intermittent sleep.

Claire de Châtelard, less impressionable, was already asleep. Fleurette slipped out of her kirtle which she laid tidily across the foot of the paillasse; then she took off her muslin kerchief. As she did so something fluttered to the ground. A piece of paper neatly folded. Smothering an involuntary cry of surprise, she stooped to pick it up. Yet she hardly dared to touch the thing at first. How had it got between the folds of her kerchief? Who could possibly have put it there unbeknown to her? This was the second time with in a very little while that Fleurette had come in contact with something that savoured of the supernatural. Still timorous, and with a trembling hand, she picked the paper up. Claire was asleep and most of the others had already stretched out their limbs upon their hard paillasses. No one paid any heed to Fleurette.

There was no direct light in the room itself, but an oil lamp which hung from the ceiling in the corridor threw a feeble ray of light through the fan-light over the door. Fleurette unfolded the paper and smoothed out its creases against her knee. She made her way to the centre of the room where she could just contrive, by that dim light from above, to decipher the handwriting upon the paper. But the first word that caught her eye, nearly caused her to utter a cry of joy; it was the signature: Amédé.

Amédé! At once her eyes grew dim with tears. Amédé! Those five letters in the clumsy, schoolboyish handwriting meant happiness and home. Amédé! Before trying to read further she pressed the paper against her cheek, fondled it; laid it against her lips.

Amédé! He had written to her. Where from? How? She did not care to think. What did it matter after all? He was thinking of her. Had written to her. And some divine messenger had conveyed his missive to Fleurette. Though he was safe and well—Bibi had assured her that he was—he had thought of her and sent her this letter through one of God's own angels.

And then Fleurette dried her eyes, for she remembered that presently the bell would clang again, when all the lights would be put out and she might have to wait until tomorrow to read Amédé's letter.

It was short, very, very short. Amédé had never been a scholar, but in it he told her how he adored his Fleurette and longed for her nearness. He also told her that whatever else happened, he implored her to trust the bearer of this note who would be the means of bringing her back one day to the shelter of his arms.

The bearer of this note? Who was he? Surely, surely, one of God's angels! and so of course she trusted him. And it was only *le bon Dieu* who would so guide Bibi that all this trouble would come to an end and she, Fleurette, would of a certainty find a shelter once more in her Amédé's arms.

She read and re-read the few brief lines over and over again, and presently when the bell clanged, and she was forced to make her way hurriedly to her paillasse before the room was plunged into utter darkness, she laid down on the hard straw with a little sigh of contentment and of peace. Her evening prayer was one entirely of gratitude to *le bon Dieu* for His gift of Amédé's love and Bibi's protection. And that night Fleurette slept quite soundly, with her cheek resting against the letter from Amédé.

Chapter 26

For two whole days Citizens Pochart and Danou of the 137th Section of the committee of Public Safety had been sorely puzzled. They had received a curt note from Representative Chauvelin telling them that he would be absent from Orange for a brief while and bidding them suspend all business until his return. Suspend all business? In very truth all business was perforce at a standstill, not because of the absence of the representative on special mission, but because of that of two high officers of State; the President of the Tribunal and Public Prosecutor.

Representative Chauvelin in his note had also alluded to this absence, stating that by direct orders from the Central Committee of Public Safety, President Legrange and Prosecutor Isnard had been obliged to proceed to Paris.

It was all very puzzling, not to say suspicious. Pochart and Danou put their heads together and came to the conclusion that here undoubtedly were some machinations at work on the part of Representative Chauvelin with a view to getting his daughter out of harm's way. The question was how to make use of these machinations. Of their knowledge that they were machinations. How in fact to turn them against the man who hitherto had carried himself with such consummate arrogance, lording it over every officer of State in Orange, with thinly veiled threats that had roused ire, malice and hatred in these men, whose rule of life was "strike ere you yourself be struck."

One thing, however, was crystal-clear. Representative Chauvelin was hard hit. He put on an air of lofty indifference; he continued to bluster and to threaten but he was hard hit by the arrest of his daughter, as indeed any family man would be. Pochart and Danou did not care one worthless assignat what became of the daughter, but they did feel that the pleasure of threatening and terrorising the representative on special mission, perhaps even of dragging him down from his exalted position and sending him in his turn to the guillotine, was not one to be missed.

Up to the hour when Lieutenant Godet had arrested the wench Fleurette on suspicion, Representative Chauvelin had been a living threat to every patriot in Orange. He seemed, as it were, to be always walking hand in hand with the guillotine, or else in its shadow; sheltered himself, yet a menace to others. But now the tables were reversed, and Pochart and Danou had in one hour learned to substitute threats for soft words, arrogance for servility. And they vastly enjoyed the substitution.

But the trouble was that they were void of imagination. Representative Chauvelin could be brought down, they knew that. But how? Judging other men by themselves, they quite envisaged the possibility of a father sacrificing his own daughter in order to save himself. And there was also the possibility that a representative on special mission was powerful enough to save both his daughter and himself. Strong forces would have to be marshalled against him. Pochart and Danou with heads together passed these forces in review.

There was Lieutenant Godet who hated Representative Chauvelin with a hatred born of fear—the deadliest hatred of all. There was that rat-faced little spy, Adèle, a mixture of petty spite and malice. She would be useful. Others might be found, for Representative Chauvelin had many enemies who had not until this hour dared to come out into the open, but who would readily show themselves once the powerful representative was attacked.

And in the meanwhile, the business of purging the countryside of *aristos*, suspects and traitors was at a standstill. With no Public Prosecutor to frame indictments and no President to try the accused, the order: "*Que la Terreur soit à l'ordre du jour*": "Let Terror be the order of the day," had become a dead letter. This could not go on, of course. Pochart and Danou, quite apart from their schemes against Representative Chauvelin, felt that a solution must be found—and that quickly—for this impossible situation. If allowed to continue they stood in very great risk of a reprimand from Paris for allowing the business of the State to be at a stand-still. They might be accused of want of zeal. Those great patriots up in Paris were so unreasonable, one never knew what they might do. Having sent for President Legrange and Public Prosecutor Isnard, they probably expected "the order of the day" to go on just the same. But how, *nom de nom?* How?

They were still seeking a solution, these two, Pochart and Danou, on the third morning, when to their surprise Representative Chauvelin walked in, as calm and indifferent as you please.

He had completed his business, he explained to them, sooner than he had anticipated. President Legrange and Public Prosecutor Isnard on the other hand had continued their journey to Paris.

Danou, suave as ever, expressed satisfaction in the return of the citizen representative. It was indeed a matter of congratulation, he added, for them all, seeing that the business of the State was so completely at a standstill.

Pochart was somewhat more emphatic.

"There are at least one hundred and sixty traitors," he said, "who should have been dealt with days ago. Your absence, citizen, and that of two other public servants should not have occurred at this critical hour—"

"It was inevitable, Citizen Pochart," Chauvelin broke in drily. "Orders from Paris, you know—"

"I was just proposing to Citizen Pochart," Danou put in mildly, "that we send a message to Paris by this new aerial telegraph to ask for further orders. There is one installed at Avignon, and a courier—"

"The aerial telegraph is required for more important business than yours, Citizen Danou," Chauvelin once more broke in, and this time with some impatience.

"What can be more important than the suppression of traitors?"

Pochart argued with an obvious sneer. "I marvel at you, citizen representative, that you should think otherwise."

"The very latest decree of the National Convention," Danou added, "was that Terror be the order of the day. I too marvel at you, Citizen Chauvelin."

"There is no cause for marvel," Chauvelin rejoined with well assumed indifference. "I have not been in Orange more than a few hours. I have not had time to devise for this new situation."

"Well, then, tomorrow, citizen," Danou suggested, "will you be ready to consult with us on the best means of meeting this impossible situation? Otherwise, I am still of the opinion that the aerial telegraph, or perhaps a courier to Paris—"

He went on mumbling for a few seconds. His tone had been quite suave, not to say deferential; but Chauvelin's keen ear had not failed to detect the threat that lurked behind those smooth, velvety tones.

"Tomorrow, as you say," he concluded dryly.

All through the wearisome journey back from Valence he had been busy scheming and planning; alternately adopting and rejecting one plan after another. He knew well enough that Pochart and Danou were stalking him like wild beasts, ready to pounce on him, come to grips with him in a life and death struggle in which his darling Fleurette would also be involved.

Now after his interview with the two men, he knew that already they scented victory, that they too were scheming and planning, planning his overthrow, and using Fleurette as the deadliest weapon against him. These last three years of titanic struggle of man against man, of the strong against the weak, of the weak against the strong, had taught him that he could expect nothing, neither mercy nor consideration, from enemies whom he himself would never have hesitated to sacrifice to his own whim or his own tyranny. His only hope lay in his avowedly superior brain power. He no longer could dominate these snarling wild beasts, now that they were showing their fangs, but he could outwit them, before they sprang and devoured him. Brainpower as against blind lust. And Chauvelin thought that he could win.

Chapter 27

Representative Chauvelin was quite calm, business-like, armed with sheaves of papers and documents, when he met his colleagues the following morning in the bureau of the Committee.

"I have found," he announced as soon as they were seated, "a solution to our difficulty."

"Ah?" Danou ejaculated simply. And Pochart also said "Ah," but in a different tone.

"I have here," Chauvelin continued, and selected and official document from the pile which he had deposited upon the table. "I have here a decree which exactly meets our case. It was promulgated by the National Convention on the motion of Citizen Cabot on the 6th of Brumaire last."

Leaning back in his chair, he began to read from the official document in his hand. The others, elbows on the table, chin cupped in hand, listened with what we might call mixed feelings.

"Should it occur that through any cause whatsoever, one of the chief officers of State be absent from duty for a period exceeding seven days, the Representative on special mission shall then assume his functions and continue to discharge them for as long as seems expedient. And in the event of more than one important officer of State being so absent, the Representative on special mission shall himself appoint a substitute who will also discharge such duties as the Representative on special mission shall have assigned to him for the time being."

Having finished reading, Chauvelin put the document down, and with a gesture of finality let his thin, clawlike hand rest upon it.

"The decree is clear enough, methinks," he said coldly.

There was a pause. A silence lasting perhaps thirty seconds; then Danou said mildly:

"I have never heard of this decree."

"Nor I," Pochart echoed.

"The Central Committee in Paris," Chauvelin put in drily, "has often remarked on the strange ignorance displayed by avowed patriots, of the decrees promulgated for the welfare of the State. The Committee deems that such ignorance amounts to treason."

"May I look at the document?" Danou rejoined simply, choosing to ignore the reprimand—and the thin veiled threat.

"Certainly," Chauvelin replied, and handed the document over to his colleague.

"Is it a copy?" Pochart asked, looking over his friend's shoulder.

"An attested copy, as you can see," Chauvelin replied. "It is countersigned by Citizens Robespierre, Billaud, Couthon and Saint Just. You are not thinking of disputing the order, Citizen Danou?"

Once more and still that arrogance, those veiled threats. The situation being entirely different from what it was yesterday, Danou and Pochart dared not persist in their mood of defiance. Not before they had consulted one another, marshalled those forces—Godet, Adèle, the proofs against the wench Fleurette—and decided on the mode of attack. Representative Chauvelin must have something up his sleeve, some hidden power, or he would not be so arrogant, so threatening.

Danou wiped the sweat from his bald cranium and handed the document back to Chauvelin. Pochart shaking himself like a wet dog, returned to his seat.

"I'll take over the office of President Legrange." Chauvelin said calmly, "and preside over the Tribunal until his return."

"Then I," Danou put in boldly, "had best take over the work of the Public Prosecutor."

"Impossible, citizen," Chauvelin rejoined firmly; "I must have a lawyer for that office."

"But—"

"You do not seem to have listened very carefully, Citizen Danou," Chauvelin broke in quietly, "to my reading of the decree, or you would remember that it is for the representative on special mission to appoint a substitute, in case of absence on the part of a second important officer of State."

"And whom do you propose to appoint, citizen representative?" Pochart inquired with a sneer.

"I will let you know my decision as to that tomorrow."

"The sooner the better, citizen representative," Danou concluded unctuously. "Remember that it is my colleague and I of the 137th section of the Committee of Public Safety who will have to collect the evidence against the accused and place it before the Public Prosecutor whom you will appoint. That is a duty from which only the Central Committee can relieve us. There are one hundred and sixty prisoners, arrested under the Law of the Suspect. Some of them gravely accused, and by witnesses to."

"I am well aware of that, Citizen Danou," Chauvelin replied calmly. Not by the quiver of an eyelid did he betray the fact that the shaft had gone home. With a perfectly steady hand he collected his papers and placed a weight upon them. After which he dismissed the others with a curt nod.

"Your pardon, citizens," he said, "I have still work to do. You too doubtless. I shall require your attendance here tomorrow at this same hour."

When the door had finally closed behind the two men, the mask fell from Chauvelin's face. Leaning his elbow on the table, he buried his burning head in his hands; a heart-rending groan broke from his parched lips, his eyes felt as if seared with glowing charcoal. Ah! if he had not only forgotten these years past how to pray, what fervent orisons would he not have sent heavenwards at this hour. Help! where could he find help out of this web which his enemies had woven round him? How he hated them! longed to smite them before they had time to accomplish their fell purpose. They had determined on striking at Fleurette. Out of revenge or hatred or was it fear? they had determined on striking at him, Chauvelin, through this being whom he loved beyond everything in the world.

And he who had been one of the first protagonists of hatred and revenge and mutual distrust, he who had the will and the power, seemed so inextricably enmeshed that he could do nothing to save her. Fight? he would fight, inch by inch, step by step. Fight to save his Fleurette. Fight while he had breath in his body; fight until he fell vanquished by her side. For if he failed he would not let her die alone. He could not think of her being dragged through the streets in that awful tumbril which he himself had so often helped to fill; could not—heavens above no—could not think of her mounting the steps of the guillotine, which so many innocent feet had mounted at his bidding. Retribution! It had come nearer, more inexorable now! Death by his Fleurette's side seemed the only possible issue.

And even as he sat there alone, in that room wherein the hatred of his fellow-men seemed still to linger like noisome ghosts, a pale ray of sunlight found its way through the closed window and played upon the myriads and myriads of dust atoms that hovered in the air. Chauvelin's hands dropped down upon the table. His weary eyes rested vacantly upon that shaft of dust-laden light. And inside its very heart he saw a face, smiling and debonair, with lazy eyes and smiling lips mocking him in his grief. It was a vision, gone as soon as seen, but vivid enough during that one brief second to bring a savage curse upon the lonely man's lips. His claw-like hand clenched so tightly that the knuckles shown like polished ivory.

"My evil genius!" he muttered through his teeth. "Had I succeeded in bringing you down, had I seen that mocking head fall under the guillotine, this devastating misery would never have come upon me. If only I could be even with you, I would die happier—even now."

Chapter 28

Ever afterwards to Chauvelin, it seemed as if the Scarlet Pimpernel had heard his challenge and come in response to his thoughts: for hardly had a couple of days gone before the first rumour reached him of the nearness of his arch-enemy. Twenty-four hours later the hue and cry was all over Orange after a gang of English spies who, it was averred, made it their business to cheat Madame la Guillotine out of her dues.

Citizen Pochart brought Representative Chauvelin the news which already was over the town, namely that Architect Caristie and his family, consisting of his wife and the small son now aged ten, who was destined one day to become one of Orange's most distinguished citizens, had unaccountably disappeared from their tumble-down lodgings in the Rue de la République, where they had taken refuge after their house had been requisitioned by the State and turned into a prison-house.

For some time, the sectional Members of the Committee of Public Safety, Citizens Pochart and Danou, ardent patriots, had had their eyes on the Caristie family. *Aristos*, what? Architect Caristie had designed and built houses in the past for tyrants and *ci-devants*. The arrest of the entire family had been decided on. It was to have taken place that very evening. Orders to that effect were out, their place of incarceration fixed in the very house where they had once sat in luxury, whilst patriots had starved outside their gates.

And suddenly the news had spread like wildfire through the town that Architect Caristie, his wife and son had disappeared. Disappeared? Where? asked every patriot. But no one knew. One evening they had still been seen, as usual, taking walking exercise on the river-bank, and the next day when the soldiers of the revolutionary army presented themselves at the door of their lodgings in the Rue de la République and demanded admittance, lo! they received no answer: the lodgings were deserted, the birds had flown from their nests.

Nor could the guard at any of the gates of the city throw light upon this mysterious occurrence. No one had passed the gates without duly authenticated passes. Pochart was at his wits end and asked counsel of Representative Chauvelin. What was to be done in face of this mystery? Exercise strict supervision at the gates, Chauvelin advised. All passes in future to be signed by himself as well as by the Sectional Members of the Committee of Public Safety.

The news of the presence of the Scarlet Pimpernel in Orange had acted upon his nerves like a whiplash. Fate, it seemed, was hitting at him from every side: and he felt like a fighter who has been downed once, twice, and then suddenly felt the strength of giants in his blood; the agility of a cat spurring him on to a new and stupendous effort. In a vague, fatalistic kind of way the safety of Fleurette and the destruction of the Scarlet Pimpernel appeared to him as inextricably involved. If he allowed his arch-enemy to baffle him now and here, in this city, then Fleurette was doomed and he himself must perish.

This was the immediate state of mind into which the news of the Scarlet Pimpernel had thrown him. A wild desire to link the destruction of his enemy with the safety of his child, to deserve so well of the State, in fact, that the life of Fleurette would be ceded to him as a reward. A drowning man will catch at a straw, and so did Chauvelin catch at this hope, cling to it, turn the thought over and over in his mind. With feverish activity then he spurred those about him into additional vigilance, combated that superstitious terror with which every official these days regarded the gang of English spies and their mysterious chief. He brought to every man notice that the handsome reward offered by the Revolutionary government for the capture of the Scarlet Pimpernel, described the Englishman's appearance, his methods, his motives, worked up every man in Orange, aye, and every woman too, into a state of enthusiasm for the possible capture of this inveterate and daring enemy of France.

But this particular frame of mind was not destined to endure. Soon memory got to work, recalled unpleasant moments in Calais, Boulogne, in Paris, in Nantes. What if here too, in Orange, the Scarlet Pimpernel should triumph and he Chauvelin once more be forced to eat the bread of humiliation? What if baffled once more, he should lose, at one terrible swoop, both his revenge and his last hope of saving Fleurette? And then it was that first the insidious, the stupendous thought penetrated his brain. Was it Satan himself who had whispered it into his ear? or some army of mocking imps intent upon torturing him to madness? But heavens above, what a thought! The Scarlet Pimpernel and Fleurette! Was that going to be the solution of this terrible impasse? The thought feverishly driven back at first, returned more insistent. Why not? And then again, why not? A young girl, sweet, pretty, innocent, was she not one to arouse those instincts of chivalry which Chauvelin had hitherto affected to despise?

What a possibility! Heavens above, what a possibility! His very senses reeled now at the thought. But he allowed his mind to dwell upon it, to weigh his possibilities: to familiarise itself more and more with it. At first it had seemed like madness, but no longer now! His Fleurette! Already Amédé Colombe was far away, under the protection of the Scarlet Pimpernel, what more likely than that—No! no! it could not be! His daughter! His, Chauvelin's! And in a swift vision he saw himself luring Marguerite Blakeney, the beloved and beautiful wife of the Scarlet Pimpernel to her death, holding her as a hostage, threatening her, torturing her. His enemy's wife! What agonies she had endured at his hands! And now Fleurette! Would not the Scarlet Pimpernel, triumphant and revengeful, gloat over her death, rather than raise a finger to save her life? Would he not gaze with joy on the misery endured by his bitterest foe?

And then once more torturing thoughts would assail him: torturing fears and torturing hopes, hopes? Yes, hopes! "Why should you not hope, man?" Whispered an insidious demon in his ear: "the Scarlet Pimpernel does not know, cannot know that Fleurette is your daughter; the daughter of his enemy Armand Chauvelin. To him she is just the sweet, pretty, innocent victim of a system of government which he hates and which he combats. Then why not hope?" And the floating, racking visions of Juliette Marny, and Yvonne de Kernogan, of the Abbé Foquet and Madeleine Lanoy, would once more haunt the daydreams of this man already steeped in misery, and hope insidious, ever-living hope, would whisper in its turn: "To that long list of innocents snatched from prison and from death by the insolent adventurer whom you hate, why should not the name of Fleurette by added? Fleurette of unknown parentage, just a sweet girl dwelling at Lou Mas, with old Louise and a father known as Armand? Why not?"

And day after day, whilst presiding, self-appointed over a tribunal of infamy, Chauvelin's mind became more and more familiarised with the vision of his Fleurette snatched out of the jaws of death by the man with the lazy eyes and the mocking lips, the demmed, elusive Pimpernel of his daydreams and his sleepless nights.

Chapter 29

Meanwhile in Architect Caristie's house, transformed for the necessities of the State into a prison, the old routine is now restored. Daily, once more, an hour before sunset, the captain of the guard with his half-dozen men, enters the courtyard, and in a loud voice reads the names that appear upon his roll-call. They are the names of those who on the morrow are summoned before the Revolutionary Tribunal, there to answer the charges that are trumped up against them by the venal spies, who make their living out of the blood of innocent men and women and children.

Impossible to refute those charges, since the law has decreed that it is a crime to be merely suspected of treason against the State. Foucquier-Tinville, the great Public Prosecutor in Paris, no longer troubles, it seems, to prepare fresh indictments against every accused in turn. He has a printed formula of accusation, with just the name left in blank, presently to be filled in as convenience arises. Therefore, in other greater and lesser cities of France, patriots desirous of showing their zeal, can do no better than emulate the example set by so great a man. Local sections of the Committee of Public Safety prepare the indictments—set *formulæ* with the names left in blank. These they pass on to the Public Prosecutor who mumbles as he reads them before the Tribunal with the President sitting up on the dais, and the accused—names left in blank—brought up to the bar, not allowed to say a word in their own justification, nor to question the witnesses brought up to testify against them.

Abandon all hope then, ye whose names are upon that Roll-call! tomorrow the Tribunal, the next day the guillotine! And once again now, day after day, the captain of the guard comes to the house, late of Architect Caristie, and reads; and at all the windows that overlook the courtyard heads appear, men, women and little children—clutching the bars and listening. Listening for their own name or that of one who is dear. Sighing with relief if neither has been called, or with resignation if tomorrow is destined to bring this miserable existence to an end.

And day after day Chauvelin presides over this tribunal of infamy. Self-appointed he sits upon the dais and sees before him pass a daily file of doomed and dying. Sometimes ten, sometimes as man as twenty in a day, and still the prisons are full—fresh arrests make up for those whom the guillotine has claimed. Acquittals are rare, for moderation now has become a crime. Danton—aye! even Danton, the lion, has perished, he who ordered the September massacres, he who thundered forth from the tribune, "Liberty! Fraternity! Equality! or Death!" he has perished because he became guilty of the crime of moderation. The glorious revolution has no use for such of its products as Danton and Robespierre—for the reality of the one and the canting hypocrisy of the other: so, Danton it was who perished. "It is right," he had dared to say once, "to repress Royalists: but we should not confound the innocent with the guilty!"

"And who told thee," Robespierre retorted, sea-green with hatred, "that one single innocent has perished by our hand?"

And because Danton had dared to raise his voice in the cause of the innocent, Danton had perished.

What chance then has Chauvelin to defend his Fleurette? His power is great. He can make your Pocharts and your Danous, our President Legrange or Public Prosecutor Isnard, but he cannot accord special privileges in prison for his own daughter. He cannot see her in private, comfort her, warn her if need be, tell her not to be afraid for Bibi *chéri* is there, on the watch, ready to protect her with his body, to stand by her in the last hour. He cannot. Pochart and Danou are on the watch. "We must not confound the innocent with the guilty:" Danton had dared to say. And for this he had perished: and though he perished, could not save one single innocent.

And all evening, after the sittings of the Tribunal are over, and ten—or mayhap fifteen or twenty—condemned to the guillotine, Chauvelin like a pale, thin ghost haunts the purlieus of Architect Caristie's house. On pretext of his office he enters the courtyard with the captain of the guard and looks up at the windows to see if she is there. Once he saw her. Just her little face peeping behind the opulent shoulders of one Claire de Châtelard, the best noted strumpet in Orange. The woman had one arm round Fleurette's waist and when the captain of the guard read out the name of Clair known as Châtelard upon his list, Fleurette threw her arms round her and laid her head upon the trollop's breast.

Chauvelin turned away from the spectacle with a groan, and all night he lay awake thinking of his sweet flower laying her head upon the breast of a Claire de Châtelard.

Yet Claire de Châtelard bore herself bravely before him the next day, and when, on the day after that, he watched her from the window of the Hôtel de Ville mounting the steps of the guillotine, saw her standing there, superb and defiant with a coarse jest upon her sensual lips, he gloated over the thought that his Fleurette would no longer pillow her innocent head upon that breast. He tried to picture her, grieving for this friend, the propinquity, the squalor of that house of detention, from which there was but one egress, that egress the gate of Death. Claire de Châtelard today—Fleurette when? Every day the indictments are sent up to him for examination, the printed forms of accusation with the names left in blank, to be filled in as convenience demands: and every day a list of ten, perhaps fifteen names are sent along with these printed forms, and it is his business to direct the Public Prosecutor, a man of his own choosing, which of these names are to be inserted in the blank spaces, on the forms of accusation.

Up to now he has been able to keep Fleurette's name out, but it has been sent up to him on two consecutive days. The fight then was getting at close quarters, Pochart and Danou were pressing him, showing their teeth like snarling dogs ready to spring. And time was hurrying on. Time would presently bring back President Legrange and Prosecutor Isnard from Paris, time would inevitably bring to light his machinations for keeping those two men out of the way. Aye! time was hurrying on, and Fleurette's name had twice appeared upon the list.

And for the past three days not a word in the town about the English spies. After Architect Caristie and his family, it had been the widow Colmars and her daughter, and then General Paulieu and his family. Disappeared as if the earth had swallowed them up. Always traitors and aristos whose arrest was imminent, whose subsequent condemnation certain. But after that, three days' respite: The Scarlet Pimpernel and his gang seemed to have disappeared in their turn.

The hopes which insidious demons had whispered in Chauvelin's ears were once more merged in a sea of despair. He derided himself for these hopes, lashed himself into a state of fury against himself for having allowed his mind to dwell upon them.

One scheme after another now did he devise and then reject. He would defy his enemies, the jury, the populace: loudly denounce the witnesses against Fleurette as liars and perjurers, pronounce her acquittal in the face of all opposition. Had he not made a point day after day of pronouncing acquittal on one or the other of the accused? just to test his power—to see how his enemies would behave? And he saw them lying low. Sneering. Whispering. Ogling him and laughing. They knew! They saw behind his schemes and his hopes. They reserved their counter-attack. They could afford to wait, whilst he could not.

If only Fleurette bore herself well: did not allow herself to be carried away with admissions or inconsidered words, out of sentiment for that fool Amédé Colombe. Chauvelin longed to see her, if only to impress this one thing upon her; to say nothing. To admit nothing. To hold her tongue and to trust *chére* Bibi. If only she did that, he felt that he might save her yet. And obsessed by the idea, devoured with the desire to convey this message to her, without compromising her or giving yet another advantage to his enemies, Chauvelin at evening would wander like a restless ghost through the city.

That afternoon after he watched Claire de Châtelard mount the steps upon the guillotine, a joke upon her lips, this restlessness became exquisite torture, and racked with tumultuous thoughts, wrapped in a black mantle, he sallied forth into the streets. It was now early in June: nearly three weeks since that last care-free day, Fleurette's eighteenth birthday, spent with her over at Lou Mas, when the scent of almond blossom had been in the air and the nightingale had sung in the old walnut-tree. The day had been sunless and chilly, after sunset the rain began to fall. But rain and weather held no terrors for Chauvelin in his present mood. Holding his mantle tightly round his shoulders and pulling his hat down over his eyes, he wandered aimlessly through the streets, over the river and back again, down unpaved streets and lonely lanes, now and then sitting down to rest in some obscure little outlying café, where no one knew or heeded him, and then starting off again on his restless course. But always drifting back instinctively to the purlieus of architect Caristie's house.

Almost opposite to it there was a small *café*: no one sitting outside because of the rain, but the interior lighted up, and sounds of merriment proceeding from within. Chauvelin thought of going inside, feeling that if he sat down there close to the window, he could watch the walls behind which lived and suffered his little Fleurette. He did not dare to go in for fear of being recognised. He was just debating within himself whether he would go or stay, when he saw a man come out of the house of Architect Caristie, cross over to the *café*, then disappear behind its creaking door. A scavenger, no doubt, ragged and dirty—not a warder, he was too ill-clad for that—just a scavenger— but perhaps he had seen Fleurette.

The thought fascinated Chauvelin. His mind clung to it: turned it over and over. The thought that here was a man who perhaps had seen Fleurette within the last few minutes, had swept corridor or staircase when she was passing by. And with that thought there was still the burning desire to send her a message, to tell her to be brave and trust in Bibi, but above all, oh! above all, not to be led into making any admission about those valuables belonging to Madame de Frontenac, or about her association with Amédé Colombe.

Chauvelin, leaning against the wall which faced the little *café*, dwelt on his thoughts and his desire. He allowed the rain to drip upon his hat and upon his shoulders from the roof above him. He no longer felt restless. He just wanted to stand there and watch for the return of the man, who perhaps would be seeing Fleurette again within the next few minutes. He wondered if he dare approach him, always with the idea of possibly conveying a message to Fleurette. But the fear that the man might know who he was, deterred him from entering the *café* himself. He had been a fairly conspicuous figure in the courtyard of Caristie's house, standing by the side of the captain of the guard: if that scavenger was at work in the corridor, he might have looked out of the window and seen him, learned who he was. All through he had been at pains to show an indifferent attitude before his enemies: if this man happened to be a spy, would the knowledge that he, Chauvelin, was trying to establish communication with Fleurette compromise him hopelessly and do no good to her?

As he stood there pondering and debating what he had better do, he saw the scavenger come out of the *café*. For a minute or two the man stood at the door, his hands buried in the pockets of his ragged breeches, contemplating the rain. The next moment another, equally dirty and bedraggled ruffian came down the street, paused at the entrance of the *café* and passed the time of day with the scavenger. The two mudlarks remained talking for a few moments, after which they parted, each going his own way. The scavenger recrossed the road and entered the Caristie House. The other passed on in the opposite direction and Chauvelin, after an instant's hesitation, followed him. He came up with the man at the angle of the rue Longue: and putting out his arm, touched him on the shoulder. With a cry of terror, the man fell on his knees.

"Mercy! I've done nothing!" he babbled almost incoherently.

"I dare say not," Chauvelin said drily "but it will be to thine advantage if thou'lt come along quietly with me."

He seized the man by the arm and dragged him up from his knees. The poor wretch tried to wriggle himself free, but Chauvelin held him tightly, and without another word drew him within the shelter of the nearest doorway. Fortunately, though them and kept up a ceaseless litany of lamentations and cries for mercy, he did so under his breath, thus creating no disturbance nor exciting the attention of the few passers-by who were hurrying homewards through the rain-swept streets.

"Are you willing, citizen," Chauvelin began abruptly, as soon as he had assured himself that the doorway was deserted and no eavesdropper nigh, "are you willing to earn fifty *livres tournoi?*"

The man gave no immediate reply, it seemed as if he was shaking himself free from his first terror and pondering over this extraordinary proposal, so different to what he had anticipated. Then he cleared his throat, expectorated, slowly repeated the magic words: "Fifty *livres tournoi!*" and finally added in an awed whisper:

"I have not seen five *livres tournoi* for months."

"Fifty are yours, citizen, if you'll render me a service."

"What is it?"

"That friend of yours, to whom you spoke just now—outside the Café de la Lune—"

"Citizen Rémi?"

"He works in the Caristie House?"

"Yes."

"In what capacity?"

"Cleaner," the man replied laconically. "Rémi hung about for days trying to earn a bit of money. He hasn't a *sou*, you understand? Same as me. A few days ago, one of the inside men fell sick. Rémi presented himself and got the work. I know him well."

"He has access to the prisoners?" Chauvelin asked.

"I suppose so."

"Then tell him that there will be fifty *livres* for him too if he will convey a written message to number 142 in room 12."

Again, the man seemed to ponder: weighing the risks probably, and also the gain. *Fifty livres tournoi!* Immense! He had forgotten that there was such a sum of money left in the world: and then for him to have the handling of it! This led him once more to expectorate, which action apparently had the effect of stimulating his brain-power.

"It could be done," he murmured at last.

"It can be done," Chauvelin asserted emphatically, "but must be done quickly, or—"

"Rémi will be back at the Café de la Lune soon after eight o'clock. He always goes there for a sip of something after supper."

"Good! Then you can meet him at that hour and tell him to wait for you, then come at once and find me here, under this doorway. I'll have the letter ready—"

"The whole thing is very risky, citizen," the man demurred.

"If it were not," Chauvelin rejoined drily, "I would not spend one hundred *livres tournoi* in the attempt."

"Fifty *livres* is not over much, when one risks one's neck."

"You are not risking your neck," Chauvelin retorted, "as you well know. And you'll not get more from me than fifty *livres* each. Take it or leave it."

He knew how to deal with these mudlarks, apparently, for the man after he had spat once more once or twice, seemed satisfied.

"I'll be back here," he said laconically, "after I have seen Rémi again."

Then Chauvelin let him go. The darkness and the rain soon swallowed him up: but Chauvelin himself remained for quite a while standing motionless under the doorway. He had not yet burnt his boats, was still free, if he thought the risk too great, to fail in his appointment. The man did not know who he was, had not seen him in the darkness and under the wide brim of his hat: but there was the risk that this Rémi might be a spy, who would take the letter intended for Fleurette straightway to Pochart or Danou. The letter might thus betray him and so minimise his power of saving Fleurette. He had to safeguard himself against the merest breath of suspicion in order to keep his power.

The more irreproachable, detached, incorruptible he appeared before the populace, the more Spartan in his attitude towards his own child until the day of her trial, the greater his chance of saving her at the last. But his desire to warn her against unconsidered words or any kind of admissions outweighed for the moment every other consideration. He hurried back to his lodgings through the rain, and at once sat down to pen his letter to the child.

"My beloved one," he began, "at last I am able to send a word to you, which I hope and trust will reach your darling little hands. Child of my heart, this is to entreat you to continue in your trust of me, for I swear to you by the memory of your dead mother, that while you trust me I can save you. I can save the man you love. Moreover, I entreat you, beloved child of my soul, do not make any admission when brought before the tribunal, as you must be shortly, alas! If witnesses testify against you, just hold your peace; if others question you, deny everything. This I entreat you to do for the sake of the love I bear you, for the sake of the tears I have shed these past weeks, ever since your folly hath brought you to this pass."

He signed the letter "Bibi." Thus, he had mentioned no names and in addition taken the precaution of disguising his writing as far as he was able. After which he sealed the letter and slipped it in the inner pocket of his coat. Time was now hanging heavily. Like a beast in its cage, Chauvelin paced up and down the narrow room, his hands clenched behind his back, a world of soul agony expressed upon his wax-like face.

As soon as he heard the tower-clock of Notre-Dame strike eight, he picked up his hat and cloak and once more sallied forth into the streets.

Chapter 30

A quarter of an hour later two out-at-elbows ragamuffins met in-side the Café la Lune. Out-side the rain had not abated, both the men, who were clad in what were little more than rags, appeared soaked through to the skin. At this hour the little *café* was almost deserted. Citizen Sabot, the proprietor, was sitting at one table with a couple of friends; at another a couple of road-menders were sipping their absinthe, when the scavenger from the prison house came slouching in. He sat down on the bench against the wall in the darkest corner of the room and ordered a bottle of wine for himself and a friend. Presently the latter came and joined him and for a while the two men sat drinking in silence. Soon an animated discussion arose between the proprietor and his friends on the respective merits of Vouvray and Beaujolais as a table wine.

This entailed much shouting and copious gesticulations. Sabot had a deep-booming voice which reverberated from end to end of the room and caused the window-panes to rattle in their frames.

The scavenger from the prison house had apparently drunk more during the day than was good for him. His head leaned heavily on his hand, his elbow resting upon the table, his eyes had become bleary, his speech uncertain.

His friend sat opposite to him, with his back to the rest of the company, and when Sabot's voice roused the echoes in the small stuffy room, he leaned forward and whispered in the other's ear:

"I had an adventure after I left you this afternoon."

"Eh?" the scavenger murmured incoherently. "Where?"

"At the angle of the Rue Longue I was pounced upon in the dark-ness and dragged under the shelter of a door-way. A man had me by the shoulder. He had seen me talking with you. He offered me fifty *livres* and the same for you, if you will give a letter to a certain prisoner in there."

And he nodded in the direction of the high walls of the Caristie house. His friend's reply to this preliminary statement was a prolonged snore.

"The prisoner to whom you are to give the letter is number 142 in room 12," the other went on, still speaking below his breath. "Who is that? Do you know?"

The scavenger from the prison house waited for a moment or two until the discussion at the next table was specially loud-tongued, then he murmured:

"Yes! It is the girl Fleurette."

"Ah!" remarked his friend.

"Who was the man who spoke to you?"

"I don't know. It was pitch-dark. He wore a broad-brimmed hat and spoke in a hoarse whisper."

"Her father, probably. The man Armand, I have marvelled why we did not hear from him before. What have you arranged?"

"That I meet him under the same doorway, after I've seen you. He will then give me the letter."

"We'll keep to that then. But try and see the man. I might recognise him by your description."

He paused for a moment or two, yawned, stretched, emptied his mug of wine and then went on. "If I went myself I might scare him off. So, it is best you should go. But try and see his face. I'll wait here till you come."

After which he ordered another bottle of wine. Sabot broke away from his friends in order to serve his customer.

"You've had about as much as you ought to have, Citizen Rémi," he said drily, as he uncorked the bottle and set it on the table.

"That is none of your business, citizen," Rémi retorted with a bibulous laugh, "so long as I pay for what I drink."

He threw some coins on the table. Sabot picked them up with a shrug and then rejoined his friends and resumed the discussion with them on the merits or demerits of Vouvray and Beaujolais. The other ruffian took the opportunity of shuffling out of the café, and the scavenger, sprawling over the table, composed himself to sleep.

Hugging the walls, the other slunk through the street till he came to the doorway, where effectively he had appointed to meet Chauvelin.

"Well!" the latter queried impatiently as soon as the other came in sight. "Have you seen your friend?"

"Yes."

"Does he agree?"

"Yes."

With a sigh of relief Chauvelin drew the sealed letter from his breast pocket.

"Fifty *livres*, remember," he said slowly, "for each of you, when you bring me back the answer."

"Oh!" the man exclaimed, visibly disappointed. "There's an answer then?"

"Yes! An answer. You friend will see to it that you bring me back either an answer or some token which will satisfy me that the letter is in the right hands."

The man gave a short laugh.

"You do not trust me, citizen," he said.

"No," Chauvelin replied laconically. "I do not."

"I do not blame you," the other retorted. "I do not trust you altogether either. How do I know, when Rémi and I have risked our lives in your service, that the money will be forthcoming?"

"You do know that, citizen," Chauvelin rejoined drily, "and anyway you are bound to take that risk."

"Why should I?" the man retorted.

"Because you are more sorely in need of money than I of your services."

This argument appeared unanswerable. At any rate the ruffian now said with a light laugh:

"Have it your own way. Give me the letter. Number 142 in room 12 shall have it, you can wager your shirt on that."

Without another word Chauvelin handed him the letter. It was so dark under the doorway that it was only by groping that the other was able to get hold of it. He drew so near to Chauvelin that the latter, fearing that the man was trying to have a close look at him, pulled his hat lower down over his eyes. The other resorted to his habitual expression of indifference by spitting upon the floor; then he slipped the letter underneath his ragged blouse.

"Where do I find you," he asked, "after Rémi has done your errand?"

"You will go into the Rue Longue," Chauvelin replied, "To the house of Citizen Amouret, the chandler. Up the first flight of stairs, on the right-hand side, you will come to a door which is painted a slate-grey. Knock at that door and you will find me within."

"At what hour?"

"At any time tomorrow after the executions in the Place de la République," Chauvelin replied.

Chapter 31

To say that Fleurette had in the past few days become familiarised with the grim mummeries that went on in the common room, would be putting it rather strongly. But she certainly had no longer the same horror of them as she had had at first. The presentment of the mock guillotine still harrowed her, it is true, but she could not help laughing when the antics of the mock Satan and his satellites when they seized the President of the Tribunal and the Public Prosecutor and dragged them off to an imaginary hell. There was that one man in particular whom she had sometimes noticed before and who was aide to one of the warders and was very diverting.

She used to watch him turning and wriggling his huge body, which he had painted all over with soot and draped in bits of red rags. He made an ideal Satan with tail and horns complete, and sometimes it seemed to Fleurette as if he went through all his antics for the sole purpose of bringing a smile upon her lips. Moreover, in a vague kind of way, she associated him with that lovely letter from Amédé, which she had found inside the folds of her kerchief one evening.

The death of so many who had been her prison-companions at first, especially that of Claire de Châtelard had deeply affected her. The want of fresh air, of exercise, and above all of love and joy, had begun to affect her health: her cheeks had lost their freshness, her eyes their lustre, her lips their smile.

It was only in the recreation hour that she would smile sometimes. Always when that big, clumsy, hideous-looking fellow who was some kind of aide to one of the warders, set himself the task of fooling for her benefit. She came to look upon him as a friend and remembering how mysteriously that letter from Amédé had come inside her kerchief, she would look up whenever he came near her, wondering if he had another such welcome message for her. And one evening— she really had not the least idea how it happened—she found a sealed letter inside her work-basket. And the letter was from *chéri* Bibi. Oh! the joy of it!

She read, and re-read it, and kissed the paper whereon his dear hand had rested. How she had missed Bibi all these days! How she longed to reassure him that she was well and that she trusted and believed in him! As to obeying him in all things, of course she would do it. To begin with, she was not afraid, not the least bit in the world. He was watching over her, and he was so great and powerful that no danger could possibly assail her while he cared for her. She would indeed obey him in all things, hold her peace while that wicked Adèle tried to do her harm; she would hold her peace before the Tribunal just as *le bon Jésus* had done when he was questioned by his judges.

Oh! it was a dear, a comforting, an infinitely precious letter. And beside it Fleurette had found a tiny little slip of paper on which were scribbled the words: "Let me have something to take back to the writer, to let him know that you are well. Leave it in your work basket, and I will see to it that he gets it." And so Fleurette had written a few lines to *chéri* Bibi; told him that she was well and assured him that she was not afraid and would obey his commands in all things. She would hold her peace and trust in him. This little note she had hidden that evening in her work basket and by noon on the following day it had gone.

Chapter 32

"But me no butts, my dear Tony, I am sick of all these filthy rags. And if I am to see pretty Fleurette's papa then must I see him decently clad and in my right mind."

So spake Sir Percy Blakeney to his friend, late the following evening, it was in an attic under the roof of a half-derelict house in the Rue du Pont close to the river-bank. The owners of the house had long since disappeared, fled into the mountains or perished on the guillotine; no one knew or cared. Blakeney, and those members of his league who were with him, had hit upon it on their arrival in Orange, had made the attic their headquarters, whilst most of the vagabonds of the city used the rest of the house as their lair. They too were outwardly vagabonds, dressed in rags, appeared unkempt, unshaven, and unwashed, when they sallied forth in the early mornings each on an errand of mercy to succour those in need of help or those who were in danger or distress.

It was only o'nights, sometimes, that an overwhelming desire for cleanliness and nice clothes caused these English gentlemen to cast aside their rags and to venture out into the open dressed in clothes that would have caused the ragamuffins of Orange go snarl at their heels like so many hungry curs.

They had been eight days in Orange now, and already architect Caristie, with his wife and small son, the widow Colmars and her daughter, and poor old General Paulieu with his family owed their safety to this gallant League of the Scarlet Pimpernel. But there was still more to do.

"We must get that child Fleurette out of that hell," the chief had said, and since then brain and heart had been at work to find the means to that end.

Later on, Lord Tony had remarked: "I wish we could find out about that father of hers; this man Armand. He seems to hold some kind of position under this government of assassins, but I for one have tried in vain to learn something more definite about him."

"I think," Sir Andrew Ffoulkes added, "that his position must be a high one, or the girl would have been brought to trial before now."

"Unless our amiable friend, M. Chauvelin, has got this Armand under lock and key somewhere else," was my Lord Stowmaries' comment upon the situation.

Sir Percy was silent. Frankly the position puzzled him. He would have liked to get into touch with the man Armand, but for once he and his friends were baffled by this anonymity which appeared so closely guarded. Great then had been the rejoicing in the attic of the derelict house in the Rue du Pont, when Lord Anthony Dewhurst—a most perfect type of ruffian in rags and a thick coating of grime—related his adventure with the mysterious individual who, under cover of darkness and rain, had offered him and his friend Rémi, fifty *livres* each for delivering a message to a prisoner, who was none other than little Fleurette.

"At last we'll get in touch with the mysterious Armand," they all declared eagerly. It was arranged that the chief would himself take Fleurette's reply to the house in the Rue Longue. But go on this errand in the filthy rags of a scavenger he would not.

"The night is pretty dark," he declared, "and I would rather the mysterious Armand saw me as I am. I may also have a chance," he added with his merriest laugh, "of coming across my good friend M. Chambertin. It is some weeks since last we met, and not to have had a pleasant chat with him all these days, while we were within a stone's throw of one another, has been a sore trial to me. I caught a glimpse of him a day or two ago, in the courtyard of the Caristie House. He looked to be sick and out of sorts. A sight of me might cheer him up."

"You won't take any risks, Blakeney," Sir Andrew Ffoulkes remarked.

"Any number, my dear fellow," Sir Percy replied laughing. "And you know you envy me, you dog. But I feel thoroughly selfish tonight. I mean to take the note to Armand myself, and I mean to take the privilege of having a little chat with my friend Chambertin. And both these things I am going to do as an English gentleman and not as a mudlark in stinking, filthy rags."

He had completed his toilet now, looked magnificent in clothes cut by the leading London tailor, which set off his splendid figure to perfection, with snow-white stock and speckless boots.

"If a single pair of eyes should see you," Sir Andrew insisted, with an anxious sigh.

"I should have a whole pack of wolves at my heels," Blakeney admitted. "But that wouldn't be the first time any of us have had to run for our lives, eh? nor the first time we gave an entire pack of them the slip."

He picked up his hat and took a last look at Fleurette's little note which he had to deliver at the house in the Rue Longue.

"This man Armand must be a very decent fellow," he mused, "his letter to the child was really fine in spirit as well as in affection. Yes! he must be a decent fellow and we must get the girl for his sake as much as for that of our friend Colombe. What?"

On that, of course, they were all agreed. The activities of the League, since the rescue of General Paulieu and his family, were centred now on Fleurette. There were still one or two minor points to discuss, arrangements of detail to complete, but the main project for the girl's rescue could not be determined until it was definitely known whether her father, Armand, was going to be a help or an hindrance.

"Anyway, I shall know more," Blakeney said finally, as he made for the door, "when I have sampled this man."

It was then nine o'clock in the evening. The night was dark and stormy. Gusts of wind alternated with sharp showers of rain—an altogether unusual state of weather for the time of year in these parts. The few passers-by of respectable appearance on their way home from business or work did no more than throw a cursory glance on the tall figure that passed hurriedly by. A few vagabonds clinging to their rags which the wind threatened to tear off their meagre bodies, did perhaps pause, cowering against a dark wall, murmuring a threat or a curse against the *aristo*, but an unexpected coin slipped into their grimy hands, quickly silenced both curse and threat.

Blakeney knew his way well through the streets of Orange. Having kept along the river bank till he came to the bridge, he turned up the Rue de la République. Glancing up at a house on his right, a smile of pure joy lit up his anxious face. Three nights ago, on this spot, he had carried architect Caristie's small son in his arms, while Caristie and his wife followed him down the street to the market cart which awaited them at the top of the bridge. Three hours later an officer of the revolutionary army was hammering at the door of Caristie's lodgings, only to find that the birds had flown. It had been a merry night, and merrier morning, while he, Blakeney, drove the market cart out of the city with Caristie and his wife concealed amidst the sacks of haricots and peas, and the boy thrust into an empty oil-jar.

Well! something equally daring would have to be devised for the girl Fleurette, and perhaps for her father, the mysterious Armand. Blakeney, throwing back his head in the teeth of rain and wind, drew a deep breath of delight. This was life in very truth. To plan, to scheme, to accomplish. Alternately hare and hound, to revel in this case with human lives as the goal. And if at times the thought of beautiful Marguerite, lonely and anxious in far-off England, caused a pang like a knife-thrust to his heart, her soothing voice, her reassuring smile came to him as a swift vision from the spirit-land to encourage and console. In suffering and anxiety, as well as in the joy of reunion, Marguerite always understood.

Now he turned from the Place de la République into the Rue Longue, and the next couple of hundred yards brought him to the house of Lucien Amouret, corn-chandler. The outside door was on the latch. Pushing it open he found himself in a narrow hall, with an inner door leading into the shop on his left and a staircase in front of him. A lamp hung from the ceiling and shed a dim light on stair and hall. From the shop came the sound of voices in conversation, but though the stairs creaked under his tread, no one came out to see whose the step might be.

Sir Percy ran lightly up the stairs, and on the first landing came to the door, painted a slate grey. This part of the house appeared silent and deserted; the upper floors wrapped in dead gloom. A rusty bell-pull hung beside the door. Sir Percy gave it a pull, and a discordant clang roused the sleeping echoes of the chandler's house. A moment or two later he caught the sound of shuffling footsteps, the door was opened, an old woman in cap and shawl mutely inquired what the visitor desired.

"Is Citizen Armand within?" Blakeney asked.

The woman, he thought, looked at him rather curiously for a second or two, then shrugged her shoulders. Without wasting words, she shuffled off down a dimly lighted passage, leaving him to enter or not, as he pleased. The next moment he heard a woman's voice—the same woman probably—say: "An *aristo* is asking to see Citizen Armand." Again, a moment's silence, then the woman came shuffling back, signed to him to enter and closed the door behind him.

"In there," she said laconically, and nodded towards the end of the passage where a half open door revealed a shaft of more brilliant light. Then she shuffled off again, presumably to her kitchen, leaving the visitor to his own devices.

Sir Percy took off his hat and coat and laid them down on a chair close by; he then walked the length of the passage to the half-open door, pushed it open and found himself in a small room, comfortably furnished, lighted by a lamp which stood upon a centre table. The table was littered with papers. Behind it sat a man writing. At sound of Sir Percy's footsteps, he looked up. The eyes of the two men met, and it almost seemed to one of them at least that time for a few seconds stood still.

And then a pleasant laugh broke the silence, and a gentle lazy voice said slowly:

"Egad! if it is not my engaging friend M. Chambertin! The gods do indeed favour me, sir, for there's no man in the world I would sooner have seen at this hour than your amiable self."

After the first paralysing second, Chauvelin had jumped to his feet. He had thought that once again his feverish fancy was playing his senses a mocking trick, that the face which ever haunted his day-dreams and his sleepless nights had only come to him on the wings of imagination. But the merry laugh, the lazy voice were all too real. His enemy was truly there, not a vision, but a cruel, mocking reality. Swiftly his clawlike hand shot out, fastened on an object that lay amidst a litter of papers, and would have lifted it, had not another slender and firm hand shot out likewise and fastened itself upon his wrist with a grasp like a vice of steel.

Chauvelin had the greatest difficulty in the world to smother a cry of pain. His fingers opened, spread out fan-wise, the pistol which he had seized fell back upon the litter of papers. With a soft laugh Sir Percy sat down on the edge of the table, picked up the pistol, withdrew the charge and swept it into the sand-box close to his hand, the while Chauvelin watched him greedily, hungrily, as a caged feline might watch a prey that was beyond its reach.

A white-faced clock on the wall struck the half-hour. Sir Percy laid the pistol down upon the table, and flicked his fine, well-shaped hands one against the other.

"There now, my dear M. Chambertin," he said gaily, "we can converse more comfortably together. Do you think it would have been wise to put a charge of powder through your humble servant? We should both of us have missed much of the zest of life."

"It is always your pleasure to mock, Sir Percy," Chauvelin said with an effort. "There are various popular sayings which I might recall to your mind, such as that the pitcher went once too often to the well."

"And Sir Percy once too often to visit his friend M. Chambertin, eh?"

"I think you will find that this is so," Chauvelin rejoined trying, none too successfully, to ape his enemy's easy familiarity. "Orange is not a healthy place for English spies these days."

"Possibly not," Blakeney retorted lightly. "Nor for some unfortunate children of France, I am thinking."

"Traitors and spies, you are right there, Sir Percy. We have no use for them in Orange—or elsewhere."

"Or for honest men, eh, my friend? for chaste women and innocent children. That is why your humble servant and the league of which methinks you know a thing or two, propose to remove these from this polluted soil."

Chauvelin had rested this elbow on the table. His hand shading his face against the glare of the lamp, effectually concealed its varying expressions from the keen eyes of his enemy.

"You have not told me yet, Sir Percy," he said after a few second's silence, "what procures me the honour of your visit at this hour."

"Pure chance, my dear sir," Blakeney replied, "though the honour is entirely mine. As a matter of fact, I came to find one Armand."

Twice did the pendulum of the white-faced clock tick the seconds before Chauvelin said quietly:

"My colleague? Have you business with him?"

"Yes," Blakeney replied slowly. "I have a message for him."

"I can deliver it."

"Why not I? since I came on purpose."

"My colleague is absent."

"I can wait."

"From whom then is the message?"

"From his daughter."

"Ah!"

Once more there was a pause. The white-faced clock ticked on but the two men were silent. Chauvelin's face was shaded by his hand, and it needed all the energy, all the strength of his will to keep that hand absolutely steady, not to allow a finger to tremble. In the other hand he held a long quill pen and with it he traced a geometrical pattern upon a blank sheet of paper. Sir Percy Blakeney, still sitting on the edge of the table watched him, motionless.

"Pretty drawing that," he said abruptly. And with a slender finger pointed to the design that grew in intricate lines under Chauvelin's aimless pen.

The other gave a start, the pen spluttered, scattering the ink in spots all over the paper.

"There now, you have spoilt it," Sir Percy continued lightly. "I had no idea you were such a master draughts-man."

Chauvelin threw down his pen. He had his nerves under control at last, was able to drop his hand, to lean back in his chair, and with both hands buried in the pockets of his breeches, to throw back his head and look his enemy squarely in the face.

"About that message, Sir Percy," he said with well-feigned indifference.

"What about it, my dear M. Chambertin?" Blakeney rejoined lightly.

"My colleague, Citizen Armand, has been called away—to Lyons on State business."

"But how unfortunate!" Sir Percy exclaimed.

"I am sending a courier to Lyons this very night."

"Too late, my dear M. Chambertin! Too late, I fear!"

Chauvelin frowned. "What mean you by too late, Sir Percy?" he asked slowly.

"Armand's daughter is sick, my dear M. Chambertin," Blakeney rejoined, speaking very slowly, as if to weigh his every word. "Before your courier can possibly reach Lyons, she will be dead."

"My God!—"

It was the most heart-rending cry that had ever come from a man's throat. Chauvelin had jumped to his feet; his two hands, claw-like, as if carved in marble, gripped the arms of his chair; his knees were shaking, his pale eyes stared like those of a maniac, his cheeks were the colour of lead.

For the space of ten seconds he stood thus, with his whole body quivering, his senses reeling, his eyes fixed on those finely moulded lips that had dealt this appalling blow. Then slowly consciousness returned, a veil seemed to be lifted from before his eyes, knowledge had entered his brain. He knew that he had fallen into the trap set for him by this astute adventurer. He realised that he had betrayed the secret which he would have guarded with his life.

"So," Sir Percy said at last very slowly, "'tis you are Citizen Armand, and the sweetest flower that ever bloomed in this putrid atmosphere has its roots in polluted soil?"

Still quite slowly and deliberately he drew Fleurette's note out of the breast-pocket of his coat; for a second or two he held it lightly between slender finger and thumb, then laid it on the table in front of Chauvelin.

"She is not sick," he said quietly, "nor yet dying. If you have not forgotten how to pray, man, pray to God now, pray with all your might, that the same power which enabled you to torture my wife and well-nigh to break her brave spirit, will aid you to save your daughter from those tigers whom you have called your friends."

Chauvelin had sunk back in the chair. His head was buried in his hands. Tumultuous thoughts rushed through his brain until he felt that his reason must be tottering. A haze was before his eyes Perhaps it was caused by tears. Who knows? Only the recording angel mayhap. Even wild beasts cry in agony when deprived of their young.

Only after a few minutes did he become aware of the note penned by his little Fleurette and laid in front of him by his bitterest foe. The Scarlet Pimpernel! The only man in all the world who might perhaps have saved Fleurette, who would have saved Fleurette, if he, Chauvelin, had not betrayed the secret of his heart.

Like one waking from a dream, Chauvelin picked up the note, and looked fearfully about him, dreading to meet those mocking lazy eyes, which, no doubt, at this hour gleamed with malicious triumph.

But Sir Percy Blakeney was no longer there.

Chapter 33

The stage was now set for the last act of the tragedy, which the chief actor himself knew could only end one way. He had schemed and planned until he felt that his reason would give way, until he feared that he would lose the nerve and the power of which he had such sore need. He had thought of everything, weighed every possibility from the bribing of prison warders, to the suppression—by murder if need be—of the two witnesses Godet and Adèle. He had thought of turning the tables on Pochart and Danou, by launching accusations against them. But all these plans had to be rejected one by one. Fleurette liberated today through the success of one or the other of these schemes would only be re-arrested on the morrow. The suppression of the witnesses, the arrest of his more powerful enemies, would only rouse more bitter antagonism against himself and failing in the end to save his Fleurette, would end in precipitating her doom.

Driven by despair, he had at one time pinned his hopes of salvation for the child on the possible interference of the Scarlet Pimpernel, but even that fond and foolish hope had been shattered by his betrayal of his jealously guarded secret. What was there left to hope for? That his power was great enough at the Tribunal to force an acquittal in spite of the witnesses, in spite of Pochart and Danou and all the mob whom they had already gathered round them. The Public Prosecutor, a man of his own making, would not dare to side against him. But there was the populace, the rabble, the swinish multitude, who, now that even the worst type of venal and corrupt jury had been abolished, were judges and jury, advocate and prosecutor all in one. The last word always rested with them, and Pochart and Danou, egged on by envy and revenge, would know how to sway the rabble.

Chauvelin was not the man to indulge in illusions. He knew well enough—none better—that the passions of hatred and of spite which he himself had engendered and fostered in the hearts of his fellowmen, were turned against him, as they had been turned on all the makers of this bloody revolution, on your Brissots and your Carriers, your Philippe d'Orléans, and your great Danton. They would destroy his exquisite Fleurette as effectually as they had destroyed thousands of others, equally innocent.

And now the end had come. No longer could the day be put off. President Legrange and Public Prosecutor Isnard might be arriving in Paris any hour when the new aerial telegraph might be set in motion, or a courier sent down to Orange poste-haste and burst the bubble of Chauvelin's machinations.

And then on that afternoon of the 15th of June two things occurred. To begin with when the Public Prosecutor placed before him the printed forms of accusation with the names left in blank, and with them a list of the names of those awaiting trial, Chauvelin with a hand that appeared quite steady, wrote in one blank spaces the name of Fleur Chauvelin, *nommée* Armand. Secondly when, an hour later, the captain of the guard stood in the courtyard of the Caristie house reading out the names of those who were to stand their trial on the morrow, Fleurette heard the sound of her own name.

She was not frightened, nor did she weep. Tears were a thing of the past for her. Twenty days had gone by since she had been happy, more than a fortnight since she had been brought into this house and deprived of air and sunlight and joy. One by one those who had been kind to her in this prison house had gone: Claire de Châtelard, Madame de Mornas, poor Eugénie Blanc, and kind M. de Bollène. Their names had been on the roll-call. The next day they were gone, and Fleurette never saw them again. Lately she had been lonely too. No one had taken the place in her unsophisticated heart of Claire de Châtelard. The only friend she had left was the warder's aide, the rough scavenger who had brought her the two welcome letters. Amédé's and Bibi's. He still continued his antics, joined in the gruesome mummeries which still went on in the common room, and Fleurette somehow had a sense of re-assurance when he was nigh. But this night of all nights, after she had heard the captain of the guard read her name upon the roll-call, her grimy friend was not there. Fleurette missed him, and disappointment over his absence was the only sorrowful feeling of which she felt conscious, when she realised that her fate would be decided on the morrow.

She was not afraid. Had not Bibi enjoined her, begged her to trust him and not to be afraid? She wondered when she would be allowed to see Bibi, whether he would be there tomorrow, at her trial, encouraging her with his presence and with his glance when she was made to stand before the judge. She knew that in a sense she had done wrong. She had taken *Madame's* valuables and handed them over to Amédé. This she had no right to do, and since Adèle had seen her with M'sieur Amédé that evening, and spoken ill of her because of that, she supposed that she would be punished.

It was only vaguely that she marvelled what the punishment would be. But she was not afraid because she trusted Bibi. Nor did she regret her actions. If it had all to be done over again, she would act in precisely the same way. The mysterious voice often rang in her ear even now. She had obeyed the commands of *le bon Dieu*, and it was *le bon Dieu* who had chosen a still more mysterious way for saving M'sieur Amédé from the consequences of her actions.

Thus, did Fleurette envisage the day that was to come, with love and trust in her heart for Bibi, and the certainty after all these trials and tribulations of a happy reunion with him and old Louise at Lou Mas.

Not to mention the reunion with M'sieur Amédé.

Chapter 34

The first thing that struck Fleurette's perceptions when she entered that huge room, was that up at the further end of it—upon a raised platform and behind a tall desk, sat Bibi *chéri* himself. Two other men sat there with him, but Fleurette hardly saw them. It was on Bibi that she looked. She had slept very little during the night. Excitement had kept her awake, as well as the tears and lamentation of two of her room-mates who were to appear with her this day before the tribunal.

And it was Bibi who was to be her judge. Well then obviously she had nothing to fear. One of some fifteen of her fellow-prisoners, she was bustled with them across the room to a wooden bench where they were roughly ordered to sit down. As they crossed the room boos and hisses, and one or two louder cries of execration, greeted them. A few remarks, all of them malevolent, rose above the murmurs.

"That old man there, I knew him once. Old tyrant. He's getting his deserts at last."

"Do you see the woman next to him? Five free-born French-women she had at a time once, to wait on her and do her hair. *Aristo, va!* It won't take long to do thy hair tomorrow. One snick with the scissors, what?"

"That young wench too. Not much more than eighteen, I warrant."

"I hear she is a thief as well as a traitor."

"Pity they should have abolished the whipping-post. That would have done the young traitors a world of good."

"Me, I prefer the guillotine; quickest work, eh?"

Fleurette had blushed with shame to the roots of her hair. She tried not to look in the direction whence these voices, harsh and coarse had come. She tried to think of M'sieur Amédé and of the joy she would have when she saw him again. But she could not shut the gates of her consciousness against all these people who had gathered here for the sole purpose of seeing their fellow-creatures suffer. Men and women and even little children. The women for the most part had brought their knitting, for everyone was knitting socks these days for the brave soldiers who were fighting against the enemies of France, and through the murmur of voices, the monotonous *click-click* of the needles acted as an irritant upon the nerves.

All around there appeared to be a sea of faces. And eyes. Innumerable eyes that glared, and mouths that grinned and decided. And above the faces, a sea of red caps with tricolour cockades. Fleurette tried hard not to look. She closed her eyes and tried to murmur the prayers she and M'sieur Amédé used to say together when M. le Cure prepared them for their first communion.

Bibi wore a hat with feathers. He had a bell in front of him, and this he often tinkled, when the noise from the crowd all around became too great. Once or twice he was addressed as "Citizen President." Fleurette had never seen him look so stern. The words which he spoke to the accused were not only bitter but terribly cruel. He seemed so unlike her real *chéri* Bibi, that she caught herself marvelling whether her fancy was not playing her aching eyes some strange and horrible trick.

One after the other the names of her fellow-prisoners were called, and one by one they were made to stand up and then walk to the centre of the room and up a couple of shallow steps to a small raised platform round which there was a wooden railing. In every instance as soon as the prisoner mounted this platform and became as it were the centre of attraction for all these innumerable eyes, he or she would be greeted with groans and hisses and cat's calls, until Bibi tinkled his bell and loudly demanded silence.

A man in a red cap who sat just below Bibi's desk then stood up and read something out aloud, which Fleurette never understood, but which the crowd apparently did, for the reader was frequently interrupted by more boos and hisses and often cries of execration. After this reading Bibi, or one of the two men who sat beside him, asked the prisoner questions. These were sometimes replied to, but not always. The crowd invariably threw in loud comments on both questions and answers, and Bibi was then forced to tinkle his bell in order to demand silence. And through the noise, the sound that was never drowned, and never was still, was the *click-click* of hundreds of knitting needles.

The first batch of prisoners to face the Tribunal, were men and women almost unknown to Fleurette. They had not long been brought into the Caristie House, had replaced others who had been Fleurette's early companions in prison. She had seen them in the common room, acting in the grim farces that were the fashion there, but she had not made friends with them as she had done with Claire de Châtelard or Madame de Mornas. But when came the turn of a woman who had actually been her room-mate, who had sat next to her on the bench of the accused and squeezed her hand ere she was led up to the raised platform with the wooden railing, then, Fleurette felt all her resolu-

187

tion of bravery and trust in Bibi, giving way.

The heat in the room had become unbearable. The stench of dank and grimy clothes, of perspiring humanity, of hot breaths charged with hate, acted as a pungent soporific. Fleurette's head fell forward once or twice, her eyes involuntarily closed. For a time, she lost consciousness. It was her own name spoken in a stentorian voice that brought her back to reality.

"Fleur Chauvelin, *nommée* Armand."

Someone nudged her elbow. An impatient voice rasped out a sharp: "*Allons! allons!*" and she found herself dragged to her feet and led by the arm to the raised platform, amidst a din which fortunately was too great to allow her ears to catch individual sounds.

She looked straight across to Bibi, who was as pale as a waxen image.

"Fleur Chauvelin, *nommée* Armand."

Chapter 35

There is no doubt that everything would have gone well, had it not been for Fleurette herself. Perhaps "well" is the wrong word: "differently" would be better. Nothing could have gone "well," because even though Chauvelin had succeeded in obtaining an acquittal, his enemies would have returned immediately to the charge, and forced on the girl's re-arrest even before she had left the Tribunal. There had been cases during the past few weeks, in Paris, in Lyons and so on, when prisoners were acquitted and re-arrested, re-tried, acquitted again, and again re-arrested. A regular cat-and-mouse game, at which Chauvelin himself was an adept.

Nevertheless, with a first acquittal there might have been some hope. And he practically had obtained that acquittal, when Fleurette herself ruined her chance and caused her own condemnation. Chauvelin could have struck her for her folly. His love for her always pertained to that of a wild beast for its young; the instinct to devour in moments of peril. If she was destined to perish, then it should be by his own hand, not as a spectacle for the rabble to gloat on.

The *Moniteur* of the 22nd Messidor gives one or two interesting details concerning the trial of a country girl named Fleur Chauvelin, daughter of a Citizen Armand Chauvelin of the Central Committee of Public Safety, and member of the National Convention, and relates at full length the extraordinary incidents which marked its close. Looking back upon that memorable day, and on the solemn hour which saw the girl Fleur Chauvelin, *nommée* Armand called to the bar of the accused, we visualise Chauvelin the father, presiding over that Tribunal of infamy, and having sent within the last half-hour half a dozen fellow-creatures callously to death, now seeing his own daughter, the only being in all the world whom he had ever loved, standing there before him, accused, condemned already in the eyes of the canaille.

There was no time wasted during the proceedings, wherein the accused was allowed neither jury nor advocate. The State as represented by its three nominees who sat as judges, was judge and jury and prosecutor all in one. It was men like Chauvelin who had invented this travesty of justice and eliminated all procedure devised by civilisation for the protection of the accused.

The Public Prosecutor opened the proceedings by reading the indictment in mechanical monotone; it was identically the same as that framed against hundreds of others—guilty or innocent alike—the printed formula invented by the odious Foucquier-Tinville in which the words "Traitor" and "Enemy of the Republic" were alone intelligible. All else was a jumble of words. The crowd was not listening. Their attention was fixed on the accused whose modest bearing and spotless attire seemed to arouse their spite and their derision, more than the rags and filth displayed by a previous prisoner had done.

When the reading of the indictment came to an end, Pochart sitting beside the Presiding Judge asked the usual question:

"Is the prisoner accused publicly or in secret?"

And the Public Prosecutor replied: "Publicly."

Danou, the third judge then asked: "By whom?"

And again, the Public Prosecutor gave reply:

"By one Adèle," he said, "of unknown parentage, and Citizen Lieutenant Godet of the Revolutionary Army."

"And to what will these persons testify?"

"To the treason committed against the State by the accused and to her connection with the enemies of the Republic."

After which Adèle was called. Her small rat-like face looked wan and pinched; her hands trembled visibly, and she wiped them continually against the ragged apron which she wore. She was obviously very nervous and never looked once in the direction of the accused, but she spoke clearly enough in a shrill, high-pitched voice. Questioned at first by the Public Prosecutor, she presently embarked more glibly upon her story, relating the events which were intended to condemn

Fleurette. Chauvelin already knew the tale by heart. The soldiers on the ridge. The raid on the *château*. Fleurette's halt that evening in the cottage of the widow Tronchet. Her assignation, through Adèle, with Amédé Colombe. The casket and wallet underneath her shawl, then transferred into young Colombe's keeping.

Ofttimes Chauvelin tried to break into the girl's narrative; he put stern questions to her, tried to intimidate her, to trip her into mis-statements or obvious contradictions. But Adèle held her ground. In-former, ingrate, wanton though she was, she was speaking the truth and was not to be shaken. Hisses and boos from the crowd oft greeted the President's cross-questionings, cries of approbation greeted Adèle's spirited rejoinders. In the wordy warfare between herself and Chau-velin, she scored nearly every time. Encouraged by the sympathy of the rabble, she lost her nervousness, whilst he gradually lost his self-control. He had so much at stake, and she nothing but the satisfaction of vanity and of spite.

"Be not intimidated, citizeness," Pochart put in forcefully at one moment, "let not powerful influences sway you from your duty."

"*Vas-y,* Adèle of unknown parentage!" one of the women shouted from above. "'Twas some *aristo* doubtless who betrayed thy mother. Let this *aristo* at least pay for her kind."

Amidst thunderous applause Adèle stepped down from the bar. Chauvelin tried in vain to command silence, he was shouted down by the crowd.

"Thou'rt a true patriot, Citizen Chauvelin," one woman called out lustily. "To have a traitor for a daughter is a curse. Her death will not be for thee a sacrifice."

He waited in seeming patience, white to the lips, until the tumult had subsided, then calling all his reserves of strength, moral and men-tal, to his aid, he said in a calm firm voice:

"The witness has lied. The events which she has described could not have taken place in her presence seeing that on that day and at that hour she was in my house, at Lou Mas, half a league away."

This pronouncement was greeted with mighty uproar. Derisive laughter, cat's calls, whistling, strident shouts made riotous confusion. Only two persons in the room appeared serene. One was the accused, the other her judge. The *Moniteur* says that throughout the whole proceedings the attitude of the accused was astonishingly calm: "*d'une sérénité étonnante.*" She looked straight before her, sometimes at the President, but more often her eyes appeared to be fixed on the tricolour flag draped over the wall above his head and ornamented with a red cap and the words writ largely: "*Liberté, Egalité, Fraternité ou la Mort.*"

And so too was the President equally serene. Outwardly. He stood upright whilst the turmoil continued, with head erect and hands held behind his back. Insults and jeers flew at him from every side. But he never winced. The rabble called him, "Traitor, Liar, Tyrant!" and various other names impossible to record. But he waited in seeming patience, until the crowd, eager to hear more, fell to comparative still-ness once more. Then Pochart's rasping voice cut through the silence, like the sound of a file against metal.

"You'll have to substantiate that statement Citizen President," he said.

"My statements need no substantiation," Chauvelin retorted cool-ly. "The word of a representative of the people is sufficient against any witness."

And while Pochart was considering a suitable repartee, Danou put in smoothly:

"Should we not hear the next witness, Citizen Lieutenant Godet, before we discuss the matter?"

"Yes, yes!" the crowd yelled in response.

Scenting the unusual, the crowd was more excited than was its wont. Of late these hasty trials, six to the hour, with condemnation as a foregone conclusion, had become monotonous. One condemna-tion had been very much like another. But here was something novel. The rumour had already spread like wildfire that the accused was no less than the daughter of the President, Citizen Chauvelin, who was well-known in the councils of State, a prominent member of many committees, and, some said, a personal friend of the great Robespierre. Here in truth was a test of supreme patriotism; a judge called upon to condemn his own daughter if she be guilty.

And of course, she was guilty, or she would not be here. There was no sympathy for either of them, only interest in the issue of this amazing trial. The crowd did not like the prisoner's attitude, what they called her aristocratic airs and disdainful ways; even the children pointed grimy little fingers at her and hurled the poisonous darts of loathsome epithets at the aristo.

Thus, was the scene prepared for the entrance of Lieutenant Go-det, who stepped up to the witness' platform with a display of self-assurance and a swagger that charmed the women. He was a man after

191

their own heart, a real *sans culotte* in grimy rags, unkempt, un-shaved, unwashed, the type of which the martyr Jean Paul Marat had been the most perfect exponent.

Conversations, objurgations, murmurs even were stilled; the *click-click* of knitting needles alone made a soft accompaniment to Citizen Godet's replies to the Public Prosecutor's preliminary questions. It was indeed a remarkable, an amazing, an almost unbelievable tale, which he had to tell. And gradually as he unfolded the various details of this extraordinary adventure a hush fell over the crowded room, very like the calm which nature assumes ere she sends forth the thunders of her wrath.

Godet, still with this air of self-assurance, related how he and the soldiers under his command, as well as the whole commune of Laragne had been tricked by a band of English spies whose actions proved them to have been in league with Amédé Colombe and with the accused. He told of the magnificently dressed soldiers. Their raid on the premises of Colombe the grocer of the Rue Haute. Their march through the village. Their captain's swagger. His orders to himself, Godet, and to the real soldiers of the revolutionary army.

Still the crowd gave no sign of approbation, or disapprobation. Only that ominous, expectant hush which presaged a storm. The accused always serene, smiled—so the *Moniteur* avers—as she encountered the President's glance. Smiled cheerfully and trustfully. But the President's face was inscrutable, and the colour of wax.

And then Godet went on to relate the long, weary tramp along the mountain roads. The dust. The fatigue. The want of food. He told how the *ci-devant* Frontenac and Amédé Colombe wrested from the hands of justice, were presently taken to some unknown place of safety, while the soldiers of the Republic were left by the wayside to perish of fatigue or inanition.

He had finished speaking, and still the *click-click* of the knitting needles was the only sound that broke the silence. The witness, sensing this silence, feeling its menace, had lost something of his arrogance; the hand with which he stroked his shaggy moustache trembled perceptibly. The accused, overcome by the heat, wiped her forehead with the corner of her apron, then she smiled once more across at her father.

And suddenly through the solemn stillness a woman's shrill voice was raised:

"Those English spies did make a fool of thee, I am thinking, Citizen Godet!"

This suddenly relieved the tension. It was like a dam let loose. In a moment every kind of call and of cry of laughter and of groan rang from end to end of the room.

"The English have made a fool of thee!"

Within a minute or two this became a general cry, accompanied by the stamping of feet, and loud and prolonged laughter, both malevolent and derisive. Godet, ludicrous in his bewilderment, rolled terror-filled eyes, whilst vainly trying to raise his voice above the din. The *Moniteur* says definitely that the accused put her hands to her ears. The uproar was in truth deafening.

A few moments of this confusion, and the next, Chauvelin was on his feet clanging his bell. His stentorian voice rose above the tumult, demanded silence, and in the lull that presently ensued, that same voice now subdued to a lower, though no less impressive key, rang clear and calm.

"Is it not an insult, citizen patriots to ask you to listen to the words of a fool, when the life of a French girl is at stake?"

The passionate earnestness with which he spoke, the burning indignation expressed in that calm, subdued voice, had the effect of awing the screaming rabble. They turned to gaze on him, as he stood there, facing them all, calm, proud, almost majestic, despite his small stature. Seizing this sudden advantage, he began to speak. Without a gesture, hardly raising his voice, he began quietly, not choosing his words, or striving after eloquence, but only as a man speaking to his friends. And by one of those inexplicable reactions which will so often change the temper of a crowd, men, women and children ceased to curse and to deride. The innumerable eyes were fixed with more curiosity than malevolence upon him, the mouths, agape, uttered no further groan, and once more the click-click of knitting needles was momentarily stilled.

"Citizens," he said, "you have heard two witnesses against the accused. One of these, the wench Adèle I myself, representative of the people, have convicted of deliberate falsehood, spoken to the prejudice of a French patriot. The other your own words have condemned for a fool, and an easy tool in the hands of English spies. You called him a fool, citizens, but I call him a traitor. Lieutenant Godet was not a tool in the hands of the English spies, he was their confederate, their help. Can you bring yourselves to believe, citizens, that a loyal soldier of the Republic could be deceived by false uniforms, by French words spoken by alien lips? Can you believe this story of a forced march, of starvation by the wayside in the company of English spies whose every action, every word, every gesture almost, must have betrayed them as the foreigners they actually were. Citizens, I appeal to that reputation for clear thinking and for logic, for which French men and women are famous throughout the world. At this hour when our beloved country is threatened on every side, is this the time, I say, for allowing yourselves to be duped by traitors who would sell you and your land, your dues and your liberty for English gold——?"

"No! no!" came a lusty shout in response. And the crowd took up the cry. "No! We'll not sell our liberties for English gold."

"Say on, citizen representative."

Pochart had jumped to his feet; once or twice he had tried to break in on Chauvelin's peroration, with cries of: "Thou'rt slandering a soldier of the Republic!" or: "Traitor! thou'rt in league with thy daughter!"

But he was not listened to. There was something about Chauvelin which fascinated the mob. His white, calm face, his pale, piercing eyes, his voice, dull, even monotonous, but penetrating to the most distant corners of the room. And there was also that welcome element of novelty. This pleased the women. Trials and condemnations in incessant routine had begun to pall. Here was something new. Witnesses summoned, then discredited, and finally accused. Such a thing had never been witnessed before in Orange.

And so, the crowd would not listen to Pochart or Danou, they wanted to hear Chauvelin; they did not particularly wish to see Fleurette *nommée* Armand acquitted, but they did relish the prospect of the two witnesses being sent to the bench of the accused. That was novelty for them, and it was what they wanted for the moment. Moreover, they did think that the citizen lieutenant with all his swagger had been such a consummate fool, if no worse, that it would be distinctly amusing to see that stupid head of his roll down into the basket of the guillotine.

Neither Pochart nor Danou, however, were men to give up the struggle quite so easily. In the fight against the representative on special mission, who had threatened them and lorded it over them for so long, they only contemplated one issue: victory. Victory! which would mean satisfaction of pride and of revenge. They had set out to win and did not consider themselves beaten. Not yet. Already Pochart was on his feet, and his rasping voice rose booming above the tumult. As soon as a slight lull gave him an opportunity he seized it, and cried in thunderous accents:

"Citizens! Frenchmen! French women! All of you!" And then again: "Citizens all! Let me put the same question to you, that the President asked you just now: will you allow yourselves to be duped? Will you go like sheep whithersoever traitors may lead you?"

The crowd murmured and shrugged shoulders, would have shouted Pochart down only that the rasping voice of his rose above the cry of: "À *la lanterne*, all traitors and fools!"

Pointing an accusing finger at Chauvelin, Pochart took up the cry.

"So, say I," he roared in a terrific straining of his powerful lungs: "À *la lanterne* all the traitors who try to throw dust in your eyes. Have you forgotten that the citizen President is the father of the accused? And that he knows well enough that if the child be guilty, then is the parent guilty too? To save himself he is trying to shield a traitor. Do not allow yourselves to be duped by him. Look on the Citizen President, my friends, and ask him how it comes about that he lavished all the treasures of his eloquence upon this one traitor, when yesterday and the day before that, he sent to the guillotine every man, woman and child who came before the Tribunal, and on a mere suspicion of treason."

A dull murmur greeted this peroration. There had been something in Pochart's eloquence which caused the crowd not to veer round just yet, but at any rate to look on the President of the Tribunal with rather less awe, and something approaching suspicion.

"That is true," a woman said loudly. "The President showed no mercy to traitors yesterday. And it is treason now to be as much as suspected of treason, we've been told."

"It is my duty to protect the innocent," Chauvelin retorted firmly, "as well as to punish the guilty."

"Methinks," Danou now broke in, and his slow, and suave tones came in strange contrast to the clamorous eloquence of his colleagues: "methinks that the traitor Danton made some such remark too, ere justice put her hand on him."

"Danton was a traitor, and thou too, Citizen Danou, art a traitor for speaking his name in this hall of justice."

"Justice!" Pochart cried, pallid with rage, for he had felt that the word "traitor" hurled at Danou was meant to strike him also. "Justice! hark at the traitor, who should be standing in the dock beside his brood."

"*Vas-y*, Citizen President," the woman cried excitedly. "It is thy turn now."

They had cast aside their knitting, so palpitating had this duel become between these three men. Insensate, doltish as they were, they scented the tragedy that underlay this wordy warfare; they guessed that the man who presided over this infamous tribunal and who with a casual stroke of the pen had sent hundreds indiscriminately to death, had one soft corner in his callous heart, and that his colleagues, consumed with envy and hatred were hitting at that vulnerable spot and had already succeeded in making him writhe in agony.

At the same time, such is the psychology of a multitude as against that of individuals, there was still a wave of sympathy tending in the direction of this father fighting so desperately for the life of his child. Strictly speaking it was not sympathy, rather was it mere instinctive understanding of family ties. Five years of this awful revolution, during which every cruel lust in man or woman had been sedulously fostered, every softer mood repressed, had not yet succeeded in crushing altogether that feeling for family solidarity which is the most distinctive characteristic of the French nation. And this spectacle of a father sitting in judgment over his own child, actually expressed to pronounce the death-sentence over her, did undoubtedly for the time being sway the crowd in his favour. He was given a more respectful hearing than either of his colleagues or either of the witnesses, and when Godet's name recurred on the tapis, it was greeted with derisive cries of "*Cet imbécile!*" and when Adèle was mentioned, most of the women shouted spitefully: "Liar!"

Chauvelin, sensitive of course to the slightest wavering in the temper of the populace, felt his advantage and strained every nerve to press it home. The whole situation was of course terribly precarious. At any moment a look, a word, a false move on his part, might cause the crowd to veer right over against him. Even after an acquittal sometimes, the populace would suddenly demand that the accused be re-arrested: a second trial, more of a mockery and a travesty of justice than the first, would be insisted on, after which condemnation was a foregone conclusion. All this Chauvelin knew, none better, and there were moments when he felt as if madness or death were preferable to this terrible fight that in the end could have but one issue. And yet fight he must, fight for every inch of ground, fight with the last breath in his body, and with it silence the vituperations of those fiends who had raised their noisome voices against his Fleurette.

Even now Pochart was on his feet again, shouting, gesticulating, banging his fist upon the table.

"Citizens," he reiterated for the third time, "do not let yourselves be duped by men who are ruining your country by pandering to traitors. Look at the accused! I say she is nothing but a wanton, who should be tied to the whipping-post ere she be sent to the guillotine. Look at the aristocrat, I say, with the demure airs and the folded kerchief; she, forsooth, goes forth o' nights to meet her lover under the almond-trees, there to concoct treason with her lover against the Republic. She was seen, remember, seen, I say, in spite of what interested parties may aver. You have heard the witness, a humble, simple girl, the victim of aristocratic lust and of tyranny. That witness spoke the truth. She saw the accused and her lover at dead of night whispering and embracing. I ask you, does a clean-minded, respectable woman, citizen of our glorious Republic, spend her nights in the company of her lover? Rather is it not the wanton, the traitor, who shuns the light of day and seeks the darkness, for the hatching of treasonable plots against the State? Look at the witness, citizens. Humbly and simply did she speak the truth—"

"She lied as well you know it, Citizen Pochart," Chauvelin broke in forcefully. "Liar, forger and thief, I decree her accused and command that she stand her trial for these offences against the Republic. Look at her, my friends, citizens all," he went on, and pointed an accusing finger at Adèle whose pinched little face had become the colour of lead, and who sat in a corner of the witness; bench, cowering within herself, her trembling hands, now and then, lifting a handkerchief to wipe the sweat of terror that had risen to her brow. "Look at her," Chauvelin continued, appealing to the sea of faces before him: "And now look at the accused. She is serene, because she is innocent; whilst the guilty trembles because she knows her treachery has come to light at last. Look at those two women, citizens, and yourselves pronounce which is the traitor and which is the stainless."

Of a truth all would have been well after that. Chauvelin passed a quivering hand across his brow. It was streaming with moisture. The strain had been immense. Mentally he felt broken by the effort. But he also felt that for the moment at least he had won the day. The *Moniteur* states definitely that: "*il y eût tout lieu de croire qu'un acquittement eût été applaudi.*" At any rate the applause at the moment was deafening, and if Chauvelin could have obtained a hearing for another sixty seconds he would have put the acquittal to the populace vote, and, as the *Moniteur* says, it would have been carried.

What would have happened afterwards nobody can say. The most fickle entity in the world is a multitude, and of all the multitudes, an audience watching the suffering of a fellow-creature is the most fickle and the most callous. For the next two or three minutes at any rate, Chauvelin held the sympathy of the crowd. Fleurette did not count either way. For the spectators of this heart-rending pageant she was just a thing, an insentient object placed there for their entertainment, the pivot round which circled their excitement. But Chauvelin, the father pleading for his daughter's life had won their sympathy— the sympathy of tiger-cats, satiated for the moment and licking their chops in the intervals of snarling.

All then would have been well but for the action of one of the sympathisers who stood leaning up against the wall in the crowd; a giant he was, coated with grime—coal heaver or scavenger probably, only half clad in ragged shirt and torn breeches, with dirty feet thrust stockingless into *sabots*, a red worsted cap over his unkempt hair, his face streaked with sweat and coal-dust. In one hand he held a large raw carrot which he was munching with loud snapping of the jaws and smacking of the lips. He was one of the noisiest in his approval of the President's peroration.

"*Vas-y*, President," he shouted. "À *la lanterne*, the fools and traitors. Where is that trollop? Let her stand up. We want to look at her, eh, citizens?"

"Yes! Yes! we want to see her! Stand up, Adèle of unknown parentage! Let's look at you."

The women, or course, were the loudest in their demand for the unfortunate Adèle. Bred by misery, often out of degradation, trained by five years of an execrable revolution, the women of France were not *féministes* these days. The spectacle of one of their own sex on the guillotine gave them more satisfaction than that of a man. Now they wanted to see Adèle of the pinched, rat-like face, Adèle with the trembling hands and the shrinking shoulders, they wanted to see her squirm before their wrath, they wanted to see her wriggle like a worm prodded with a pin. Incidentally they had almost for gotten Fleurette.

Louder and even louder they clamoured for Adèle, and at an order from the President, two soldiers of the National guard did presently drag Adèle from the corner of the witness' bench where she was cowering like a frightened rodent and dragged her—or rather carried her—to the bar of the accused. The crowd seeing that its dictates were being obeyed, restrained its frenzy for an instant and, through the comparative stillness that ensued, a piercing shriek rang out from the unfortunate Adèle.

"Mercy! Mercy!" she cried and struggled fiercely to free herself from the men's grasp. "I am innocent! I spoke the truth."

A thunderous shout of derisive laughter greeted her cry. The women, with their hands on their knees, were literally rocking with laughter. They thought that Adèle with a face like a rat, wisps of lank hair poking out from underneath her cap which sat all awry, with mouth wide open uttering shrieks which no one could hear through the deafening tumult, was supremely funny.

The President made no attempt to quell the disturbance. It was all to the good. The greater the hatred against Adèle, the greater his chance, not only of forcing wave of sympathy for himself at full-tide, until he had the opportunity of getting Fleurette out of Orange. He was striving with all his might to catch his darling's eye. But Fleurette's glance was fixed on Adèle. She seemed to him to be fascinated with horror, mute and paralysed. She was looking on Adèle, and her dear little hand was fidgeting the corner of her kerchief.

Through the ear-splitting uproar led by the women, Pochart and Danou, their sympathisers, men of their own choosing, vainly tried to get a hearing. As well try to shout down a tempestuous sea as these hundreds of women gloating over the spectacle of one of their own sex writhing in an agony of terror.

"*Hein!*" came in a stentorian shout from the grimy giant in the rear of the crowd; "thou wouldst slander the innocent girl with lies. Take that for thy pains."

And he hurled the remnant of his raw carrot over the head of the intervening crowd at the unfortunate Adèle.

It missed her by a hairbreadth, but the action delighted the crowd. They took up the cry: "Take that for thy pains!" and sent various missiles flying at the girl, who, crouching down on her knees, lay there like a bundle of goods just below the bar of the accused where Fleurette stood, gazing down at her, fascinated with horror.

Looking back later on that terrible moment, Chauvelin felt that it was the action of the grimy coal-heaver—or scavenger, whatever he was—that precipitated the catastrophe. He it was who egged on the rabble to virulent hatred against Adèle. It was he who by hurling that first missile at the girl brought in a further, more immense element of cruelty and horror into the situation. Certain it is that up to that moment Fleurette had appeared more dazed than horrified. She must even in her own gentle heart have felt a burning indignation against

Adèle for the treacherous part which she had played, and if the girl's arrest had been effected outside the Tribunal, she would perhaps never have actually realised what had brought it about. But with that shout of "Thou wouldst slander the innocent girl with thy lies," full consciousness returned to her, and with it the recollection of everything that had gone before. Chauvelin, who watched her with the devouring gaze of his love, saw as in a flash, through the quick glance which swept form Adèle to himself and thence over the sea of perspiring faces, the full workings of her mind.

He tried to keep the tumult going; he hoped that Fleurette would faint, so that she might be carried out of court. He prayed that the roof of the gigantic building would come crashing down and bury him and Fleurette and all that swinish multitude in its ruins ere she spoke the words which he saw hovering on her lips.

But none of these things happened. Rather by that perversity which is peculiar to Chance, a sudden lull broke in on the mighty uproar, a lull through which Fleurette's calm voice rang clear as water poured into a crystal glass.

"Adèle was not lying, nor did she slander me, I did give some valuable articles into the keeping of my beloved M'sieur Amédé Colombe, at the hour spoken of by her, and I have no doubt that she did see me, as she says."

Chapter 36

One must of necessity turn once more to the *Moniteur* of the 22nd Messidor year II of the Republic One and Indivisible. There in the *Choix des Rapports XXV*. 516-17, despite its sobriety of language and paucity of detail, there is ample proof that throughout the proceedings it was the action of one unknown that precipitated the final catastrophe. "*Un géant,*" we are told, "*fût le premier à lancer l'accusation fausse contre le Président du Tribunal, et on tumulte irrépressible s'ensuivit.*"

"False," you observe. But on that 16th day of June, 1794, Chauvelin of the National Convention, member of committees and confidant of Robespierre, did, we know, stand in danger of being dragged out into the open and hung on the nearest lamp post. The crowd was in no mood even to wait for the paraphernalia of the guillotine. They wanted to see the arch-traitor, the perjurer, who had sworn false oaths and lied in order to save himself and his brood, hang then and there. The giant spoken of in the *Choix des Rapports* had, it seems, hardly waited till the words were out of Fleurette's mouth, before he pushed his way to the forefront of the crowd, with vigorous play of his powerful elbows. Down he was now, in the body of the court. In the struggle, his ragged shirt had been half torn off his shoulders, and his broad chest and sinewy arms could be seen, nude and immense, and coated with grime. Out of one of the pockets of his tattered breeches he produced another uncooked carrot, and into this he bit lustily, then with a wide sweep of the arm he launched one by one against the President of the Tribunal the damning invectives which the *Moniteur* has characterised as false. "Traitor!" he cried. "Liar and perjurer! Citizens all, have you in all your lives ever witnessed such infamy?"

The *Choix des Rapports* describes the tumult as irrepressible. Indeed, at that moment it would have been easier to dam a raging torrent with one pair of hands, than to suppress the riotous confusion that ensued. Fleurette of a truth stood there forgotten, so did Adèle and Godet. All eyes were fixed on the President, every menacing gesture tended in his direction, all the strident cries, the insults, the varied and foul epithets were hurled against him. There were but few sober tempers in that crowded room at the moment. A dozen perhaps; no more. Older men, one or two women who watched rather than yelled. And what they saw interested and puzzled them, so much that, when the time came, when everybody else was shouting themselves hoarse to the verge of mania, they still kept cool and silent.

Like everybody else these few were gazing on the President. They saw him standing there on the bench like a figure carved in stone, and, like a stone, his face was of a grey, ashen colour. His eyes looked dim and colourless as if a hand had drawn a film over them; his lips were parted, his nostrils distended. The breath seemed to come with difficulty out of his lungs. A figure, in truth of terror and despair. But calm and still. Motionless as a stone. The giant munching his carrot had waved his huge arms about and yelled himself hoarse until he had lashed all the spectators into a state of frenzy. Finally, he strode across the room, and came to a halt close to the judges; bench facing the President.

The three judges had been watching him all along: Pochart and Danou with undisguised glee, and President Chauvelin with that stony stare out of his colourless eyes. But even as the giant approached, Chauvelin though apparently motionless, seemed inwardly to sink within himself, to crouch as a hunted beast in face of the menacing enemy. And suddenly like that of an automaton, up went his arm. With finger outstretched he pointed at the giant and one word escaped his trembling, rigid lips.

"You!"

Those who were watching him could not understand the word, for it was spoken in an alien tongue. Nor could they understand what happened afterwards. But what actually did happen was that the grimy giant threw back his head and gave a quaint and altogether pleasant laugh.

"Why yes!" he said in the same alien tongue, which no one present understood. "At your service, my dear M. Chambertin."

And Chauvelin murmured almost under his breath:

"You have your revenge at last, Sir Percy."

"Hitting back as you see, my friend."

It all passed unperceived in the midst of the irrepressible tumult, save by those few who sober-tempered chose to watch rather than to yell. It is doubtful whether even Pochart and Danou, who sat close by, saw anything of this brief, this mysterious scene.

The very next moment the grimy giant, this time with a hoarse and not at all a pleasant laugh, had hurled his half-munched carrot straight into the President's face. Then facing the crowd once more he threw up his great arms high above his head.

"Why should we wait, citizens?" he shouted louder than the rest of the yelling crowd. "À la lanterne, I say, the traitor and his brood. The guillotine is ready outside the Place. The executioner is to hand. Why wait?"

Nothing could have pleased the crowd better. They were all like tigers scenting blood, demanding it, licking their jaws in anticipation.

"Who is for a front place for the spectacle?" a man shouted from the rear of the crowd.

"À moi! the front place," a woman cried in response.

"À moi! À moi!" came from every side.

Then the general scramble began. A stampede down the gradients. The clatter of wooden sabots against the floor. The screams of women and children pushed and squeezed by the crowd. The grounding of arms, the click of bayonets, the words of command from the officer in charge of the guard, who were here to maintain order and who were quite powerless. They did of a truth try to stem the mob, to prevent the mad rush, the trampling, the stampede. But there were in reality too few of them for the task. All available fighting men being required for the army abroad, these were for the most part too inexperienced and too incompetent; raw recruits, half-trained for a wholly inadequate corps of *gendarmerie*.

The officers did what they could, but the men themselves were soon caught in the vortex. Having no idea of discipline or duty, they soon became just a part of the mob, allowed themselves to be carried along by the crowd. They were just as excited, just as eager to see the President of a revolutionary tribunal sent summarily to the guillotine, as anyone else. Their lust for the spectacle was as keen as that of any ragamuffin in the place. They were but half-trained ragamuffins themselves, and as every man these days was at least as good as his officer and owed him neither obedience nor respect, it was small wonder that in emergencies like these, the soldiers got out of hand, whilst the officers, shrugging their shoulders, viewed the scene with indifference.

In the meanwhile, the grimy giant had effectually fought his way along the floor of the house as far as the bar of the accused, where Fleurette, wide-eyed, deathly pale, half-crazy now with terror, had just fallen forward unconscious across the railing, drooping like a lily that is battered by the storm.

"And *à moi* the traitors," the giant shouted, and it was marvellous how his booming voice rang above the uproar and the confusion.

He dragged Fleurette's inanimate body from the bar and flung it over his shoulder, as if it were a bundle of goods. Then with two huge strides he was right in front of the judges; bench, and there turned back to face the crowd again.

"Take your places for the spectacle," the Titan shouted, "and I'll bring along the actors for you."

And so, they rushed out in a compact, struggling mass, hurrying, scurrying, fighting and pushing and struggling. Out in the open, in the Place de la République, into the sunshine and under the blue vault of heaven they rushed. The guillotine was set up there ready for its afternoon work, but, as the grimy giant had said, "Why wait?" Why indeed. No one was in a mood for waiting. The blackest traitor this town had ever seen had tried to save himself and his brood by slandering worthy citizens of the République. By the by, where were they? Adèle of unknown parentage and the swaggering Lieutenant Godet? Ah bah! they were forgotten. Lost in the crowd. Who cared? Time enough to cheer them when the traitors and slanderers were punished. Who cared indeed? For the moment the most important thing in the world was to secure a place of vantage for witnessing the wonderful spectacle.

The President of a revolutionary tribunal, a representative of the people in the National Convention, was not often to be seen in Orange mounting the steps of the guillotine. That spectacle was reserved for the Parisians—lucky people!—who saw the heads of *ci-devant* kings and queens, of generals and dukes and duchesses and of countless other *aristos* roll into the basket. Therefore, everyone scrambled for a good seat. The houses all round the Place were invaded by the mob; windows and balconies were soon filled with eager faces; boys and men swarmed on the roofs, clung to the rain-pipes, the gargoyles on the Hôtel de Ville, the guillotine reared its gaunt arms, painted a vivid red. The officers of the *gendarmerie* had succeeded by dint of threats, in restoring some semblance of order in the tenue of their men. They now stood at attention round the guillotine on the platform of which the executioner was busy with his grim task.

The crowd around was very still. Something oppressive, unconnected with the heat of midday sun, seemed to hang in the air. People were still pouring out of the Hôtel de Ville, though not in such compact numbers. Gradually these numbers too were thinned. Those that came out last appeared more sober, less excited than the mob that had spread itself all over the Place shrieking and gesticulating in the manner habitual to these natives of the South. Some of the last to come out were a group of men well known in Orange, one was the butcher from the rue Longue, another the innkeeper of Les Trois Abeilles, a third kept the haberdashery shop over the bridge. Citizens Pochart and Danou were with them. They were all talking eagerly together as they came down the steps. A group of women were standing close by.

"Are they bringing the traitors?" they asked.

"Yes, Citizen Tartine," the butcher replied, "that fine patriot Rémi, one of the scavengers at the Caristie house is close behind us, with some of his mates. They've got the traitors between them. We are to give the sign by firing this pistol when the executioner is ready."

He showed the women the pistol which he said Rémi himself had given him.

"The executioner is ready now," the women said, three of them speaking at once.

Citizens Pochart and Danou and the others then walked across the Place to the foot of the guillotine, one of them spoke a few words with the executioner. The crowd of spectators watched with feverish excitement. And presently Citizen Tartine, the butcher, raised his arm and fired a pistol in the air. A number of women shrieked. The excitement was so tense that the loud report sent the others into hysterics. Soon, however, the rumour went round that the pistol-shot was the signal that everything was ready for the spectacle and for the entrance of the chief actors in the play. After which every noise subsided. The multitude held its breath; a thousand pairs of eyes were fixed on the wide-open portals of the Hôtel de Ville waiting for the grandiose appearance of Rémi the scavenger and his mates bearing the traitors upon their shoulders.

Up, on the platform of the guillotine, the executioner was giving a last look to the pulleys. The soldiers stood at attention.

The huge crowd waited.

Chapter 37

The *Moniteur* does not say much about what happened afterwards. "*La foule attendit avec assez de patience*," is all it says, "*mais personne ne vint.*"

The portals of the Hôtel de Ville which should have been a frame for the entrance of the principal actors in the last act of the drama, showed nothing but the yawning black emptiness beyond. The crowd waited, says the *Moniteur*, with sufficient patience. They did wait quite happily for ten minutes, agitatedly for twenty. But nobody came. Citizens Pochart and Danou, also Citizen Tartine, the butcher, and three or four others, were seen to make their way back across the Place, to run quickly up the steps of the Hôtel de Ville and subsequently disappear inside its portals. Still the crowd waited, very much as a crowd will wait in a theatre when the entr'acte is too long; some of them hilariously, others with impatient yawns, others again with tapping of feet and presently with murmurs of: "*La Lanterne! La Lanterne!*"

The next thing that happened was the reverberating clang of the portals of the Hôtel de Ville being suddenly closed. Then only did the crowd realise that they were being cheated of the spectacle. Murmurs were loud, and there were some hisses and boos and cat's calls. But on the whole, they took the event with extraordinary calm. There was no rioting as indeed might have been expected. A few hot-heads tried to create a disturbance demanding that the executioner be given something to do. *Madame la Guillotine* should not be cheated of her dinner.

"She's hungry, give her something to eat," was the catchword these hot-heads used in order to excite the rest of the crowd. Somehow it did not work. There certainly were a few bouts of fisticuffs, one or two broken heads, the soldiers round the guillotine and those on guard at the street corners did use their bayonets with some effect, but on the whole the crowd was strangely subdued, more inclined to whisper than to shout.

For quite a little while after the portals of the Hôtel de Ville had been closed, they still waited, thinking that perhaps something more was being devised for their entertainment. But as time went on and nothing happened, they thought they might as well get home. It was dinner time. The children were hungry, and though there was little enough in the larders these days, one had to get home and give them what there was. The whole thing had been strange. Very strange. As men and women wended their way homeward, their thoughts reverted to that titanic figure with the grimy face and the huge bare chest, one sinewy arm encircling the body of the wench Fleurette *nommée* Armand, which hung limp across his massive shoulder. He was no mere mortal, that was certain.

And though the government up in Paris had abolished *le bon Dieu* and declared that it was Citizen Robespierre who was the "*Être Suprême*," something of the old superstitions imbibed at their mothers' knees, still lingered in these untutored, undisciplined minds. That the Titan with the flashing eyes and grimy face should have vanished with the traitors whom he and his satellites had seized, was but the fitting ending to his meteoric appearance. The government might forbid belief in God and the Devil, in heaven and in hell, but here was proof positive that the Devil did exist. He was black and he was of abnormal stature, he had a great bare chest and strong muscular arms, and—clearest proof of all—he had before the very eyes of the citizens of Orange seized upon two traitors and carried them away with him to limbo.

Nothing would take that idea out of the people's mind, and long after these horrible days of the revolution had passed away and men and women had returned to sanity, those who were present on that day in June at the trial of one Fleur Chauvelin *nommée* Armand, would recount the marvellous story of how the devil had entered the courthouse and spirited the accused away. Only a few knew the true facts of the case, and even so a great deal was left to surmise. Among those who knew was Citizen Tartine, the butcher. And this is what he told his friends when they pressed him with questions.

It seems that when the crowd stampeded out of the Hôtel de Ville, he, Tartine, together with Citizens Pochart and Danou who had stepped down from the judges' bench, and three or four other notabilities of the city among whom was Motus, the chief warder of the Caristie House, put their heads together for moment or two, wondering if something could not be done towards sending the wench Fleurette and her father by a back way to one or other of the prison houses, with a view to bringing them up for formal trial on the morrow. They did feel, however, that given the present temper of the populace, such a move might prove dangerous to themselves. "The people will demand a victim, two victims, perhaps more," Danou said with a doubtful nod of the head. "They might vent their wrath on us."

That was sound logic, and the project was abandoned almost as soon as it was formulated.

Motus, it seems, then turned familiarly to the giant and said:

"*Tiens*, Rémi, is it thou?"

"Myself, citizen," the giant replied.

In response to inquiries from the others, Chief Warder Motus then explained that Rémi was a scavenger whom he himself had taken on in the Caristie House for extra work when the regular man fell sick. A splendid patriot, Motus averred. There was, therefore, not the faintest cause for suspicion.

"Come along, all of you," Pochart now said addressing Rémi and is mates. "Bring along the prisoners. The people are waiting."

"Give them time to settle down," Rémi replied with a shrug and laugh. "We are the chief comedians in this play. Do you all go and prepare everything for our entrance."

"You won't tarry?" Danou admonished.

"Not we," Rémi replied. "We're as eager as you for the spectacle, eh, citizens?" he added, turning to his mates who had the President of the Tribunal still between them.

Rémi then took a pistol out of his ragged breeches and handed it to Citizen Tartine.

"When the executioner is ready," he said, "and everything prepared for our entrance, just give us the signal by firing the pistol. We'll be with you a few minutes after that. We've yet another surprise for the spectators," he added with another laugh, "which will delight them and you."

Tartine vowed that not the slightest suspicion entered his head or that of his companions. How could one suspect a patriot vouched for by no less a person than Motus the chief warder? In the end, however, Pochart decided that two men of the *gendarmerie*, one of whom was a sergeant, who were still standing at attention below the judges' bench, should remain with Rémi and his mates and escort them when the time came, on to the Place.

After which the group of notabilities followed the rest of the crowd out into the open. When looking back upon what followed, they all agreed that some fifteen minutes must have gone from the time when they finally left the court-house and took their last look at Rémi and his mates, to that when they returned and found the place empty. They all said that even then, at first glance, no suspicion entered their minds and they stood about for a few minutes talking together, thinking that Rémi was preparing the surprise spectacle which he had promised them. Thinking too that every moment would bring the scavenger back with his mates and the prisoners. Tartine, the butcher, was the first to suspect that there might be something wrong. He crossed the floor of the room and made his way to the private door which was at the back of the judges' bench and led to some corridors and private rooms, and also to the back of the premises of the Hôtel de Ville, and to a back door which gave on a narrow street that ran parallel with the façade.

The private door was locked, with no key to be seen. But even then, so remote was suspicion from their minds that Tartine and the others hammered away on the door and called loudly to Rémi. The door was made of solid oak, but Pochart and Tartine were both of them powerful men. Receiving no answer to their call, they searched amidst the litter left pell-mell by the crowd upon the gradients and found an axe and a leaded stick. Thus, armed they attacked the panels of the door, whilst Danou and one of the others wisely thought of closing the portals of the Hôtel de Ville. The oak panels yielded after a while. The door battered in, fell under the heavy blows dealt by Tartine the butcher with the axe. He and Pochart and two or three of the others striding over the debris, found themselves in a dark corridor.

Some twenty paces down the corridor on the right, they came to another door. It was locked, but behind it came a vigorous sound of banging and the door shook now and again as if under heavy blows. Once more the axe was brought into play, the door was smashed in and as it fell in with a crash, it revealed the two men of the *gendarmerie*, with arms and legs securely pinioned, and their crimson caps stuffed into their mouths. One of them had succeeded in rolling along the floor, near enough to the door to kick against it with his otherwise helpless feet.

There could no longer be any doubt. The public had been hoaxed either by an impudent imposter, or by a traitor, bribed to aid the prisoners to escape. The words: "English spies," soon cropped up as did those of Amédé Colombe and architect Caristie and a host of others. This too, no doubt, was their work. At least this was the opinion of some, whilst others, headed by Danou, shook their heads dubiously. Citizen Chauvelin was known to be the sworn enemy of those English spies—weren't they called the League of the Scarlet Pimpernel?—and it was Citizen Chauvelin and his daughter Fleur who had been so insolently spirited away.

Having hastily released the men of the *gendarmerie*, they all ran down the length of the corridor as swiftly as they could, chiefly because one of the soldiers said that this corridor led ultimately to a back entrance of the Hôtel de Ville. But the building itself was something of a maze, the passages were dark and narrow, it took them all some time to find that back door, and when at last they came upon it, they found it locked.

Once more the axe had to come into play, and time had in the meanwhile slipped by to the tune of some twenty minutes. Nor did the narrow back street reveal any of the secrets of this amazing adventure. Impostors, traitors or English spies, Rémi the scavenger and his mates had disappeared with the two prisoners and taken their secret with them. On the other side of the road there was a row of one-storied, tumble down houses, inhabited by some of the poorest families in the city. Inquiries at each house in succession revealed but little. Nearly all the inmates had spent their morning as usual watching the trials in the Hôtel de Ville and were not yet home; but in one of the houses a sick woman had, it seems, been standing at the window when she saw four or five men come out of the building opposite.

One of them, she said, was very tall and was carrying what she thought was a large bundle on his shoulder. The others were hustling a short, thin man who wore a blue coat and had on a tricolour sash round his waist. They turned sharply to their right and she soon lost sight of them. She thought nothing about the incident, one saw so many strange things these days.

In the meanwhile, the crowd on the Place had begun to disperse, the first stragglers were wending their way to their homes. Pochart and Danou holding high functions in the administration of justice, did not feel that it was incumbent upon them to go hunting for spies. That was the business of the *gendarmerie*, and they parted presently from their friends, declaring their intention of sending immediately for the Chief Commissary of Police. The others, feeling that it was not part of their duty either to run after escaped prisoners, found that they had pressing business to see to at home.

As far as Citizen Tartine, the butcher, was concerned, the incident had no further interest for him save for the pleasure of recounting his share of the adventure to his numerous friends. A couple more traitors escaped from the clutches of justice, a few more English spies when already the country swarmed with them, was nothing to worry one's head about.

Pochart and Danou did, on the other hand, worry their heads considerably about it all. They had a burning desire to know just what the English spies did ultimately do with their colleague Chauvelin. They hoped—oh! very ardently—that as soon as the much-vaunted Scarlet Pimpernel discovered that it was his inveterate enemy whom he had rescued from the guillotine, he would either hand him back straightway to the tender mercies of justice, or simply murder him in some convenient and out-of-the-way corner of the district. Pochart and Danou would have preferred the former alternative as being more satisfactory to their wounded vanity and their baffled spite.

Unlike Tartine, they seldom spoke of their experiences in connection with the affair. But their hopes did rise to their zenith when a week or so later President Legrange and Public Prosecutor Isnard returned from their fool's errand to Paris; there could be no doubt that even Robespierre, friend of Chauvelin though he be, would order the punishment of such a consummate liar and traitor.

Chapter 38

An immense lassitude had held Fleurette in a kind of semi-consciousness, a dreamless sleep from which she woke at intervals, only to open her eyes for a moment, and immediately let the lids, heavy with sleep, fall over them again. It was the reaction insisted on by health and youth against the terrible nerve-strain of that awful day.

During the brief intervals while she had a certain consciousness of things about her, she found herself nestling against *chéri* Bibi's shoulder! And when, with half-dimmed eyes she looked up at him, and tried to smile between two yawns, she always saw his pale, grave face turned away in profile, gazing straight out before him into the dark recess of the post-chaise, in which apparently, they were travelling. She called softly to him once or twice, but he never turned to look at her, only his hand, which felt cold and clammy, would gently stroke her hair.

How long all this lasted, what happened to her in the intervals of sleep, Fleurette never knew, but there came a time when the chaise rattled unpleasantly over the cobble-stones of a city, and lights darted to and fro through the darkness as the vehicle lumbered along through fitfully lighted streets. Fleurette sat up straight; all the sleep suddenly gone out of her eyes.

"Where are we going, *chéri* Bibi?" she asked. "Do you know?"

"No! I do not," Bibi replied, and his voice sounded hoarse and hollow. "Would to God I did."

Fleurette had never heard him invoke *le bon Dieu* before, and she tried through the gloom to peer into his face.

"But we are out of danger now, *chéri?*" she asked wide-eyed, the old terror which had caused her to lose consciousness in that awful courthouse, once more clutching at her heart.

"I do not know," he murmured mechanically; "would to God I did."

And then as if recalled to himself by the half-drawn sigh of terror from Fleurette, he seized hold of her, and pressed her head against his breast.

"No! No!" he said hastily, "they cannot harm you whilst I'm here to guard you."

Just then the coach came to a halt, and a moment later the door was thrown open and a gruff voice said:

"Will you descend, citizeness?"

Fleurette, frightened, clung to Bibi. She made no attempt to move. Whereupon the gruff voice resumed:

"If you don't come willingly, I shall have to send someone to fetch you."

Fleurette buried her face against Bibi's coat. His arms held her tightly. A minute, perhaps less, went by, and then—suddenly—she heard a voice—a very gentle, very timid voice this time, saying:

"Mam'zelle Fleurette! Oh, Mam'zelle Fleurette, I pray you to turn to me. It is I—Amédé."

What had happened? Was she dreaming? Or had she died of fright and gone straight up to heaven? Certain it is that she felt a timid hand upon her shoulder, whilst Bibi's hold upon her relaxed.

"Hold up the lantern, man," the gruff voice now broke in upon the delicious silence that ensued, "and let her see that she is not dreaming."

The light of a lantern flashed across Fleurette's eyes, she opened them and turned her head, and found herself gazing on M'sieur Amédé's pink and moist face, into his kind eyes full of anxiety and of tenderness, upon his mouth which had taught her how to kiss. Gently, slowly, she extricated herself from Bibi's embrace. Gently, slowly she seemed to glide into Amédé's arms.

He carried her whither she knew not. All she knew was that presently she found herself snuggling in a deep, cosy arm-chair, and that Amédé was kneeling beside her, with his eyes fixed ecstatically upon her as if she were *la sainte Vierge* herself.

"Where am I, dear M'sieur Amédé?" she asked.

"At Ste. Césaire, Mam'zelle Fleurette," he replied.

"Where is that?"

"Just outside Nimes. Your chaise passed through the streets of Nimes."

"I daresay," she said with a tired little sigh. "I was so sleepy; I didn't know where we were."

"We are under the protection of the bravest men that ever lived," Amédé said slowly. "They saved me from death. They have saved you, Mam'zelle Fleurette."

A shudder went through her. She closed her eyes as if to try and shut away the awful visions which his words had conjured up. But his kind, strong arms encircled her closer, and she nestled against him and once again felt comforted and safe. He told her the entire odyssey of his rescue, from the hour when the mock soldiers entered his father's shop at Laragne, until when his brave rescuers took leave of him outside the derelict cottage by the banks of the Drôme, and he, seeing the pale crescent of the moon rise above the snow-capped crest of La Lance, had solemnly bowed nine times, praying for that joy which today was his at last.

He had spent a few very lonely days in the cottage after that, devoured with anxiety as to the fate of his beloved. He could not eat, he could not sleep. For hours he would watch the filmy crescent of the moon, whose pale light mayhap illumined the window behind which his own Fleurette would also be watching and praying. And three days ago, he received the message which he was waiting for. It appeared mysteriously early one morning outside the cottage door. A missive, with a stone put upon it to prevent its being blown away by the wind. How it got there Amédé never knew. It came from the leader of that gallant little league of Englishmen who devoted their lives to helping those in distress.

In it he, Amédé, was ordered to walk as far as Crest, to the house of Citizen Marcor the farrier, where he could hire a horse. And then to hie him straightway hither to Ste. Césaire, not sleeping in any wayside inn, but rather in the fields, under shelter of hedges of forest trees, getting food for himself and his horse as best he could.

The missive further directed him, on arriving at Ste. Césaire, to seek out an empty house situated in the Rue Basse, and there to wait, for of a surety within two days he would hold his beloved Fleurette in his arms. Amédé had obeyed these commands to the letter. This very morning, he had arrived at Ste. Césaire and found the house in the Rue Basse. It was neither empty nor uninhabited. There was furniture in the house, and what's more there were two friends, two fine English heroes, who had been expecting Amédé and who made him welcome when he arrived. Oh! and didn't Mam'zelle Fleurette think that these Englishmen were the finest and bravest men that ever lived? As for their chief who was known amongst them as the Scarlet Pimpernel (*le mouron rouge*, M'sieur Amédé called it), he surely was more like one of the mythological gods rather than a mere mortal.

M'sieur Amédé seemed very anxious to know what Mam'zelle Fleurette thought about all these marvellous adventures, but how could she tell him, how could she talk at all when every time she raised her blue eyes to him, he broke off in the midst of a most exciting narrative in order to ask her in a voice vibrating with passion: "*Tu m'aimes Fleurette?*"

Chapter 39

Chauvelin, after he had seen Fleurette safely carried away in her lover's arms, sat for a while in the dark interior of the coach, starting into the gloom, his folded hands clasped between his knees. His thoughts were in such a whirl that it almost seemed as if he were unconscious. He certainly was insentient; he neither saw, nor heard, nor felt anything save the joy of knowing that his Fleurette was safe. It was only a few minutes—fifteen perhaps—later that a pleasant laugh broke in on his riotous thoughts, and that he became aware of a tall figure sitting beside him in the coach.

"You see, my dear M. Chambertin," the voice which he dreaded most in all the world said suddenly in his ear, "I would not forgo the pleasure of bidding you *au revoir.*"

Chauvelin half turned to his enemy, the man whom he had so persistently wronged, so persistently pursued with hatred and with spite. Through the gloom he could just see the outline of the massive figure, wrapped in a dark, caped coat, and of the proud head so nobly held above the firm, somewhat stiff neck.

Did all that this man stood for in the way of heroism and selfless-ness, strike a chord of shame in the heart of this callous, revolutionary tyrant? Why shall say? Certain it is that for the moment Chauvelin felt awed, and sat there in the gloom, silent, motionless, staring into the black vacancy. But after a second or two his lips uttered mechanically the name that was uppermost in his mind:

"Fleurette?"

"She is under my care," Blakeney said slowly. "Tomorrow at break of day she and her sweetheart will set sail for England with some of my friends. There she will be under the care of the noblest woman in the world, Lady Blakeney, who will take her revenge on you for all the wrong you did her, by lavishing the treasures of her sympathy upon your child."

"Then Fleurette will be happy?" Chauvelin murmured involuntar-ily.

"Happy, yes! she will soon forget."

"Then I am ready, Sir Percy."

"Ready? For what?"

"My life is at your service. My enemies are waiting for me over in Orange. You have but to send me back thither and your own venge-ance will be complete."

For a second or two after that there was silence in the old post-chaise; only Chauvelin's laboured breathing broke the utter stillness of the gloom. Until suddenly a pleasant, mocking laugh struck upon his ear.

"Egad man, you are priceless," quoth Sir Percy gaily. "You must indeed credit me with a total lack of the saving grace, if you think it would amuse me to hand you over to your genial friends over in Orange."

"But I am at your mercy, sir."

"As I and my beloved wife have been once or twice, eh? Well! I am hitting back now. That's all."

"Hitting back?" Chauvelin exclaimed. "You have the power now. I admit it. I am in your hands. My life is at your command."

"*La* man!" Sir Percy retorted lightly, "what should I do with your worthless life? For the moment all I want is to make that sweet child up there completely happy by telling her that you are safe and well. After that you may go to the devil for aught I care. You probably will."

"Then," Chauvelin murmured aghast, "you grant me my life,

you—"

"I am sending you back safely as far as Nimes. What happens to you after that I neither know nor care. You have tried to do me such an infinity of wrong at different times, you still hate me so cordially, you—"

He paused for a moment with firm lips tightly pressed together and slender hand clutched upon his knee.

"You are right there, Sir Percy," Chauvelin murmured between his teeth. "God knows how I still hate you, even after this. You have the power to hit back. Why the devil don't you do it?"

Whereupon Sir Percy threw back his head and his merry, infectious laugh woke the slumbering echoes of the sleepy little town.

"*La*, man," he said, "you're astonishing. Can't you see that this is my way of hitting back?"

A Child of the Revolution

Contents

This is the story which Sir Percy Blakeney, Bart., told to His Royal Highness that evening in the Assembly Rooms at Bath.

The talk was of the recent events in France, the astounding fall of Robespierre: the change in the whole aspect of the unfortunate country: and His Royal Highness expressed his opinion that among all those men who had made and fostered the Revolution, there was not one who was anything but a scoundrel, a reprobate, a murderer, and worker of iniquity.

Sir Percy then remarked: "I would not say that, sir. I have known men—"

"You, Blakeney?" His Royal Highness broke in, with an incredulous laugh.

"Even I, sir. May I tell you of one, at least, whose career I happened to follow with great interest?"

And that is how the story came to be told.

Chapter 1

"In Heaven's name, what has happened to the child?"

This exclaimed Marianne Vallon when, turning from her wash-tub, she suddenly caught sight of André at the narrow garden gate.

"In Heaven's name!" she reiterated, but only to herself, for Marianne was not one to give vent to her feelings before anyone, not even before her own son.

She raised her apron and wiped her large, ruddy face first and then her big, capable hands, all dripping with soapsuds; after which she stumped across the yard to the gate: her *sabots* clacked loudly against the stones, for Marianne Vallon was a good weight and a fair bulk; her footsteps were heavy, and her movements slow.

No wonder that the good soul was, inwardly, invoking the name of Heaven, for never in all his turbulent life had André come home looking such a terrible object. His shirt and his breeches were hanging in strips; his feet, his legs, the whole of his body, and even his face, were plastered with mud and blood. Yes, blood! Right across his forehead, just missing his right eye, fortunately, there was a deep gash from which the blood was still oozing and dripping down his nose. His lip was cut and his mouth swollen out of all recognition.

"In Heaven's name!" she reiterated once more, and aloud this time, "thou little good-for-nothing, what mischief hast thou been in in now?"

Marianne waited for no explanation; obviously the boy was not in a fit state to give her any. She just seized him by the wrist and dragged him to her washtub. It was not much Marianne Vallon knew of nursing or dressing of wounds, but her instinct of cleanliness probably saved André life this day, as it had done many a time before. Despite his protests, she stripped him to the skin; then she started scrubbing.

Soap and water stung horribly, and André yelled as much with impatience as with pain; he fought like a young demon, but his mother, puffing like a fat pug dog, imperturbable and energetic, scrubbed away until she was satisfied that no mud or dirt threatened the festering of wounds. She ended by holding the tousled young head under the pump, swilling it and the lithe, muscular body down with plenty of cold water.

"Now dry thyself over there in the sun," she commanded finally, satisfied that in his present state of dripping nudity he couldn't very well get into mischief again. Then, apparently quite unruffled by the incident, she went back to her washtub. This sort of thing happened often enough; sometimes with less, once or twice with even more disastrous results. Marianne Vallon never asked questions, knowing well enough that the boy would blurt out the whole story all in good time: she didn't even glance round at him as he law stretched out full length, arms and legs outspread, as perfect a specimen of the young male as had ever stirred a mother's pride, the warm July sun baking his skin to a deeper shade of brown and glinting on the ruddy gold of the curls which clustered above his forehead and all around his ears.

"What a beautiful boy!" strangers had been heard to exclaim when they happened to pass down the road and caught sight of André Vallon bending to some hard task in garden or field.

"What a beautiful boy!" more than one mother in the village had sighed before now, half in tenderness, half in envy. And "André Vallon is so handsome!" tall girls not yet out of their teens would whisper, giggling, to one another. If Marianne Vallon's heart swelled with pride when she overheard some of this praise, she never showed it. No one really knew what went on behind that large red face of hers, which some wag in the village had once compared to a bladder of lard. People called her hard and unfeeling because she was not wont to indulge in those "*Mon Dieu!'s*" and "*Sainte Vierge!'s*" when she passed the time of day with her neighbours, or in any of the "*Mon chou*"'s and "*Mon pigeon*"'s when she spoke to her André.

She just went about her business in and around her cottage, or at the *château* when she wanted up there to do the washing, uncomplaining, untiring, making the most of the meagre pittance which was all that was left to her now of a once substantial fortune. Her husband had died a comparatively rich man—measured by village standards, of course. He had left his widow a roomy cottage, with its bit of garden and a few hectares of land whereon she could plant her cabbages, cultivate her vines, keep a few chickens and graze a cow. But, bit by bit, the land had to be sold in order to meet the ever-growing burden of taxes, of seignorial dues, to be paid by those who had so little to others who seemed to have so much, of tithes and rents and rights, all falling on the shoulders of the poor toilers of the land, while the *seigneurs* were exempt from all taxation.

Then came two lean years—drought lasting seven months in each case, resulting in a total failure of the crops and poor quality of the wine. André was ten when the last piece of land was sold, which his father had acquired and his mother tended with the sweat of her brow; he was twelve when first he saw his mother stooping over her own washtub. Hitherto, Annette from down the village had come daily to do the rough work of the household; then one day she didn't come. André took no notice. It was nothing to him that at dinner-time it was his mother who brought in the soup tureen, that it was she who carried away the plates and the knives, and that she disappeared into the kitchen after dinner instead of sitting in the old wing chair sipping her glass of wine, the one luxury she had indulged in of late. Annette or *Maman*, what cared he who brought him his dinner? He was just a child.

But when he saw his mother at the washtub with a huge coarse apron round her portly person, her sleeves tucked up above those powerful arms, the weight of which he had so often felt on the rear part of his person when he had been a naughty boy, then he began to ask questions.

And Marianne told him. He was only twelve at the time, and she did not mince matters. The sooner he knew, the better. The sooner he spared her those direct questions and those inquiring looks out of his great dark eyes, the sooner, she thought, would he become a fine man.

So, she told him that the patrimony which his father had left in trust for him had all dwindled away, bit by bit, because the tax collector's visits were getting more and more frequent, the sums demanded more and more beyond her capacity to pay. There were the imposts due to the *seigneur*, and the tallage levied by the king; there were the rates due to the commune, and the tithes due to the Church.

Pay! Pay! Pay! It was that all the time. And two years' drought, during which the small revenues from the diminished land had shrunk only two palpably. *Pay! Pay! Pay!* And there were the *seignorial* rights. No corn or wine or livestock allowed to be sold in the market until *Monseigneur's* wine and corn and livestock, which he wished to sell, had all been disposed of. No wine press or mill to be used, except those set up by *Monseigneur* and administered by his bailiffs, who charged usurious prices for their use. *Pay! Pay! Pay!* It was best that André should know. He was twelve—almost a man. It was time that he knew.

And André had listened while *Maman* talked on that cold December afternoon three years ago, when the fire no longer blazed in the wide-open hearth because wood was scarce and no one was allowed to purchase any until *Monseigneur's* requirements were satisfied. André had listened, with those great inquiring eyes fixed upon his mother, his fingers buried in the forest of his chestnut curls, and his brows closely knit in the great endeavour to take it all in. He wanted to understand; to understand poverty as his mother explained it to him: the want of flour with which to make bread, the want of wood wherewith to make a fire, even the want of a bit of thread or a needle, simple tools with which his breeches and shirts—which were forever torn—could, as heretofore, be mended.

Poor? Yes, he was beginning to understand that he and *Maman* were now poor as Annette and her father down in the village were poor, so that Annette had to go and scrub floors in other people's houses and wash other people's soiled linen so as to bring a few *sous* home every day wherewith to buy salt and bread. Not that this primitive idea of poverty worried the young brain overmuch. It was not like a sudden descent from affluence to indigence. It was some time now since his favourite dishes had been put upon the table and since he had last wore a pair of shoes. The descent into the present slough of want had been very gradual, and, childlike, he had not noticed it.

Nor did his mother's lengthened homily make a very deep impression upon his mind. From a race of children of the soil he had inherited a sound measure of philosophy and a passionate love of the countryside. While he could run about in the meadows or watch the rabbits at evening scurrying away across the fields, while he could pick black berries in the hedgerows and gather the windfalls in the neighbouring orchards, while he could scramble up the old walnut trees and furtively touch the warm smooth eggs in the nests among the branches, he was perfectly happy.

What he didn't like was when Marianne set him to do the tasks which used to devolved on Annette. He didn't like scrubbing the kitchen floor, and he hated wringing out the linen and hanging it up to dry. But it never as much entered his dead to disobey. Mother was not one of those whom anyone had ever thought of disobeying, André least of all. She was large and fat and comfortable, and—especially in the olden days—she loved a good joke and would laugh heartily till the tears rolled down her fat cheeks, but she knew how to use the flat of her hand, as André had often learned to his cost. She was not one of those who believed in sparing the rod, and many a time had André gone to sleep on his narrow plank bed lying on his side because it hurt him to lie on his back.

But the fear of his mother's heavy hand did not really keep him out of mischief. As he grew older the desire for mischief grew up with him. A vague sense of injustice would, moreover, inflame that desire until it led him to acts which caused not only Mother's hand to descend upon him, but, also, of a certain hard stick, which was very painful indeed.

That time when he chased Lucile Godart, the miller's daughter, all down the road and then kissed her in sight of Hector Talon, her *fiancé*, who was short, fat, and bandy-legged, and was too slow in his movements to come to her rescue, was a memorable occasion, for, though Hector had not felt sufficiently valiant to administer punishment to the young rascal, Godart, the miller, had no such qualms.

And André got his punishment twice over, Mother's being by far the more severe. But he said that it was worth it. To kiss a girl, he declared, when she is placid and willing was well enough, but when she was a little spitfire like Lucile and fought and scratched like a wildcat, then to hold her down, kiss her throat and shoulder and, finally, her mouth, that was as great a lark as ever came a man's way—and well worth a whipping, or even two. What Lucile thought about it he neither knew nor cared.

Chapter 2

The incident with Lucile Godart had occurred two years ago. André was thirteen then, and already the girls were wont to blush when their eyes met his, so dark and bold.

Since then Lucile had married her Hector, who was now an assistant bailiff on *Monseigneur's* estate and lived with his young wife in a stone house on the edge of the wood. At the side of the house there was a field, which at eventide was alive with rabbits. That field exercised an irresistible fascination over André Vallon. He would cower behind the hedge and for hours watch the little cottontails bobbing in and out of the scrub. More than once he had been warned off by Hector Talon; once he had actually been caught unawares and driven off with some hard kicks.

But today a tragedy had occurred.

Lying on his back at this moment on the hard stones not far from his mother's washtub, and in the state in which God first made him, he was perhaps wondering whether in this instance the game was going to be worth the candle. He was too old now to get a whipping from Mother, and he did not think that what he had done was punishable by law. Still, Hector Talon was a spiteful beast, and Lucile... Well, the little she-devil would get her deserts one day, on the faith of André Vallon.

While the hot July sun was baking his skin and staunching the blood of his wounds, his brain was working away on the possible consequences of today's adventure. He wondered what his mother thought about it. For the moment she appeared to be immersed, both with hands and with mind, in her washtub. Her broad back was turned towards him, and André thought that it looked uncompromising. Still, Mother would have to know sooner or later, so better now, perhaps, while she was busy with other things. And before he knew that he had begun to think aloud, words were pouring out of him a kind of passionate outburst of resentment.

"Rabbits! Rabbits! —Why! there are thousands and thousands of them in that field," he went on with childish sense of exaggeration. "M. Talon himself is obliged to put fencing round his kitchen garden to keep them away. And I didn't put up any snare or trap—I swear I didn't. There was nobody about, and I just got over the fence to see— Well, I don't know. I just did get over the fence, and there in the long grass was the tiniest wee rabbitkins you ever saw! He was all crouching together till he looked like a ball of brown fur, and his round eyes were wide open, looking—I suppose he was horribly frightened—so frightened that he couldn't move. Anyway, I just stooped to pick him up. The house was all quiet, there didn't seem to be anyone at home, and that brute of a dog of theirs was on the chain."

André paused a moment; his hand had gone mechanically up to his forehead, to his lips, his shoulder, all of which were smarting horribly. Perhaps, he thought, it was time Mother said something, but she just went on with her washing, and all that André saw of her was that large, uncompromising back.

"How could I guess?" the boy went on; and suddenly he sat up, his brown arms encircling his knees, his chest striped with the red of the blood oozing from his shoulder. "How could I guess that that little vixen Lucile was spying from the window? I had got the young beggar by the ears, and I remember just thinking at the moment what luscious strew he was going to make. Of course, I had no intention of putting him down again, and I was trying to tuck him out of sight inside my shirt. And then, all of a sudden, I heard Lucile's voice calling to that dog of hers: '*Hue!* César! *hue!*' What a devil! My god! what a devil! That great brute César! He was on me before I could drop the rabbit and take to my heels. He was on me and got me on the shoulder. Then I did drop the rabbit, and it scooted away. I wanted both my hands to defend myself. I knew it would be no use trying to run, and César would have had me by the throat if I hadn't got him. And there was that little devil Lucile, running down the field and shouting, '*Hue! hue!*' all the time."

André was warming to his story. He was fighting his battle with César over again. His nostrils quivered; perspiration glistened on his forehead; his eyes, wide open and dilated, were as dark as the blackberries in the hedgerows.

"I got César by the throat," he went on in a shaky, hoarse voice, his words coming out jerkily, interspersed with gasps that were half laughter and half tears. "I squeezed and I squeezed, and all the while his horrid hot breath made me feel so sick that I thought I should have to let go. Once he got me on the forehead, and once I felt his nasty slimy teeth right inside my mouth. That gave me the strength to squeeze tighter, for I thought that if I didn't he would probably kill me. Then that little devil Lucile began to laugh, and I could hear bits of words that she said, 'That will teach you to insult honest girls. César also thinks it a lark to get a boy down a kiss him on the shoulder, what? And on the mouth. *Hue*, César! *hue!*' Isn't she a troll, Mother, a witch, a vixen, a she-devil, nursing vengeance like this for two years—or is it three?—but I'll kiss her again. I will! And what's more, I will—"

Once more André paused. His mother's broad back was still turned towards him, but she had turned her head, and through the corner of her eye she was looking at him. That is why he did not complete the sentence or put into words the ugly thought that had taken root in his brain. He remained quite still and silent for a moment or two, then he said abruptly:

"I never let go of César's throat till I had squeezed the life out of him."

But at this bald statement of fact, Marianne Vallon's outward placidity gave way. "*Jésus! Mon Dieu!*" she exclaimed and faced that naked young daredevil with horror and anxiety distorting her squab features. "Not content with poaching in M. Talon's field, thou hast killed his dog?"

"He would have killed me else. Would'st rather César had killed me, Mother?" André retorted with an indifferent shrug of his lean shoulders.

"Don't be a fool, André!" Marianne Vallon went on once more, in her usual placid way. "M. Talon—dost not know it?—has only to go before the magistrate and denounce thee—"

"Well, they can't hang me for killing a dog in self-defence, and I didn't poach the rabbit."

"No, but they can—"

It was the mother's turn to leave the phrase incomplete which involuntarily had come to her lips. Just like André a moment ago, she did not wish to put into words the thoughts that had come tumbling into her brain and were filling her heart with the foreknowledge of a calamity which she knew she could not avert.

If she could she would have packed André off somewhere, to friends, relations, anywhere; away from the spite of Talon, who already had a grudge against the child and who would feel doubly vindictive now. But when Marianne Vallon first fell on evil days she lost touch with her former friends or relations, who, in their turn, were content to forget her. André must stop at home and face the calamity like a man.

It came soon enough.

Talon, who was a man of consideration in the commune, laud a complaint before M. le Substitut against André Vallon for poaching and savage assault on a valuable dog, resulting in the latter's death.

André, in consideration of his youth—he was only fifteen—was condemned to be publicly whipped. M. le Substitut told him that he could consider himself most fortunate in being let off with so mild a punishment.

Chapter 3

A blind unreasoning rage, an irresistible thirst for revenge; a black hatred of all those placed in authority; of all those who were rich, or independent, or influential, filled André Vallon's young soul to the exclusion of every other thought and every other aspiration.

He was only fifteen, and in his mind, he measured the long years that lay before him in which he could find the means, the power, to be even with those who had inflicted that overwhelming shame upon him. It was not the blows he minded—Heavens above! that lithe, young body of his was inured to every kind of hardship, to every kind of pain. It was not the blows, it was the shame. Talon, who was influential and who was egged on by his wife, had prevailed upon the magistrate to make an order that all the inhabitants of the commune who were not engaged in work were to be present in the market place to see justice done on the young reprobate. And these were still the days when no one dared go against an order, however absurd and however unjust, framed by M. le Substitut du Procureur Général.

Monseigneur also came in his coach and brought friends to see the spectacle. There were two ladies among them who put up their lorgnettes and stared at the straight, sinewy young body, so like a statue of the Hermes with its slender, perfectly modelled limbs and narrow hips, and its broad shoulders and wide chest, smooth and dark as if cast in bronze.

"But the boy is an Adonis!" one of the ladies exclaimed in ecstasy.

"*Quelle horreur!*" she exclaimed a moment later when the stripes fell thick and fast on the smooth back she had admired. The days were not yet very far distant when ladies of high degree would crowed on balconies and windows to watch the execution of conspirators who perhaps had been their friends before then.

But for André Vallon, the bitter, humiliating shame!

His mother was waiting for him when he got home. She had prepared a little bit of hot supper for him, to which sympathisers in the village had also contributed: things he liked—a little hot soup, a baked potato, a bit of bread and salts. André ate because he was a young, healthy animal and was hungry, but he never said a word. Silent and sullen, he sat and ate. Not a tear came to those big dark eyes of his, in which there burned a fierce hatred and an overpowering humiliation.

Marianne, of course, said nothing. It was never her way to talk. She saw to it that André had his supper, and when he had finished she took him by the wrist and led him to his little room at the back. She undressed him and washed and dried his poor aching young body; then she wrapped him up in one of her wide gingham skirts which had become soft as silk after many washings and laid him down on his narrow plank bed with his head resting on an old coat of his father's, which had survived the dispersal of most of the household goods. Before she had finished tucking him up in her wool shawl he was asleep.

She watched for a moment or two the beautiful young face, with the blue-veined lids veiling in sleep the sullen, glowering look of the eyes; stooped and softly touched the moist forehead with her lips. Two heavy tears found their way down her furrowed cheeks; a heavy sigh came though the firm obstinate lips, and slowly she came down on her knees. With clasped hands flung across the bed, she remained kneeling there for some time, praying for guidance, for strength to fight a brave fight with this turbulent young soul, and for power to guide it in the path of rectitude.

This was the year of grace 1782, and Marianne Vallon, in common with many men and women in the land these days, was not blind to the tempest which already was gathering force in every corner of France, framed by the ardour of young enthusiasts with a grievance like her André, or by the greed of profligate agitators, soon to burst in all its fury, sweeping before it all the old traditions, the old beliefs, the old righteousness of this country and its people, and inflicting wounds that it would take centuries to heal.

Chapter 4

M. le Curé de Val-le-Roi, in the province of Burgundy, where they make such excellent wine, was a kindly and worthy man. He came of a good family—the Rosemondes of Nièvre, and though his intelligence was perhaps not of the highest order, his piety was sincere and his human understanding very real.

On the tragic day of André Vallon's public punishment he stood beside the whipping post the whole time that Marius Legendre—the local butcher employed by the Commune to administer punishment to juvenile offenders—was lamming into the boy. André, with teeth set and eyes resolutely closed, appeared not to hear the *curé's* gentle words, exhorting him to patience and humility.

Patience and humility, forsooth! Never was there a vainer exhortation.

It was only when it was all over and he was freed from the post that André opened his eyes and cast a glowering, rankling look around the market square. Legendre had thrown down the whip and was handing the lad his shirt and coat. André snatched them out of his hand, and Legendre—a worthy man, not unkind—smiled indulgently. The two *gendarmes* stood at attention, waiting for orders, their faces wooden and impassive. Part of the crowd had already dispersed: the men silent and sullen, the women sniffing audibly. The younger ones—girls and boys—muttered words of pity or of wrath. *Monseigneur* was standing beside the door of his coach, helping the ladies to step back into the carriage. One of them—the one with the *largnette*—cast a final backward glance at André; then piped in a high-pitched, flutelike voice:

"See, my dear Charles, so would a fallen angel have looked had the Almighty punished the rebels with thongs."

A man in the forefront of the crowd, close to *Monseignuer's* coach, laughed obsequiously at the sally. André saw him. It was Talon. Lucile stood beside her husband. When she met André's glance, she, too, gave a laugh, but quickly turned her head away. Then only did a groan rise from the boy's breast. It was a groan of an overwhelming, impotent rage. His breath came whistling through his teeth. He made a movement like a wild beast about to spring, but instinctively the *gendarmes* had already placed each a hand upon his shoulder and held him down. André was weak after the punishment, though he would not have admitted it even to himself; but his knees shook under him, and he nearly collapsed under the heavy hands of the *gendarmes*. M. le Curé murmured gentle words. "My son, remember that our Lord——"

André turned on him with a cry that was like a snarl. "Go away! Go away!" he muttered hoarsely. "I hate you."

But the *curé* did not go away. He stayed to help the lad on with his shirt and coat; then, when André, avoiding the crowd, went staggering round a back street and then down the lane towards his mother's cottage, the kindly old priest followed him at a short distance, ready to render assistance should the boy be seized with giddiness and collapse on the way. Only when he saw Marianne standing at the narrow garden gate waiting for her son did he went his way back to his presbytery. Contrary to his usual habit, he did not take his breviary out of his pocket or murmur orisons while he walked. With his *soutane* hitched up around his waist, he strode along, obviously buried in thought, for now and again he would shake his head and then nod, as if in secret communion with himself.

The results of *M. le Curé's* agitation were, firstly, a lengthy interview with *Monseigneur,* and secondly a summons to Marianne Vallon to bring her son André up to the *château. Monseigneur* desired to see him.

André, of course, refused to go. "I hate him!" he declared when *M. le Curé* came to announce what he thought was great news for Marianne and the boy.

"*Monseigneur,*" the priest had explained, "was interested. He is always so kind and so gracious, but when I spoke to him of André he was pleased to be genial, facetious; he toyed, as one might say, with the idea of doing something for the boy. Then there were the ladies. Madame la Marquise d'Epinay put in a word here and there, so charming she was, so sprightly. She spoke of André as the bronze Hermes, and though the latter we know is nothing but a heathen god, and I would not care to think that our André had any likeness to such idolatrous things, I could not have it in my heart to reprove the witty lady, especially as *Monseigneur* appeared more and more diverted. Then Mademoiselle Aurore came in—such a pretty child—her governess was with her, and I gathered at once she knew something about our André—domestics will talk, you know, my good Marianne—and *Mademoiselle* was even more interested than *Monseigneur.* She put her little hands together and begged and begged of her father that André might come up to the *château,* as she desired to see him. And *Monseigneur,* who since the death of Madame la Duchesse gives in to all the child's whims, gave me permission to bring our André to him."

The good *curé* spoke thus lengthily and uninterruptedly, for Marianne, absorbed in her knitting, said never a word: she was never much of a talker, and André only glowered and muttered unintelligible words between his teeth. There was perhaps something a little unctuous, a little complacent in *M. le Curé's* verbiage. He was not forgetting that besides being the incumbent of this poor little village, he was also by birth a Rosemonde de Nièvre, and that by tradition and upbringing he belonged to the same caste as Monseigneur le Duc de Marigny de Borne, whose gracious sympathy in favour of "our André" he had been fortunate enough to arouse.

"I hate him! I will not go!" was all that could be got out of André that day. "You can drag me to that accursed *château,*" he went on sullenly, "as you did to the whipping post, but willingly I will not go."

"But, my dear child," the *curé* protested, "*Monseigneur* said—"

"Whatever he said," the boy broke in with a snarl, like an animal that is being teased, "may his words choke him!—I hate him!"

"You are overwrought and agitated, my boy," the priest said placing his well-manicured podgy white hand on André's shoulder, who promptly shook it off. "When the good God and your dear patron saint have prevailed over your rebellious spirit, you will realise how much *Monseigneur's* kindness and Mademoiselle Aurore's intercession—"

"Don't speak to me of those women up at the *château*," André cried hoarsely, "or I shall see red!"

Marianne Vallon at this point put down her knitting. She knew well enough that to carry on the discussion any further today would only drive the boy to exasperation. All that he had gone through in the past few days had, in a way, made a man of him, but a man with all a child's unreasoning resentment at what he deemed an injustice.

M. le Curé took the hint. With characteristic tact he changed the subject of conversation, spoke to Marianne on village matters—the washing of surplices which she had undertaken to do for a small stipend, and finally took his leave, deliberately ignoring André's ill manners and glowering looks. At the door, however, he turned once more to where the boy sat, chin cupped in his hand, staring dully into the gathering shadows.

"Remember, my dear child," he said with gentle earnestness; all his small, worldly ways drowned in a flood of genuine sympathy, "that your future does not belong entirely to yourself: your sainted mother works her fingers to the bone so that you should be clothed and fed. She performs menial tasks to which neither by birth nor upbringing was she ever ordained. Think of her, my lad, before you spurn the hand that can help you up the ladder that may lead you to an honourable career and give you the chance of repaying part of your debt to her."

Mother and son spoke little to each other during the rest of the day. Marianne appeared more than usually busy with knitting and sewing and spoke even less than was her wont. After sundown André went out from a tramp in woods and fields. Ever since the fatal day he had made a point of wandering over the countryside only after dark. He dreaded to meet familiar faces in the country lanes, dreaded to see either compassion or ridicule in the glances that would meet his.

Tonight, his young soul was brimful with bitterness. Never before had he felt such an all-embracing hatred for everything, and every human being who had made possible the humiliation that had been put upon him. Childlike, he wandered down the lane past the house where lived Talon and his wife, the prime authors of the whole tragedy. He stood for a long time looking at the house. There were lights in one or two of the window. The Talons were rich, they could afford candles. They were people of consideration. They got the ear of the Substitut and engineered his, André's, lasting disgrace. He hated them—hated their house, their garden, their flowers; he wished with all his might that some awful calamity would overtake them.

The fields around were bathed in moonlight; the air was fragrant and warm; a gentle breeze fluttered the branches of the forest trees, causing a gentle murmur to fill the night with its subtle sound. The scent of hay and clover rose from the adjoining meadows, and from the depths of the wood there came from to time the melancholy call of a night bird or the crackling of trigs under tiny, furtive feet.

Only a very few days ago André would have revelled in all that: the little cottontails scurrying past, the barn-door owl flying by with great flapping of wings; fantastically shaped clouds veiling from time to time the face of the moon. All would have delighted him, those few short days ago. Now he had eyes only for that house of evil. He watched its windows till the lights were extinguished one by one, and then wished once more with all his might that hideous nightmares should disturb the sleep of those whom he hated so bitterly.

Chapter 5

When André finally turned to go home again, it was close on midnight. Coming in sight of the cottage, he was surprised to see that, contrary to his mother's rigid rules of economy, there was still a light in the parlour. He pushed open the door and peeped in. Mother was sitting sewing by the light of a tallow candle. She looked up as he came in and gave him a welcoming smile. He thought she looked quite old, and her eyes were circled with red, as if she had been crying. But he pretended not to notice. Still, it was funny, her burning a candle so late at night when candles were so dear. And why did she look so tired and so old?

He asked no questions, however. Somehow, he didn't feel as if he could say anything just then. He knew that presently his mother would come into his room to hear him say his prayers, to tuck him up in the old wool shawl and give him a last goodnight kiss.

Of late he had refused to say his prayers. *Le bon Dieu*, he thought, only bothered Himself about rich and powerful people—nobles, bishops, and such likes—what was the good of murmuring prayers that were never listened to and asking for things that were never granted? When Mother said her prayers as usual beside his bed in spite of his obstinacy, he turned his head sullenly away. He had even caught himself wishing that she would leave him alone, once he was in bed: alone, nursing his thoughts of future retribution on all those whom he hated so.

Strange that he never had the desire to talk to his mother about all that went on in his mind these days. Strange, seeing that hitherto he had always blurted out everything that troubled him, poured into her patient ear the full stories of his peccadillos, his adventures, anything and everything that passed through his mind. But now André had succeeded in persuading himself that his mother would not understand his feelings. She was, he thought, so patient and so devout that she would not sympathize with a man—a man!—who had been so deeply injured as himself. He felt that he had suddenly become a man—a man suffering an infinite wrong; and that Mother was only a woman, weak under the influence of priests and of their everlasting teachings of gentleness and humility. Men couldn't be gentle these days. They had suffered too long and too bitterly: crying wrongs, injustice that called to heaven for vengeance—only that heaven wouldn't hear. Well, if *le bon Dieu* wouldn't help the poor and the downtrodden to defend themselves against injustice, then they would fight on their own without help from anywhere.

Monseigneur and his sycophants! And those women with their perfumes and their silk dresses and their *lorgnettes* and their high-pitched voices! André hoped to God that he would live long enough to see them all eat the bread of humiliation as he himself had been forced to do.

At this point in his meditations Mother did come in. André did not hear her at first, for she had taken off her *sabots* and was in her stockinged feet. It was only when she stood close beside his bed that he turned his head and saw her.

Of course, he felt sorry for her. Women were women, and therefore weaker vessels, unable to take in the vast thoughts and projects of men. But they were dear gentle creatures whose ministrations were essential to the well-being of the stronger, more intellectual sex. Therefore, André felt very kindly disposed towards his mother just now: he would not have admitted for the world, even to himself, that at sight of her dear old face, with its furrowed cheeks and eyes to often stern, and yet always full of love, a great yearning seized him to bury his head in her ample bosom, to forget his manhood and be a child again. However, all he said for the moment was: "Not yet in bed, Mother? Isn't it very late?"

To which she replied cheerily, "It is, my cabbage, and fully time you were asleep."

She then knelt down beside his bed. André ought then to have jumped out of bed and knelt beside her to say his prayers. This had always been the rule ever since he was old enough to babble his "Gentle Jesus, meek and mild—" and clasp his baby hands; even when he began to feel himself a man, he had readily complied with the rule. But for days now, when Mother knelt beside his bed and murmured, "Our Father which art in Heaven," he had turned his head stubbornly away, nor had he looked at her till she had finished her prayers. Tonight, however, though he still felt wrathful and was too big a man to get out of bed, he kept his head turned towards her so that he could see her face. There was such a bright moon outside that he could see her quite plainly: her found flat face, her thin hair already streaked with grey, parted in the middle and fastened in a small tight bun on the top of her head. Her eyes were closed while she prayed with hands tightly clasped, her lips murmuring softly, "Forgive us our trespasses"; then all at once she raised her voice and said quite loudly, "As we forgive them that trespass against us."

"I won't! I won't!" André broke in involuntarily. "I'll never forgive them, never!"

But Marianne did not seem to hear. She finished her prayers and then remained for a time on her knees, gazing on the beautiful young face that meant all the world to her. Almost distorted now with wrath and obstinacy, it was none the less beautiful; with those large dark eyes that seemed forever to be inquiring, to be groping after something unattainable. Marianne's large, capable hand wandered lovingly over the hot, moist forehead and brushed back the unruly curls which fell, rebellious, over the brow. Without another word she pressed a kiss on the eyes, closed as she thought in sleep, and on the mouth through which the young passionate breath came in slow, measured cadence. Then she tiptoed out of the room.

André was not asleep. He had felt the kiss and tasted the salt moisture of his mother's tears on his lips. For a long, long while he remained lying on his back, with widely dilated eyes staring into the darkness above him. Through the chinks in the ill-fitting door he could perceive the feeble light of the tallow candle which still burned in the adjoining room. He heard the old church clock strike one, then the half hour then two. The moon had gone, the tiny room wherein stood the boy's small plank bed was in complete darkness, save for that dim streak of light underneath the door.

As noiselessly as he could André rose and tiptoed across the room. For a few seconds he listened, his ear glued to the keyhole, but all that he could hear was an occasional sigh, and once a sound like a broken sob. The door hung loosely on its hinges, he pulled it open. His mother was still sitting sewing by the feeble candlelight. André, leaning against the door jamb, stood mutely watching her.

She seemed very busy and never looked up once in his direction. She had a pair of breeches in her hands, had evidently been at work on them. Now she fastened off the cotton, broke it off, put down her needle. André watched her. She did look old, and there was a tear which had settled on the tip of her nose. She wiped it off with her apron and then held the breeches up with both hands to see if more darning was needed. Satisfied that they were quite in order, she laid them down on the table, smoothed them out with both hands, then folded them carefully and put them to one side.

André thoughts: "Those are my breeches. She has tired herself out mending them." And the words which *M. le Curé* had spoken earlier in the day came hammering into his brain: "Remember, my child, that your future does not belong entirely to yourself. Your sainted mother works her fingers to the bone that you should be clothed and fed."

That was true, for there she was, working for into the night, mending his breeches, while he—

"Mother!" he said abruptly. "Do you wish me to go up to the *château* and see those people?"

She didn't give a start; obviously she knew that he was there. She was standing now with one hand resting on the table and peering over into the darkness to try and see him with her blinking, tired eyes.

"André! Why aren't you in bed?" she asked. "Go back at once."

"Mother!" he insisted.

"Yes, André?"

"Do you wish me to go to the *château* and see those people?"

"It might lead to something good for your future, my child. *M. le Curé* said that *Monseigneur* was kindly disposed."

"I have no decent clothes in which to go," the boy muttered, his sullen mood not yet quite gone.

"There are your new stockings which I have quite finished," Marianne rejoined quietly, "and I have done mending your best breeches. You can wear your father's Sunday coat and his buckled shoes—fortunately he was a small man, and you are near as tall already."

"Mother!" André exclaimed.

"Yes, André?"

"You have been working your fingers to the bone so that I should be clothed. *M. le Curé* said so."

"No, my child," Marianna said, smiling through an involuntary little sigh, "not to the bone."

"And did you sit up tonight because you—you—"

"I knew that you would want your best breeches—soon."

"You knew I would change my mind and go to the *château?*"

"Yes, André, I knew."

"How could you know, Mother?"

"I suppose your guardian angel must have told me. He knew."

"Mother!"

This time the cry came straight from the boy's heart. With one bound he was beside his mother and with his arms was encircling her knees. His tousled head was buried in her voluminous skirt. She fell back into her chair and drew the hot, aching young head against her breast. There, resting against that warm, downy pillow, all pretence at manhood was swamped in the grief of a child. André burst into a flood of tears, the first that had welled out of the bitterness of his heart since that awful day of disgrace. Marianne, with her kind fat arms wrapped round her most precious treasure, thanked God for those tears.

The tallow candle flickered and died out. The room was in darkness, only a pale light, the first precursor of dawn, came shyly peeping presently through the small uncurtained window. The distant church clock struck four. It was more than an hour since Marianne had moved. The child had cried himself to sleep, squatting on the floor, with his head on her lap, her hand resting on his curls. From time to time a sob shook the young frame; then even the sobs were stilled, and Marianne, stiff with sitting motionless, would not move for fear of waking him.

Chapter 6

If you should ever visit the Bourbonnais do not fail to go as far as Le Borne, on the outskirts of which stands the princely Château de Marigny. It is one of the most sumptuous survivals of medieval splendour, with its unique position on a spur of the Roches du Borne, commanding a gorgeous view over the valley of the Allier with its rippling winding stream, its spreading forests of beech and walnut and sycamore, its vine-clad slopes and picturesque villages—Val-le-Roi, Le Borne, Vanzy, and so on—peeping shyly through the trees.

Originally built in the twelfth century by Jean Duke of Burgundy, it was enlarged and enriched by each of his successors, until the great Duke Charles—known to history as the Connétable de Bourbon—as great in treachery as in doughty deeds, completed the work of making the Château de Marigny second to none in grandeur and magnificence. It was to him that King Henry VIII of England referred when he remarked to François I of France on the occasion of the meeting on the Field of the Cloth of Gold: "If I had so opulent a subject, I would soon have his head off."

François I had no occasion to follow his English friend's advice, for it was soon after that that the illustrious Connétable de bourbon became a traitor to his country and sold his sword to the enemy of France, which was quite sufficient excuse for the king to declare the duke's estates forfeit to the Crown. Some of these were subsequently sold and passed from hand to hand. The *château*, then known as Château de Borne, came into the possession of the Duc de Marigny, first cousin of King Henry of Navarre and a direct descendant of the Connétable who renamed it Marigny and added to his many titles that of De Borne.

Though the magnificence for which the old *château* was famous in the past—when 'twas said that Duke Charles kept five hundred men-at-arms within its precincts—was somewhat shorn of its dazzling rays, the present Duc de Marigny did, nevertheless, live there like a prince and entertain with lavish hospitality. These were the days, closely following on those of the *grand monarque*, when the king set the pace in splendour and prodigality and the great nobles thought it incumbent on them to emulate royal ostentation. It was the era of beautiful furniture and of exquisite silks and laces, of stately ceremonials both at court and at home, of gorgeous banquets, expensive food and wins, as well as of the aesthetic enjoyment of pictures, music, and the play. Money flowed freely into the coffers of those who had landed estates: The State favoured them, for not only were they free of taxation, but one privilege after another was conferred on them, and, quite naturally, they grasped these with both hands and then asked for more.

Cradled in the lap of luxury, wrapped up in cotton wool by syco-phants and menials, they shut their eyes to the gather clouds of the inevitable Revolution. The cataclysm found them unprepared, scared, and astonished, like children wakened out of a dream. Most of them had not done blinking their eyes under the shadow of the guillotine. When they died, they died like heroes. They would have lived like heroes had they been given the lead, had they understood that the distant thunder of growing discontent among the people, the flashed of lightning of menace and revenge, were the precursors of a raging storm that threatened them, their traditions and their caste.

In this year of grace 1782 Monseigneur le Duc de Marigny, one of the richest and most distinguished members of the old French ar-istocracy, connected with the royal houses of Bourbon and Orléans, was certainly one of those who thought that most things were for the best in this best possible world. The only thing that ever troubled him was the occasional tightness of money. This was an unheard-of thing. The Duc de Marigny, cousin of kinds, short of money! in his father's day, my gad, sir! if there were no Jews to skin there were always those lazy, good-for-nothing peasants whose whole excuse for being alive at all was that they should provide their *seigneur* with everything he was pleased to want.

Those were the good old days. Now there was nothing but grum-bling in the villages. Bad weather, poor harvest, bad luck. *Eh, morbleu!* *Monseigneur* knew well enough that the harvests were poor. If they weren't, he wouldn't be so terribly short of money; just when Aurore's birthday was coming on, too, and the *château* was going to be full of the most distinguished visitors that he had ever assembled under one roof. He was an amiable old gentleman, this descendant of the great Connétable: he did not aspire to have five hundred men-at-arms un-der his orders, but he did expect his house to be second to none in the matter of hospitality and of splendour. And Aurore meant half the world to him. He had been married three times: the first two duch-esses had failed in their duty of presenting him with an heir, the third one turned her face to the wall and died when a tiny baby girl was first put against her breast.

Monseigneur quickly consoled himself and would no doubt have brought a fourth duchess home to grace the head of the table only that his reputation of Bluebeard had made the eligible young ladies of his own rank chary of accepting so dangerous a position. Moreover, little tiny Aurore had already entwined himself around his fickle old heart. He forswore the delights of matrimony for the more durable ones of fatherhood and devoted all the time that he could spare from the study of his own comforts to the furtherance of Aurore's enjoyment of life.

It is, perhaps, a little difficult to imagine a girl in her teens taking pleasure in games and pursuits which in these modern days would rouse the scorn of a child of seven—difficult to visualize that bright sunny day in July, 1782, when Aurore's birthday party, consisting of twenty or thirty of her friends in ages ranging from thirteen to twenty-three, spent their afternoon in playing blindman's bluff or hide-and-seek in the terraced gardens of Marigny. In and out the *bosquet* and *parterres* they darted like so many gaily plumaged birds, filling the air with their laughter and childish screams of delight, the while Monseigneur le Duc in his *boudoir* was giving M. Talon, his bailiff, a bad quarter of an hour.

"*Mort de Dieu!* you old muckworm!" was one of the many pleasant ways in which *Monseigneur* addressed the unfortunate Talon. "Have I not told you that I must have five thousand *louis* before the end of the month?"

"Yes, *Monseigneur*," Talon replied obsequiously, "but—"

"There is no 'but' about it, my man, when I said 'must'—" *Monseigneur* broke in drily.

"The tallage has all been paid—the salt tax, the window tax—"

"Call it the harvest tax or any cursed name you choose, but find me the money, or else—"

"*Monseigneur!*" protested Talon, who was quaking in his buckled shoes, knowing well enough what menace was being held over his head.

"Or else," *Monseigneur* went on slowly, emphasizing his words, "you and your precious family quit my service; I have no use for incompetent menials."

"*Monseigneur!*" Talon protested again, and with hands upraised called Heaven to witness his loyalty and his competence.

"Eh, what? There is no '*Monseigneur*' about it; and your sanctimonious airs, *mon ami*, are no use to me. I have thirty guests in the house; it is *Mademoiselle's* birthday. I have told you that before, have I not?"

"As if I could forget—"

"Very well, then. Even with your limited intelligence you must be aware that in order to entertain such distinguished persons I must have my larder and my cellars full. Well! I'm short of wine. You know that.

You know that we sent to that thief in Nevers for some, and that the mudlark refuses to send the wine unless he is paid beforehand."

"I know that, *Monseigneur*."

"You also know that I am giving *Mademoiselle* a ruby necklace for her birthday. You wrote the order out yourself."

"Yes, *Monseigneur*."

"Well, then! that also has to be paid for," *Monseigneur* concluded with what he felt was unanswerable logic. "So, do not dare to appear before me again without at least—mind! I say at least—five thousand *louis* in your filthy hand. Now you can go."

Talon's narrow hatchet face, usually sallow and bilious, took on an ashen hue. Through narrow deep-set eyes he cast a furtive glance at his irascible master. But *Monseigneur*, having delivered his ultimatum, no longer troubled his august head about his unfortunate bailiff. No doubt experience had taught him that under threat of dismissal Talon had always contrived somehow to produce the necessary money. *Monseigneur* never troubled his head much whence that money came. He had never been taught to troubled his head about anything so mean and sordid as money. He paid Talon a liberal salary, gave him a good house, productive land, and every facility to rob and cheat him, in order that this man should take all such burdens to enjoy life without care or worry. Many a time had Talon heard this philosophy propounded to him by his master: he knew that argument and protests were worse than useless, and it is to be supposed that in an emergency like the present one it was safer to incur further hatred from *Monseigneur's* tenants than the displeasure of *Monseigneur* himself.

M. le Duc for the moment appeared to have forgotten Hector Talon's very existence; he had caught sight through the wide-open window of his darling little Aurore at play with her friends. There was a grand game of blindman's bluff going on, and the sight would have gladdened any old man's heart, let alone that of a doting father. *Monseigneur's* eyes gleamed with pleasure; the misfortune of "blindman" who measured his length on the sanded path drew a delighted roar of laughter from him. Talon thought and hoped that he was momentarily forgotten and that he could achieve his exit without hearing further abuse or further threats. As noiselessly as he could he turned on his heel and made for the door. Just as he was about to slip through it *Monseigneur's* pleasant voice once more reached his ear:

"That reminds me, Talon," he said lightly, "that my cousin M. le Marquis d'Epinay had a splendid idea last year when he was short of money. There was all that stony land on Mont Oderic and Mont Socride, you remember? It was no use to him, he couldn't make anything out of it. So, he made the neighbouring communes buy it of him at his own price. I believe the rascals have done very well with it since. Well! there's that bit of land the other side of Rocher Vert. I don't want it. Let the communes of Val-le-Roi and Le Borne buy it of me. They can have it for three thousand *louis* and you can make up the other two out of the hoard which you have amassed through robbing me, you blackguard."

"The communes couldn't pay, *Monseigneur,*" Talon protested, and then added very injudiciously: "As for me, how can *Monseigneur* think-"

"That you are a thief and a liar?" *Monseigneur* broke in, with a careless laugh. "Why, you villain, if you were a decent man you would have left my service long ago. You know that I only employ you to do my dirty work, which I couldn't ask others who are clean and honest to do for me. As for the communes, what I propose is a sound bargain for them: those peasants can make a good thing out of land, which you are too big a fool to turn to account. Anyway, that's my last word, and now, get out of my sight. I am sick of you."

Talon was as thankful to go as *Monseigneur* was to be rid of him. He slipped like a stealthy cat through the door, while *Monseigneur,* throwing cares and money worries off his broad shoulders, returned to the more agreeable occupation of watched his daughter playing at blindman's bluff.

Perhaps, if he had been gifted with second sight, M. le Duc de Marigny would not have felt quite so carefree: for then he would have seen his bailiff, Hector Talon, the other side of the door, pausing for a moment with clawlike fingers resting on the handle. On his sallow face there was neither humility nor servility, only a cunning, mocking glance in the narrow, deep-set eyes and a sneer upon the pale thin lips. What went on in the man's mind it is impossible to say. Did he long to turn on the hand that fed him? Did he foresee that, on a day not very far distant, he would be the one to command and *Monseigneur* the dependent on his good-will? All unconsciously now, even good-humouredly, *Monseigneur* chose to snub and humiliate him.

There was no conscious feeling of arrogance in so great a gentleman's treatment of his subordinates; just the belief amounting to a certainty that he and his kind were made of a different clay from the rest of humanity, and that God had preordained them to rule and the others to obey. All these thoughts and hopes did, no doubt, course through Hector Talon's mind as he stood on the other side of the door with his fingers on the handle. But *Monseigneur* knew nothing of that. He was not gifted with second sight and did not see the change of expression in his bailiff's face—just as he had only given one casual and careless glance at the boy at the whipping post whom the ladies had so aptly named "the rebel angel."

Chapter 7

On this same afternoon when André Vallon, still rebellious in spirit, followed M. le Curé de Val-le-Roi up the wooded slopes that led to the *château*, the picture that was revealed to his gaze when he came in sight of the gorgeous old building, with its sumptuous gardens, its marble terraces, its towers and battlements, its stately trees and wealth of flowers, was one he never forgot. Vaguely he had heard the *château* spoken of by those who knew, as "magnificent"; vaguely he was aware that *Monseigneur* lived there in a state of splendour of which he, a village lad, had no conception, even in his dreams; and from the valley below, where on the outskirts of Val-le-Roi his mother's cottage lay *perdu*, he had often gazed upwards to the heights, where at sunset the pointed roofs glistened like silver and the rows of windows sparkled like a chain of rubies; but he had never been allowed to wander up the slope and see all that magnificence at close quarters.

Heavy gilded iron gates shut off the precincts of the *château* from prying eyes and vagabond footsteps; stern janitors warned trespassers against daring to set foot inside the park; and thus the place where dwelt those unapproachable personages, *Monseigneur* and his friends, had hitherto appeared to André like fairyland, or rather, like the ogre's castle of which he had read in the storybooks of M. Perrault—the ogre who devoured all the good things of this earth and always wanted more.

André was dazzled. The same enthusiasm that made him love the moonlight, the cottontails, or the hedgerows caused him to utter a cry of pleasure when he first caught sight of the *château*. He came to a halt and allowed his eyes to feast themselves on the picture. M. *le Curé* was delighted; he thought that the boy was showing a nice spirit of reverence and of awe.

"It is beautiful, is it not, André?" he remarked complacently.

But André's mood was not quite as serene as the worthy priest had fondly hoped. He turned sharply on his heel and retorted with a scowl:

"Of course, it is beautiful, but why should it be his?"

"What in the world do you mean?"

"You call that man up there '*Monseigneur.*' Why? This all belongs to him. Why?"

"Because..."

The good *curé* droned on. André certainly did not listen; he stalked on once more, irritable and silent. He had asked a question for which, in his own mind, there could not possibly be an answer. True that something of the bitterness of intense hatred had, as it were, flowed out of him with the tears which he had shed on his mother's breast, but the spirit of inquiry, of blind groping after mysteries which were incapable of solution had, for good or ill, replaced the childish acceptance of things as they were. To him henceforth his mother's penury and *Monseigneur's* wealth were not preordained by God; they did not form a part of the scheme of creation as God had originally decreed. They were the result of man's incapacity to grapple with injustice; the result, in fact, of the weakness of one section of humanity and of the arrogant strength of the other.

Very wisely, M. le Curé had not pursued the contentious subject. Together the two of them found their way across the wide, paved forecourt and up the perron. Lackeys in gorgeous liveries opened wide the gates of the *château*, and André, feeling now as if he were in a dream, silent, subdued, all the starch taken out of him, all the rebellion of his spirit overawed by so much splendour, kept close to the *curé's* heels.

They went through the endless rooms, across floors that were so slippery that André, in his thick shoes, nearly measured his length on them more than once. He caught sight of himself in tall mirrors, full face, sideways, walking, sliding, pausing, wide-eyed and scared, thinking that the figure he was coming towards him was some strange boy whom he had never seen before. At length the *curé* came to a halt in what seemed to André like a fairy's dwelling place, all azure and gold and crystal, where more tall mirrors reflected a somewhat corpulent old man in a long black soutane, and a tall, clumsy-looking boy in an ill-fitting coat, with tousled hair and large hands and feet encased in huge, thick buckled shoes.

On one side of the room there were three tall windows through which André saw such pictures as he had never seen before. At first, he didn't think that they were real. There were marble balustrades and pillars, *parterres* of flowers and groups of trees, and a fountain from whose sparkling waters the warm sunshine drew innumerable diamonds. This fairy garden appeared peopled with a whole bevy of brightly plumaged birds that darted in and out among the *bosquets* and the *parterres* with flutelike calls and rippling music. At least, so it seemed to André at first. *M. le Curé*, tired out, hot and panting, had sunk down in one of the gilded chairs and was mopping his streaming face; André, attracted and intrigued by the picture of that garden and those birds, ventured to go nearer to one of the tall windows in order to have a closer look. The window was wide open. André, leaning against the frame, stood quite still and watched.

A merry throng peopled the garden; ladies in light summer dresses, some with large straw hats over their powdered hair, others with fair or dark curls fluttering about their heads, men in silk embroidered coats, with dainty buckled shoes and filmy lace at throat and wrist, were chasing one another in and out of the leafy *bosquets*, just like a lot of children, playing some puerile game of blindman's bluff, which elicited many a little cry of mock alarm and silvery peals of merry laughter. How gay they seemed! How happy! André watched them, fascinated. He followed the various incidents of the game with eyes that soon lost their abstraction and sparkled with responsive delight. He nearly laughed aloud when an elegant gentleman in plum-coloured satin cloth, his eyes bandaged, tripped over a chair mischievously placed in his way by one of the ladies—a girl whose pink silk panniers over a short skirt of delicate green brocade made her look like a rosebud: so, at least, thought André.

He quite forgot himself while he stood and watched. Like a child at a show, he laughed when they laughed, gasped when capture was imminent, rejoiced when a narrow escape was successful. *M. le Curé*, overcome by the heat, had gone fast asleep in his chair.

André, absorbed in watching, did not even notice that the crowd of merrymakers had invaded the terrace immediately in front of the window against which he stood. "Blindman" now was the young girl with the fair hair, free from powder, whose dress made her look like a rosebud. With arms outstretched she groped, after the clumsy fashion peculiar to a genuine blindman, and her playmates darted around her, giving her a little push here, another there, all of them unheedful of the silent, motionless watcher by the open window. And suddenly "Blindman," still with arms outstretched, lost her bearings, tripped against the narrow window sill and wound have fallen headlong into the room had not André instinctively put out his arms. She fell, laughing, panting, and with a little cry of alarm, straight into him.

There was a sudden gasp of surprise on the part of the others, a second or two of silence, and then a loud and prolonged outburst of laughter. André held on with both arms. Never in his life had he felt anything as sweet, as fragrant, so close to him. The most delicious odour of roses and violets came to his nostrils, while the downiest, softest little curls tickled his nose and lips. As to moving, he could not have stirred a muscle had his life depended on it.

But at the prolonged laughter of her friends the girl at once began to struggle; also, she felt the rough cloth beneath her touch, while to her delicate nostrils there came, instead of the sweet perfumes that always pervaded the clothes of her friends, a scent of earth and hay and of damp cloth. She wanted to snatch away the bandage from her eyes, but strong, muscular arms were round her shoulders, and she could not move.

"Let me go!" she called out. "Let me go! Who is it? Madeleine—Edith, who is it?"

The next moment a firm step resounded on the marble floor of the terrace, a peremptory voice called out: "You young muckworm, how dare you?" and the hold round her shoulders relaxed. André received a resounding smack on the side the face, while the girl, suddenly freed, staggered slightly backward even while she snatched the handkerchief from her eyes.

The first thing she saw was a dark young face with a heavy chestnut curl falling over a frowning brow, a pair of eyes dark as aloes flashing with hatred and rage. She heard the voice of her cousin, the Comte de Mauléon, saying hoarsely:

"Get out! Get out, I say!" And then calling louder still: "Here! Léon! Henri! Some of you kick this garbage out."

It was all terrible. The ladies crowded round her and helped to put her pretty dress straight again, but the girl was too frightened to think of them or her clothes. Why she should have been frightened she didn't know, for Aurore de Marigny had never been frightened in her life before: she was a fearless little rider and a regular tomboy at climbing or getting into dangerous scrapes; but there was something in that motionless figure in the rough clothes, in those flashing eyes and hard, set mouth which puzzled the child and terrified her. Here was something that she had never met before, something that seemed to emit evil, cruelty, hatred, none of his had ever come within sight of her sheltered, happy life.

Pierre de Mauléon was obviously in a fury and kept calling for the lackeys, who, fortunately, were not within hearing, for heaven alone knew what would happen if anyone dared lay hands on that incarnation of fury. The boy—Aurore saw that he was only a boy, not much older than herself—looked now like a fierce animal making ready for a spring; he had thrust one hand into his breeches' pocket and brought out a knife—a miserable, futile kind of pocketknife, but still a knife; and his teeth—sharp and white as those of a young wolf—were drawing blood out of his full red lips.

Some of the ladies screamed; others giggled nervously. The men laughed, but no one thought of interfering. Inside the room, *M. le Curé*, roused from his slumbers, had obviously not yet made up his mind whether he was awake or dreaming.

Just then the two lackeys, Léon and Henri, came hurrying along the terrace. A catastrophe appeared imminent, for the boy had seen them; knew, probably, what it would mean to him and all these bedizened puppets if those men dared to touch him. He was seeing red; for the first time in his life he felt the desire to see a human creature's blood. With jerky movements he grasped the flimsy, gimcrack pocketknife with which he meant to defend himself to the death. He met the girl's eyes with their frightened, half-shy glance and exulted in the thought that in a few seconds, perhaps, she would see one of her lackeys lying dead at her feet.

Not even on that fatal day when he had tasted the very dregs of humiliation had his young soul been such a complete prey to rebellion and hatred. Why, oh, why had he allowed his heart to melt at sight of his mother's wretchedness? Why had he ever set foot across this cursed threshold? *Pay! Pay! Pay!* Those were once his mother's words. Pay, while these marionettes laughed and played; pay, so that their bellies might be full, their pillows downy, their hair powdered and perfumed. He hated them all. Oh, how he hated them!

These riotous thoughts were tumbling about in André's brain, chasing one another with lightning speed while he was contemplating murder and hurling defiant glances at the pretty child, the cause of this new—this terrible catastrophe.

Ever afterwards he was ready to swear that not by a quiver of an eyelid had he betrayed fear or asked for protection. Asked? Heavens above! He would sooner have fallen dead across this window sill than have asked help from any of these gaudy nincompoops.

Be that as it may, there is no doubt that it was the girl's piping, childish voice which broke the uncomfortable spell that had fallen over the entire lively throng.

"*Ohé!*" she cried, with a ripple of laughter. "How solemn you all look! Pierre, it is your turn. Come, Véronique, you hold him while I do the blindfolding; don't let him go—it is his turn."

Her friend to whom she called was close by and ready enough to resume the game. Before Pierre de Mauléon had the chance to resist she had him by the hand, while Aurore tied the handkerchief over his eyes. A scream of delight went up all round. All seriousness, puzzlement, was forgotten. Pierre tried to snatch the handkerchief away, but two of them held onto his hands; the others pushed and pinched and teased. They dragged him along the terrace; they vaulted over the marble balusters; they were children, in fact, once more, tomboys, madcaps, running about among the *bosquets* and the flowers, irresponsible and irrepressed, while André, without another word, another look, turned on his heel and fled out of this cursed *château*, leaving *M. le Curé* to call and to gasp and to explain to *Monseigneur*, as best he could, what, in point of fact, had actually happened.

Chapter 8

There are several biographies extant of André Vallon, some written by friends, others by enemies. No man who has played a *rôle* on the world stage has ever been without his detractors, and only a few have been without their apologists. To have really complete conception of Vallon's temperament, character, and subsequent conduct, it would be necessary to know something of his life during the ten years that followed.

He was little more than fifteen when he left his village of Val-le-Roi and went up to Paris under the aegis of M. l'Abbé de Rosemonde, who had obtained for him, after much tribulation, countless petitions, and untiring zeal, a scholarship in the College of the Oratorians in Paris, where a few years before this a young scholar named Georges Danton had pegged away at the classics, and where many young minds began nursing those thoughts of rebellion and agitation which were to render them famous or infamous in the annals of the greatest revolution of all time.

Some of these men, at the time that André Vallon went to the Oratorians, were already prominent in the public eye. Danton at this date was *Conseiller du Roi*, was calling himself Maître d'Anton and had a fine practice and a pretty young wife. Maximilien de Robespierre had finished his studies at the Collège Louis-le-Grand and was now a leading light of advocacy; and Camille Desmoulins was a notorious journalist. André, who had developed a hitherto latent ambition, and with such examples before him of success won by hard work, became as model a scholar as he had been a turbulent village lad. That it took all *M. le Curé's* eloquence and floods of his mother's tears to persuade him to go to college at all goes without saying, but he did go in the end.

How much it cost his mother to keep him in decent clothes while he was at college remained forever a secret within her ample bosom. As André grew to be a man he made a pretty shrewd guess at the hardships which she must have endured in order to put by a few *louis* every year so that he should not cut too sorry a figure among his schoolfellows. Luckily for him, he never felt any sense of humiliation at his own shabby clothes or want of money to spend. He was so firmly persuaded that his mother's poverty and his own empty pockets were only transitory states which would be remedied by himself when he was a man. And then, again, some of those whose names at this hour were on everybody's lips had been as poor as himself. Camille Desmoulins never had a *sou* from his avaricious father to spend on leisure or finery, and Robespierre's clothes were invariably threadbare.

Moreover, as the years went on, poverty became so much a matter of course, except in the case of a privileged or a dishonest few, that it ceased to have any significance. It was a matter of caste, that was all, and became such an accepted fact that for a family man not to be hungry, to have fuel on his hearth or shoes on his feet was to be something of an alien among his own class. Nor was it shame that stirred André's young blood to boiling when he saw his mother in her old age, still scrubbing floors or toiling up to the *château* to do the family washing; it was only passionate rage at his own impotence to drag her out of her penury, and ever growing better resentment at a social system which permitted the few to have all the good things of this world and allowed the many to go under for want of sufficient nourishment. That this resentment should lead a young mind to wholesale condemnation of the present *régime* was only natural, seeing that the king was an autocratic monarch, and that his word, and his word alone, made and unmade the laws.

In 1788 André Vallon was called to the bar and delivered, as was customary, his diploma speech in Latin. The subject set for the year was the social and political condition of the country and its relation to the administration of justice. A ponderous subject for a village lad to tackle, but even Vallon's detractors—and he already had a few—were ready to admit that he acquitted himself adequately, and that his Latin was faultless. The grave and reverend *seigneurs* of the law, on the other hand, sat up in amazement and rubbed their lack-lustre eyes when they heard this young advocate from the back of the provincial beyond spout grandiloquent phrases, such as Salus *populi suprema lex esto*, and with wide gestures of delicately modelled hands strike a note of warning to those in high places—to all who had inherited power, influence, or riches.

"*Qui habet aures auriendi*," he thundered. "*Audiat.*"

There could be no two opinions about it: it was an incendiary speech, even though there were no actual words in it that could be construed into excitation to reprisals or insurrection. On the contrary, it even concluded with a passionate appeal to those who had the ear of the malcontents to pause before they led the people blindly along the paths that led to revolution.

"Woe to him," he fulminated in conclusion, "who for his own advancement plays on the passions and the prejudices of the people. Woe to the instigator and the maker of revolutions!"

Thus, ended his impassioned harangue, delivered in the language of Ovid and Virgil, leaving his learned audience marvelling at this young Cicero sprung out of a remote village, and gravely shaking their heads at the unorthodox sentiments to which they had been compelled to listen.

A week later André was at home, telling his mother all about it, courting her approval more ardently than he had done that of the leading lights at the Paris bar. There was something in Marianne Vallon's calm philosophy, in her acceptance of the inevitable, which by its very contrast appealed to André's rebellious spirit.

"You help me to keep my balance, Mother," he would say with all youth's impatience, when she talked as she often used to do in the past, of resignation and humility. "And God knows we shall all of us want it presently," he added, with a careless shrug and a laugh.

He went through all the fatigue of translating his Latin speech into French for her, so that she might understand and criticise. But he was quite proud of his achievement; he knew that he had left his mark on the somewhat somnolent brains of his fellow advocates.

"Maître d'Anton was present, Mother," he related, bridling up at the recollection of that proud moment when he saw the popular orator make his way into the hall. "I think he liked my speech, for I saw him nod with approval once or twice, and at the end he clapped his hands together, and I heard his stentorian voice shouting, 'Good! Very good indeed!'"

"A selfish and a cruel man," Marianne muttered under her breath.

"How can you say that, Mother *chérie?*" André protested. "He is a model husband and a devoted father."

"He was born lucky. Wait till misfortune overtakes him–"

"I hope it won't," André broke in gaily, "for he has offered me a clerkship in his office."

"Don't take it, André!" Marianne cried involuntarily.

"Why in the world no, Mother? It will be the making of me. Clerk to Maître d'Anton, *Conseiller du Roi!* Think of it!"

Marianne shrugged: "*Conseiller du Roi?*" she said with what would have been a sneer round a mouth less kindly. "That man, Danton, *Conseiller du Roi?* When he dreams of nothing but deposing his king—if not worse."

"He dreams of changing the whole aspect of the world," André protested with unwonted earnestness, "and God knows this old world wants a change."

Old Marianne shook her head. She was too old to imbibe all those principles which men with fine oratorical powers like Georges Danton poured daily into the ears of the young; too old also to hope for a change in the system which had brought her to her present state of indigence. In Danton's ways she foresaw disaster. "Once you set an avalanche sliding down the mountain side," she would say, "you cannot possibly stop its mad career. You are bound to be crushed beneath it in the end."

But André would retort proudly: "A man like Danton does not count the cost. He says and does what he believes to be right, and if he cannot carry his principles though, he will die like a martyr."

"And drag all those whom he has fooled to perdition with him."

"What grander death than that of a martyr?" André demanded, flushed with enthusiasm.

But Marianne, wise old peasant that she was, muttered: "Martyr? And for what cause, *mon Dieu?* For what?"

"The happiness of mankind!"

And so, the boy would argue. He was only a boy still, after all, in spite of his Latin, and hero worship was in his blood. He became a clerk to Maître d'Anton, *Conseiller du Roi*, one of the greatest lights at the moment of Paris advocacy: a man, too, wholly unspoilt by success and prosperity. He had a way of persuading all those who knew in him intimately that his was a large, all-embracing nature, which only pined to see everyone around him smiling and happy.

He had a fine property in the country, a well furnished house in town, a pretty wife and a boy whom he worshipped. Danton was at this time the most popular man in France, and André one of the happiest, for he felt that he had his chance, a chance coveted by every budding advocate who had delivered his Latin thesis that year. He walked hand in hand with the man who was called the Lion Tamer of France, for he held the savage pack of snarling felines on the leash. Marat, Desmoulins, and the others bowed to his moderate, sensible views.

"Wait," Marianne had said, "till misfortune overtakes him."

It did. Soon after André entered his office his only child died, the boy whom he adored. His wife was broken hearted; sought consolation in religion. Georges Danton, who worshipped her, would escort her daily to church, then rush round to the club and, in a hoarse voice, broken with sobs, would prophesy now the coming cataclysm. Shrewd, fat Marianne had proved indeed to be right.

In the wake of misfortune, Danton's moderation went to the wind, and during the most impressionable years of his life André's ears were constantly filled with his chief's ever more violent diatribes against the social regime, the ignorance and ineptitude of the king, and the venality of his ministers.

"They have eyes and see not; ears they have and hear not," Danton would thunder forth whenever news of riots in the provincial towns, already of frequent occurrence, looting of shops, firing of *châteaux*, were brought to his office. "Fools they are! all of them fools! Can't they see that their whole world is falling to dust about their feet, and that soon the rivers of France will be running with blood?"

André, whose young soul had always been inclined towards rebellion, would listen wide-eyed, trying with all his might to disentangle the right from the wrong in those tempestuous tirades. Danton was a man of immense influence. In the clubs his power was supreme, and it was the clubs that governed France these days; for it was in the clubs that ministers were made and unmade. Men of all ages, men of wide experience, bowed to Danton as to their greatest leader. And André Vallon was little more than a boy, with a boy's enthusiasm and generous impulses, and young blood ready to boil at sight of injustice and cruelty.

"Get me out an article for *l'Ami du Peuple*, André," Danton would often say to him when he came home, hoarse and tired from a noisy *séance* at the Cordeliers. "Revolution is in the air; it gathers strength. At Versailles the king fashions padlocks and the queen plays at hide-and-seek. The people starve. Make no mistake: at this moment thousands of men are seeing their wives and children dying of hunger. Write it, André. Write it. Dip your pen in gall. Marat will print anything you write. For God's sake, don't mince matters! Up at Versailles they must be made to see, or the most awful cataclysm the world has ever known will drench this country with blood."

After which outburst he would go home to his young wife and with his ardent love-making help her and himself to forget their own grief and the misfortune of their country. But André would go back to his own dingy lodgings and try to put into words the turbulent thoughts of his chief. And whenever his mother shook her wise old head over these youthful lucubrations, he would excuse the more passionate passages by saying:

"It is impossible to stem the fury of the people now, Mother dear. All we can do is to lead it into as reasonable channels as we can."

"Your Danton tries to cure evil with worse evils, my child," Marianne retorted. "How can good come from evil? Take care, André! Men like Danton have set their world rocking; when it falls together with a crash it will drag them along, too, into the abyss."

"They must take their chance, Mother," André rejoined with an impatient sigh. "We must all take our chances, for we cannot foresee what the end of it all will be."

But it was not often that he was in such a serious mood. Whenever he could obtain leave he would take the diligence to Nevers, and thence the country chaise to Val-le-Roi. He would burst in on his mother with the gentleness of an exploding bombshell, and thereafter for a few days, not only the cottage, but the country inns around, the lanes, the woods, the village streets would echo with his laughter and his big, sonorous voice.

Chapter 9

The worst of the great political storm had not yet touched the outlying villages. The people, of course, were desperately poor, for the year had been one of the hardest the unfortunate country had ever known; a prolonged drought had been followed by terrible hailstorms on the very eve of harvesting; the price of corn was prohibitive, and the winter that ensued was so severe that even forest trees suffered from the frost. Poor? Of course, they were poor! There was no such thing as a plump girl to be seen in any village: children were emaciated, their growth stunted, their future health hopelessly impaired. But life had to go on just the same. There was marriage and giving away in marriage; babies were born and old people died; and those that were not old clung to life in spite of the fact that it promised nothing but misery.

André Vallon's visits to Val-le-Roi were always something of holiday for all. He was so gay, so light-hearted. The news which he brought from Paris always seemed reassuring.

He would meet his friends around the bare tables of the village inn where, over sips of thin, sour wine, he would try to put heart into the men.

"It can't last, can it, André?" they would ask.

"Of course, it can't. The darkest hour always comes before the dawn. There are some good times head for all of us. You'll see."

Then he would call to Suzette, mine host's pretty daughter, and sit her on his knee.

"Come, Suzette," he would say gaily, "help us to talk of something cheerful: of your pretty self, for instance, and of Jerome, whom you met last night in the lane. You did—don't tell me you did not—Give us a kiss, no, this instant, or I'll tell your worthy papa just what I saw in the lane last night."

And in the sunshine of his irrepressible gaiety some of them would momentarily forget their troubles.

"There goes that madcap, André Vallon," the older people would say when he went down the village street, singing at the top of his voice; "he was always a good lad, but his skin is too tight to hold him."

And they would tell each other tales of André's misdeeds when he was a boy, and of the worry which he had been to his mother: not a lad in the village whom he had not licked at some time or another, not a girl from whom he had not snatched a kiss. Twice he had been within an ace of being drowned; three times he had nearly smashed himself to pieces by falling from a tree or a rocky height; once he had tackled farmer Lombard's bull which was after him, and with just his two hands he had squeezed the life out of Bailiff Talon's savage dog.

"Such a beautiful boy, he was," the women said.

255

And the girls giggled as he went by, for those great dark eyes of his would look them up and down with disturbing, provoking glances. And some of them would pause and return the glance with a look which was more than a hint, but André would only smile, showing a gleam of white teeth. But ne'er a look of tenderness did he cast in response, nor did the faintest whisper of love ever cross his lips.

Love-making? Yes! Any amount of it. André's young arms were forever reaching out for white shoulders or a slim waist; his full laughter-loving mouth was always ready for a kiss, but it remained at that: there was no girl for leagues around who could boast that she had meant more to André Vallon than the old mother whom he worshipped.

But the old mother knew—or rather guessed—that there was always something behind her son's flippancy in the manner of women and of love. She didn't know what it was, but there was no deceiving her—there was something. And there came a time when she made a pretty shrewd guess. She asked no questions, of course, but whenever the subject of the Château de Marigny and its inmates cropped up, a strange reserve seemed to tie the boy's tongue. He would become moody and silent, and if Marianne then pursued the subject, spoke of the hardships so bravely borne by *Monseigneur*, or said something of Mademoiselle Aurore and her angelic patience in all her misfortunes, André would suddenly jump to his feet and cry out with extraordinary vehemence:

"Don't talk to me about those people, Mother. I hate them!"

Chapter 10

But the time soon came, even in these remote villages, when agitator and demagogues would rub their hands with glee. They would stretch out their legs in front of their own hearths and declare complacently that the revolution which they had foretold had not only come but come to stay. Distress had become general; with it stalked resentment and a fury of reprisals.

In the provincial towns bread riots were of constant occurrence; the starving people had taken to looting granaries and stores; in several cases shops, house, *châteaux* had been fired. Tub thumpers were shouting daily to willing ears the deadly slogan: "Liberty and Equality."

Paris was full of men and women who had wandered to the capital from the neighbouring towns and villages, armed with scythes and other agricultural implements which had become useless, since there were no crops to harvest; starving, wrathful, and determined, they paraded the streets shouting for redress. At street corners, in the clubs, in public bars, malcontents waved their arms and spouted magnificent phrases about Liberty and the sovereignty of the people. Danton thundered forth his call to arms, to bloodshed and revenge.

Misery had sown discontent and reaped revolution. Less than a year later butchery had begun.

In September, '92, a brutish crowd, armed with pikes, scythes, old blunderbusses, and rifles, rushed through the streets of Paris, stormed the houses of detention that were overcrowded with unfortunate prisoners, and in cold blood massacred hundreds of men, women, and children, while Danton, the darling of the crowd, the all-powerful party leader, did not raise a hand to stop the carnage.

André Vallon, long before then, had given up his profession in order to join the army. France was besieged on every side: the whole of Europe had taken up arms against her, outraged at the excesses of this revolution which aimed at regicide and achieved wholesale butchery. The onus of carrying on a world war now rested upon the shoulders of men with no experience of organisation or government. The responsibilities which hitherto had devolved solely upon the king and his ministers were theirs now; and they were already finding out that to depose the king, to wrest from him the control of civil and military administration, was quite one thing, but to defend the country against the foreign invader, with troops whom they themselves had taught to mutiny, was quite another. To rouse the people to insurrection had not been difficult, famine and misery had helped in the task; but to feed a whole nation and, at the same time, to raise an army strong enough to fight both Austria and Prussia, was not quite so easy.

Already these new masters of France hated and despised one another. Five out of the six ministers who formed the Executive were timid and vacillating. Danton alone dominated them. He, too, was ignorant of the essentials that make up a stable government, but at any rate was a man—a lion amid a flock of sheep.

His impassioned oratory, his powerful voice, his immense patriotism, helped to raise an army of recruits, to send them to the frontiers, insufficiently armed, insufficiently clothed, empty bellied and undisciplined, but full of enthusiasm for *la patrie* in danger. There is nothing in the world that quite comes up to the love of a Frenchman for his country. France is a beautiful country; every corner of it is beautiful, and its sons love it with a love that in a way transcends the patriotism of every other nation. *La patrie* is a word that cannot be rendered in

257

any other language—it is not a question of home, of family, of race! it is just France! And there are few pages in the world's history so pathetic and yet so magnificent as this epic of raw, untrained, famished recruits, dragging their shoeless feet along the muddy woods of Champagne, on whose sacred soil the King of Prussia was advancing with his well-trained, highly equipped army, and, with the sheer enthusiasm of love for their country and determination to defend her against foreign invasion, keeping the whole of Europe at bay.

At home now there remained, in addition to the women and children, only the halt and the maimed, a few youngsters too *débile* to bear arms, the only sons of widowed mothers, who were exempt from military service, and the fathers of growing families. Quite a crowd, nevertheless, and one that, in the opinion of the Executive up in Paris, must be made to bear its part in furthering the glorious Revolution.

Inflammatory placards were posted up at every street corner and every crossroad, proclaiming the sovereignty of the people and headed by Danton's declaration: "We must govern by fear."

Terror had become the order of the day. Men and women—peaceable and respectable citizens—went in fear of their lives. Every crime had become permissible; every act of violence was considered patriotic; every outrage was not only condoned but commended; so long as they were directed against those who, through their selfish enjoyment of life, their riches, their contentment and luxury, had proved themselves traitors to their country and enemies of the people.

And men in three-cornered hats and cloth coast ornamented with brass buttons, potbellied and bleary eyed, were sent round the provincial towns on a tour of active propaganda. Hoisted on tables outside the taverns they harangue the famished crowds, denouncing the traitors that caused all the sufferings of the people, and foretelling an era of plenty, which certainly would soon come if only France were swept clean of king and aristocrats.

At first the crowds listened in sullen silence, and in some places, it took the rogues some time to work the people up to a state of effervescence. They were all so poor and so hungry that in most cases all they wanted to do was to sit still and brood over their wrongs. But the demagogues were no fools; they knew their business. It was not inertia they wanted, or acceptance of penury. They were out to make trouble and to stir up strife. Within half an hour they had hurled sufficient invectives against the owner of the nearest *château*—his hoard of wheat and fuel, his cellar full of good wines—to work up the lethargic blood of these ignorant folk into a state of frenzy. The poisonous suggestion of reprisals began to filter down into receptive brains, and men who saw their wives and children dying for want of food began lending a more attentive ear to these prophecies of a panacea for all their ills.

"Liberty!" and "The sovereign will of the people!" The great slogans, thundered at them day after day, began to make an appeal to their empty stomachs and frozen limbs. If liberty meant taking what you want, eating your fill, and drinking good wine; if it meant covering your wife's emaciated shoulders with a warm shawl and putting shoes on your children's feet, then liberty by all means!

In the villages the tavern orators were for the most part local malcontents or ambitious rascals who had nothing to lose and everything to gain by a complete upheaval of the social system. Subsides for carrying on the propaganda came from the clubs in Paris. It was a paying game, carried on in one village by a defaulting clerk, in another by a dishonest servant or perhaps it would be an absconding lawyer, or even an unfrocked priest.

At Val-le-Roi it was Hector Talon.

Talon was still nominally steward to Monseigneur le Duc de Marigny, but the place had become a sinecure. The estates had become so impoverished that they were no longer worth administering. Talon knew well enough that the days of Marigny in its present condition were numbered. Either the owner would emigrate—as so many of his kind had done, in which case the whole of the property would be confiscated—or he would be arrested on some pretext or other and sent to the guillotine. And it was quite a usual thing for faithful servants to share the fate of their masters.

Now, Talon was quite determined not to share any untoward fate with his employer or with anyone else. He wanted to be on the right side. Not only now, but in the future.

Indeed, Hector Talon was no fool. He knew as well as anybody that the present state of affairs could not possibly last; that presently—in three, four, or even ten years, perhaps—tempers would quieten down, and when all these assassins who were now in power had butchered one another, an era of moderation would then assert itself. And—who knows?—it was just possible that the reaction would be so great that the political pendulum would swing right over to the old regime.

Fortunately for him, Talon was an adept as dual *rôles. Monseigneur*— or *ci-devant* Marigny, as he was contemptuously designated by his former sycophants—lived a solitary life up at the *château*, like an eagle in its eerie, with only his daughter for company and a couple of his old servants to wait on him. Talon was, as it were, the only link between him and the seething world down below. It was easy enough to throw dust in his eyes and to persuade him that the interests of respectable citizens, be they bailiffs or ex-dukes were identical. There certainly was the Curé of Val-le-Roi, the Abbé de Rosemonde, who had kept up friendship with De Marigny and who might have enlightened him as to the real worth of Hector Talon; but the old priest was one of those entirely childlike natures which never see anything that is not thrust under their very noses, who never seem to know anything of what goes on around them, and whom it is the easiest thing in the world to hoodwink.

Talon, therefore, had a clear field up at the *château* for his *rôle* of faithful administrator entirely devoted to his employer's interests. But in the village taverns, surrounded by all the malcontents of the countryside, adulated and puffed up with his own importance, he gave lip service to Danton and Marat, spouted insults at every man or women who had ever owned a hectare of land, and spat out the venom of malice and envy which was the accumulation of years.

Of a truth, he was on the safe side. During the past lean years his corpulence had melted away; he was thin now and more bandy-legged than ever, with wide, bony shoulders and hollow belly. His head rolled about on his long, lean neck, crowned with a stubble of short, tawny, ill brushed hair; his lips were thin and his mouth awry; his chin was pointed, and his hollow cheeks were darkened with the bristles of an unshaven beard. And under overhanging brows his eyes, which had a yellow tinge in them, were always veiled by heavy, blue-veined lids. Unlike the regular army of tub thumpers, he affected the meanest and dirtiest of clothes, a ragged shirt which had not seen the washtub for months, breeches that hardly covered his lean thighs; his shanks were bare, and his feet were thrust in sabots stuffed with straw.

But he had a powerful voice and a good delivery and an easy choice of words. For the most part he drew his inspiration for his most inflammatory speeches from articles which he picked out of various Paris journals.

"Liberty! The time has come, citizens, not only to talk of liberty, but to fight in her sacred cause!" his was one of his favourite tirades. And then he would go on: "Let us take up arms like our brave soldiers on the frontier and engage in a hand-to-hand struggle against tyranny, against all those vampires who suck our blood and strive to break our will. France needs you, citizens, every one of you; she needs your help to gain that freedom for which she pines; she needs all your strength, all your courage. She needs the patriotism of self-sacrifice. To arms, citizens, to arms! Think no longer of yourselves or of your wives or children! Think only of liberty. And if in your heart you should reckon the cost of your lives, then remember that there are forty-thousand palaces, *châteaux*, and abodes of the rich, half the wealth of France, that will become yours in payment for your valour and for your loyalty."

And after he had delivered himself of this oratory he would go home, put on a cloth coat and breeches, woollen stockings and buckled shoes, and make his way up to the *château*, and fill *Monseigneur's* ears with protestations of his loyalty.

His wife sometimes gave him a word of warning.

"If the old crow should hear of your oratory..." she would say.

"He wouldn't believe anything against me," Talon retorted with a complacent snigger.

"Rumours do travel," Lucile insisted. "I heard in the village, for instances, that it was you who egged that crowd on last night to set fire to the mill and the granaries."

Talon nodded. "Quite true," he said drily. "I did."

"What was the good? The granaries were empty, and they'll want to burn the *château* down next."

"I hope they do."

"What? Set fire to the *château*?"

"No. Only threaten to."

Lucile Talon was silent for a moment or two. By the feeble light of a flickering tallow candle she could only partly see the expression on her husband's face. It was not pretty at this moment, and Lucile gave a slight shudder as she turned away and busied herself for a time with her household affairs. But presently she came back into the parlour and sat down at the table opposite her husband.

"You have a plan in your head, Hector," she said decisively. "What is it?"

Then, as he made no reply, only stared and stared into the flickering flame, she added: "You won't tell me?"

"It is too vague at present," he replied at last, "for you to understand."

And Lucile saw the yellow gleam in his eyes, shining like the light in the eyes of a cat.

Chapter 11

It was eleven years almost to a day since M. l'Abbé de Rose-monde, Curé de Val-le-Roi, had toiled up the slope to the Château de Marigny with his young *protégé*, André Vallon. Then, as now, a hot July sun flooded the pointed roofs with silvery lights. Only a few white fleecy clouds flitted across the cobalt sky. The birds sang in the forest trees; the branches of walnut and sycamore quivered under the breath of a gentle summer breeze. In the valley below, the Allier gurgled softly among the reeds, and the weeping willows along its banks set forth their sweet, sad sighing through the noonday air.

Nature, lovely and impersonal, seemed by her serene beauty to mock at all the turmoil, the hideousness created by men. "Look at me," she seemed to say. "My laws are immutable. I destroy nothing without cause. Death in my infinite wisdom is only the maker of life."

M. le *Curé* looked about him and sighed. He could almost have wished that God's world would cease to be beautiful since men no longer had eyes to see the glory of His creations. He was an old man now. These last few years had put a heavy burden upon him. Torn between his hatred of the present godless regime and his desire to do what little good he could among these poor misguided folk to whom he had ministered for more than thirty years, he had at last decided to take the oath of allegiance to this impious government which he abhorred, simply because he did not wish to leave Val-le-Roi to its fate. In spite of threats, in spite of persecution, he had managed so far to keep his church open, to hold occasional services, to visit the sick, and to administer the sacraments.

On this beautiful morning in mid-July when he came in sight of the *château*, he experienced the same heartache which assailed him every time he noted the slow but sure ravages of neglect upon the magnificent pile. It was many years now since flowers had graced the parterres of the garden and thrown their gay note of brilliance against the subdued colouring of the age-old stonework. The *bosquet* now were withered; the fountains still; marble balustrades and terraces were covered with the soil and litter of years.

The *abbé* sighed again and wearily made his way up the perron. The monumental gates opened at a touch; the cracked bell which he pulled echoed weirdly through the silent halls. There were no servants in gorgeous liveries now to wait on visitors; no sound of gaiety or laughter came reverberating through this silence, which seemed as solemn as that of a tomb. The old priest crossed the vast hall and made his way up the great marble staircase and through the length of the gorgeous apartments, which stretched *en enfilade* to the farthest angle of the *château*. Here he came to a halt and knocked at the door that faced him. A woman's voice called, "*Entrez!*" and he stepped into the room.

At sight of him a young girl jumped up from the low stool whereon she had been sitting, threw down a book, and came to greet him with hands outstretched.

"*M. l'Abbé!*" she cried. "How kind of you to come, and in this heat, too! Do sit down. You must be tired. Papa and I were just saying that perhaps you would not come till later in the day."

The good *curé* took the two soft white hands that were so eagerly tendered him and then turned to pay his respects to *Monseigneur*. Like the *curé* himself, Monseigneur le Duc de Marigny had in the past few years become a very old man. Misfortune and anxiety had put a quarter of a century onto his years. Like so many men of his generation and caste, he had made a splendid effort to bear with outward fortitude the terrible calamities that well-nigh overwhelmed him, but obviously the fortitude had only been on the surface. Every line on his face showed that he had suffered and was suffering terribly. He had the appearance of a martyr, conscious of his martyrdom. He had seen his friends, his relatives, one by one, either driven to exile or to death, and calmly awaited the hour when he would be called to share their fate. Were it not for his daughter he would have welcomed that hour, nay! even have gone forward boldly to meet it.

But there was Aurore, his child, the darling of his shrivelled heart. Because of her he was willing to shelter beneath the protection which his near relationship with that infamous Duc d'Orléans, who had cast his vote in favour of the death sentence on his cousin and king, had so far given him. Because of his cousinship with that man he had escaped persecution at the hands of the Committee of Public Safety: his name had not as yet appeared on the list of the "suspect." He accepted this slur upon it for Aurore's sake, but had suffered agonies of humiliation for this immunity. In his eyes today, dimmed not so much with age as with unshed tears, there smouldered the fire of bitter resentment. Not even to his daughter, not even to the kindly priest, his one remaining friend, did he open out his innermost thoughts, his desperate longing for revenge.

On this occasion, as indeed always, he greeted the *curé* with the greatest friendliness. Cut off from all his friends and all his kindred, the

Abbé de Rosemonde seemed like a last link with the happy past. They had become like two old cronies, these two, not talking much to each other, because there were so few pleasant things to talk about, but they often had friendly bouts at chess or piquet, and instinctively the old duke felt the soothing influence of his friend's Christian philosophy.

Aurore had put a chair in a convenient position, and the *abbé* fell into it, panting and blowing, for the day was hot and the climb up the hill steep.

"I wish I could offer you a glass of wine," *Monseigneur* said with a fretful little sigh, "but I have not a bottle left in the cellar."

Aurore poured out a glass of water for the old priest, who drank it eagerly, and then set to with great energy to mop his streaming face and neck.

"The best wine in the world, *Monseigneur*," he said cheerfully, "is this fresh water from the well. I am not tired, I assure you, my dear little Aurore, and even if I were, your smile would comfort me more thoroughly than the finest bottle of Burgundy."

Monseigneur gave a significant grunt and turned his head away.

"Well!" the priest went on after a moment or two. "What news?"

"The very best," Aurore de Marigny said eagerly. "I found the box I told you about, and, oh! M. *l'Abbé,* it is full, full of lovely things—stockings and shirts and petticoats. They will be so useful for many of the poor mothers this winter."

She chattered away in great excitement, her eyes sparkling and her cheeks flushed.

"And they won't as much as say 'Thank you!' for them," *Monseigneur* put in drily.

"Oh, yes, they will!" the girl asserted. "And even if they don't—"

She gave a little shrug. What cared she if she got thanks or no, so long as she could find something to do, something in which to interest herself, to make time slip by a little more swiftly? The days were so long and so dreary! Nothing to do, nothing to think of or to hope for, save to bring now and again the ghost of a smile on Papa's face. To help M. *l'Abbé* in his charitable work was a perfect godsend, now that she saw her youth slipping by before she had begun to understand the true and inner meaning of such things as happiness and love. She was barely nineteen when her world began to crash about her feet, when she first came face to face with ill-will, malevolence, even hatred. Until that hour the world had been one great thing of beauty. Loveliness was the very essence of her young life. She inhaled love and adulation with every breath she drew. When she took her walks abroad people got out of her way to allow her to pass. Glances of admiration accompanied her all the way she went. Gentle expressions of respect, often a murmured blessing, were the words that most often rang in her ears.

Then suddenly came the crash: an awful cataclysm seemed to sweep the whole of her past into an immeasurable abyss. Glowering looks, sullen glances, objurgations, even insults were cast at her, until she no longer dared to set foot beyond the precincts of the castle. One by one the servants, who she thought loved her, who had seen her grow up from babyhood, fled from the *château* as from a plague-ridden spot. And slowly her childlike mind began to unfold: it had been closed hitherto to outward things as is a flower bud sheltered beneath a canopy of leaves. But soon her quick intelligence grasped the true significance of what was going on around her, and the Abbé de Rosemonde, with the utmost gentleness and care, helped in the development of her understanding.

Aurore de Marigny never took a gloomy view of life. She accepted a great deal which was rousing her father's bitter resentment as inevitable; as she was very young, she never gave up hope. These years of indigence and anxiety were only transitory: of this she was sure. But while she did her best to infuse some of that hope into her father's soul, she would in the loneliness of her little bedroom shed many a bitter tear over her lost youth. Better times might come presently—they certainly would come, she knew they would—but she would be old by then; her beauty would be gone along with her youth; she would no longer be desirable; she would never learn the great lesson of life, the lesson of Love.

Chapter 12

Aurore had dragged the good old *curé* along interminable corridors, and up interminable stairs to a distant attic, where, beneath the old oak beams, covered with dust and cobwebs, and ancient black leather trunk stood open, with most of its contents already scattered about the floor.

Aurore went through them methodically, and M. le Curé nodded approval, or the reverse, as she held up the garments one by one to the dim light.

"These stockings are strong," she said. "They'll do for Legendre's children. This shawl we'll give to Marianne Vallon; she has nothing of the sort, poor thing. These silks are not much use, but what do you think of these cloth breeches? They are just the right size for Chabot's boy. Oh! and do look, *M. l'Abbé*, here is a beautiful travelling coat, warm and thick. You'll have to think of someone for whom it would be really useful."

She was squatting back on her heels, turning a great heavy cloth coat over and over.

"It is rather moth-eaten in places," she said ruefully, "but that wouldn't matter much. I believe it was Papa's travelling coat when he and *Maman* used to post in Paris—"

She paused with the coat in her delicate hands and looked up at the priest with a troubled expression in her eyes.

"*M. l'Abbé*," she said abruptly, "do you think it would be possible to warn Papa against that awful Talon?"

The *curé* looked astonished, not to say shocked.

"My dear child!" he exclaimed. "An old and faithful servant!"

"He is not," Aurore said decisively. "I am sure he is not. He is a hypocrite—he talks softly to Papa-"

"My little Aurore, you must not say those things. Where is your Christian charity? What has poor Hector Talon done?"

"He incites the people down in the village against us."

"But what makes you say such a thing? You really haven't the right-"

"*M. l'Abbé*, listen to me," Aurore rejoined firmly. "You know Marianne Vallon down in the village?"

"I do. A good woman and—"

"She is a good woman, I daresay, though she seems to hate us."

"No, no, my dear child. You must not jump to conclusions like that. Marianne is a very unhappy woman. Her only son, whom she adored, went to the war a year ago and has not been heard of since. She feels rather bitter about everything. But hatred? No! no!"

"Well, that is as it may be," Aurore rejoined with some impatience; "but she said something yesterday which has confirmed my opinion about Talon. I suspected him long ago, but since yesterday..."

"Well? And what did Marianne say?"

"That it was Talon who egged on those people to fire the mill and the granaries."

The *curé* raised his hands in protest.

"Oh!" he exclaimed. "I cannot believe that."

"Then you think that Marianne Vallon deliberately told me a lie?"

The old priest felt cornered. His brain, which was not over-brilliant, though intensely kindly, had to make a choice between calling a man a traitor or a woman a liar. He shrank from either conclusion; he hummed and hawed and did his best to avoid Aurore's searching eyes. In the end he compromised.

"Talon," he said, "may have said something that those poor people misunderstood. And there is no doubt, alas! that, with their minds turned away from God, the devil has a great hold over their souls. But I am sure," he added hopefully, "that they have already regretted their action of the other night."

"Only because they found the granaries empty," Aurore concluded with a shrug.

What was the use of arguing? This incorrigible optimist was as surely courting disaster as was her father with his bitter resentment. She gave an impatient little sigh and returned to the more pleasing subject of stockings and petticoats.

Chapter 13

Indeed, Aurore de Marigny's anxiety would have turned to real alarm could she have guessed Talon's purpose in coming up to the *château* today.

He made his way quite unceremoniously to the small *boudoir* where *Monseigneur* usually sat, entered without knocking and with all the assurance of a privileged guest, rather than of a servant. Charles de Marigny always writhed at this show of independence on the part of his once obsequious bailiff. In spite of his outward stoicism, he had not yet become accustomed to those principles of equality which placed the caitiff on a level with the *seigneur*. Every time that Talon came into his presence with the swaggering air of an equal, and the suggestion of sympathy and protection more galling than enmity, *Monseigneur* would grind his teeth and clench his hands in an effort not to strike the insolent varlet. But he had enough sense to realise that, as far as the future was concerned, his safety, and perhaps his life and that of Aurore were dependent on this man's goodwill: so, he swallowed his wrath and returned Talon's casual greeting with as much heartiness as he could.

With scant ceremony the bailiff took the chair lately occupied by the *abbé*, poured himself out a glass of water, drank it down, and remarked with an attempt at jocularity:

"No more Burgundy in the cellar, eh? Well! never mind, better times will be coming soon."

Then he talked about the weather, commented on the latest news from Paris, seeming not to notice *Monseigneur's* absorption. At last Charles de Maringy broke in impatiently:

"Well, what about the granaries?"

Talon sighed and dolefully shook his head.

"Burnt to the ground. Nothing saved."

"And the mill?"

"Alas!"

Monseigneur had made a vigorous effort to control his temper, but with each curt answer from his bailiff the veins on his temples stood out more and more like cords, and he pressed his lips tightly together because he felt that his breath was coming and going with a hissing sound. All of which Talon did not fail to notice, even while he appeared absorbed in picking at the nails of one hand with those of the other.

"And," *Monseigneur* asked, after a moment or two when he thought that his voice would sound steady, "what have you done about it?"

"I, my dear sir!" Talon exclaimed, "what do you suppose I can do?"

This easy familiarity, this jaunty "my dear sir" required yet another effort on De Marigny's part to keep his temper. He did it, nevertheless, forced himself to appear at ease with this man the very sight of whom he detested, and after a moment he said with quiet deliberation:

"I ordered you, some time ago, when that raffish mob fired my bakery, to let the miscreants know that for every building of mine which they destroyed I would raze one of their cottages to the very ground."

"But, my dear friend—" began Talon in protest.

"I am not your dear friend," Charles de Marigny broke in, on the fringe of exasperation, "but your employer! I gave you certain orders. Did you execute them?"

"I did my best. I threw out hints. I warned them, but I dare not do more."

"Your warnings were no use, apparently. Two valuable granaries have been wantonly destroyed: also the mill, which cost thousands to build only have a dozen years ago: find me a handful of honest men— men who will do what they are paid to do. Choose any two cottages in the village you like, evict the tenants, and let not one stone remain upstanding."

"*Monseigneur!*—" Talon exclaimed with a gasp.

"Ah!" De Marigny rejoined with a sneer. "It has brought you to your senses, too, has it? You realise that I am not your dear friend but a man who has not forgotten either his position or his rights? Those devils up in Paris talk of a government by terror. Terror, they say, is the order of the day, and they remain in power because they govern by fear. Terror is going to be the order of the day on my estate. An eye for an eye; a tooth for a tooth. A cottage for my granary; a house for my mill. Find me the men, Talon: I'll show those dastardly ruffians down there that I am still their lord and master."

Charles de Marigny had worked himself up into a state bordering on frenzy. All his common sense, his stoicism had fled to the winds. He had nursed his resentment, his longing to hit back, for so long that all this wanton outrage against his property he lost all sense of proportion, and seized the opportunity to strike, and strike again, not counting the cost of the deadly danger. If he had been perfectly sane at the moment he not only would have realised the folly of such arrogance, but he would not have failed to notice that his bailiff, far from appearing horrified at the monstrous suggestion or frightened at its probably consequences, sat huddled up in his chair with his bony hand across his mouth.

Talon was doing his best to conceal the sneer that lurked around his lips and the gleam of triumph that shot through his eyes. For months now, he had worked for this: to bring this arrogant fool to a state of exasperation had been the aim and object of all his scheming and his double game. Those whom the dogs wish to punish they first strike with madness. Talon knew no Latin, but he did know that he had at last succeeded in bringing to the point of frenzy the man on whom depended the success of all his well laid plans.

"*Monseigneur*," he murmured again. "You don't seem to realise the temper of the people—"

He had shed his easy familiarity as he would a mantle; he was obsequious, servile, cringing now.

"It is time they realised mine," De Marigny retorted proudly. "I or that rabble. One of us must be the master here."

"Unfortunately, they have the power—and the numbers. You are alone."

Monseigneur said nothing for the moment. He sat staring out of the window through which he could perceive over the treetops the ruins of his mill and his granaries. It seemed as if his outburst had tired him out. He looked, all of a sudden, like a sick and weary old man; the blood was ebbing out of his temples; he closed his eyes for a moment or two, and a long sigh broke through his trembling lips.

Talon drew his chair a little closer to him, and, sinking his harsh voice to an insinuating whisper, he said:

"Why not turn your back on the rabble? Get away to England or Belgium—emigrate. So many of your friends have done it—"

Monseigneur made no reply; but Talon, whose keen eyes were watching every change on the proud, expressive face, saw a sudden softening of its lines, as if an invisible hand had passed over them and erased all that were hard and cruel. And in the eyes, there crept a look which was almost one of yearning.

"So many have done it," Talon reiterated. "It is the only road to safety."

But, as quickly as they had come, softness and yearning had already vanished from De Marigny's expression; once more the eyes became hard, the mouth obstinate.

"I'll not go, Talon," he said forcefully, and brought his clenched fist down on the arm of his chair. "I will see this devilry through to the end. I will hold the fort against this rabble, though, as you say, I must do it alone, but nobody shall lord it over Marigny while I live."

"It wouldn't be a case of anyone 'lording' it," Talon murmured, "only of a temporary arrangement. Scores of gentlemen have done it—and it is the safest plan."

He waited a moment or two, then he added:

"The safest plan for you and Mademoiselle Aurore."

This time the blow had gone home. Charles de Marigny could not suppress a cry of anguish.

"Aurore!"

"But," he went on slowly, speaking as if to himself, "if we go—if we—if we emigrate—those devils will confiscate the whole of my property, and—"

Talon had to make a great effort to conceal the gleam of satisfaction that shot through his yellow eyes: *Monseigneur* had started to argue the point—and that was the first sign of defeat.

"Only nominally," he said. "The whole plan is of the simplest—as I said just now—a temporary arrangement—"

"What temporary arrangement?" De Marigny asked with a frown.

"A paper making the property over to—to—a faithful servant—just a temporary arrangement, as I say—the other party undertaking to restore the property to its original owner on demand. It is done every day, my friend. Half the estates in France, at this moment, are nominally the property of men who have undertaken to administer them on the quiet, till times are better. . . . "

"In this case you mean yourself?"

"Oh, I don't know that, my good sir. The risks are very great, you must remember."

"How do you mean—the risks? There are no risks, except for the unfortunate owners who put themselves at the mercy of knaves."

"Only for the time being—always supposing that those others are knaves. But when life is at stake—and not only one's own life, but that of others who are very dear—well, one must take certain risks. And there is little risk in trusting a faithful servant who has looked after your interests for twenty years."

Talon had a persuasive tongue, and as soon as he noted that his suggestion had made a breach in *Monseigneur's* armour of pride and obstinacy, he pressed his point home. It was done every day. The sale of the estate was nominal. The price paid in worthless bits of government bonds. Talon had once more dropped his show of servility. He "dear sir"-ed and "my dear friend"-ed De Marigny because he had not rejected the proposal with scorn but was pondering over it. Half the battle, then, was already won, and Talon saw himself in possession of Marigny, at any rate for a number of years, long enough to build a good nest egg and then to flit out of the country if times changed back to the old regime and he was summarily dispossessed.

"You, as the owner, would run no risk," he went on more glibly. "The risks would all be mine, if I undertook the task, for I might be denounced as a traitor for my devotion to you. But you! Why, my dear friend, you could go away to England or Belgium with Mademoiselle Aurore, and when you came back to Marigny four or five years hence—the present state of things cannot last longer than that—you will find your estates impoverished, no doubt, but your house standing where it did."

He rose, preparing to take his leave. He knew well enough that he had sown the right seed in fairly receptive soil and that to say more just now might imperil the happy issue of his fight. Whether, when once more left to himself, Charles de Marigny would return to his state of arrogance and frenzy or ponder more deeply over his bailiff's suggestion was on the knees of the gods. It was no use thinking that the battle was already won. It was not. There was a chink in the armour of obstinacy, and that was all.

"I'll bring you the papers in a day or two," he said casually, as he took his leave. "It is quite a simple affair. You acknowledge having received a certain sum from me for the sale of all your properties wheresoever situated, and I sign an undertaking to restore them to you on demand and the repayment of the money."

"On demand?"

"Why, yes! You are not likely to return to this hell upon earth, are you? Unless times have much changed."

And Charles de Marigny, as if wear of struggle and argument, assented somewhat lamely.

"Yes, yes, Talon. Quite right! You are right, I am sure, and you mean well. Bring me the papers; I'll look at them."

"In the meanwhile, I'll give it out more decidedly that if any more arson occurs on your property you will give as good as you get."

"Yes, yes!" *Monseigneur* assented, his exasperation getting, at last, completely the better of his good sense. "Do what you like, but, for God's sake, get out of my sight now! I am sick of you and your ugly face."

Talon grinned. Memory took him back to those days before the great upheaval, when Monseigneur le Duc de Marigny was in the habit of thus dismissing his obsequious bailiff. Times had changed, but not *Monseigneur*. Talon knew well enough that beneath a great deal of show of stoicism the old Adam could always be reckoned with. Because of that old Adam of arrogance and tyranny he would gain his point. *Monseigneur* would be forced to yield Marigny up to him or perish at the hands of an infuriated mob.

And Hector Talon made his way home, satisfied with the morning's work.

Chapter 14

By the time that Aurore and the Abbé Rosemonde had finished sorting out the treasures of the old leather trunk Talon had left the *château*. Aurore found her father looking thoughtful.

"That rascal Talon," he said presently, speaking as it were to himself, "is no fool. His advice is sound." He drew the girl to him and looked searchingly into her eager young face. "My little Aurore," he went on wistfully, "would you like to put all these horrors behind you and seek refuge somewhere where we could have peace?"

"You mean—emigrate, Father?"

"Why not?"

"And lose Marigny? They confiscate everything if one emigrates."

"If it could be done without losing Marigny?"

"Even so——?"

"You don't want to go?"

"I want to do whatever you think is right; but—I love Marigny." And Aurore's dreamy eyes, full of a vague yearning, swept over the beautiful *vista* around, the wooded slopes, the distant ribbon of the Allier whispering among the reeds, the steeples of the village churches peeping out between the clumps of sycamore and walnut. All this meant home to her. She had never known another. Even the palace in Paris had been but a *pied-à-terre* for her: Marigny alone was home. "I love it," she reiterated with a sigh. "I know every tree in the forest, every shrub in the coppice, the call of every bird. To go away into the unknown frightens me, somehow."

"Now, that is sheer childishness, Aurore," her father said sternly. "My dear *abbé*, help me to get those silly fancies out of her head."

The old priest had stood by in discreet silence, ostensibly engrossed in looking over again the old clothes he was going to distribute in the village. At Aurore's outburst he looked up, and now that *Monseigneur* appealed to him he came and placed a hand on the girl's shoulder.

"I should miss you terribly in the village, my child," he said, "but I agree with your father. If it can be done, it would be wiser to go away. It will only be for a time."

"Do they hate us here so much as all that?" she asked. Probably she would have broken down then and had a good cry. It seemed so cruel that, in spite of every effort towards forgiveness and charity, it was impossible to combat that hatred which a lot of irresponsible and cruel demagogues had instilled into the hearts of the people of France. But Aurore met her father's anxious, loving glance fixed upon her: young as she was, she knew that he depended on her for every tiny gleam of joy or happiness that she was able to give, and also that at sight of her grief his bitter resentment and suffering would increase a hundredfold. So she swallowed her tears, gave her father a good kiss, then turned once more to the old priest, smiling through her tears:

"Let us go straightway to the village now, *M. le Curé*," she said. "I do want the Legendre children to have those stockings soon. And," she added with a light laugh, "I have not yet done my marketing today."

It was late afternoon when Aurore de Marigny made her way back from the village toward the *château*. Jeannette was with her and carried her market basket. She was an elderly woman who had served the ducal family almost from childhood, when she began life as a scullery wench. She had lost mother, father, kindred, one after the

273

other, and gradually her whole life became entirely dependent upon the *château*. When approaching middle age, she had married Pierre, one of the men-servants, and after that had carried on just as before. She never had any children. Somehow, she had never wanted any. And then when, one by one, the other servants of the *château* ran away, terrified lest they should be identified with unpopular *aristos*, Pierre and Jeannette had stayed on, chiefly because they had nowhere else to go. What few services were required of them—the little bit of cooking and cleaning—they did quite ungrudgingly but without enthusiasm. They seemed to have become a pair of automatons, with undeveloped brains and a vague protective instinct towards Aurore de Marigny and *Monseigneur* who gave them shelter and food.

Together Aurore and Jeannette walked rapidly along the road, which at this point follows the river bank until it branches off to the wooded slopes which lead up to the *château*. They had gone past the last two or three outlying cottages, and the road stretched out before them like a white ribbon, sun-baked, dusty, and solitary. They had seen no one for some time when, suddenly, a man came into view around a bend, walking slowly towards them. He looked wearied, ragged, and dirty, but in this was no different from many other wayfarers on the high roads these days; but there was something in his limping gait, in his stooping shoulders, and in his head, which fell forward on his chest and rolled round and round as if insecurely held by his neck, which gave the idea of fatigue verging on complete collapse.

As the man drew nearer Aurore perceived that he wore a military coat and breeches, both in the last stages of decay, and that he had no shoes on his feet, which were bleeding and covered with grime. His head was bare, and a shocked of chestnut-brown tousled hair fell like a mop over his face. Aurore noted, also, that the right sleeve of his tattered coat was hanging empty.

Obviously, a miserable soldier, making his way home from the way. As he came close up to the two women he stumbled and would certainly have fallen had not Aurore put out her arms. Instinctively, with his one hand he seized hold of hers, and remained quite still for a moment or two, trying to steady himself and clinging blindly to this unexpected support. Then he raised his head and shook the mop of hair away from his face. Aurore encountered a pair of dark eyes, lack-lustre and glassy, and with an unseeing vagueness in their dilated pupils. She did not dare move for fear of seeing the man fall at her feet, but she half turned her head to Jeannette and said quickly:

"That drop of wine in the small bottle—give it here—"

At sound of the voice the glassiness went out of the man's eyes. The pupils contracted, and a deep frown appeared between his brows. He seemed suddenly to realise that the prop which supported him was a woman's arm, and with a great effort he steadied himself on his feet. A curious light flashed from his eyes, which seemed to sweep Aurore from head to foot.

Jeannette muttered something about wasting good stuff which had cost so much to procure, but Aurore spoke impatiently:

"The bottle, Jeannette! Quick!"

Under the man's curious sweeping glance, she felt her cheeks flushing, but still she did not move, holding out her arm quite stiffly until his hold on it relaxed. Then she frowned and turned her head away, for the man was staring at her still, and there was something in that stare, a certain contempt or even enmity, which almost caused her to take to her heels and run. But she held her round, and when, presently, Jeannette handed her the bottle, she took it and held it out to the man. With a sweep of his arm he brushed it away, then threw back his head and laughed.

It was a strange laugh, hard and mirthless, which caused the suspicion of a shiver to run down Aurore's spine—a shiver not of fear (for what was there to fear in this miserable, maimed creature?), but of recoil, as if in the presence of something weird and not altogether earthly. But that was only a momentary weakness: the man looked so unutterably wretched that tears of pity, never absent from the depths of Aurore's sympathetic head, welled up to her eyes. Instinctively she felt, however, that pity in this case would be unwelcome; repulsed, perhaps, with that contempt which still lingered in the man's eyes; so, she closed her own for a moment or two, lest the tears trickle down her cheeks.

When she opened them again the man had passed by.

"Come, Jeannette," Aurore said quickly, "let us get home."

Jeanette, stolid and silent, had rearranged the market basket and started to walk beside her mistress.

"Thank goodness," she said, "this good wine was not wasted. It would have been a sin to deprive *Monseigneur* of it for the sake of that down-at-heel vagabond."

After a while she added: "You know who that was, don't you, *mademoiselle?*"

"No," Aurore replied. "How should I?"

"It was André Vallon. I knew him at once, though he looks a miserable bag of bones now."

"André Vallon?"

"Marianne's son. *Mademoiselle* must recollect."

"But, how should I?" Aurore reiterated frowning.

Mechanically, however, she had paused for a moment and turned round to look at the retreating figure. Strangely enough, the man, too, had paused and looked back; and once more their eyes met. There was a distance of some ten metres between them now: the man, whoever he was, shrugged and laughed as soon as he had caught her glance; then he turned and went his way; but Aurore was again conscious of that vague sense of terror, as if something fateful and irresistible had come across her path. It was nonsense, of course.

Again, and again she said to herself: "What is there to fear?" Unfortunately, these days, inimical glances were more familiar to her than kindly ones; she was accustomed to looks of derision, even of hatred, to threatening words and menace of violence. The wretched vagabond who had just gone by had not spoken; had threatened with neither word nor gesture; but never in all these fateful days had she encountered a glance so full of latent contempt and almost unearthly hatred.

"Tell me about this—this André Vallon—was that the name?" she said presently to Jeannette, while together the two of them walked up the slope.

Jeannette, whose powers of narration were limited, began a long and involved tale on the subject. She talked of André and his mother; of the boy's early turbulent life in the village which ended abruptly and violently in a public whipping in the market square for disorderly conduct. Jeannette could not remember the details, but she had heard it said in the village that young Vallon had sworn deadly enmity against all those who had been present and seen his humiliation.

"He went up to Paris after that," Jeannette went on to relate, "and got under the thumb of that murdering blackguard Danton. So, I shouldn't wonder if he has become just such another assassin himself. I shouldn't care to meet him alone on the road. But, as I used to say to his mother long ago, she would spoil him. She let him think he was somebody, though he was nothing better, even in those days, then a young ne'er-do-weel. And the woman spoilt him, too, because he had flashing eyes and a way with him. Dirty young blackguard, I call him."

She went meandering on, not caring whether her mistress listened to her or not. She had the usual anecdotes to tell of André's turpitude, and the perpetual mischief he would get into, causing his mother endless worry.

Aurore only listened with half an ear. Vague memories floated through her mind of a glorious day such as this in mid-July. Her birthday. Her young friends. A game of blindman's bluff. And then the face of a boy with flashing black eyes, a shock of chestnut hair from which the hot sun drew glints of shining copper, and of a brown, slender hand holding a futile, useless pocketknife.

It all seemed like a dream now. Later on, she had heard the story of the same boy being publicly whipped in the market square for having killed Hector Talon's savage dog, and she remembered feeling sorry for him, because already in those days she had instinctively disliked Talon. How it all came back now! Her pity for the boy, her dread at sight of his flashing dark eyes and of his beautiful face convulsed with rage because Pierre de Mauléon had slapped his cheek. And the heavy scent of earth which had offended her nostrils when, blindfolded, she fell against his breast.

Chapter 15

Soon the news was all over the countryside that André Valon had come home from the war, and the very next day Marianne's doorstep was besieged with people who not only wanted to see the boy, but wished to know just what was going on over in Champagne or Verdun; whether the King of Prussia was really marching on Paris, or whether he had been defeated by the brave national army and was now in full retreat.

Somehow, too, it had become known that André had both won his epaulettes and lost his left arm at Valmy, where the King of Prussia had suffered a severe defeat. Rumours of that victory—one of the rare ones—had penetrated as far as Val-le-Roi; Danton had made grandiloquent allusions to it in the National Assembly, had talked volubly about "our glorious troops, our valorous soldiers who were sweeping the whole of Europe clean of tyrants and militarism." He spoke of "their heroic deaths, fighting in the glorious cause of liberty," and "sacrificing their noble lives with the smile of martyrs going to glory, so that the world might, at least, be safe for democracy."

What he did not talk of were the unspeakable privations, the almost unbelievable hardships which, indeed, had been endured by the troops with a stoicism and heroic obstinacy almost without parallel in the history of the world. André himself never spoke about that. That he had suffered, and suffered terribly, along with the troops which he had helped to lead to victory, could be seen by the unnatural glitter that came to his eyes whenever friends pressed him to tell them something of that well equipped and well fed army of Prussians and Austrians who were attacking France just because she had thrown off the shackles of tyranny and led the vanguard to an era of equality and of liberty.

An almost cruel curve would then distort André's lips when he spoke of the Austrian officers in their smart uniforms, or the Prussian troops with their good boots and well filled bellies, all fighting in the cause of those *aristos* who had so complacently shaken the dust of starving France from their high-heeled shoes and were disporting themselves in comfort and safety in Belgium or England. And he would glance up into the distance, where, outlined against the summer sky, the pinnacles and pointed roofs of the Château de Marigny towered above the treetops, and the look in his eyes became almost one of frenzied hatred, whilst words such as Danton himself would have emulated came hoarsely from his parched throat. He hated them. Heavens above, how he hated them all! It was a hatred akin to physical anguish, one that had been born in his heart when he was a mere child, on that day of bitter humiliation when he had stood naked at the whipping post, exposed to the mocking gaze of those *aristos* with their perfumed hair and bejewelled *lorgnettes*. That had been a boy's hatred, but now it was the hatred of a man filled to the soul with bitter resentment and the yearning for some measure of revenge.

But it was when the gleam of that resentment glittered most vividly in her son's eyes that Marianne's podgy, toil-hardened hand would descend with a soothing pressure upon his shoulder. Her calm philosophy would express itself in a few clumsy words, and André would pat that kindly hand and kiss it and make a big effort to subdue the paroxysm of his fury.

"All I long for, *Maman chérie*," he would say, as calmly as he could, "is that I may live long enough to see the destruction for this old world and the rebuilding of the new. Nothing else will do, my dear one, but complete annihilation of everything. There is corruption everywhere; uncleanness, crying evils too deeply rooted to be remedied. The world is overgrown with tares; nothing but a world conflagration can render it clean again."

At which Marianne would nod her head and reply gently: "The worst tare of all, André, is hatred. How can you reap anything but conflict if you sow that?"

"It is not hate, Mother, that will set the world aflame, but justice. Something has got to be done. Those who have mocked at misery and done nothing to alleviate it must be made to suffer. Those who have enjoyed life, who have always eaten and drunk their fill—they have got to learn what it feels like to be so cold—so cold that your chattering teeth seem ready to fall out of your jaws and to feel your belly so hollow that you would gnaw the flesh off your own limbs. They have got to know something of suffering, Mother. It is justice, and it has got to be."

But Marianne would still shake her wise old head. Justice? When had there ever been justice in this old world in which she had lived long and endured so much? There had been no justice in the days that were past, when up at the *château*—whither she trudged day after day, in order to do the family washing—she saw buckets full of meal and skim milk thrown to the pits, and fat, meaty bones given to the dogs, which would have kept her and her boy free from hunger. Was there justice now, when soldiers who were fighting for France were allowed to starve while the great orators up in Paris held banquets and feasts in the name of Liberty?

Justice? God alone held its scales, and no man knew how He would administer it in the life that was to come.

Chapter 16

It was while the excitement of André Vallon's homecoming was at its height, and the imagination of the countryside stirred by his account of the heroism and endurance of the national army, that Hector Talon took the opportunity of recruiting half a dozen ruffians to fulfil that act of madness ordered by *Monseigneur* by way of reprisals for the burning of his granaries and his mill.

With ferocious spite he had already selected the cottage of Marianne Vallon for the dastardly deed and chosen the day when André himself was absent from Val-le-Roi, having gone to Nevers on business of his own. He also selected another cottage close by, which was the property of the widow Louvet, who had four children and a small competence left to her by her husband, at one time a prosperous farmer who, some time before his death, had fallen on lean days and been forced, like so many others, to sell most of his land. Those two cottages, then, isolated from the rest of the village, had been marked by Talon for destruction.

The six ruffians, whom he had recruited in absolute secrecy and for a small sum from one of the distant villages, arrived in the early morning armed with sabres and bayonets, clad in cloth coat and breeches, and wearing red caps on their heads. They proceeded first to one cottage and then to the other and summoned the women to clear out of them at once. As they refused to move, the ruffians seized them and the Louvet children and forcibly ejected them from their homes, after which act of brutality, they set fire to the cottages. When these were well ablaze they incontinently took to their heels, and no one had set eyes on them since.

The news of the outrage spread like wildfire, and soon the entire population of three villages flocked to the scene of the disaster.

Strange how rumour does travel in these lonely districts! The firing of shops or stores, of granaries or timber sheds, were of frequent occurrence these days, and usually the crowds that gathered round the conflagrations were made up, in addition to the ruffianly incendiaries, of a few young rapscallions intent on mischief and some poor half-starved vagabonds—men and women—who hoped to pick up something out of the wreckage. There were also those who came to shout, "*Vive la liberté!*" at the instigation of the professional tub thumpers, who took the opportunity of egging the crowd to worse mischief still.

But in this case, it was different. People came from Le Borne and Vanzy, from Aubeterre and Barbuise; for hours the road, the lanes, the towpaths were dotted with dark figures hurrying to the scene. Men in ragged shirts and shoeless; women in tattered kirtles; children, half naked, clinging to their mother's hand; but there were also the farmers from Aubeterre or Vanzy, who came driving in their carts, and there was the lawyer from Le Creusot in his *cariole*, and the leech from Barbuise, who was on his rounds.

For an hour or more the cottages were ablaze. They were stone-built, with heavy wooden rafters and age-old beams, which were a ready prey for the flames. There was very little wind, and the sky was leaden. Great storm clouds, tinged now with crimson, came rolling in from the west. Huge columns of smoke rose, writhing and twisting, to the sky mingled with showers of spluttering, hissing sparks.

The men worked wonders, some of them risking their lives in a heroic endeavour to save the women's goods. There had been a prolonged drought since June and very little water in the wells, but many men defied the flames while they dragged poor bits of furniture, bedding, or clothing out of the blazing buildings. The women stood round, staring wide eyed at this disaster which they could not comprehend. It was so un-understandable, meaningless, wanton. The destruction of *bourgeois* or *aristo* property, yes! they understood that well enough, because those that were well-to-do were the enemies of the starving people of France—at least, so the great orators up in Paris were never tired of dinning into the ears of all and sundry. But cottages! the dwellings of the poor, the home of a widow and of a mother of children! That was beyond human comprehension.

The widow Louvet, with her children gathered about her knees, was squatting by the side of the road up against the hedge with a crowd of sympathizers all round her. She mostly had her apron over her face, feeling, she said, quite unable to bear the sight of that awful conflagration. She seemed quite incapable of lending a helping hand, even in the simple effort of dragging her goods out of the way of the crowd. When her apron was not over her face she just stared in front of her, or else at her children, and through quivering lips murmured agonising, "*Mon Dieu!*"'s and "*Sainte Vierge!*"'s. "What will become of us now?"

But Marianne Vallon neither cried nor prayed. In her own quiet, stolid way she did her share in endeavouring to rescue her goods. She worked like a man: and when all her little bits of furniture were in safety, she went over the Louvets' cottage and helped in the work of salvage there.

"*Voyons*, Citoyenne Vallon," one of the men said to her when she attempted to go too near the blazing building. "Keep your distance. The place is dangerous."

She said nothing, only shook the men off who tried to restrain her. There were the children's paillasses to get out of the way, and their few bits of clothing. The men had gotten these out of the cottage, but they were too near the fire still, and flying sparks might set them alight.

"Take care, Citizeness Vallon!" the women shouted to her. "Let the men do what they can."

Marianne was stooping at the moment. She had hold of a bundle of bedding with both hands and was dragging it out of the way. Her bulky shoulders were bent to the task: the scanty grey hairs clung to her streaming face. The bedding was heavy and awkward to handle, but so precious; so very precious, with all those poor sickly children wanting to sleep comfortably o' nights.

"Take care, Citizeness Vallon!" the women screamed. "It isn't safe!"

"Let the things be!"

"Take care!"

And the men all at once gave a terrific shout, "Out of the way!"

One of them tried to get a hold of Marianne to drag her to safety, but she was large and heavy and bulky, and she was bending to her task, not seeing what was going on and heedless of the shouts of warning.

And suddenly a sheet of fire came bursting from the cottage: it was followed by a thunderous crash as the roof fell in, scattering bits of wood, stones, and tiles in all directions.

A cry of horror rose from every throat, drowning the roar of the flames, the hissing of sparks, the din of falling timber and crumbling stones. Beneath a huge smouldering beam Marianne Vallon lay, huddled up and lifeless, still clasping the bundle of bedding in her arms.

Chapter 17

Now only the blackened stone walls were left standing, with the empty holes where the tiny windows had been staring out on the scene of devastation like hollow, sightless eyes. An evil-smelling sooty smoke still found its way out of the smouldering ruins, and now and then a volley of sparks rose up hissing to the stormy sky. A suffocating smell of hot paint and burning refuse hung in the air, and the lamentations of women, the whimpering of children, and the dull murmur of men's voices seemed like eerie sounds that came from the Stygian creek.

No one knew exactly what to door what to say. The catastrophe was so appalling that, beyond sullen murmurs, those who had witnessed it appeared tongue-tied. Paralyzed they were with the horror of it. The death of Marianne Vallon was the culminating point in the overwhelming disaster. And André himself was away. He had gone to Nevers the day before to see about a lawyer's business which he wanted to take over now that he was no longer fit to rejoin the army. He had been full of hopes of a brighter future for the mother whom he adored. No longer would she have to wash and scrub for him. There was so much litigation these days that any lawyer with brains was certain of a good income.

And André Vallon was well seen in his high places: he had been clerk at one time to no less a personage than Georges Danton, the idol of the people, who thought the world of him. Oh! there was no doubt about it, the world held compensations for a man like André

Vallon. He had lost an arm but not an iota of his brains, and though the terrible hardships which he had endured in the campaign against the Prussians had to a certain extent impaired his health and embittered his temper, he had still two priceless possessions—youth and an iron constitution.

He was going to be so happy! And now this awful, this overwhelming cataclysm. Who was going to tell him? Who would be bold enough to face that son with news of his mother's death under such tragic circumstances? The women discussed it but could offer no advice. All they could do was to stretch their arms up to heaven and ejaculate, "*Jésus! Mon Dieu!*" even though they knew well enough that appeals to the deity were nor forbidden by law. The men were torn between the desire to run away, now that they could do nothing to help in an active way, and the longing to fasten the guilt of the whole thing on somebody. For somebody had done this awful deed. The ruffians who had ejected the women and children from their homes had taken to their heels. True enough! But the countryside could be scoured for them, and, by dint of menace and other more forcible arguments, they might be made to confess in whose pay they were. Strangely enough, no one suspected as yet that the monstrous order had emanated from the *château*.

In the meanwhile, those among the crowd who had business of their own to attend to were gradually trying to get away. Perhaps at the back of their minds there arose the fear that some sort of mischief would surely come out of this. Vallon would turn up presently, and the devil alone knew to what lengths his fury would go. He already held the people around in the hollow of his hand and could lead them whithersoever he chose. With his mother lying dead at his feet through an outrage as yet inexplicable, something of the rage of a tiger unleashed might carry him and his sympathizers to excesses which presently might know no bounds. When the temper of the rabble was worked up no one knew how things would end, and it was best to be home and keep gates and doors well barred and bolted. And so, the farmers in their carts, the leech in his *cariole*, the keepers of neighbouring village stores, drifted away one by one.

"If you meet Vallon, tell him!" was shouted after those who were going in the direction of Nevers.

And Farmer Lameth, from over Le Borne way, going homeward in his cart, did presently meet André Vallon, who had borrowed a *cariole* in Nevers and was leisurely driving home. Farmer Lameth pulled up.

"Terrible doings up at Val-le-Roi," he called out to André. "You should be there, Citizen Vallon."

"Why? What has happened?"

"Two cottages have been fired, and families turned out of their homes."

"Name of a dog—!"

Farmer Lameth hesitated a moment or two. Already he did not much like the look in André's face. What would it be presently—when he knew?

"One of them is your mother," the worthy farmer added tentatively.

"My mo—!"

This time it was the devil himself who kindled the flame in André's eyes. He whipped up the nag, and the *cariole* started off with a bump upon the stony road. Farmer Lameth turned in his seat and called out once more:

"Citizen Vallon!"

André did not slacken speed, but he too turned in his seat and shouted back:

"Yes! What is it?"

"There's more trouble there than you think—"

But André did not really listen. He whipped that poor old nag as he had never whipped a horse before. Never had the road seemed so long. Trouble indeed! He would see to it that there was trouble and to spare for whoever had lain hands on his mother's property and turned her out of her home. Trouble? There would be trouble in Val-le-Roi such as there had never been even in Paris, even in Versailles! Trouble? My God!

Chapter 18

"Here comes Citizen Vallon."

"No."

"I tell you 'yes.'"

"And he's driving like the devil!"

Instinctively the crowd had closed up right across the road, barring the way to the smouldering cottage and standing in a dense mass round the recumbent figure over which someone had reverently laid an old tattered shawl. The men had succeeded in moving away the beam and the bundle of bedding, and Marianne Vallon now lay on one of the paillasses which she had rescued from the flames: her hands had

284

been folded across her ample bosom, and the thin grey hair smoothed away from the marble-like, wide forehead.

There was no other feeling in the heart of anyone there at this moment but intense pity for the bereaved son and an awed wonder as to what would happen next. Even such men as Tarbot, the ex-butcher of Vanzy, and Molé, the wheelwright, two of the most desperate ruffians the Revolution had engendered in any village, were silent and uncertain, and determined to delay as long as possible the terrible revelation that would bring such overwhelming grief to a devoted son.

So, they all stood like a solid *phalanx*, shoulder to shoulder, around that still and inert mass, while a *cariole* came rattling down the road, and a miserable nag, all skin and bones, thick with dust and lather, charged straight into them. It is very difficult to stand up to a charging horse and vehicle, even though the horse is but skin and bones: the crowd gave way, and André jumped down from the *cariole*. The men tried to restrain him, but with his one arm he shook them off and forged his way to where his mother lay, with eyes closed, her hands folded across her bosom, her body covered with a shawl.

He was in the midst of a crowd, and he would not let them see what he felt. Not a word came through his lips, and the cry that had risen to his throat was smothered and deadened with a mighty effort of will. He knelt down beside his mother and, with his hand on her ice-cold forehead, he looked down on her face and listened. No need for the others to tell him. Death was all too plainly writ on those beloved features, so stark and set, and the slightly parted lips through which so many words of quiet philosophy had often passed in order to comfort and to calm him. The eyes were closed, and André bent down and kissed each rigid lid; the hands were folded as they had so often been in prayer when she had knelt beside his bed. Her heart was still—that great, big heart of hers in which there had never been room for hatred and bitterness.

Oh, no! There was no need for others to tell him. He knew the moment that the crowd parted and he saw her lying there with the tattered shawl over her that she was dead. A slight noise among the crowd, a sigh, no doubt, or a smothered sob, recalled him to the fact that there were others there. Very gently he drew the old shawl right over his mother's face, and then he rose to his feet. There was not a drop of blood in his cheeks: his face looked as pale as that of the dead woman at his feet, but in his eyes now there were smouldering flames of fury that would not be quenched save in revenge.

"What has happened?" he asked curtly.

A dozen voices were raised at once. Floods of eloquence so long held in check poured into his ears in full.

"The two cottages were fired."

"Six ruffians laid hands on the women."

"The widow Louvet and her four children are homeless."

"Your mother was killed in an endeavour to save some of the children's belongings."

"The roof fell in. A heavy beam knocked her down."

"She must have died instantly."

"Hold on!" André shouted, drowning the tumult with his stentorian voice. "Who fired the cottages?"

"Six ruffians there were—"

"In cloth coats and breeches—"

"And with shoes on their feet."

"Who saw them?"

The widow Louvet—she with the four children—had given up crying and moaning and staring into vacancy. The far greater tragedy of Marianne Vallon's death had put her own misfortune in the shade. Thus, directly appealed to, she was ready to come forward with her tale. She had seen the six ruffians, of course: had they not turned her out, her and the children, out of her home, and at the point of their bayonets? She couldn't resist. What could she do? They had turned her out, and she was afraid the children would be hurt. Then the ruffians had set fire to her cottage. They had piled up straw in the middle of the kitchen floor and set it alight. Some of them stood by to see that the straw had caught on properly; the others went on to the house of Citizeness Vallon.

"Was no one about, then, to stop them?"

Apparently not. They all shook their heads. It had all been done so quickly.

"After that the reprobates took to their heels."

"And no one after them?"

Again, they all shook their heads.

"Your mother tried to save the children's bedding—" the widow Louvet began dolefully, and suddenly paused, for the look in André's face was so terrifying that it froze the words on her lips.

"And I am not here," he murmured, "to tear their entrails out of their filthy bodies—" And suddenly he threw back his head and his glowing eyes searched the faces in the crowd.

286

"Can any of you guess," he asked quite quietly, "who is at the bottom of this?"

Not only had they guessed, but they knew. Had not Hector Talon—that double-faced hypocrite—had he not thrown out hints that more than a week ago that Marigny, up at the *château*, had threatened—nay, commanded—reprisals for the firing of his granaries? Some of them murmured the name of Talon, but André gave a harsh, scornful laugh.

"Talon?" he said. "Yes! We'll deal with Talon presently, for of a certainty he is in this villainy up to the neck. But," he went on more slowly, so that every word told and struck the ears of the crowd like the knell of an inevitable doom, "it is that devil up there who must account for today's infamy."

He paused a moment and then added:

"I am going up there, anyway, in order to make sure. Who comes with me?"

The response was unanimous. Indeed, it seemed as if a great sigh of relief went through the assembled crowd. Not only the men, but also the women. The sense of awe engendered by the magnitude of the catastrophe and the death of Marianne Vallon was beginning to wear away. There were men here who had begun to think of reprisals and who read in André's white, set face, in the almost tigerish fury in his glowing eyes, that passionate desire for revenge for which they themselves had so often thirsted. Men like Tarbot, the ex-butcher, and Molé, the wheelwright, had also brooded over the wrongs of their caste until they hungered for an opportunity to bring *aristos* to shame, or, better still, to the guillotine. They had seen around them such scenes of misery, humiliation, starvation, and tyranny that their hatred of tyrants and oppressors had turned to savage lust for the sight of blood.

There was no question here of philosophy or moderation.

How are you going to preach forgiveness and moderation to a starving crowd? There is no tongue sufficiently eloquent to find words that will pour the soothing oil of forbearance on a raging sea of rebellion. One Voice alone could do that, and did it nigh two thousand years ago, but today that Voice is still: It only speaks mutely from the Cross.

"Citizen Vallon," one of the men said decisively, "we will help you in your revenge."

André nodded in silence. He could not trust himself to say much. Not yet. There was always the fear of breaking down, of showing weakness which he was far from feeling. He hardly dared look on that so still form beneath the ragged shawl: the folded hands showed all too plainly, and the swell of the ample bosom against which he had so often as a child cried himself to sleep. No, indeed, he dared not look, for sobs threatened to choke him, and he might cry out his agony of grief. But he still had a task to accomplish, a duty to fulfil.

"A few sticks to make a stretcher," he said curtly.

"Where'll you take her, André?" one of the women asked.

"Back home."

"It is burnt to the ground."

"I know that."

They asked no further questions, for already André was busy breaking down branches of trees. The men helped: some of them had tools, others went to fetch what they could. A stretcher was soon improvised, and they lifted the dead woman on it. André and Tarbot, the ex-butcher, carried her to her ruined cottage, most of the others following.

Tarbot, looking down on the dead woman, asked:

"Where shall we put her?"

"In there," André replied.

They put the stretcher down, and André went deliberately up to the cottage door and started clearing away the charred *débris* which encumbered it. The other men lent a hand, and when the entrance had been cleared André and Tarbot went back to get the stretcher. They had just stooped to lift it when the Abbé Rosemonde was seen hurrying down the road. He had heard the news and came panting along as fast as his shaking limbs would carry him. He had tucked his *soutane* up round his waist: he was hatless, and his grey hair clung to his streaming forehead.

"I don't want to see him," André said abruptly. "Keep him away."

But the *curé* forged his way resolutely through the crowd.

"André, my child," he cried panting, "I only just heard the news. I came as fast as I could."

André paid no attention to him. In silence, with the aid of Tarbot, he carried his burden into the ruined cottage.

"We'll lay her down here," he said, "until such time as—"

"André!" the old priest called.

"Go home, Citizen Curé," Tarbot said roughly. "Can't you see that you are not wanted here?"

He and André had taken the dead woman to the centre of what

had once been her parlour. The floor was littered with rubbish. They cleared a place on which to deposit the stretcher. Above, through a wide, yawning gap in the roof, there was a vista of a leaden sky of grey clouds which hung, low and heavy, presaging the coming storm.

André collected what there was left of charred wood and spread it around the stretcher.

"Straw would be better," he muttered.

"What are you going to do, Citizen Vallon?" Tarbot asked.

The others had come to a halt all about the doorway. Behind them the old priest was still striving to elbow his way through the crowd. André drew his flint and steel out of his pocket and used them vigorously, trying to draw a spark. The men understood.

"Straw would be better," one of them said. Another added: "I know where to get some," and turned toward the road. This made a gap through the crowd, and the old priest pushed his way in.

"André!" he cried once more. "Your mother—!"

André paid no attention to him. He was busy with his flint and steel, trying to get little bits of wood alight. But the fire had done its work, the charred wood fell into ashes and would not burn.

"Young Legendre has gone to get straw," said one of the men.

"This is sacrilege," the old priest protested loudly. "André, in your dead mother's name—"

At this André looked up. "My mother is dead," he said roughly; "she doesn't want you."

"You may not want me, my child," the old priest retorted firmly, "but she would."

Then, as André said nothing more, only went on stolidly striking flint against steel, the *curé* said forcefully:

"Remember, my son, that from above she can still see you; how think you she would view this awful sacrilege? *Voyons! voyons*, André," he went on more gently, "do not harden your heart in rebellion against the will of God. Let me come near the dear old soul, and we'll pray together that she may have eternal rest. She would have wished it, you know."

And though resentment and bitterness were tearing at André's heart, he knew that the priest was right. Old Marianne, could she have said the word, would have rebelled against this desecration of her body: she would have wished for Christian burial, to the accompaniment of prayer and the ministrations of the Church. To the end of her hard life she had remained a professing Christian, clinging to the simple beliefs of her youth, weeping over the godlessness of this new regime, over the spirit of rebellion which it had fostered in her André's heart, abhorring the tyranny of man which had brought so much misery on the poor people, yet bowing with quiet philosophy to the inscrutable will of God.

André knew all that. "She would have wished it, you know." The priest's words found an echo in his aching heart. For a few seconds still did he hesitate, did his pride war with his love for the dead. The others watched him in silence while the women wept. Here was something that was past their comprehension, something that awed and silenced them and for the time being made them forget their passions and their hatred. Then André, without another word, put his flint back into his pocket and rose to his feet. He stood aside, and when the priest knelt down beside the dead and began murmuring his prayers, he watched him silently for a while and then walked quietly out of the cottage.

Chapter 19

But under the stormy canopy of the sky the spell was broken.

"We'll help you, citizen Vallon. Let's to the *château!*" was the universal slogan.

"But first of all, for Talon!"

The cry came from André. It was harsh and cruel like that of a young tiger scenting its prey. They others did not quite understand.

"Talon? Why Talon?"

"Because," André said, "such an abominable deed could never have been carried out without the aid of Hector Talon."

Why indeed Talon? Because he was the man whom André hated only one degree less than the people up at the *château*. Why Talon? Because André had a longing to see him dragged here by the heels through the dust and to see his yellow eyes turn glassy with the agony of deathly terror. Talon the hypocrite! The mealy-mouthed sycophant!

"Who will go and fetch Talon?"

There were any number of them there willing enough to start the day's work by baiting Talon. They went off in a body to fetch him. They dragged him out of his house. Pushed along, heckled and jostled, they brought him to the scene of the disaster, face to face with André Vallon.

They had dragged him along, and he had come, and on the way, he had mapped out his line of action. Not without due deliberation had he planned the monstrous outrage, nor without due regard to the consequences, unpleasant to himself, that might ensue. He had foreseen the rage of these people, their lust for revenge; he had reckoned on their passions as a lever for finally persuading Marigny to emigrate. He had even been prepared for a certain measure of danger to himself—danger which he would know how to combat. But what he had not reckoned on was the death of Marianne Vallon.

Nevertheless, he faced the crowd boldly. Whatever terror he felt he did not let them see; nor did he flinch when André, towering above him, laid such a heavy hand on his shoulder that his knees gave way under him.

"So, there you are, Citizen Talon," André apostrophised him coolly. "I suppose you know who I am?"

Talon looked up at the young face, dark and distorted with fury, and blinked his yellow eyes.

"How should I not know you, Citizen Vallon?" he said smoothly. "I have known you ever since—"

"Ever since you had me whipped for killing your brute of a dog, eh?"

"That is past history, Citizen Vallon," Talon said jocosely; "you are a man now."

"While you have remained a worm," André retorted: "such a worm that I have a mind to tread on your face, just for the pleasure of seeing you wriggle."

The men laughed, but Talon did not flinch. He even contrived to shrug and to smile. He was clever enough to know that a bold face and an arrogant air would be his best safeguard against aggression. Some of these men here—the rougher ones—were his friends. They knew him to be a man of influence. They had listened to his oratory outside the village taverns and had heard men in high places speak of Citizen Talon as a good patriot. And Talon knew that they would not dare touch him, even though André Vallon, the savage young brute, did his level best to incite them to murder. He kept up his jaunty air, and, only pulling a wry face, he said indulgently:

"You were always good at jesting, Citizen Vallon."

"I am not jesting now," André rejoined. "I want to know who gave the order for this abominable outrage."

"You mean the firing of the cottages?"

"Who ordered it? Tell us! Speak, why don't you? Speak, or I'll tear the words out of your filthy throat."

Talon put up his hands and gazed at André with an air of innocence.

"Easy! easy! my friend," he said, "how should I know?"

"You are Marigny's menial—you must know—"

"Then if you've made up your mind—"

"It was Marigny who gave the order?"

"I don't know," Talon protested. "I swear I don't know."

"You lie!"

Talon shrugged his lean shoulders.

"You lie, I say," André reiterated roughly. "Speak the truth, man," he went on more calmly, "it will be better for you. The *aristo* gave the order, is that it?"

But Talon would admit nothing. He knew nothing, he declared: vowed that he could not believe Marigny capable of such a thing. As for himself, he knew nothing. Nothing. He had been more shocked, more distressed than anyone when he first heard of the disaster.

"Lies! lies!" André retorted roughly. "Shall we to the *château*, citizens, and find out the truth for ourselves?"

A murmur of assent went the round. The truth? Why! they all knew the truth. André had known it all along, from the moment when he saw his mother lying dead and that awful red mist rose before his eyes. Marigny! It was Marigny who had done this loathsome deed. Murder, deliberate and most foul, lay at the door of that arrogant man up there, who, like his kindred and his king, had not yet learned that the people would no longer bow the neck to the yoke of their pride and their tyranny. Well, he, at any rate, would be taught a lesson that day: he would be made to mourn with tears of blood the deadly wrong which he had committed. He and his brood! Let them look to themselves! Men and women had gone to the guillotine for less, had watered their marble floors with bitter tears for crimes which were as venial sins compared to this morning's outrage.

Already the crowd had begun to move in the direction of the *château*; they had all been impatient enough to go. What cared they if the *aristo* "up there" were guilty or not? They wanted to march, to shout, to threaten, as others had done in Paris and Versailles. In the far distance from over the mountains came, from time to time, the dull rumbling sound of thunder; occasional flashes of lightning lit up the heavy storm clouds with a weird purple light. The air grew hotter and more oppressive every moment, but they all wanted to be up and doing—the storm was finding an echo in their hearts.

"To the *château*, André!" they said. "We'll help you in your revenge."

Talon made feeble efforts at protest.

"And you come with us, Citizen Talon," André concluded grimly.

Tarbot and Molé took Talon by the elbows. There was a general movement along the road. Men, women, children: they all joined in the procession. The men, earnest and determined; the women, bitterly vindictive; the children, innocently curious. There were fourscore of them at least, fourscore bent on demanding reprisals for an unparalleled wrong.

And André, silent and absorbed, with eyes aglow and mouth set, saw, through a veil of red, a woman's face with large, innocent eyes and soft fair hair—a woman, just a girl, in a rose-coloured silk which made her seem like a flower bud. He hadn't seen her for many years. She must be a woman now.

Bah! what had he to do with women, and visions of women seen through a mist the colour of blood? The one woman in the world he had ever cared for lay stiff and stark now, silent in her ruined home. And all that misery, all this injustice and unbounded sorrow lay at the door of those people "up there"!

Heavens above! how he hated them all.

Chapter 20

The Abbé Rosemonde, having finished his orisons, bethought himself of Marigny and little Aurore up at the *château*, ignorant, mayhap, as yet of the storm that was about to break with raging fury over their heads. At one moment he had thought of speaking to those poor misguided children who were being led away by disaster into acts of violence, the terrible consequences of which God alone could foresee. He had thought of admonishing André Vallon, who bitter resentment was causing him to whip up the tempers of his sympathizers.

The worthy *curé* shook his head dolefully: that poor lad! led astray on the very threshold of manhood by his obstinacy and wilfulness: full of generous impulses, and such a good son! He would have made a kind and faithful husband if only the times had been different. And now that this awful grief had descended upon him his obstinacy would harden his heart still more against the comfort which religion along could give. A pity! a sad, sad, pity that this catastrophe had happened. It was the will of God, of course, and he, poor, humble priest, bowed meekly before it, but, oh! how he wished that it had not happened. He couldn't imagine who had conceived such an inhuman project, for never for a moment would he contemplate the idea that *Monseigneur* would act so cruelly.

"*Mon Dieu! mon Dieu! Sainte Vierge Marie!*" he murmured fervently, "turn the hearts of those poor, ignorant people of France to a better knowledge of religion and virtue."

Thus, the old man prayed while he tramped up the familiar woodland path toward the *château*. He had been able to reach the slope without being seen by the crowd, who were still standing outside the ruined cottage, talking and murmuring. At one moment the *abbé* thought that he heard the voice of Hector Talon. Well, of course, as a priest and a Christian he wished no harm to come to anyone, but if it pleased God to punish Talon, Talon who had the ear of *Monseigneur* and was such an evil counsellor, he, as a man, would not complain.

Now, as he tramped upward, the good *curé* could hear echoing from the valley below the distant clamour of the angry crowd: André's sonorous voice and the hoarse shouts that rang with the promise of mischief.

The atmosphere was terribly oppressive; there seemed to be no air here under the trees; not a leaf stirred, and an evil smell seemed to rise from the dust in the road. The *abbé* hurried on. He knew that he could do nothing "up there," but he could warn *Monseigneur* of what was brewing against him. It might be wise to seek safety in flight while there was time.

There was the width of the terrace and the gardens, with the distant postern gate which gave on a lonely part of the wood, where it might be possible to await quietly a better turn of events.

Indeed, the *abbé* had to hurry. Looking down from a point of vantage, into the road below, he could see that the crowd had begun to move. To the priest it seemed as if their number had swelled. But his eyes were short-sighted, and many months ago he had broken his spectacles; he had never had any money since with which to buy new ones, so he couldn't see very well. He hoped that the crowd was not great and that Talon was with them. Surely Talon would act as a restraining power over the others.

Mon Dieu! Mon Dieu! how foolish it all was! If only Mademoiselle Aurore and Jeannette were out of the way, for arguments with noisy crowds were not fit for women's ears.

Fortunately, he was well ahead of the misguided lambs. He almost ran up the perron, pushed open the great gate, and hurried across hall and corridor and up the marble staircase to the distant small withdrawing room, where *Monseigneur* usually spent the best part of the day.

Aurore was there with her father. She was busy sewing, and *Monseigneur* was reading a paper which seemed highly to incense him, for just as the *curé* entered the room he crushed it in his hand and threw it on the floor with an oath. The priest sank, puffing and panting, into a chair:

"Those poor people! those poor miserable fools!" he began and mopped his streaming forehead.

Monseigneur looked at him and laughed.

"You need not tell me," he said curtly. "I know."

Aurore looked up from her sewing; she looked first at her father, then at the *abbé*; then she put down her work. Something terrible had happened. The strange glitter in her father's eyes, the anxiety and distress in the *curé's* face, but, above all, her intuition and a sense of foreboding told her that something terrible had happened.

"What is it?" she demanded.

"Those poor people," the priest murmured, "they are so foolish—so ignorant-"

"Ruffians and devils!" *Monseigneur* declared, and struck the table with his fist, "they have learned at last that I, for one, am not to be defied."

Aurore took hold of his hand; the one with which he had struck the table.

"What has happened?" she demanded again.

There was a moment's silence. Only a few seconds. But during those seconds she heard. The window was open, and she heard the clamour—the sound of feet tramping up the slope and of a dull murmur that mingled with the rumbling of the distant thunder. She knew what it meant. Without doubt an in a moment, she knew what it meant. Newspapers, pamphlets, rumours had found their way to this lonely corner of France. Aurore de Marigny knew that all over the country demagogues—men like that André Vallon—spent their time in inciting all the ruffians they could get hold of to do acts of violence against persons of property. She knew that. And she knew what the outcome of such provocations had often been. Outrage. Death. Sometimes worse than death.

She questioned her father. She had the right to know. They would all hold their lives in their hands in a few minutes when the crowd reached the *château*. She had the right to know, she declared. Something had roused the village folk to frenzy: what was it?

Monseigneur shrugged and said nothing. The glitter in his eyes was like that of a madman. The old priest, overcome with emotion and the heat, could do nothing but mop his forehead. And the clamour from the valley grew louder and louder, the dull murmur of voices and the tramp of naked feet in the dust of the road.

And suddenly Pierre came bursting into the room, with Jeannette weeping and trailing behind him. They knew everything. Pierre had heard it all—Heaven knew how—but he had heard so he ran up—like the old *curé* had done—to warn *Monseigneur* and *Mademoiselle*. He was breathless and inarticulate, but *Monseigneur* did not interrupt him while he blurted out the whole terrible tale: the six ruffians, the eviction of the women and children, the firing of the cottages, the death of Marianne Vallon.

Charles de Marigny appeared indifferent to the whole thing and entirely disdainful. He did not even wince when Pierre spoke of the death of Marianne. The priest moaned and ejaculated: "*Mon Dieu!*" and looked to Heaven for guidance, while Aurore listened wide-eyed, horrified. At first, she was incredulous and turned to her father with an appealing and mute: "Is it true?" But his glance was obstinately averted. He stared out of the window—listening—listening for the coming of that rabble which he despised so utterly, even though their approach now probably meant death to him and to Aurore.

A few minutes later the crowd had invaded the courtyard. The shuffling of naked feet, mingling with the clatter of *sabots* and the tramping of shoes, sounded like the breaking of surf on a pebble beach. The voices were subdued, like the distant murmur of an angry sea. There were no shouts, only murmurs and occasionally the whimpering of a child.

Monseigneur rose.

"The gate——" he said curtly to Pierre.

"Barred and bolted, *Monseigneur*. Oh! *Monseigneur* didn't think that I would allow——"

Charles de Marigny did not listen. He had opened the drawer of the table against which he now proceeded to examine carefully. Aurore's large troubled eyes watched him as he drew his tall figure to its full height and then turned to the door. With a sudden little cry, she ran and stood between him and that door. "You are not going to meet them, Father!" she exclaimed impulsively, and put out her arms to stop him, but he pushed her roughly aside.

"You don't imagine," he retorted coldly, "that I would allow that rabble to come in here?"

"If you go," she protested, "I come with you."

He took hold of her wrist with such violence that she nearly cried out with pain. Who was she, he demanded, to stand in his way? How dare she pit her feeble woman's will against his determination to deal with those ruffians as they deserved?

"I order you to stay here," he commanded; and not heeding the servants' look of horror or the *curé* mild protest he dragged her roughly from the door.

"Are you trying to defy me," he thundered, "like that riffraff over there?"

And the look which he cast on her—on her, the child of his heart, the apple of his eye—was so laden with fury that she shrank from him as if he had struck her in the face.

Then he opened the door. It gave on one of the great reception rooms, used as a ballroom in the olden days. A long *vista* of parquet flooring, of mirrors and girandoles, of tapestries and consoles, stretched out to the other great doors opposite. Aurore turned a last appealing look to the *curé*.

"You must obey your father, my child," he said. "God will protect him, and you can do nothing."

He struggled to his feet and beckoned to Pierre. Charles de Marigny had already gone through the door, and now the Abbé Rosemonde and Pierre went out in his wake.

Chapter 21

The great room was empty. Silent and majestic, with its gilded mirrors and chandeliers and rows of chairs ranged round the walls as if ready to receive the ghosts of the grand ladies and gentlemen who had chatted here a few short weeks ago, had flirted and laughed and fluttered their fans and danced the minuet in their high-heeled shoes before they made their way up the steps of the guillotine or sought safety in an obscure corner of some foreign land.

But Charles de Marigny had no mind for sentimental recollections just now. He strode across the room to the great central window and threw it open. Like the sudden bursting of a dam, the sound of the surging crowd rose in a strident cadence. *Monseigneur* stepped out on the balcony and looked down on them. How ugly they were! Dirty, unkempt, clad for the most part in filthy rags! He loathed them! Oh! how he loathed them! The men! The women! Those half-naked, unwashed children! Were they human at all? In the olden days he would have classed all that rabble as lower and of less consequence than his cattle or his dogs.

He stood there for quite a few moments looking at them, his arms resting on the marble balustrade, the pistol in his hand. They had come to a standstill in the vast forecourt and were evidently debating what to do next. Then a man's figure detached itself from the rest. He wore an old military coat, one of the sleeves of which was empty and fastened to a button on his chest. He wore shoes and stockings, but his head was bare, and his hair was the colour of a horse-chestnut when it bursts its green prickly shell.

There was something vaguely familiar in the face, those dark eyes and chiselled features, which recreated in *Monseigneur's* memory a vision out of the past—a boy half naked, with straight young back and firm limbs standing at the whipping post, while he and Hélène de Beauregard looked on rather amused. Hélène had put up her *lorgnette* and compared him to a rebel angel. He looked more like a demon now.

He strode across the forecourt and up the perron. Two others, more swinish than the rest, followed him. Charles de Marigny watched them. No one had caught sight of him yet, for the balcony was thirty feet from the ground and twenty from the top of the perron. The three men came to a halt in front of the great wrought-iron and gilded gates.

Pierre whispered to *Monseigneur*:

"Good thought I had of locking them. They'd want a cannon to break them open."

The men, seeing that the gates were locked, appeared to hesitate, and suddenly the man with the empty sleeve looked up.

"Marigny!" he called out and pointed to the balcony. The crowd at once gazed upward. They say "*Monseigneur.*" They shouted, "Assassin! Open the gates!" The women waved their arms; the men shook menacing fists. But Charles de Marigny remained motionless and detached, with an expression of withering scorn on his pale, aristocratic face.

"Open the gates, Marigny," André Vallon commanded. "The people here want a talk with you."

De Marigny's sole response was a peremptory:

"Get out of there! All of you, get out!"

"Don't be a fool, Marigny!" André retorted loudly. "The people will not stand your arrogance. They have come to speak with you, and speak with you they will, if they have to pull down these stone walls about your ears."

"Get out!" Charles de Marigny called out in reply. "The gates through which you came are open! Get out!"

"Open the gates!" they all shouted.

"Get out!"

The tumult was waxing fast and furious down below. Murmurs had long since turned to raucous shouts, in which the words, "Traitor! Tyrant! Death!" came clearer than the rest. But "Death!" clearest of all. The Abbé Rosemonde tried in his feeble way to restrain *Monseigneur*, but Charles de Marigny shook himself free with a loud oath from the kindly hand on his shoulder.

"Open the gates!" André's voice rose above that of the others, and Tarbot and Molé, like a pair of savage dogs on the leash, cried out, "Open the gates or we'll burst them open!" Whereat a boy's voice in the crowd rose shrilly:

"If we burst them open there'll be no talking: only death for the traitor."

"Death! Traitor! Assassin!"

"The guillotine!"

Pierre's teeth were chattering with terror. He kept on murmuring, as if to give himself courage: "They can't burst them open! They can't! They'd want a cannon!"

Charles de Marigny drew himself up. Only his hand now, the one which held the pistol, rested on the marble balustrade. He wanted them to see him better, to see the contempt with which he regarded them and their futile efforts to intimidate him. He turned half away from the balcony as if that rabble down there was not even worth a glance. He shrugged ostentatiously when the words, "Assassin! the guillotine!" rose more and more insistently from below.

"Let us go back, *M. l'Abbé*," he said calmly, "and see what Aurore is doing. When these muckworms are tired of shouting they'll clear out fast enough."

As far as he was concerned that was all! Rabble! riffraff! the scum of humanity! That is what they were! And trying to frighten him? Ludicrous, of course! Contemptible! What a fool to have brought his pistol! As if those cravens would ever dare—

A simultaneous cry from the *abbé* and Pierre caused him to swing back suddenly.

The man with the empty sleeve had clambered up to the balcony.

299

With the aid of projections in the stonework and the age-old ivy which, untended, had spread over the wall, he had pulled himself up. Tarbot and Molé were following him, but he, André, had got there first. One arm can be as good as two when fury whips up the blood. With the aid of his one arm and a sinewy pair of legs he was soon over the balustrade, even before the cry of alarm spent itself in the old priest's throat.

Monseigneur swung round. The pistol was in his hand, even with André's head.

"Another step and I shoot!" he called.

"Shoot and be damned!" André retorted, and with a bound was on the floor of the balcony. His arm shot out; his fingers, hard as steel, closed round De Marigny's wrist and forced his arm up, up, and back from the shoulder. The pistol went off with a loud report and then dropped from the nerveless hand to the ground.

From the crowd below came an infuriated yell.

"À *moi*, Pierre!" Charles de Marigny shouted. And then, "Let go my arm, *canaille!*"

Before Pierre could come to his master's rescue, Tarbot and Molé were over the balustrade, too, and onto him. They took no notice of the *curé*, for he had fallen on his knees, poor old man! and was imploring God to protect *Monseigneur*; but they held Pierre down while André forced De Marigny, step by step, back into the room. Like a vise, that one hand of his was nearly wrenching the upturned arm out of its socket.

"*Mon Dieu, ayez pitié!*" the priest murmured fervently, whilst *Monseigneur*, though half swooning with pain, reiterated obstinately, "*Canaille! Canaille!* Get out!"

The crowd, baulked of the sight of their enemy, had resumed their cry of "Assassin!" A few of them, more vigorous than the others, tried to follow their leader's example by climbing up the ivy-covered wall. The other's shouted, "Open the gate!" whereupon Molé, the wheelwright, seized Pierre by the arm and said curtly:

"You hear them, citizen? Come and open the gate."

"Pierre, I forbid you," *Monseigneur* attempted to command, but Molé had already marched Pierre out through the door, while André, step by step, pushed De Marigny back into the room.

When he had got him right over to the other end, with his back to the door of the small *boudoir*, he released his arm. It fell, nerveless and numb. Obviously, the man was in great pain, but pride kept him on his feet. Obstinate and arrogant he was; he could be cruel, too, where his dignity was at stake; but he was no coward, either morally or physically. He did not regret the firing of the cottages, that act of madness which had brought this yelling horde about his ears. He felt faint and giddy, but with a mighty effort he kept himself upright. There was a chair close by, but he would not allow himself to sing into it, and even while André stood towering above him like a statue of wrath and vengeance, his lips continued to murmur mechanically, "*Canaille!* Get out!"

André gave a contemptuous shrug:

"*Canaille* we are," he said with a sneer, "that's understood, but we are a *canaille* who today demand justice. You have committed an outrage which calls to Heaven for vengeance, and we have come here to show you that we mean to get it."

"Murder, I suppose?" De Marigny said coldly.

"Killing is no murder when justice demands it. A few hours ago, two defenceless women and a crowd of children were turned out of their homes by your orders. My mother gave up her life to rescue the few belongings of a poor widow and her children. As sure as that I hold your worthless life in my hands, her death is at your door. Killing is no murder, Marigny, when it means justice."

Still De Marigny did not flinch. He made no reply, and for a few seconds they stood facing each other, these two men, each the product of his own upbringing and of his century; each imbued with the passion and cruelty of men when they defend what they hold most dear. Charles de Marigny, unbending and imperious, seemed at this moment to be entrenched within the last outpost of his caste, and to be safeguarding his right of property and the privileges of his birth. Immaculately dressed, his hair carefully powdered, his fine linen scarcely disarranged even after a hand-to-hand struggle with this renegade, his pale face betrayed no emotion, only a withering contempt.

And André Vallon, the typical child of this bloody revolution, the son of a people who for generations had suffered and toiled like beasts of burden and looked with patient, submissive eyes on the pomp and luxury that never could be theirs; who had never eaten their fill while others feasted; who had wallowed in poverty and ignorance with hardly the promise of Heaven to save them from despair: André with shabby coat and empty sleeve, with glowing eyes and heart overflowing with resentment for past tyranny and unavenged wrongs, André stood for those stirrings which men like Rousseau had first infused

301

into their blood.

And as De Marigny worshipped privilege, so did these youngsters worship at the shrine of the newly discovered goddess, Liberty. A new dawn had arisen for them, and they fell on their faces and adored. They ate the fruit of the Tree of Knowledge. They learned and they pondered, and from out the depths of their soul they evolved the consciousness of the dignity of man.

"*Canaille* we are!" he had thrown back the challenge in De Marigny's face: "low, unwashed, and ignorant, but men for all that. For centuries your cast denied us the right to live as we desired, to share in what goodness the world holds—the right to hold our homes sacred, our wives and daughters inviolate. But now we are your masters at last. We're butchered, we've despoiled, we've killed, but the measure of justice is not yet full. Hundreds of you have mounted the guillotine, and hundreds more shall do the same until we get what we demand—justice!"

All that he said and more, while Charles de Marigny's face expressed nothing but disgust at being in such close contact with this filthy horde.

Chapter 22

And now the crowd came pouring into the *château*. Pierre had been made to open the gate, and they all rushed up the marble staircase. They invaded the hall and the vast reception rooms. Awed at first by so much magnificence of which they had no conception, by the gliding and the crystals and the damask chairs, and by the mirrors which reflected their dark faces and their rags and made their numbers seem so much greater than they were.

But the awe soon wore off. So much magnificence! And there were the Louvet children homeless; and Marianne Vallon lay dead in her ruined home.

"Well, André!" one of the men asked. "What says the *aristo*?"

"Not much to say, I imagine," said another.

"I am for slitting his throat at once and have done with him." This from Tarbot, the ex-butcher, who always kept a knife in his belt.

"I prefer the guillotine," declared Molé sententiously. "It's more effective. An example to others, what?"

"Let's hear what he's got to say first, and then we'll see."

De Marigny's fine white hand felt in his pocket and drew out a lace-bordered handkerchief, which he raised to his nose. With a rough gesture André tore it out of his hand.

"Play-acting, Marigny!" he said with a sneer.

"Let me slit his throat, André!" Tarbot demanded.

"Murder, by all means," De Marigny retorted coolly.

"Murder? No," André declared. "I too am for the guillotine. The people want to see you die a dog's death. Murder? Bah! Will one moment's anguish in your miserable life give us back our youth spent in toiling so that you might feast; gives us back our health impaired by starvation while you ate and drank your fill? The last drain of your life's blood, Marigny, cannot make good your tyranny. It cannot! It cannot! You cannot make good, for you have nothing now—no power, no riches, none of the claptrap that made you think you were a creature apart while we were just swine."

His words acted like a gust of wind on a smouldering flame. Some were for immediate murder, others like the thought of the more protracted agony of the guillotine, but all wanted this man's death. They hungered for it. They ached for a sight of his blood. There was not a man or a woman there who did not see that pale, proud face through a veil of crimson. But they still help their breath like wild beasts when they have sighted their prey and are ready to spring. Like felines they were, licking their jaws, enjoying to its full the sublime sense of power over the life and death of a fellow man.

"Strike him, André!" one of the men shouted. "I am for instant death."

"Remember your mother, André!" yelled another. "Why wait for the guillotine."

And suddenly the door behind De Marigny flew open, and Aurore rushed in, a vision pale and ethereal, with fair hair loose and eyes as dark as the midnight sky in June. In an instant she was beside her father, her arms were round him, her head was against his breast. Her slender body was a shield between him and his enemies.

André had uttered one loud, savage oath, and then remained dumb, staring at the girl, while the crowd, taken aback for a few seconds, soon began to laugh and jeer. A fresh spectacle this: this fine lady with her laces and her frills. The wolves in expectation of the slaughtered sheep rejoiced at sight of the lamb.

"For God's sake, Aurore, go back!" *Monseigneur* exclaimed. At first, he had been half dazed, hardly believed his eyes when he saw Aurore. He was like a man in a trance, not fully wakened from a dream. "*Monsieur l'Abbé*, take her away!" he added, vainly trying to perceive the *curé's* face in the midst of the crowd. He himself did what he could to drag Aurore's arms away from his shoulders, whilst the old priest made a vain effort to reach her. But all this was of no avail. It was Molé, the wheelwright, who seized hold of Aurore by the waist and dragged her away from her father. In a moment she was surrounded. The women in the forefront pulled at her gown and tore at the lace of her sleeve.

"How much did your gown cost, my cabbage?" one of them jeered.

"As much as would keep a family in food for a year," declared another.

"Strip it off," suggested one of the men with a coarse laugh.

One of the women grabbed at her *fichu*; another tugged at the ribbon in her hair; the older ones lifted her dress and pulled at the lace petticoats, the dainty stockings and silk garters. Obscene jests went round:

"Strip off her clothes!" called Legendre, the young imp with the game leg.

"Pigs! Curs! Let her go!" De Marigny cried at the top of his voice, and tried to reach his daughter, but the whole crowd was in the way, laughing and jeering, pressing round the girl with shouts of derision and of glee. They elbowed De Marigny out of the way. One of the men struck him on the face with his fist, and he fell bleeding to the ground. He tried to drag himself up again until another man kicked him and he lost consciousness.

Aurore gave an agonised cry of horror, the first she had uttered since she had faced the crowd. Wildly, like a young animal at bay, she looked about her, and her eyes met those of André Vallon.

He as outside the crowd, had stood there ever since she first came into the room, vaguely retracing in his mind the childish features of ten years ago in that lovely face, contorted with fear. With a mechanical movement his hand went up to his breast, where all those years ago her head had rested for one brief moment, on the very spot where they empty sleeve was now attached. Her soft fair hair had tickled his cheeks; the scent of violets and roses had risen to his nostrils. He had been in a dream until the rough blow on his face from the hand of an insolent fop had awakened him and kept him awake all those years with the memory of a crowning insult.

He had been in a dream then; he was in a dream now, until her eyes met his. Then suddenly he pushed his way through the crowd. With his one arm he seized Aurore round the waist and lifted her off her feet.

"The wench is mine!" he called aloud.

Holding her closely to him, he pushed his way back as far as the door of the *boudoir* to the accompaniment of vociferous shouts and laughter from the astonished crowd. Here was a novel spectacle, forsooth!

"He was always a madcap, that André!" the women declared, while laughter brought tears to their eyes. Laughter, perhaps, or something a little softer, more gentle: a vague sense of romance never quite absent from the hearts of a Latin race.

André had allowed the girl to slide out of the shelter of his arm. She collapsed on the floor right against the door like a pathetic bundle of laces and frills. She was not quite conscious. Terror and horror combined had obscured her senses. With her small trembling hands, she grasped the corner of a console as she slid down on her knees, and through her bloodless lips came pitiful moans and whispered murmurs, "Father! My father!"

André stood guard over her like a desert beast over its prey. He stood, tall and erect, with head thrown back and legs wide apart, a vivid presentment of the conquering male. The crowd was certainly amused. Some of them tried to push forward to peer once again closely at the *aristo*, her silks and her laces, but André with his stentorian voice kept them all at bay.

"Hands off! The wench is mine!"

"What will you do with her, André?" a voice called laughing out of the crowd.

"Take her for wife, *pardi*," André retorted. "I must have someone to wash and cook for me. The wench pleases me. She's mine!"

This sally was greeted with a wealth of coarse jests from the men, but the women were all on the side of André. They liked his looks, his flashing eyes, darker than ever in his pale, determined face. They liked his full red lips which showed a glimmer of white teeth like those of a young cat.

"Let him be, he was always a madcap!"

"If he wants the wench, why shouldn't he have her?"

And whisperings went the round: stories of André Vallon's pranks before he left the village to seek fortune in Paris. Not a boy for leagues around he had not licked, not a pretty girl whom he had not kissed.

"Let him have her if he wants her."

The men agreed. Even Tarbot, whose lust for killing had a few moments ago turned him into a savage brute, shrugged his wide shoulders and said coolly with a coarse jest:

"Better than the guillotine, anyway!"

One of the men who had worked at the *maire* in Nevers added sententiously:

"If he likes to take her for wife there would be no guillotine for her."

"Is that so?" the others asked.

"The new law," the man from Nevers declared curtly. "A patriot may save an *aristo* from the guillotine if he chooses to marry her."

They discussed this matter from several points of view. Those big-wigs up in Paris were always framing new laws, but this was not a bad one. France was in need of children. The men, at any rate, were all in its favour because, forsooth, they were well-favoured, those *aristos*— soft skins, fluffy hair, better nourished than the poor village wenches. The women, on the other hand, liked the romance of it, especially if the patriot was young and handsome, like André Vallon.

André himself listened to all the comments and the murmurings with a vague smile on his lips. Perhaps he only half heard what was said. His glance more often than not wandered round to that motion-less figure, crouching against the door, and when a pitiful moan came to his ears, a look almost of ferocity flashed out of his eyes.

The priest had contrived to get near to Aurore. He stooped and put his hand on her shoulder. He whispered comforting words to her, but the only response she gave was a pathetic murmur: "My father? Where is he?"

André, at sight of the priest, had become more and more impa-tient, and suddenly, like a man who has come to the end of his tether, he turned and kicked open the door. The small withdrawing room beyond was in semidarkness. Jeannette was in there, squatting on a low stool, weeping into her apron which covered her face. There was a book on the floor, an open workbox, a piece of embroidery on the table with a thimble and scissors beside it. The room looked cosy in the half-light with all these little intimacies. André glanced into it, then down on the crouching figure at his feet. God in heaven! how he hated it all! The beauty, the cosiness, and the perfume as of a bouquet of flowers that seemed to dull his senses!

"Stop your mumblings," he said roughly to the priest, "and take her in there."

Aurore wouldn't move, though she looked up for a moment when she heard the door open behind her. Not seeing her father, she turned on André.

"My father!" she demanded.

He took her by the wrist and dragged her roughly into the *boudoir*. "I'll look after your father," he said curtly. "He's safe enough for the moment."

The Abbé Rosemonde slipped in after them and closed the door. Strangely enough, the crowd did not attempt to follow. They stood outside jeering and sniggering, vastly amused at the turn of events. So unexpected this romance of the *aristo* and that madcap André! It might turn to tragedy, some of them thought, but even so, it was better than the guillotine.

Some of the men gazed down on De Marigny lying unconscious in a corner of the room with a bleeding wound on his face: Bah! he was hardly worth a kick now. A miserable rag of humanity, trampled in the dust as he had been wont to trample those whom he despised. His very life he owed to one of the despised rabble, and his daughter, who was his pride and joy, would be the property of a man whom in the past he would have looked on as lower than his dog. She would have to cook and wash for him as Marianne Vallon had cooked and washed up at the *château*. It was that, or the guillotine for the lot of them. Ah! this revolution was indeed a great thing. It had turned the tables on those proud *aristos* with a vengeance. More power to its elbow, and long life to Georges Danton and all its makers.

Long life above all to the child of the Revolution, André Vallon.

Chapter 23

At first Aurore had made futile efforts to free herself from André's grasp. Then, feeling helpless, she gave up the struggle, whereupon he immediately released her wrist. She turned at once to the door.

"Open, *M. l'Abbé!*" she called. "I must find *Monseigneur*."

The priest would have obeyed, but André barred the way.

"I said that I would look after Marigny," he said curtly. "You stay here with her."

Aurore's hand was on the door knob.

"Wait here, *M. l'Abbé*," she said, "while I speak with *Monseigneur*."

André was quite close to her, looking down on her half quizzically, yet wholly in scorn. She threw back her head and returned his mocking glance with defiance and cold contempt, and when he put his hand over hers she withdrew it quickly, as if she had been touched by some noisome animal. A grim smile curled round André's set lips.

"If you go out through this door," he said coolly, "it means death to your father, to this priest, to your servants and to you."

Defiance in her eyes gave way to horror. She did not know what had become of her father. The turmoil in the next room had subsided to such an extent that she had not realised there was still danger there from the crowd. This male ruffian here, with his brute strength and mocking ways, seemed to be the only living creature that she need fear. Apparently, he had divined her thoughts, for without another word he turned the knob and gently opened the door. A murmur of many voices came to Aurore's ears. There were no longer any shouts, no imprecations or threats—only that steady murmur, and now and then a laugh. Just as the moment a man's voice rose above the rest, and a phrase, coarse and hideously offensive, accompanied by a cruel laugh, brought a blush of indignation and of shame to the girl's face. It suffused her cheeks, her forehead to the roots of her hair; only her lips remained bloodless. The glance which she cast up at André was almost one of appeal.

Miserable and helpless, she gazed round the room, longing to find something—weapon, anything wherewith to end this terrible situation. Again, he seemed to divine her thoughts, gave a light laugh and a shrug, then pointed to one of the chairs across which lay *Monseigneur's* elegant sword, with its jewelled hilt and chiselled scabbard. As she made no movement—indeed, she could not have moved a limb just then—he went over to the chair and picked up the sword. He made pretence to examine it; with his one hand he worked the blade out of the scabbard, and with that irritating, quizzical glance of his held the hilt out to her.

"Will this answer your purpose?" he asked.

Strangely fascinated by that blade from which, at the moment, the evening light drew dull fantastic rays, she raised her hand and took hold of the hilt. Here was the weapon to her hand: what should she do with it? The brute stood there, waiting and mocking: oh, for the strength to plunge this blade into his cruel, callous heart!

"Aurore, my child!" the priest exclaimed, for, acting on blind impulse, Aurore had stretched out her arm and was holding the point of the blade to her throat.

"Let her be, Citizen Curé," André said coolly. "Reason has already told her that with her death my wish to save her father—and you—will vanish. Look, what did I tell you? Even proud ladies listen to reason sometimes. And, anyhow, that sword was both futile and ridiculous."

The sword fell out of Aurore's hand. Futile and ridiculous! How true and how humiliating! Helpless, hopeless, and ashamed, she buried her face in her hands.

"André, my son!" the priest entreated, "you must have pity on us all."

"Pity?" André retorted lightly. "*Pardi!* Am I not showing you all pity of which any man is capable? Have I not snatched her and her miserable father, and you, my good friend, out of the jaws of death? Has not my pity for her stayed the murderous hand of our friend Tarbot and saved her from outrage?"

"Yes, my son," the *curé* admitted, "and of a certainty God will reward you; but surely you do not intend to carry your cruel intention to its end?"

"What cruel intention? I have no other intention with regard to this wench save to take her for wife."

"But, André, my son, that is impossible."

"Impossible? Why?"

"Look at her, my child. Does she look like the wife of—"

"—of a rapscallion?" André broke in with a sneer. "That is as may be and for her to decide. If the prospect is so very displeasing, all she need do is to open this door and let the rest of the *canaille* have its way with her, with her father, her servants, and with you."

Then, as neither Aurore nor the *curé* spoke another word, he went on, with an impatient shrug:

"Perhaps you are right, Citizen Curé: the scheme will not work. It is impossible, as you say, and I'd better let our friend Tarbot have his way with you all."

Once more he turned to the door; but it was Aurore this time who barred the way. A dull, half-choked cry came involuntarily from her throat:

"No! no!"

She put out her hand, and he seized it.

"Ah!" he said with a sigh of satisfaction, "reason has spoke more loudly this time. Well! which is it to be, my fine lady? Death at the hand of Tarbot or marriage with the *canaille?*"

The grip on her waist was like a tentacle of steel, but she welcomed the physical pain almost as a solace to the mental agony of the moment. She would not look at him, but turned appealing eyes to the old priest, who, of a truth, could offer neither advice nor consolation.

It was for her to decide and he, for one, was content to leave it all in the hands of his Maker. He clasped his hands and prayed as he had never prayed before.

"Look at me, Aurore," André commanded. "The decision rests with you and not with the priest."

With what seemed like a refinement of cruelty, he once more gently opened the door. They were still laughing and jeering out there.

"My father!" she murmured.

And then added under her breath:

"For his sake, if you'll swear—"

She could say no more, for she was on the point of swooning. André's powerful arm encircled her drooping body, while an immense sigh of satisfaction rose from his breast.

"*Par Dieu!*" he said lightly. "I had no idea you were so beautiful, *ma mie!*"

And of a truth she was exquisitely beautiful, with those deep, unfathomable eyes of hers filled with terror and with hate, her red lips parted in a final appeal for mercy. She had been on the point of swooning, but now that he raised her to him—that she saw his face, his dark eyes, his cruel, sneering mouth closer and ever closer, a moment's consciousness returned to her with the horror of it all.

"Let me go!" she gasped. "I hate you!"

"Of course, you do, my dear," he retorted. "We hate each other—that is understood. But Fate has decided to link us together until, like two wildcats, we shall have torn one another's soul to shreds. In the meanwhile, in the presence of our friend, the Citizen Curé, we will seal our mutual promise to one another with a kiss."

She felt helpless and stifled as his arm held her closer and closer; with her two hands she tried to push against him—his face, his breast. But her struggles only seemed to amuse him; his eyes flashed mockery instead of passion, while they seemed to search the very depths of her soul.

"You are beautiful!" he reiterated slowly—very slowly—while those mocking eyes of his drank in every detail of her loveliness: her blue-veined lids, her perfect mouth, the exquisite contour of throat and chin. "You are beautiful, but, on second thoughts, *ma mie*, I'll not kiss you yet. Not today. I'll wait," he added with a light laugh, "till those perfect lips ask mine for a kiss."

And suddenly he slackened his hold on her, lifted her off the ground, and carried her to the sofa. He called peremptorily to Jeannette, who was whimpering under cover of her apron, and ordered her to look after her mistress.

Then, without another word, he strode out of the room.

Chapter 24

The crowd in the meantime had worked its will in the old *château*. With the exit of the hero and heroine of a brief romance, reaction had set in. The fury of reprisal, merged for a moment in laughter and coarse jests, reasserted its domination. The *aristos* were ashamed and punished; the *ci-devant* Marigny lay half dead on the floor; but this seemed hardly compensation enough for two smouldering cottages and the death of a valiant woman. Not enough, of a truth, with all this magnificence flaunted in these gorgeous halls, with tapestries and sconces and mirrors, all accessible to eager, needy hands. Not much notice was taken of Marigny. Once kicked conveniently aside, he was allowed to remain lying there. Dead or alive? Who cared, when there were damask curtains to be had for the taking?—useful things to replace shawls and blankets long since worn to rags.

Down came the curtains, one after the other, torn down by vigorous hands. In the vast banqueting halls there was not much that was useful, but there were chairs and tables to replace humble ones that had been used for fuel when other wood was so dear. And in the bedrooms, there were beds and mattresses and pillows and blankets; there was china and there were carpets. The crowd wandered from room to room, from stately hall down to pantries and kitchens and bakehouses. The cellars were empty, and so were the larders, but there were pots and pans galore. Where silver and gold were hidden they knew not. Perhaps they never even thought of such things. It was the chairs and the tables, the curtains and the pots and pans that they needed and that they took.

Who shall judge them? Who condemn? They had nothing, and they took. For generations successive governments had taken from them all that they had. Human nature will always try and hit back when it has the chance. They were not evil, these people here; they were not really cruel and rapacious by nature: hunger and want had made them so, and the sense of oppression and injustice. Who, of a truth, shall condemn them?

When they were tired of looking and had their arms full, when they were wearied with the day's work and emotion, they wandered homeward. The evening was drawing in, and squalid homes called to them, and the longing to gloat over stolen treasure and find use for it all. One by one, or in groups of twos and threes, they trudged back through the vast halls, shorn now of much glory, down marble stairs, and across the forecourt. Their naked feet were sore with tramping; they wanted to get home.

André stood for a long time by the door, listening and watching. The great reception room was deserted by now, but he could hear the crowd wandering about the *château*; he could hear cries of delight and laughter and guessed what was going on. He made his way across the room to the window, staggering in the darkness like a man drunk. Leaning against the window frame, he gazed out into the fast-gathering gloom. From the distance, now and then, there still came the dull rumbling of faraway thunder, and from time to time the treetops were lit up with the reflex of distant lightning, but the storm never broke over Marigny on that never-to-be-forgotten day in July.

André watched the crowd, as, one by one, they came through the gate, bearing their loot—furniture, tapestries, clothes. The women staggered under their loads; the men looked like beasts of burden, dragging their shoeless feet over the paved forecourt. Slowly, wearily, they made their way down the wooded slope. André, through the darkness, could still distinguish some of them: the women in their faded kirtles; the naked bodies of little children; Tarbot and his red cap, Molé and his ragged shirt. He thought of his mother, lying on the old paillasse, with a ragged shawl to cover her body, and all around her the ruins of her home. And with thoughts of her there came into his soul an immense wave of shame.

The large empty room with its torn tapestries and gilded chairs lying topsy-turvy about the floor became filled all at once with imps and demons who hopped all around him and cried, "Shame!" in his ears. They called him a fool and coward. Why not have allowed the mob to have its way with the *aristos?* Were they not his friends? Riff-raff, like himself? Then why have interfered? There might have been some satisfaction in seeing justice done. A life for a life! Those miserable aristos for the saintly woman who lay silent and stark in her devastated home.

With a rough gesture he brushed those imaginary demons away. Shame had brought the blood beating in his temples. "Coward!" and "Traitor!" he called himself, and then signed with a great unexplainable longing. "Justice! Truth! My God! where are they now?"

The room was so still! So still! André strained his ears to hear any sound that might come from the *boudoir*. After a moment or two he heard a soft grating; the door was opened very gently, a narrow shaft of light pierced the gloom, and the old priest tiptoed stealthily into the room. André listened without stirring: the old man had left the door slightly ajar and now groped his way cautiously about in the darkness. A moment or two later soft murmurings came to André's ears; then a sigh—a struggle. And the priest's kindly words:

"Lean on my arm, *Monseigneur*—"

And then another sigh. A whisper: "Aurore!"

"She is safe, *Monseigneur*. Shall we go to her?"

"Has that *canaille* gone?"

"There is no one here now, *Monseigneur*—"

"My head! My head! May God punish those ruffians!"

"Do lean on me, *Monseigneur*—I am quite strong—Don't be afraid."

André's eyes, accustomed to the gloom, could now perceive the two old men moving slowly towards the door. Instinctively he stepped back from the window farther into the shadows, and thus, hidden from view, he waited until the priest had piloted De Marigny back into the *boudoir*.

As the *curé* was about to follow, André called to him:

"Citizen Rosemonde!" The priest paused with his hand still on the door knob, and André called again: "Close that door. I want to speak with you."

The voice was low, scarcely above a whisper, but so peremptory that the priest, after a few seconds' hesitation, closed the door and came across the room. With the passing of immediate danger to Monseigneur and Aurore he seemed to have recovered something of his natural dignity. He approached André not as a servant beckoned to by his master, but as a minister of God, with a mission to mediate between warring souls.

"What is it you wish, my son?" he asked.

"Only to give you a word of warning, citizen," André replied curtly. "You must understand once and for all that my mind is made up. I have decided to take that woman in there for my wife. As you have taken the oath of allegiance to the Republic, you are bound in law to perform the marriage ceremony. You know that, do you not?"

"I know it, my son, but—"

"There is no 'but' about it. If you refuse you forfeit every privilege which your oath of allegiance has conferred upon you. Your church will be closed, and you may or may not escape with your life. But even that is beside the question, for if the marriage is not solemnised in your church it will be done in the *maire* which, as you also know, is all that the law requires."

"André, my child," the priest protested, "I implore you to think over what you propose doing. I beg it of you in your mother's name——"

"Do not speak of my mother, Citizen Curé," André broke in harshly, "or I swear to you that I will call the worst of that rabble back and hand over that damned assassin to them to be dealt with as they choose."

"But such a marriage is an outrage, André!"

"Was not the eviction of two defenceless women and a pack of starving children an outrage? Was not the ruin of their homes an outrage? My mother's death—was that not a murder most foul?"

"Ah!" the priest exclaimed, "then you admit it, André?"

"Admit what?"

"That your whole purpose is one of revenge."

"Call it justice, Citizen Curé. You'll be nearer the mark."

"And you, my son, will be the first to suffer."

André shrugged with cynical indifference.

"Bah!" he said. "Your friend Marigny would tell you that muck-worms such as I are made to suffer."

The priest was silent for a moment or two. His heart ached for this man whom he had seen grow up in this village—a merry, care-free lad whom the cruelty of fate, and perhaps of men, had rendered bitter and cynical. But it ached also for the exquisite girl whose every instinct of pride and aloofness would be outraged by this monstrous union.

"You will kill her, André," he sighed, "if you persist."

"Bah!" André retorted drily. "She's young. She will get used to being the wife of a *caitiff*. And anyhow, her life and that of her father will be safe. I can see to that."

"Alas!"

"Why alas?"

"They would sooner be dead."

André gave a scornful laugh.

"The *aristo's* sword," he said, "is still handy."

"I forbid you to mock, André," the priest retorted with energy. "Religion which you choose to ignore still holds sway in the hearts of many, and religion forbids——"

"Suicide," André broke in. "Yes, I know! Well, the rabble only needs recalling——"

"André, in Heaven's name, don't talk like that! I am appealing to your pity—"

"Pity? Would you call it pity to let a pack of snarling hyenas loose once again on this house, to stand by and see that arrogant old madman in there massacred before his daughter's eyes, to see her brutalised and outraged as a prelude to death? Is that what you would choose for her, Citizen Rosemonde?"

The old priest's head fell upon his breast. He felt utterly helpless and ashamed of his helplessness. A little while ago he believed in his mission of conciliation, but that mission had failed. His simple faith in divine interference had received a rude shock, as did his earnest belief in the justice of the Royalist cause. For here was a rebel who gloried in his rebellion, who demanded justice from God and man with as much right as the most earnest adherent to the old *régime*. Like André himself a while ago, the Abbé Rosemonde could have signed with unutterable longing, "Truth? Justice? Where are they now?"

"I suppose," he said with a doleful shake of the head, "that you've said your last word, and that nothing which I can say-"

"No, citizen," André broke in impatiently, "nothing. I have said my last word. Go down into the village, if you have a mind, and talk to the men there. Tell them that religion bids them forego revenge, and that if a man smite you on the cheek, to hold out the other so that he might smite you again. Tell that to men who have toiled and starved and sweated and seen their wives and children die for want of food, while the tax collector stood at the door and seized the few *sous* that would have bought them bread. Tell it to men who have seen their brides dragged from their arms to satisfy the caprice of their *seigneur*. Talk to them of forgiveness, Citizen Curé, now that they are the masters of France and have the power to give back blow for blow the and outrage for outrage."

Again, the priest was silent. There was so little that he could say. Never before had he been made to feel that there was something after all to be said for those terrorists who had earned for themselves the obloquy of half the world, but who had, of a truth, been the first to instil into a downtrodden people a sense of their power, both as men and as guardians of their families' welfare and of their family honour. Demagogues they were, and stirrers up of infinite trouble. They had let loose on the sacred soil of France a horde of savage brutes bent on ruin and persecution. All that was true enough, but there had been such an infinity of wrong to put right that nothing short of this im-

315

mense upheaval could possibly have done it all. But dominating all other thoughts and fears in the old man's heart were those for Aurore.

"You will be kind to her, André," he implored, "if she consents."

"I care not if she consents or no," André retorted. "Either she is mine or I let loose the floodgates of the people's wrath on this house till there remains nothing of it but a few blackened stones like those of my mother's cottage, nothing but a memory of all the arrogance and the cruelty which have turned us all into the wild beasts that we are."

André had spoken all along in a kind of hoarse murmur and without making a single gesture. Now his voice broke into a sob. He stood there in the darkness by the open window with the last glimmer of the western light outlining his clear-cut profile, the firm jaw and noble forehead with its crown of chestnut hair. And while he spoke he looked out into the distance, where far away in the peaceful valley below a puff of smoke still hung in the heavy storm-laden air. Just a puff of smoke there where the cottage once stood, where he, André, had spent the thoughtless years of childhood, where he had first learned the bitter lesson of manhood, where he had dreamed and planned and waited for this hour which had struck at last.

"You have not yet told me, André" the *curé* said at last, "what you wish me to do."

"I want you to be prepared to give my bride and me the nuptial blessing in your church tomorrow."

"Blessing!" the priest exclaimed with the nearest approach to sarcasm he had ever in his life expressed.

"As you please, of course—or as she pleases, for the matter of that. I am satisfied with the *maire*, as the law directs."

"I will do as God wills," the priest concluded with gentle dignity. "But let me tell you this, my son: your union with Aurore de Marigny is on the understanding that her life and that of her father and servants will be safe. God is long-suffering, remember, but believe me that He will know how to punish you if you should break your word."

He turned and slowly groped his way across the room. André watched him till the door of the *boudoir* finally closed upon him.

Then he, too, went his way.

Chapter 25

In an angle of the staircase André came across Pierre, concealed behind a marble column, crouching there in the dark like a frightened rabbit.

"Come and lock the gate after me, citizen," he said, and with scant ceremony dragged the man out of his hiding place.

Pierre, trembling but obedient, followed him. When the great gates fell to with a clang behind him, André stood for a moment on the perror, breathing in the heavy air of this summer's night. It seemed as if he longed to be rid of the scent of perfume and of flowers which clung to his nostrils and made his head ache with its cloying fragrance. Once or twice he passed his hand across his brow and through the thick mop of his hair. His talk with the priest which had resolved itself into a kind of profession of faith had left him in a state of bewilderment. He felt that he had become a puzzle to himself.

"Am I a brute?" he murmured. "A wild beast—a pitiless savage beast? Or just a man who has lost the being dearest to him in all the world and has nothing left in his heart but the very human desire for some measure of revenge?"

He wondered what his dead mother would have said had her precious life been spared and she had been a witness to this afternoon's tragedy. She, with her quiet philosophy and sober common sense, what would she have said in face of the homeless Louvet children and her own ruined home? Would she still have preached her favourite doctrine that evil cannot be cured with more evil? And would she still be hugging the fond belief that those *aristos* "up there" had learned something from the terrible events which had precipitated their king from his throne and left him and their kindred to the guillotine? If he had eyes to see and ears to hear, would that arrogant madman "up there" have infuriated the people to the point of seeing his daughter insulted before his eyes?

"They have learned nothing," André murmured to himself. "The lesson has, it seems, not yet been driven home."

He cast a look back on the stately pile, majestic still, in spite of approaching decay. All the windows were dark save one at the end, and here a feeble light glimmered behind a drawn curtain. They were in there. All of them. The *aristo*, the priest, and the girl. The priest had told him by now of the ultimatum which meant life and safety in exchange for union with one of the *canaille*. And André then pictured to himself what they would all say: imagine Marigny's vituperations, the priest's exhortations, and the girl's tears. She would weep, of course, and protest; beat her wings like a bird caught in a trap; and André wondered how she looked when she wept. Women were usually ugly when tears trickled down their cheeks and their noses became red.

Did those great unfathomable eyes become red and swollen, he wondered, or did the tears make their depths more mysterious still?

"Bah!" he exclaimed impatiently, "as if I cared!"

He strode down the steps and across the flagged forecourt. He was on the point of turning into the bridle path which led down to the valley through the woods when he spied a dark figure which slipped quickly past him and then through the gates into the forecourt. André watched the figure as, presently, it mounted the perron and, in a moment, disappeared through the great gates into the *château*.

Now the gates had been locked by Pierre when André left the *château* a few minutes ago. Pierre must have opened them again almost directly, which meant that the nocturnal visitor was a familiar of the house and was apparently expected.

"Talon, of course," André thought. "Now I wonder what the rascal is up to. He gave us the slip this afternoon. Then why has he come now?"

The result of his cogitation was that he retraced his steps and turned back into the forecourt just at the moment when a dim light travelled past the row of windows on the front of the *château* and stopped short at the door of the *boudoir*, where it was suddenly extinguished.

Chapter 26

André was wrong in his supposition. Talon was not expected at the *château*: it was by chance that Pierre had stood for a time by the gate, busy with lighting a couple of lanterns which he usually carried with him about the house. He had spied Hector Talon and opened the gate for him. He gave him a lantern, and Talon made his way across the hall and up the stairs with a catlike tread. He was one of those men who have carried the trick of walking noiselessly to a fine art: he made no sound as he went across the great reception room and came to a halt outside the *boudoir* door. Here he extinguished the lantern, then waited. Stooping, he glued first an eye and then an ear to the keyhole. What he heard seemed to please him, for his hatchet face broadened into a leer.

He knocked softly at the door, heard *Monseigneur's* voice and Jeannette's shuffling tread. The door was opened, and with a timid: "May I enter?" he stepped into the room.

Monseigneur was half sitting, half lying across the sofa: his cravat was undone. Aurore was behind him, intent on placing a white linen bandage over his forehead. M. l'Abbé de Rosemonde was sitting at the table in the window with his breviary open before him. No one said a word to Talon as he entered, but after a moment or two Jeannette, still at the door, turned to Aurore and asked: "Can I see about supper now, *mademoiselle?*" Aurore nodded, and Jeannette went away.

Talon ventured a step or two farther into the room.

"*Monseigneur*—" he began in his most obsequious tone.

De Marigny raised his head slightly, half opened his eyes, and looked Talon up and down as if he did not know who he was.

"Why are you here?" he asked at last. "Get out!"

"*Monseigneur*," Talon reiterated in a gentle, persuasive voice, "you know you can command my devotion. I am here to offer you my services."

"There is nothing you can do," Charles de Marigny said wearily. "Go away."

Talon glanced from one face to the other. The *abbé* appeared absorbed in his breviary. Aurore had not once glanced at him. Talon thought the *abbé's* attitude looked the least uncompromising.

"*M. l'Abbé*," he pleaded, "do, I entreat you, persuade *Monseigneur* that it is in his best interests and those of Mademoiselle Aurore to listen to me. I have come with the best and most loyal intentions."

Thus, directly appealed to, the *abbé* said, not unkindly: "Even so, my good Talon, I don't see what you can do. I don't suppose you know all that happened here this afternoon. You were so very safely out of the way."

"I do know, *M. l'Abbé*," Talon rejoined. "Everything."

At which Aurore's tired, swollen eyes shot a quick, suspicious glance at him.

"I met that blackguard André Vallon just now," Talon went on glibly, "coming away from here—alone. He chose to jeer at me for my loyalty to *Monseigneur*, and to threaten me with denunciation as a traitor if I did aught to cross his villainous schemes." He paused a moment, measuring the effect of his outrageous lies, and then went on, dropping his voice almost to a whisper: "He openly boasted before me of—of his coming marriage with Mademoiselle Aurore."

Again, he paused, waiting for a word, a sign, either from *Monseigneur* or from the girl. He felt sick with apprehension and found it terribly difficult to keep up this appearance of obsequiousness, the habit of which he had lost in these past few years. He also felt very tired. He had had a very trying day, both physically and emotionally. His head ached, and his feet were sore; his knees scarcely bore him. He wanted to sit down, to fall back into the easy familiarity to which he had accustomed himself of late, but he had too much at stake to dare risk offending *Monseigneur* or *Mademoiselle*. He had garnered scraps of information from the crowd as he met them wending their way homeward, but had scarcely believed his ears when, with much jeering and laughing and obvious satisfaction, they told him of Citizen Vallon's extraordinary project to marry the daughter of the *aristo*.

The last thing in the world Talon could have foreseen! The last thing in the world he would have wished. De Marigny's daughter married to a man like Vallon—well known in influential places as a friend of Danton—and "goodbye" to his beloved scheme of obtaining possession of the estates. There would no longer be the slightest need to emigrate or to transfer the property for worthless bonds to him. The situation was perilous because it was imminent. The women in the crowd had talked of the legal marriage taking place on the morrow. Talon had hurried up to the *château*. He wanted to clear up this dangerous situation. If Aurore de Marigny had indeed agreed to the marriage in order to save her father's life and her own, she must as quickly as possible be made to realise that such a sacrifice was unnecessary while there was a faithful and loyal bailiff at hand to show an easier and more dignified way out.

It was a little disconcerting to see her so calm and silent, and *Monseigneur* more disdainful than ever, when he had thought to find them both distraught and verging on despair. In spite of his aching feet and tired back Talon did not sit down, and as the *abbé* appeared to be more approachable than the others, Talon kept his attention fixed on him:

"*Monsieur l'Abbé*," he began, "you are a holy man; your loyalty to *Monseigneur* is as great as my own. Surely you will not allow this monstrous union to take place."

"You know as well as I do," the *abbé* replied simply, "that I am powerless to prevent it."

"I know nothing of the sort, *M. l'Abbé*," Talon retorted with well feigned vehemence. "Anyone who, like yourself, has *Monseigneur's* complete confidence can prevent it. You especially."

"My ministration," the *abbé* said, "is not imperative. André Vallon is a lawyer, and he knows that. If I refuse-"

"I did not mean that, *M. l'Abbé!*" Talon broke in impatiently. "We are none of us lawyers here, and yet we all know that by the new marriage laws a declaration before the *maire* is all that is necessary. I did not mean anything so futile."

"Then what did you mean, my good Talon?" the *curé* asked, naïvely.

"That *Monseigneur* and *Mademoiselle* must get away while there is still time."

"Get away?" The old man was puzzled, for he had never heard of *Monseigneur's* half-formed project to emigrate. "Get away? How? Where?" He closed his breviary and leaned forward, listening eagerly, while even *Monseigneur* seemed to forget his pain and weariness and sat up to gaze inquiringly on Talon, and Aurore's great tired eyes seemed indeed to probe to the very depths of the man's soul.

Talon glanced round, satisfied. He thought he time had come when he might sit down, and he sank into a chair with a great sigh of satisfaction. He beamed on *Monseigneur*, with arms outspread, like a kind and benevolent father talking to weeping children: " *Voyons, Monseigneur*," he said, "*mademoiselle!* did you really think that Talon would abandon you in the hour of your greatest need? Why, ever since that awful rabble set out to intimidate you up here, I have been scheming and planning to encompass your safety."

"Don't talk so much drivel, Talon," *Monseigneur* put in drily, "but tell us what you want."

"To get you away from here as soon as possible."

"Too late," *Monseigneur* sighed involuntarily.

"Why too late? It wants three more hours before midnight and eight before the dawn."

"What do you mean, Talon?"

"That I will have a covered cart here at your door about three o'clock of the morning. One of my farmhands will drive you to Nevers. There you can get the diligence to Bourges. It starts soon after dawn. At Bourges you can easily get a further conveyance as far as Tours—You have money, I suppose?"

"Yes, some—but no papers, no passports—nothing!"

"I have both," Talon continued eagerly. "I have papers and passports which were made out six months ago for my brother-in-law, who was a widower, and his daughter. He died before he could undertake the journey, and she has gone to live with relatives somewhere in the South. I found the papers among his effects without ever thinking that they would be of use. They are yours, if you like to use them. You can easily make up to look like the owner of the passport, Achille Vérand: he was about your age and build; and young ladies," he concluded jocosely, "can always be made up to look like one another."

The whole thing was a lie, of course. It was more than six months since Hector Talon had nursed hopes that Charles de Marigny would one day decide to emigrate. He had forged or stolen the papers, or mayhap just acquired them from some influential friend. Men like Talon always contrive to get what official documents they want. Anyway, there they were, the blessed, blessed passports! Talon laid them on the table, and the table was then dragged across to the sofa so that *Monseigneur* could look at them at his ease. *Monseigneur, Mademoiselle*, and *M. l'Abbé* all pored over them. Those blessed, blessed passports!

They were made out in the name of Achille Vérand, doctor of philosophy, aged sixty, native of Vanzy in Nièvre, and of Mariguérite Vérand his daughter, spinster, aged twenty-two. The descriptions? Well, they certainly did tally in a wonderful—an unexplainable manner. And all the papers had the official seal of the *maire* of Vanzy and the countersign of the local member of the Committee of Public Safety which sits at Nevers. Everything was in perfect, in absolute order. It was a most marvellous, a most heaven-sent coincidence that *Monseigneur* and *Mademoiselle* could make up so easily to resemble Achille and Marguérite Vérand.

Aurore, even Aurore, in her eagerness forgot all her prejudices against Talon. He was no longer to be suspected of evil intentions. He was the harbinger of hope. Captives, they were being shown he way to deliverance; drowning, they felt a hand stretched out to drag them to the shore. *M. l'Abbé* was once more getting convinced that God was on the side of the Royalist cause. And Talon was entirely in his element. Easy, familiar, jocose, he propounded his plan, satisfied that at last, not only was he in sight of the life's desire, but actually held the prize in his hand.

"You could go too, *M. l'Abbé*," he said, "if you wish. I can arrange papers for you also."

He had friends in Paris, he explained. Certain services which he had rendered the country had forced men in high places to recognise his worth, so if *M. l'Abbé* desired—But *M. l'Abbé* gently shook his head.

"While the altar of God stands in Val-le-Roi," he said, "I shall be there to administer the Holy Sacraments. But, *Monseigneur*," he exclaimed in no ecstasy of hope, "my dear Aurore, to think that freedom can, with the will of God, be yours!"

She talked of not going without him, but he said earnestly: "Your father is your first consideration, my child. It is his life and your honour that are in peril. Your father must be your first and, indeed, your only thought."

And frankly, *Monseigneur* agreed with him. Probably he did not think that the *abbé* would be in any danger, once he and Aurore were out of the way. It was against them that the fury of the mob and of that brutish ruffian Vallon was directed. And to his proud spirit any human life was worth the sacrifice to save the daughter of De Marigny from the outrage of a union with an André Vallon.

Presently some of the excitement subsided, and Talon's plan was soberly discussed. Aurore went out of the room to put a few necessities together for herself and her father. The cart, Talon explained, would be at the gate one hour before the break of dawn. Two hours' drive, and they would be in Nevers. At six o'clock the diligence started for Bourges. Talon had thought of everything, and the farm hand who would drive the cart was loyal and reliable.

Only one more matter had to be settled: the assignment of the Marigny estates to Hector Talon, bailiff, native of Val-le-Roi in Nièvre, for the sum of two million *livres*, payable in State assignats, receipt of which was hereby acknowledged by the vendor Charles Henri Marigny, *ci-devant* Duc de Marigny. *Monseigneur* hardly did more than glance at the papers. The horrors which he had gone through that afternoon had somewhat sobered that arrogant sense of possession and prerogative which theoretically he would have guarded with his life. But when it came to Aurore's future—her future with that brutish ruffian—by God! Charles de Marigny would have assigned all his worldly belongings, without counting the cost, to any man who saved her from such a fate.

He signed the papers, and Talon solemnly laid on the table assignats with the face value of two million *livres*. He had sufficient self-control not to show too plainly how intense was his satisfaction. He folded up the papers most carefully and tucked them inside his coat.

"This is a step which you will never regret, my friend," he said.

"Perhaps not," De Marigny retorted drily, "but let me assure you of one thing, my man, and that is that you will regret it—bitterly—if in any way you play me false."

"My dear sir," Talon protested. "How can you think–"

"Oh! I know more about the laws of this hellish government than you suppose. I know, for instance, that these assignments are not valid if the assignor dies within the year. The State in that case takes possession of the property. So, it is not in your interest, you rascal, to play the traitor, and you know it."

"My good friend—"

"Enough! *Mademoiselle* and I are safe from your double dealings for one year. Long before then, please God, we shall be in Belgium. And when sanity once more reigns in this demented land, and the king—God save him!—comes back into his own, your rule over my property will automatically cease."

"I know that, my good sir!"

"A sound-minded government will soon make you disgorge."

"I am taking that risk."

"Well, so long as you know that you are taking it—I only wanted you to understand that I am not the fool you fondly imagine. I am taking a risk, I know—but I am banking on the not far distant future when rascals such as you and ruffians like that Vallon will get their deserts."

"In the meantime," Talon concluded with undisguised sarcasm, "you deign to accept the use of my cart and horse, my farm hand, and the passports which I obtained for you at my own risk and peril to help you to flee this country and seek safety in Belgium."

To this Charles de Marigny vouchsafed no reply. The shaft had probably gone home. He despised this man, called him at pleasure a rascal and a thief, but he was at this moment the only being in the whole land who could save him and his daughter from death and worse than death. Talon, having had his say, was now ready to go.

"We meet in happier times, my friend," he said drily, "times happier for you, I mean. When you are safe in Belgium you will, perhaps, remember to whom you owe your safety. I will administer this estate as if it were my own for good and all. The wretched brat whom you call your king may come into his kingdom someday. Personally, I doubt it, or I would never have done this deal. The cart will be here at the hour I have named. Goodnight! Pleasant dreams! *M. l'Abbé*, your servant."

He shuffled out of the room, and for some time his footsteps, gradually dying away in the distance, were the only sound that broke the stillness of the night.

Chapter 27

The Abbé Rosemonde had resumed his orisons. *Monseigneur* was lost in a brown reverie from which the creaking of the massive gate as it was opened and then shut again roused him after a while. He lent an ear to Talon's footsteps as they echoed faintly along the flagstones of the forecourt.

A moment or two later Aurore came back.

"That awful Talon gone?" she asked with a sigh of satisfaction.

"Yes, thank God!" De Marigny replied. "I hate the sight of the rogue."

"He has saved us—"

"I know that," De Marigny was ready to admit, "but he has done it for his own ends. He has saved us, as you say, my dear. And for this I suppose we should be grateful."

"There is no possibility," Aurore queried anxiously, "of his playing us false?"

"It would be entirely against his own interests if he did," De Marigny replied drily.

"And at three o'clock we go!" she said with a long-drawn-out sigh. And then added under her breath: "I am glad that it will still be dark. I hope it will be very dark."

"It will make it safer, of course."

"Not because of that," she murmured.

"Then why—?"

"I would rather not see Marigny when I go."

"You will see it when you return, my child," the *abbé* put in cheerily. "This state of things cannot last. It will not last. I believe in God, and He will soon be avenged."

Aurore smiled on the kindly old man and quickly wiped her eyes. She loved Marigny and dreaded the long farewell—dreaded, even now, going into the unknown. The priest had risen and was looking for his hat.

"I don't think you had one, *M. l'Abbé*," Aurore said, smiling at him through her tears.

But suddenly both tears and smile vanished. She looked frightened. Her eyes dilated, her cheeks became the colour of ashes.

"What was that?" she murmured hoarsely.

"What, my dear?"

"What is it, Aurore?" *Monseigneur* asked frowning.

She seemed to be listening and put up her hand with her finger pointed towards the window.

"Didn't you hear?" she whispered.

Both the men shook their heads. She tiptoed to the window and softly pushed aside the curtain. Again, she listened. The two men remained silent, for she had put her finger to her lips. But no sound came from outside, and after a little while Aurore allowed the curtain to fall back in its place. She still looked very white, and her knees appeared to be shaking under her, for she sank into a chair.

"But what was it, Aurore?" her father asked.

"I thought I heard a sound," she murmured, "just outside the window, as if—"

"As if what?"

"I don't know. As if someone had been there—listening."

"It was Talon's footsteps you heard going across the forecourt."

"Perhaps," she admitted reluctantly, and once more tried to smile.

The *abbé* had finally turned to go.

"You are going, M. *l'Abbé?*" she asked, trying to speak calmly, though her lips were still quivering and bloodless.

"Yes, yes, my child. I'll go home now and prepare everything."

"Prepare what, M. *l'Abbé?*"

"To celebrate for you both," the old priest replied with fervent earnestness. "The church will be quite ready for you directly you pull up. You will tell the driver to stop at the churchyard gate. I will say Mass and give you both Holy Communion. After that, you can go on your long journey fortified by God's blessing. Now, if there's anything else I can do—"

Monseigneur also had risen. In spite of his vaunted self-possession, he, too, was feeling keenly the separation from his ancestral home. He felt that in going away from Marigny, in joining the large crowd of *émigrés* who had turned their backs on their country and found refuge in foreign lands, he would leave behind him something of his pride of caste, something of his dignity, something subtle and indefinable which, even if he came back one day, he would never again recapture. The old priest no doubt knew what went on in the heart and mind of his old friend. He took his leave in silence, grasping the hand which, perhaps, he would never touch again. Aurore continued to smile as she bade him farewell.

"Soon after three o'clock," she said, "we'll be outside the church door."

The hand which she gave him felt cold, and her eyes still looked dark and filled with terror. The priest patted her hand reassuringly.

"There was no one, I am sure," he said, nodding in the direction of the window. "But I'll have a good look as I go out and shoo the malefactor away. Don't be frightened, my child. I have the feeling that you are under the special protection of the holy angels this night."

He looked so serene and so reassuring that Aurore felt comforted. She found a candle and lighted it.

"I'll see you to the gate," she said.

Together they went out of the room, Aurore holding the candle high above her head. As she crossed the threshold, she could not repress a shudder: all that she had gone through that afternoon in this great gilded room came back to her with a rush of memory. Pierre had closed the window, but the night was no longer dark outside. The storm clouds had drifted away, and the waning moon had risen and tipped the treetops with her silvery light.

"It won't be so dark, after all," the priest remarked.

They had gone down the stairs and crossed the hall. The priest opened the gate.

"Go back, my little Aurore," he said as he once more bade her goodnight. "You must have lots to do, and your father will be getting anxious."

After he had gone she stood for a moment at the gate, watching while the priest walked briskly across the forecourt. A soft breeze fanned the flame of the candle, and she shielded it with her hand so that the light fell on her face and the loose golden strands of her hair. And suddenly she had the feeling that a pair of eyes was watching her out of the gloom. Hastily she blew out the candle. She was ashamed of her nervousness, for, in very truth, she was shaking with terror, while her reason told her there was nothing to fear. The *abbé's* serenity put her to shame, as did her father's coolness; she tried to steel herself against this humiliating weakness, but her teeth chattered persistently, while her head felt heavy and hot. At last she heard Pierre's voice behind her; he came shuffling across the hall, carrying a lantern. Aurore left him to close the gate and ran back as fast as she could across the hall.

Chapter 28

Aurore had considerable difficulty in getting together the few necessities which she and her father would need for their long journey. With acting heart and burning indignation she beheld the havoc which vandal hands had wrought in the *château*. Her bed had been stripped, her clothes stolen, her father's belongings had all been looted. Fortunately, there were attics and hidden recesses in the old mansion where, in the days of plenty, many things had been stowed away. With the help of Jeannette, Aurore searched for and found dark travelling clothes for herself and her father, also some changes of linen; and together they dragged down a couple of old valises in which they packed the travellers' most pressing future needs.

Aurore and her father did, after this, contrive to snatch a few hours' sleep—he on the sofa, she in an armchair. At three o'clock they were both up; washed and dressed. Half an hour later the covered cart was at the gate.

Pierre and Jeannette were going as far as Val-le-Roi to assist at the service of Holy Communion which *M. le Curé* had promised to hold in his little church. They wept copious tears while they hoisted the valises into the cart and then climbed in, in the wake of Monseigneur and Mademoiselle Aurore.

Precisely at half-past three Monseigneur le Duc de Marigny and his daughter looked their last upon their stately home. Slowly the cart lumbered down the wooden slope. A quarter of an hour later the driver pulled up at the gate of the churchyard of Val-le-Roi.

The waning moon was low in the western sky, and over in the east the first faint streak of dawn tinged the horizon with silver. The little church was dimly lighted from within. Aurore jumped down lightly from the cart, and Charles de Marigny followed. After them came Pierre and Jeannette. The little procession thus formed went through the gate and across the flagged path through the churchyard.

They were within a few metres of the porch when a dark figure came out of the shadow and then stood still, as if waiting for them. Aurore gave a quickly smothered cry of alarm and clung, trembling, to her father.

"Who is there?" she called in a hoarse whisper.

"Only the bridegroom, citizeness," came a mocking voice in reply, "waiting for his bride."

Aurore and De Marigny, numbed with terror, had come to a halt. Neither of them felt able to move. André Vallon emerged fully out of the shadow and came a step or two nearer to them.

"Come, *ma mie!*" he said coolly. "The church is ready. The *curé* waits. Shall we proceed?"

He put out his hand to take hers. De Marigny, shaking himself free of his torpor, tried to interpose.

"Do not touch her!" he cried peremptorily.

But André seemed not to notice him. He glanced over his shoulder, called aloud: "Citizen Tarbot!" and calmly took Aurore's cold, limp hand in his.

Then only did she perceive that there were other people here, moving in the shadows. A man came forward. It was that awful Tarbot.

"My witnesses for our wedding, *ma mie*," André said coolly. "Your servants will do for yours. Come!"

A small group of people had emerged from under the porch. Aurore felt like a dumb animal, helpless in a poacher's trap. She couldn't see her father, for those awful men were all around him, but she heard his voice, peremptory at first, then hoarse and smothered. She felt herself lifted off her feet and carried into the church. The flickering tallow candles on the altar showed her the Abbé Rosemonde on his knees with his head buried in his hands. Behind her there was the sound of feet shuffling along the flagstones. The voice she dreaded most in all the world whispered in her ear:

"You didn't think, *ma mie*, that I should be such a fool as to let you run away?"

She realised then how futile had been this attempt to flee, how she had never really believed in its possibility. Even during those few moments of sleep, she had been conscious of Fate that was both inevitable and relentless. It was no use praying to God: God was cruel and meant her to go through with this sacrifice. She had thought to escape, and the trap had closed on her once more, more firmly, more inexorably than before. All she could long for now was her father's safety—the certainty that this awful sacrifice would not be in vain.

As once before, André seemed to divine her thoughts.

"There are friends here," he said coolly, "looking after your father's safety. And," he added, "once the knot is tied between us, you need have no fear whatever for him."

She glanced up into the face of this man whom she hated with the intensity of a suffering martyr for a ruthless tormentor. She saw nothing in his eyes but cruelty and mockery. She had the feeling that, try how she might, she could not combat his will; that, like a ferocious brute, he had marked her for his prey, and that she was his thing, his property, the trophy of his victory not only over her but over her kindred and her caste. Nothing but death could ever set her free again. Were it not for her father, how gladly would she have welcomed death, if death could have been swift and sudden, an act of God without the agency of that brutish crowd, whose gibes and snarls and insults still rang in her ears.

Through the stillness she heard a distant rumble of wheels and a driver's call to his horses, and then her father's voice once more, uttering that awful word "*Canaille!*"

In a moment she would have turned, ready to run back to him, but André had her by the wrist, and she could not move.

"They are taking him back to Marigny," he said drily. "He was doing no good here and might have come to harm. When Pierre and Jeannette have done their duty as witnesses, they can go and join him there and serve him as they did before."

"Let me go with him," she pleaded involuntarily. "Give me one more day, and I'll swear——"

"You are going to swear loyalty to me at the altar first, *ma mie*," he rejoined lightly. "After that, we shall see."

He led her to the altar rails, where a couple of chairs had been placed ready for them. Aurore followed as if she were in a trance, hypnotized by this powerful will which dominated her and broke her spirit. She despised herself for a coward, and yet knew that she was, in fact, utterly helpless, caught in toils which no power on earth could now sever until this monstrous sacrifice had been offered up on the altar of filial devotion.

The Abbé Rosemonde was already waiting for them at the rails. He had his breviary in his hand. He had prayed to God for guidance, and God had remained dumb. Half an hour ago André Vallon had come to him and demanded his services for his marriage with Aurore de Marigny as the law ordained, and the priest, as a citizen of the new Republic, was forced to obey this law which his heart condemned.

Prayers and admonitions were all in vain. Even the old man could not fail to realise that the sacrifice of Aurore was the only means to save her life and that of her father. With heart half broken with pity he began to read the Latin prayers which his church prescribes for the blessing of those who desire its ministrations when entering the bonds of matrimony.

"*Deus Israel conjugat vos——*"——"May the God of Israel unite you——"

It would be impossible to say what went on in Aurore's heart. She stood at the altar, mute and passive. Her lips murmured no prayer, nor did she glance in the direction of the tall, motionless figure by her side. She was only conscious of that intense fear of him which at moments caused her teeth to chatter and her hair to cling matted to her moist forehead. Close beside her Jeannette and Pierre were weeping and mumbling, while a small crowd of village folk—women and men—clustered around the bridegroom.

Surely a more strange pair never stood before God's altar for such a purpose. Victim and tormentor, with hearts overflowing with resentment and bitterness. To André the Latin words, the Gospel, the Creed, the Offertory prayers seemed like sounds out of dreamland, phrases belonging to the land of memory, to a land which he had not visited since boyhood and which seemed divided from the present by an ocean of injustice and wrong.

Anon the Abbé Rosemonde came down the altar steps. He had a small plate in his hand which, as he arrived at the rails, he held out to the bridegroom. André sought in the pocket of his coat for the two gold circlets which in the midnight hour he had taken off his dead mother's fingers. Her wedding ring and that of his father, dead when he, André, was still a baby. She was lying so still, so still in her ruined cottage, with a peaceful smile around her lips.

What André had thought and felt when he knelt down beside her and forced those stark fingers to yield up those tiny gold emblems of a happy union he himself scarcely knew. All that he remembered afterwards was that bitterness seemed for the moment to give way in his heart to the immense sorrow in which he had not yet been able to indulge. Just for those few moments he felt free to give rein to tears. There was no one there to see him, no one to pity him or, perchance, to mock. And now, when he took the rings out of his pocket and put them on the plate, it was only by the greatest effort of will that he choked back those tears which again rose insistent to his eyes.

A sound like a long sigh came to Aurore's ears. She heeded it not, did not know whence it came. She was staring—staring at those two gold circlets, the material presentment of what her self-immolation would mean for the rest of her life. Jeannette and Pierre were sobbing audibly; the crowd of village folk were down on their knees, trying to recollect forgotten orisons. Abbé Rosemonde took the small, cold white hand and the other, strong and rough, and placed one within the other. Aurore felt a shudder pass through her body; every drop of blood fled from her cheeks and gushed back to her head, and André felt her hand in his, fluttering like the wings of a captive bird.

With a steady hand he slipped the ring upon Aurore's finger and in the clear voice echoed the Latin words murmured by the old *curé*. They were the old familiar words, heard so often at the weddings of friends, a good deal about love, something about sickness and death. Then came Aurore's turn. The crowd of village folk craned their necks to see what she would do. Would she recoil at the last moment in the face of the magnitude of the sacrifice? There were women there who vaguely understood what went on in her soul and who marvelled if at the last she would rebel. But with a mighty effort of will Aurore held herself erect and did not flinch. Something had occurred during the past quarter of an hour while she knelt at the alter rails which gave her the strength to go through with this holocaust of herself until the end. Perhaps it was a retrospective vision of what she had endured yesterday, of the outrage from which she had been rescued by the man beside her, of her father's arrogance and madness which had brought all those horrors about.

Certain it is that she did not flinch, not even when she in turn echoed the words murmured by the *curé*. She murmured the Latin words not understanding them altogether, and the Abbé Rosemonde in the simplicity of his heart barely mumbled those wherein she should have sworn to cherish her tyrant, the cruel wrecker of her happiness.

Soon it was all over. André Vallon, the demagogue, the child of this bloody revolution, was the lawful lord and master of Aurore de Marigny, the descendant of kings. The village folk gave a sigh of satisfaction. They felt that now they were the equals of those great people up in Paris whose will was law, whose voice was the voice of God. Abbé Rosemonde whispered a few last words in Aurore's ears. He placed his hand in reverent benediction upon her head. André stood by, obviously impatient. His friends pressed round him and tried to grasp his hand. The women wept, why they knew not. Through the coloured window glass, the dawn was creeping in, and the tallow candles on the altar flickered more and more dimly.

"You will be kind to her, André," were the last words the good priest spoke before he left the sanctuary.

André gave an impatient shrug.

"Come, *ma mie*," he said curtly, and with his habitual peremptory gesture he put his arm round Aurore's waist and led her out of the church.

The waning moon was nothing now but a half circle of filmy white vapour. Out in the east a July dawn had already set the fires of heaven alight. The horizon was aglow with crimson and gold, with emerald and chrysoprase, and tiny fleecy clouds, blood red and splendent, lay like streaks of flame across the sky.

Chapter 29

When Aurore awakened from a long dreamless sleep it was evening. She was lying in a bed, the soft white sheets of which smelt of dried roses and lavender. Facing her were two tall windows masked by delicate lace curtains through which the light of a street lamp came dimly peeping.

For a long time, she lay here, with aching head buried in the sweet-smelling downy pillow, while, one by one, the events of this fateful day came back to her mind on the wings of memory.

The market cart. The last glimpse of the old home. The little church of Val-le-Roi. The figure that came out of the shadows. The bridegroom awaiting his bride. After that there was something of a blank, a veil through which floated the figure of Abbé Rosemonde, the altar, the flickering tallow candles, and a dark face with compelling eyes and cruel, mocking mouth. Spirit voices echoed words which her ears at the time had only vaguely heard.

"*Deus Israel conjugat vos*—"

"You are going to swear loyalty to me first, *ma mie*—"

"Wilt thou take this man to be thy lawful husband?—"

"Once the knot is tied between us you need no longer fear—"

Then the ring upon her finger. Jeannette's weeping farewells. The murmurings of the village folk. The *cariole* outside the churchyard gate. The long drive in silence, with her eyes fixed on the strong brown hand close to her which handled the reins and the whip—the hand of André Vallon, her husband!

Yes, it all came back now! She had slept for a while and had mercifully forgotten, but now it all came back. After the interminable drive in the *cariole* over the jolting roads they had reached Nevers when the sun was already high in the heavens. In the fields just outside the town there was a stretch of ripening corn, from which a lark suddenly rose with joyful song up to the sky.

The *cariole* came to a halt in a nice broad street outside a house, the door of which bore on a metal plate the names JULES MIGNET and below it *DOCTEUR EN MÉDÉCIN*. André put up his whip, threw the reins over the horses' backs, and jumped lightly down from the *cariole*.

"Come, *ma mie*," he said, and held out his arm to help her descend.

In answer to the clanging of a bell, a neatly dressed maid opened the door and greet André with a smile.

"The Citizen Doctor?" André asked. "Is he in?"

"He is busy at the hospital just now," the girl replied, "but the citizeness is upstairs."

The small paved hall and stone staircase smelt of ripe apples and of soap. André ran up the stairs. This time he didn't say, "Come!" but Aurore nevertheless followed. She had no longer any will of her own. It seemed as if that strong brown hand was driving her with whip and reins as it had done the two horses in the *cariole*.

Double doors on the first landing were wide open, as André's firm footsteps rang out on the tiled floor an elderly woman came out of the room beyond. She was small and frail-looking and had slender white hands which she held out to André with the friendliest of greetings.

"Had a good journey?" she asked.

André kissed her hand and then stood aside, disclosing Aurore.

"And that is your young wife!" the old woman exclaimed, and this time her two arms extended towards Aurore, and a sweet smile lit up her pale wrinkled face. "You are right welcome, *citizeness*," she said. And Aurore felt two kindly arms encircling her shoulders and a friendly kiss pressed on both her cheeks.

"This is the Citizeness Mignet, *ma mie*," André said. "A dear, kind friend who has offered us hospitality until we can continue our journey to Paris."

"For as long as you will stay in my house, my dear," the old lady said, fondling Aurore's hand but gazing on André with eyes full of deep affection. "I don't suppose he ever told you, but your husband saved my son's life at Valmy. He lost his arm while he carried him to safety under the fire of Prussian cannon. Not only my house, but all I possess in the world is his and yours for the asking."

But while she spoke André had made good his escape. Aurore heard him clattering down the stairs.

"He is always like that," the old lady said, with her gentle smile. "He can't bear me to say a word about what we owe him, Jules and I. But one day when André is not there my son shall tell you about it, and you will be prouder of your handsome husband than you ever were before."

"But you are tired, my dear," she went on, "and here I am chattering away instead of looking after you. Come and sit down here in the sunshine while I get you a nice cup of hot coffee, or would you rather have some nice sweet chocolate?"

She led Aurore to an armchair placed by the window, through which the warm July sun came in smiling. Aurore thanked her with a wan smile, and she was not really tired and that she would prefer coffee, whereupon the old lady tripped out of the room.

And Aurore had remained sitting there with the sunshine caressing her hair and cheek, looking about her as in a dream. The room had not a great deal of furniture in it, but the few pieces that were there revealed a fastidious taste. Fine work of the Louis XIV period was displayed in a splendid bureau and a fine Boulle table, in the Aubusson carpet and tapestried chairs. There were two or three pictures on the wall which suggested the fantastic brush of Lancret, and above the fireplace a delicate mirror which must have hailed from Venice.

Aurore had the feeling that this could not be reality; that this was some kind of dreamland out of which she would presently emerge fully awake. Did people who were country doctors and *bourgeois* possess Boulle furniture and Lancret pictures? Of course not. At least, Aurore had never supposed that they did. Louis XIV bureaus and Aubusson carpets were to be found in ancestral *châteaux* and not in the plebeian houses of small provincial towns. And this old lady, who now came tripping back in her dress of soft grey silk with the exquisite lace *fichu* round her shoulders and beautiful cap covering her grey hair, she of a certainty was not the mother of an obscure country leech, the sort of man who, if he had been called in to attend a sick person at Marigny in the olden days, would not have been admitted to eat at *Monseigneur's* table. "Citizeness Mignet!" That awful word *"citizeness,"* which had the power to arouse the most bitter resentment in the heart of every aristocrat, could surely not be applied to her.

She held in her fine which hands a cup of exquisite Sèvres china from which arose the delicious scent of steaming Mocha. Aurore took the cup with a grateful if pale little smile. She drank the coffee eagerly and felt a little better after it. Only with half an ear did she listen to the old lady's pleasant chatter, out of which only a few disjointed sentences penetrator to her inner consciousness.

"Your room is quite ready, my dear—I shall take an old woman's privilege and call you Aurore—When you wake up in the morning—How proud you must be of your husband—Prodigies of valour at Valmy—My son says—"

Surely, surely, none of that could be real! The old lady was just one of those fairies of which Aurore had read when she was a child in the books of M. Perrault—the fairy godmother in "Cinderella" or "The Sleeping Beauty." She would vanish presently, and she, Aurore, would wake to find herself back in her bed with the blue damask curtains in her room at Marigny. Dear, dear Maringy!

Nor was the gold ring on her finger real. There was no such person as André Vallon, who had dared to call her *"ma mie"* and looked down on her with such a cruel, mocking glance. She gazed down on her own hands, her left hand with that narrow gold circlet round the fourth finger; and oddly, with her right hand, she toyed with the ring, twisting it round and round.

"And now I shall take you to your room," the old lady said in her smooth, gentle voice. "Come with me, my dear."

She smiled, and her old eyes twinkled as she gave Aurore's cheeks a little pat. "You will want to be alone with your husband," she said.

And now, after all those hours, and lying on this sweet-scented bed, Aurore supposed that she did then follow the old lady out of the room and up some stairs. But of that she remembers nothing. She did not even recall her first impression of this room with the tall windows veiled behind delicate lace curtains and hangings of rose Du Barry damask. Here again memory registered a blank until the moment when André Vallon came into the room.

Chapter 30

Memory can be terribly cruel!

Aurore, lying numb and tired after a few hours' heavy sleep, felt the full force of this cruelty.

One by one, pictures which she would long all her life to blot out from her mind rose before her aching senses. Visions of shame and of cowardice which she felt would forever after leave a stain upon her soul. Even now memory most cruel brought the blush of humbled pride to her cheeks.

She, Aurore de Marigny, daughter of one of the proudest houses in France, claiming kinship with Royalty, the apple of her father's eyes, the worshipped mistress of a regal ancestral home, she had grovelled at a plebeian's feet; on her knees she had begged him to set her free, entreated him with words that in the past she would only have spoken to her king.

She had begged him, on her knees, with hands clinging to his rough clothes, to let her go back to Marigny and to her father; begged him to look on his vengeance as complete, since he had broken her spirit and humiliated her so that she would never dare look one of her own caste in the face again.

And memory mocked her with that picture of herself, lying like a crumpled heap of silk and laces at the feet of the man whom she hated and loathed and despised beyond what she would have thought herself capable of feeling. And through it all he had remained cool, sarcastic, indifferent.

"Do not cry, *ma mie*," he had said once: "you will make your eyes red."

And another time: "In Heaven's name, do not raise your voice. You don't want our friends down below to know that we have already embarked on matrimonial quarrels."

But the words that memory recalled more insistently were more fateful than all:

"While you are my submissive wife no one dare touch your father or you; but if you choose to leave me, no power on earth will save either of you from the guillotine. I care naught," he added presently, "about that arrogant father of yours: let him die a dog's death, for aught I care, but I do not choose to see my wife's pretty head roll into the same basket as those of the enemies of France."

"I hate you," she had murmured once. "I shall always hate you."

"I have no love for you, either," he had retorted coolly, "but we shall get used to each other."

And when in her agony of mind, she had cried out, "Why—why have you done this? You hate me, you say—then why not let me go?"

"Because—" The word had escaped him, vehement and fierce; the cruel expression she had learned to fear had flashed for a few seconds out of his eyes. But the next moment he pulled himself together, seemed, indeed, to shed his fury like a mantle. A mocking smile chased away the ferocious glance, and he said lightly:

"Because you are beautiful, *ma mie*; you are my wife and I wish to keep you. That is all."

In the olden days Aurore de Marigny, even when she was little more than a child, had been wont to despise the airs and graces, the megrims and mild hysterics in which her elegant friends so often indulged. She had always been a fearless child: at games, on horseback, nothing frightened her. In an age when women affected the weaknesses of their sex as a sign of aristocratic birth, she would find joy in breaking in an untamed colt or accompanying her father in his shooting expeditions after wolf or wild boar in the forests of Ardennes.

She had never known fear until now, when a beggarly *caitiff* held her like a slave in thrall. But with memory's cruel insistence there came back to her the knowledge that she was afraid; that there was one man in the world the sight of whom caused a quiver of abject fear to go right through her body, the sound of whose footfall caused every drop of blood to flow back to her heart. Why, she couldn't say.

It was that despicable fear which at this fateful hour had taken such hold of her that, even while his formidable arm encircled her waist and raised her from the ground where she had been cowering like a frightened beast, her senses suddenly forsook her, her head fell back, her teeth chattered as if in ague, her limbs felt as cold as ice. Broken and bruised by the terrible mental and physical struggle, she was numb and limp, had not one spark of fight left in her, or the strength of a kitten. She felt herself lifted off the ground and laid down somewhere, where it was soft and warm and sweet smelling. She heard the dreaded footfall receding from her, the opening of a door, and then a call.

There were other people in the room presently—a man and a woman. Aurore couldn't see them; she had not the energy to raise her eyelids; but gentle kindly hands undressed her, took off her shoes and stockings, combed her hair and moistened her face with sweet-smelling water. She felt herself being tucked up in a soft downy bed, and soft murmurs that sounded pitiful and motherly soothed her throbbing senses.

A man's voice, persuasive and authoritative, said, "Try and drink this, *citizeness*, it will make you sleep." She obeyed and drank the slightly bitter liquid that was held to her lips. After that she lay placid and quiet and, presently, must have dropped off to sleep.

Chapter 31

The stay in Nevers was made endurable for Aurore through the absence of her husband.

Her husband!

The Mignets explained to her that André had left for Paris on the very day of their arrival, while she was lying asleep. He wouldn't have her disturbed. He had gone in order to make arrangements for their new home, and he had gone full of joy and hope, because Citizen Danton had sent a courier over from Paris confirming the happy tidings already sent to Val-le-Roi a few days ago, that he would be overjoyed to see his old friend and colleague André Vallon again. There was work and to spare for young hands and young brains who had the welfare of the people at heart. The education of the young and the reclaiming of the unfit were the two questions that occupied the minds of the committees at the present moment, and Danton held out hopes of an important post for André in connection with these questions.

"It is the sort of work that will appeal to your clever husband, *citizeness*," the doctor said, "now that the loss of his arm has compelled him to leave the army. The illiterates in France have been reckoned by the million in the past. Whatever else the present great upheaval may do, it will certainly remedy that crying evil."

"They are opening schools all over France," the old lady continued, "not only for the young, but also for the afflicted: the deaf and dumb and the blind."

"Schools?" Aurore remarked with a slight lifting of the eyebrows. "To teach what?"

"The elements of education," Madame Mignet replied quietly. "These must no longer remain the privilege of the few."

"And is my—my husband taking a hand in this scheme of education for the million?"

"Indeed, yes," the doctor said. "I understand that Citizen Danton has obtained an important post for him in connection with the schools for the blind."

"Citizen Danton is the most influential man in France," Madame Mignet went on to explain to the somewhat bewildered Aurore. "He has a charming young wife. Madame Roland is one of their intimate friends. You and your husband will move among the most brilliant and most intellectual society in Paris."

Aurore was indeed bewildered. She gazed on this fastidious-looking old lady with the aristocratic features and delicate hands, who talked so calmly of Danton, the hideous master butcher of this awful slaughterhouse, the man whose large plebeian hands were stained with the blood of hundreds of his fellow men. Madame Mignet, or Citizeness Mignet as she preferred to be called, could talk of that man and his circle as "intellectual" and "brilliant," and took it for granted that she, Aurore, daughter of Monseigneur le Duc de Marigny, would find pleasure in their society. Pleasure? Aurore could only marvel whether she would have sufficient courage to show her horror and loathing should the hands of those butchers be extended in friendly welcome to her.

It seemed impossible that people like the Mignets should look complacently on the wholesale butcheries which were turning the fair city of Paris into a shambles; that they could condone the hideous crime of regicide about to culminate in the still more deadly sin of the execution of the queen; that they could utter such names as Danton or Robespierre, Carrier or Desmoulins without a shudder. And when, after a few days of quiet intimacy, Aurore ventured to put the question to Madame Mignet, the old lady replied with strange earnestness:

"My dear, since the beginning of all times men have perpetrated horrors against one another. It is the devil in them, but the devil would have no power over men if God did not allow it. Could He not, if He so willed, quell this revolution with His Word? Must we not rather bow to His will and try to realise that something great, something good, something, at any rate, that is in accordance with the great scheme of the universe must in the end come out of all this sorrow?"

"But, surely," Aurore protested, "you must look with horror on these wholesale murders."

"I look with horror on every act of violence committed by man against his fellow creatures. I look with horror on every war where men are trained and encouraged to kill or maim one another. I look with horror upon the slave owners in our colonies, where men drive their fellow creatures with whip lash and torture to toil so that they themselves may reap. All these, my dear child, are horrors which we women condemn and shudder at. But wars there will always be, because man will always defend his property against aggression, and there will be revolutions in this world so long as men use their power in order to enslave others."

Aurore hotly defended her caste. On her father's estate the people were content and prosperous.

"I am sure they were," Madame Mignet admitted, with an indulgent smile, "but throughout the history of the world, the innocent have suffered together with the guilty. Great evils need desperate remedies. The children of France, egged on by centuries of misery and spurred by starvation, have struck blindly about them in their scramble for food. In the *mêlée* noble heads have fallen along with some that were heavy with guilt. But it is God's will, and we must have patience. France is a great and glorious country. This is the period of her travail. From it she will bring forth liberty and progress which, as the years roll on, will cause her children to forget what they have endured in the cause."

It was amazing to hear a woman of refinement talk so placidly about it all. In fact, Aurore could not help remarking to herself how strangely like this old lady's philosophy of life was that of Abbé Rosemonde. Resignation to the will of God. Contentment in leaving everything in His hands. She felt a kind of mild contempt for this placidity, and yet, what right had she to scorn anyone? She, the miserable coward who shrank from the hurt that her father's death would cause her, and to save herself and him had grovelled at the feet of one whom she despised?

But it was only toward the end of her stay at Nevers that she spoke of all this to Madame Mignet. She wondered how much of her history the old lady and the doctor knew; if they realised that as far as she was concerned the greatest horror she had ever experienced was when she found herself the wife of one whom her father had so justly dubbed "*Canaille!*" They, of course, would not understand how her entire being was in revolt against this slavery. André Vallon was admittedly a poor man, which would mean that she, Aurore de Marigny, would be little better than a servant to a despicable knave. Ignorant of the commonest elements of household work, she would be a constant suffering victim to his gibes and his tyranny. But it was not the work that she feared, it was the mental, the moral, the physical contact with one whom she hated.

And all the while that she was at Nevers, her ears were constantly filled with his name. Though absent, he seemed always to be there in this home of culture and refinement, as he was ever present apparently in the hearts of his friends. From beginning to end, Aurore was forced to listen to the story of André's heroism when he carried Doctor Mignet on his back out of range of the Prussian cannon; how a chance musket shot had shattered his arm and he had dragged himself and his swooning comrade back to the French lines, only to return to the scene of danger and bring to safety half a dozen more of his wounded comrades until, stricken with a raging fever, more dead than alive, he in his turn had completely lost consciousness.

With a wealth of detail and a plethora of exciting incidents did Doctor Mignet recount not only this story, but others in which André Vallon was the hero and had accomplished prodigies of valour.

"Four citations, *citizeness*," he said with undisguised enthusiasm. "Dumouriez, before his abominable treachery, always spoke of Vallon as the bravest soldier he had ever had under his command; and when the crash came, when Dumouriez, whom the whole of France trusted as an able general and a loyal patriot, when he sold his sword to the enemies of his country, Vallon was one of those who put heart into the troops, who revived their courage and led them to a series of victories which culminated in that glorious day of Valmy."

And the old lady would then conclude with a happy little sigh:

"Indeed, *citizeness*, André is a man to be proud of as a husband and as a friend."

And Aurore wondered if all those stories could possibly be true.

Valour, loyalty, selflessness, these were the attributes of her caste. *Caitiffs* like André Vallon surely were not capable of such noble impulses. They had no educations to guide them, no tradition, none of the examples which formed the glorious history of a noble race such as hers. It couldn't be true. The whole thing was an exaggeration on the doctor's part. He was blinded by his affection for a comrade in arms, by dangers passed together, by suffering endured for the sake of France, when the whole of Europe raised its hand against her, and the Prussian hordes invaded her sacred soil.

"I look with horror on every war," the old lady had said. And for the first time in all these miserable years Aurore was conscious of a vague feeling of shame that so many of her kindred had turned their sword against their country in the hour of her greatest peril or sought refuge and safety on foreign soil.

"France, my country!" an unconscious poet had once sung. "She may have erred, she may have sinned, but still she is my country!"

Chapter 32

Indeed, these few days in Nevers in the company of two charming and intellectual people were both pleasant and peaceful. It was years since Aurore had the opportunity of listening to conversation other than the somewhat *naïve* philosophy of Abbé Rosemonde and her father's somewhat monotonous if fully justified diatribes against the new *régime*; and though she felt that she could never agree with the opinions and ideals expounded so eloquently by the Mignets, yet she could not help feeling interested, taken out of herself, made to feel that at any rate the original makers of this terrible revolution were men of high ideals actuated by the purest of motives.

The day of departure came, alas! all too soon. André came to Nevers to fetch his wife. The sight of him revived in Aurore's memory all the terrible times she had lived through. All the quietude of the past few days seemed to fly from her soul. At once she felt irritated, with her nerves all tingling and on edge. She watched the carriage drive up to the door and saw him jump down and take his valise from the driver. She thought he looked ill but supposed that perhaps the journey had been trying. It was only later that she heard that he had actually come from Val-le-Roi, whither he had gone first from Paris in order to see after his mother's grave in the churchyard there.

It was not till late afternoon that Aurore found herself along in her room with her husband. She certainly thought that he looked different, somehow: older perhaps, but certainly different. He had been to Marigny and spoke to her about his visit there.

"Your father refused to see me," he told her, "which I suppose was natural. But I questioned Pierre and Jeannette and also the Citizen Curé. They all told me that physically he was well, but not quite normal in his mind."

"*Mon Dieu!*—"

"It is nothing to be alarmed about. I spoke to the leech—Citizen Journet—whom you know. They used to call him in the olden days if any of the servants were sick. Your father, it seems, condescended to let him feel his pulse and to take the potion which he prescribed."

"If I could only see him. . . ."

"You wouldn't do him any good. On the contrary, if you were there he would let loose the floodgates of his resentment and work himself up into a delirium of fury. I put the question to the Citizen Doctor and Abbé Rosemonde: they both thought it best that he should be kept very quiet for a time, under the care of Pierre and Jeannette."

"You seem to have been very kind," she said, feeling grateful yet loth to acknowledge her gratitude.

"Only seemingly," he replied lightly, in that flippant, mocking tone of his which still had the power to irritate her. However, she kept sufficient control over herself for the moment to swallow the sharp retort which hovered on her lips.

There was a moment's silence between them, and then he mentioned Talon.

"I have got the deeds of sale out of that thief, at any rate," he said.

"The deeds?"

"Why, yes! The deeds of sale of Marigny and of all the estates registered in your father's name to Hector Talon."

"I had forgotten," she murmured.

"He hadn't," André replied drily, "not your father's."

"What does that mean?"

"That I had the title deeds registered in your name, under the plea that your father was *non compos mentis*."

"But I couldn't allow—"

"What?"

"I should be defrauding my father."

"Would you rather Talon had possession?"

"Rather he than you," she retorted coldly.

343

At the moment she hoped, rather than thought, that a slight shadow passed over his face. They had both been standing during this brief conversation, carried on with a kind of casual indifference on his side and with thinly veiled animosity on hers. She had intended to wound him with the sharpness of her tongue, and having, as she hoped, succeeded, she turned coolly away from him and sat down in the winged armchair by the window. With ostentatious care she disposed the folds of her gown about her, fiddled at her *fichu*, allowed her daintily shod foot to peep from beneath her skirt. Then she took up a piece of embroidery and started to ply her needle with the appearance of being deeply engrossed in her work.

André watched her in silence for a moment or two. Had she looked up she would have seen the mocking smile which curled round his lips.

"I suppose," he said after a while, "that my wits are specially dull this afternoon. Would you be so gracious as to explain just what you mean by 'rather he than you'? It sounds enigmatic to me."

Aurore kept her eyes fixed on her embroidery frame, drawing the thread in and out as if the destinies of France rested on the success of her work. With her head slightly tilted to one side, her fair hair free from powder, like a golden halo above her smooth forehead, a look of concentration in her deep blue eyes, she looked perfectly adorable. She knew it and felt a great measure of strength in the knowledge. A woman is soon conscious of victory when she knows that she is beautiful, and Aurore, young and inexperienced as she was, was no exception to this rule. What worried her was that she could not keep her hands entirely steady or still the beatings of her heart.

She knew that if she spoke her voice would betray the fact that she was vaguely frightened. She had hit out rather blindly and thoughtlessly because his cool indifference had exasperated her, but now she was afraid of what he might do. He was cruel and vengeful, she knew that, and she felt frightened, like a child who has been naughty and knows that it is going to be punished.

But she would not for worlds let him see that she was anything but indifferent, and so she remained silent and went on drawing her embroidery thread in and out with cool ostentation. But, suddenly, and without any warning, he came up close to her and, with an impatient oath, snatched the work out of her hand and threw it on the ground.

"Please answer my question," he said coldly.

The needle, it seemed, had slightly grazed her finger, drawing a drop of blood. She put the finger to her mouth. Then she rose from her chair and stooped to pick up her work. He put his foot on it. As she straightened again she found herself quite close to him, looking up into his face.

"I meant just what I said," she said, as coolly as she could, though she felt that her nerves were beginning to give way; "that I would sooner any man in the whole of France had Marigny rather than you."

"A very natural sentiment on your part, no doubt," he rejoined calmly, "seeing that you honour me with such active hatred. But had you equally honoured me by listening to me just now you would have heard me say that the title deeds of Marigny are not inscribed in my name but in yours."

She broke into a harsh, derisive laugh.

"A pretty bit of sophistry, forsooth," she retorted. "You must think me a food, indeed, if you imagine I do not see through your tricks. A marriage with the to humiliate her, what? and to avenge wrongs in which she had no share? Your precious friends believe that tale, do they not? But they are the fools, not I. I know enough of the laws of your murdering government. A wife's property belongs to her husband, and that is the reason why you forced this monstrous union upon me. It was in order to feather your nest, to obtain possession of the lands and *château* which if my dear father and I had perished on the guillotine would have become the property of the State. Marry the aristocrat, forsooth, to avenge a mother's death! *Par Dieu!* 'twas a pretty story to cover the grasping avarice of an upstart out for loot!"

She had succeeded in working herself up into a state of uncontrolled fury. Fear had given way to a kind of nervous exultation at her own power to wound. All unknowing, he had put the flail in her hand wherewith to chastise him. And chastise she did. Whether she believed in what she said or no didn't seem to matter: all she knew was that her words must hurt him. They must, even though he stood there close to her, entirely motionless, looking down into her glowing face with eyes the expression of which she could not entirely fathom. But that was because she was excited, unable to reason and to think, only to strike with words that must hit at what pride he possessed, as a whip lash would have struck at his face. It was only when she was forced to pause in order to draw breath that that awful mocking smile which she hated worse than his cruelty curled once more around his lips.

This goaded her beyond endurance. Her nerves were completely unstrung. She couldn't have controlled them even if she would. She was just longing for an actual whip wherewith to strike, longing with all her soul to make him cringe and suffer at last as he had so often made her suffer.

With a strange cry, as much of pain as of triumph, she suddenly raised her hand and strike him in the face—

"You little fool!"

That was what she heard. The voice did not sound quite like his. Perhaps she had expected a roar, a cry of rage, a savage oath—he was a beast, and beast usually bellowed when they were hurt; but all she did hear was a low, contemptuous laugh and those three words, "You little fool!"

But what happened was quite another matter. His formidable arm shot out, and in an instant both her wrists were tightly held together as in a manacle of steel. She felt as if her arms were wrenched out of their sockets, and in the agony of it her knees gave way under her. She felt herself sinking to the ground, and through a mist of semi-consciousness she saw his face quite close to hers—a cruel, mocking face with a gleam of ferocity in the eyes.

"On your knees, you little fool!"

What a harsh voice it had become! And then that laugh! Mockery! Contempt! Mild amusement! The whole gamut of what was most humiliating and most riling.

"Let go my wrists," she said as steadily as she could, though she was ready to cry with pain. "Let go! You hurt me!"

"Hurt you?" he went on coolly. "By God! I mean to hurt you, you infuriating little vixen! I am going to keep you here on your knees until those red lips of yours have begged for pardon."

"Let me go!" she cried aloud. "Brute! Brute! Let me go!"

"As soon as you have begged for pardon!" he retorted grimly.

"Never!"

"We shall see!"

He sat down in the winged chair and still held her by the wrists. She was on her knees, crouching at his feet, for there he held her pinioned with one foot on the edge of her gown. She could not move.

"Coward! Let me go!"

"Not I! Coward," he continued coolly, "is an attribute of mudlarks such as I, but so is obstinacy you'll find, *ma mie*. Anyway, you are going to stay here on your knees until your sweet lips have claimed and received a kiss of forgiveness."

Just for a few seconds she had an uncontrollable desire to scream

346

at the top of her voice in the hope that some member of the Mignet household would come to her rescue. But her pride revolted at the idea of being found in this humiliating position, and with all their adoration for this brutish husband of hers they might even take his part against her, and ridicule might then be piled on humiliation—a thing too awful to contemplate. She thought that he would tire; those fingers of his, which felt more and more like iron clamps around her wrists, were bound, she thought, to loosen their hold a little after a time. Manlike, he would grow weary of sitting still. The slightest movement on his part, and the tension would relax. That would be her opportunity for escape, and, of course, she would not be caught unawares again. If only she could have closed her ears to his voice, to his gibes and his sneers and, worse still, to this scornful admiration.

"So, you thought out that pretty story for yourself," he said at one time: "that I schemed to marry you in order to obtain possession of your impoverished estates. Name of a name! you have imagination as well as beauty, *ma mie*"; and then he added irrelevantly:

"When you sue for pardon I shall kiss you, Aurore, for your lips just now look as luscious as two cherries."

Involuntarily a sob rose to her throat, her pretty head fell forward, and great hot tears fell from her eyes.

"Don't cry, *ma mie*," he said gaily. "I didn't cry when that charming cousin of yours struck me in the face just because you happened to fall into my arms one day. I was only a boy, and you were a child. Do you remember that day, *ma mie*?"

His voice seemed to die away somewhere in space. The shades of evening were drawing in. It was quite dark in the remote corners of the room. Aurore felt faint and sick, dreading, yet longing for, unconsciousness. At one moment hope revived. There was a knock at the door, and she heard André's voice calling:

"What is it?"

"Supper is ready, *citizen*," came the servant girl's voice in reply. "Will you be coming down?"

"Not tonight, Marie," André replied. "My wife is fatigued, and I will stay with her. Pray the Citizen Doctor and the *citizeness* to excuse us."

After that Aurore sobbed like a child. She was tired and hungry and in pain. She sobbed, and through her sobs she heard the hated voice saying quite lightly:

"Give in, *ma mie*. You won't regret it. If I had a hand to spare I

347

would put a finger under your pretty chin and try and teach you that it is quite good to kiss."

She did give in, in the end. She felt ashamed, abject, cowardly. A brief while ago she would have scorned the idea of any woman giving in under such humiliating conditions. But it was not only physical pain that compelled her. It was something more than that, and she knew it. It was the enforcement of a will greater than her own, the absolutism of physical, moral, and mental strength which seemed to rob her surrender of its most galling sting. She raised her head and almost with an air of defiance she threw out the word, "*Pardon!*" At once her wrists were released, but her whole body was imprisoned instead. Weak and broken, with head thrown back and eyes closed, she remained motionless in the crook of his arm.

For a long, long time she remained thus, expecting and dreading that kiss. She felt that his eyes were on her, revelling—she had no doubt of that—in her beauty. And for this she hated and despised him as much as she hated and despised herself. For one instant she opened her eyes and looked into his. What had compelled her to open them she didn't know. It was still that immense power which appeared to be in the very air about her, bending her will and breaking her spirit. Had she read fury, passion, or hatred in his eyes she might, she felt, have forgiven him in her turn, have felt less ashamed of her cowardice; but all she encountered was a kind of gentle, indulgent mockery, mild amusement at what to her meant the uprooting of all that she had held inviolate, the surrender of what she held far deeper than life.

He was amused at her humiliation and could laugh at her distress. She gave him one look and then said loudly and quite steadily:

"I never knew what hatred meant until now."

"We'll call it that if you like," he retorted lightly, "but isn't it good?" And then he kissed her.

Chapter 33

Since that day many months had gone by, and Aurore, sitting once more in the large winged chair by the window in that pretty room at Nevers and watching the snowflakes slowly fluttering down from the leaden sky thought of the long, long time that separated her from the past, and of the interminable days that still lay, wearisome and monotonous, before her, until she was an old woman, too old to recollect and too old to feel.

She had been very sorry at the time to leave the quietude of the house at Nevers, not thinking that she would ever see it again. The Mignets had been so kind! So kind! She marvelled often just how much they knew. She had dreaded the journey to Paris in the company of her husband, had dreaded the life that lay before her—the great unknown! the leap into a future which she pictured to herself as dark and lonely and laden with sorrow.

But things in life have a way of not being either quite so pleasant or so unpleasant as one anticipates; and Aurore's first impression of the apartment in Paris which was destined to be her home was certainly not so unpleasant as she had imagined. It certainly was spacious and sunny. Situated on the Quai de la Ferraille, high above the noises of the street below, it had a fine view over the river and the towers of Notre Dame. She wondered who it was who had presided over the furnishing of it but didn't like to ask. She thought that she detected a feminine hand and a woman's taste in her bedroom, with its muslin curtains and flowered chintz hangings. All very simple, even Spartan, but with nothing to jar on her fastidiousness. In an adjacent small *boudoir,* she found a comfortable armchair, a work table, many appurtenances necessary for needlework. These only a woman could have selected, so Aurore thought, and wondered who it could have been.

There were also a number of books ranged on shelves on one side of the room. As soon as she had an opportunity Aurore looked to see what they were. Rousseau, of course, and Diderot, and also Voltaire and D'Alembert; the speeches of Mirabeau and reprints of the early numbers of *L'Ami du Peuple*. But there were others too: the poets and essayists of the Grand Siècle, Molière, Coidorcet, Bossuet, and many more, somehow, she felt that each one had been chosen specially for the moulding of her mind. Herein she suspected her husband and wondered how any man could be so dense or so arrogant as to suppose that she would swerve one iota from the principles and the faith, which she had been taught to believe were the only possible rules of life.

But apart from such rebellious thoughts and during those early days of August, Aurore set out resolutely to live the life which she believed was to be hers to the end of time. She wondered how she was every going to live and to endure. And yet other people did it; other women in this awful city of Paris had learned how to live and how to suffer. How amazing that was! Amazing and un-understandable! The Reign of Terror was at its height. The glorious revolution, which was going to regenerate the world and bring about the millennium with unbroken happiness for all, could now be best described as a conjugation of the verb "to fear": I fear, thou fearest, he fears, we fear, you fear, they fear! Men and women in Paris went daily, hourly, in fear of their lives; in fear of the lives of those near and dear to them. Every day accusations, trials, condemnations, and the procession of victims to the guillotine. Terror, indeed, was the order of the day, the darlings of the crowd today were the execration of the mob on the morrow.

And yet, life went on just the same.

People walked about the streets, met each other and talked over the events of the day—the death of this man, imminent arrest of that other; Robespierre's latest speech; the news from the front. They went to the theatre and the opera; they dined at restaurants. Young people made love; old people died; babies were born. Life went on just the same.

Aurore saw very little of the outside world. She went daily to market with the pleasant middle-aged woman who helped her with her *ménage*; she stood in the queues, waiting her turn to purchase the few ounces of bread which the law allowed, and spent the money which André had given her for the purchase of such food as was obtainable. Her life was Spartan in the extreme, but she had no rough task to perform. There was no question of washing and scrubbing—the nice middle-aged woman did all that; but Aurore soon found herself strangely interested in keeping her new home dainty and comfortable and her table as free from monotony as possible.

The feeling gradually came to her that this was more of a real home to her than stately Marigny had ever been. There, during its days of splendour, everything was ordained and arranged by an army of servants without any reference to her own special wishes. Probably she had no special wishes in those days, as everything went on in its own perfect routine. There was never any hitch: housekeepers and *major-domos* saw to it that *Mademoiselle* was not troubled with such trifles as the arrangement of flowers in her room or the composition of a menu.

But here, in the sunny rooms of the Quai de la Ferraille, everything depended on her, and the thrill was very real when there were a few asters to be bought in the market, or there was a possibility of obtaining a thin old fowl that made excellent soup.

Aurore heard vague rumours from time to time that men in high places kept rich tables in their homes while the people starved; that certain restaurants in the Rue St. Honoré, patronised by Robespierre, the Incorruptible, and his friends on the influential committees, served their customers with the richest of food and choice wines bought for a song from the cellars of dispossessed aristocrats. She heard that in the country there was no shortage of luxury; that Danton's house at Arcis was noted for its good cheer.

All that she heard and more, but she had soon schooled herself to know nothing, to listen to nothing, to comment on nothing. She never went to a theatre; she had never set foot inside a restaurant. She only walked for exercise, and then only in the fields round about St. Martin and Passy. It was the only way to endure life. Strangely enough, quite apart from the interest in her home, she was not really unhappy. What sorrow and anxiety she felt was purely outside herself. The fate of the unfortunate queen caused her immense grief, but she never spoke of it; through gossip gleaned in the streets, or through the placards at street corners which she could not fail to see, she learned of the condemnation and death of many whose names had been familiar to her since childhood: relatives, friends, acquaintances.

Many she knew had found shelter abroad, and more than once she half broke her heart with regret that her father had always set his face so obstinately against emigration. They would be together now—she and he—secure in England or Belgium, with only the echo of all these horrors to disturb their peace, instead of this daily agonizing contact with it all.

She remembered that a year or less before this she had heard rumours of an organisation of English gentlemen, headed by a mysterious chief who was known as "The Scarlet Pimpernel," who risked their lives in order to help those who were in danger of death, who were unhappy and innocent, and who longed to flee from this terror-stricken land. She remembered that her father had obstinately refused to get in touch with these gallant Englishmen. He hated the English, he said, and would not owe his life to any of them. Aurore, at the time, thought no more about it. She did not hate the English, but she didn't want to leave Marigny, and in that remote country district the danger to her father and herself did not appear imminent.

Until that awful day in July, which seemed now like a nightmare, she had no realised how hated she and her father were in the villages, and how intense was the enmity of the people against her caste. But here, in Paris, her eyes were soon opened to much that she had never fully understood before: she soon realised how miserable and ignorant the people were, and how easy it was to arouse in them passions of hatred, of resentment and cruelty. She also realised how helpless now were those men who, with the highest possible ideals to spur them, and an infinite understanding of the injustice under which the poor had groaned for centuries, had let loose the floodgates of this titanic revolution. They were helpless now, and, one by one, paid toll with their lives for all those dreams of liberty and justice which were going to make this word regenerate and happy, and only succeeded in making it more miserable and more foul.

Her husband, André Vallon, was one of these. He had come back from the war full of enthusiasm and of hope. Since he could no longer fight the enemies of his country abroad, he would fight them within its borders: traitors, who would sell France to her foes, who would allow the Prussian heel to tread her sacred soil; upstarts, who filled their pockets and their bellies while others groaned and starved. They were the enemies whom men like André Vallon were ready to denounce to an outraged people. The people were ready enough to have those traitors thrown to them as bait for their revenge, but, having tasted the sweets of retaliation, they soon cried for more. And Aurore watched clouds of anxiety gather over her husband's brow. Day by day he became more absorbed, more silent.

When first they had settled down in Paris he had often talked to her of the great upheaval which was convulsing the country: he spoke with great moderation, careful not to outrage her principles or her belief. He brought her books to read, pamphlets that interested her even though they could never convince. André could talk well when he liked; he knew his Rousseau and discussed him with Aurore in a manner which opened up her mind to social questions of which she had never dreamed before. She was intelligent and responsive.

She had a great desire to learn, and, in spite of herself, she caught herself more than once looking forward to a quiet evening in the Quai de la Ferraille, *tête-à-tête* with her husband, listening to his talk while she worked. He would speak very freely of the social ideals that had brought about the Revolution, of men like Lafayette and Mirabeau, of the original Legislative Assembly, the Constitution of '89, and the Declaration of the Rights of Man. But it was always of the past that he spoke. Of the present and the future, he never uttered a word, and Aurore, through innate delicacy of feeling, never mentioned the names of those demagogues who had been André's colleagues and friends at one time, and who had since been hurled down the steep path of enormity and of crime by the avalanche which they had let loose and no longer could control. She never once uttered the name of Danton, the master butcher who had been André's friend.

From time to time she had news of her father, and André held out hopes to her that she would see him soon; but he never spoke again of Marigny, though she had a strong suspicion that he was administering the estate through an agent whom he had placed there for the purpose.

Soon she had the conviction that he was taking her presence in his home absolutely for granted. She was his wife and looked after his comfort. Sometimes she was also a pleasant companion with whom he could talk of extraneous subjects. He had never once set foot inside her room.

He taught her to play chess, and now and then they would have a game in the evening. The lamp, set on a tall stand behind Aurore's chair, lit up the tender gold of her hair, the curve of her shoulder peeping through the folds of her lace *fichu*, her delicate hand supporting her chin. She was beautiful, and she knew it. But whenever she looked up from her game she invariably saw his head bent, intent upon the next move, and his eyes fixed upon the board.

He had never once kissed her since that evening at Nevers.

Chapter 34

Towards the end of September André announced to Aurore his intention to take her to Nevers.

"The Mignets," he said, "will be very happy to have you with them, and there will be a chance for you of seeing your father."

A quick cry of protest came involuntarily to her lips.

"I would rather stay here!" she said, and then could have cried with vexation, for at once that mocking smile which she hated came curling around his mouth.

"I would not wish to burden Madame Mignet with my presence," she went on, as coolly as she could. "I know from experience how difficult housekeeping has become, and a visitor must be a burden in any house."

"The *citizeness* has been longing to see you again, she tells me, and Paris is not the place for you just now."

It was not often that he assumed this air of authority over her, but Aurore was sensible enough to know that when he did any kind of resistance would be useless. In this great era of liberty, a married woman was still entirely dependent on her husband. She had no money or property apart from him, and he had complete control over her affairs and over her movements. Aurore, who had a great regard for her own personal dignity, would never have demeaned herself by argument or resistance which could only result in defeat.

As a matter of fact, she knew quite well why she was being sent out of Paris, and in her innermost heart could not help feeling thankful that there were some kind friends with whom she could stay, away in a quiet provincial town, until the terrible events which were looming ahead had come about and vanished into the past. The trial of the unfortunate queen had been decreed by the Convention. This, of course, would be nothing but hideous mockery and would inevitably end in her condemnation and her death. André did not wish his wife to be in Paris when that occurred.

He took her over to Nevers on one of the last days in September.

The drive in the diligence through the beautiful valleys of the Nièvre and the Allier, where the trees that bordered the road were already clothed in the gorgeous russet and gold mantle of autumn, was strangely soothing. More than once Aurore fell asleep in spite of the roughness of the road, the heat inside the diligence, the querulous murmur of conversation of her fellow passengers. When a sudden jerk aroused her from these fitful slumbers she usually found that in her sleep her head had fallen sideways and come to rest on her husband's shoulder. She would look up at him, half dazed and with a beating heart, only to find that he was sitting bolt upright, staring straight out in front of him, and had not apparently as much as noticed her.

The Mignets were, as usual, more than kind, and did all they could to make their guest happy. But a strange restlessness now had possession of Aurore, and the peaceful atmosphere of this refined household seemed to irritate rather than soothe her nerves. Very little news from Paris penetrated as far as this sleepy cathedral town. The diligence to and from the capital only plied once a month now, and the meagre sheets which it brought were at once snapped up by a privileged few. As Aurore never spoke with anyone outside the household she could only learn what the Mignets chose to tell her. She more than suspected that news was being kept from her when it was more than usually horrible or alarming.

She did hear of the condemnation and death of the queen, and this caused her unmitigated grief. She also heard of the wholesale execution of the Girondists, the brilliant party whose members were the first to try and cry halt to the holocaust which they themselves had set in motion. The *élite* of intellectual Paris perished on the guillotine on that awful last day of October, and with them perished the last of the moderatists who might have stemmed the tide of butchery nine months before the surfeit of carnage put an end to it at last.

Aurore could not help wondering at times how her husband would fare though all the turmoil that followed the execution of the Girondists. It was obvious, even to her who knew so little, that no man's head was safe upon his shoulders if he expressed the slightest desire to see the end of all the slaughter or showed anything but satisfaction at the orgy of blood that went on day after day. And Aurore, with all her hatred and dread of André, knew him to be entirely fearless and disdainful of his life where his ideals and his beliefs were at stake.

As in the days of his youth, when he had boldly expressed his views on the Rights of Man and the iniquity of the old social system that allowed two thirds of humanity to starve so that the remaining third might feast, as later on he had joined Danton in the denunciation of those tyrants who had learned nothing from the lesson taught them by an outraged people, so now he would with equal boldness tilt against the assassins, who through sheer fear for their own lives were vying with one another in atrocities and had turned the beautiful land of France into a gigantic shambles.

Sooner or later, thought Aurore, he would fall a victim to his moderatism. It would be a pity, she thought, because there must be so few men of sane views and true patriotism left in the country now. Once or twice she spoke about André to the Mignets and showed an anxiety on his behalf which she hoped would please them. It did. And as usual the doctor and the old lady at once embarked on their wonted eulogy of their friend.

"They daren't touch him," the doctor said decisively.

"Why not?" Aurore retorted. And then added: "It seems to me that, as they dared raise their guilty hand against the queen, they would dare anything."

"That was different," the doctor asserted.

"Why different?" she demanded.

"André's life is consecrated to the service of the poor and the afflicted. One could hardly say that of the unfortunate Marie Antoinette."

"She never had the opportunity," Aurore protested hotly.

"Perhaps not. But, anyway, while she lived she was a constant inducement to a handful of hot-headed traitors to betray their country

355

for her sake. You would be surprised, *citizeness*, if you knew the number of conspiracies, of intrigues, of treacheries that were daily hatches in order to overthrow the Republic and replace the Austrian woman on her son on the throne."

"Then do you mean to tell me that you——" Aurore retorted vehemently.

"Don't ask me that question, *citizeness*," the doctor broke in with earnestness. "I am no politician, nor am I the guardian of my country's laws. I only wanted to point out to you that the execution of Marie Antoinette in no way suggest danger to your husband."

"Unless things change very much for the worse," the old lady put in, "the country cannot afford to lose its André Vallon."

"Why not?"

It seemed a strange question for a wife to ask. Madame Mignet, for the first time since the beginning of their friendship, cast a disapproving eye on Aurore.

"My dear," she said coldly, "you know better than we do that your husband is the only man in France at this present moment who has thoroughly mastered the system of teaching the deaf and dumb. By means of signs, which he does with his one hand, he has taught scores of such poor afflicted souls how to exchange and assimilate ideas. And the same with the blind. Surely you knew all that."

Aurore's silence was her reply. She felt ashamed. How could she own to these dear, kind friends that she had not yet been on such terms of intimacy with her husband that he could speak to her about himself or his work? She had only been a pleasant acquaintance in the sunny home of the Quai de la Ferraille, one with whom a busy man could discuss the abstract theories of Rousseau or the speeches of Mirabeau. To her husband she had only been an intelligent opponent at chess or piquet, but never a confidant. Not hers the sympathetic ear into which a man could pour the tale of his struggles, his strivings, his disappointments. Not hers the loved voice whose gentle tones could soothe the nerves jaded by fatigue.

Much against her will, a few hot tears rose to Aurore's eyes. She rose quickly and turned away lest those kind friends should see them.

But after that she no longer tried to disguise from the Mignets the fact that she and André were two beings apart. They had guessed it, of course, but out of delicacy had never given her a hint that they knew. The full circumstances of her marriage were, of course, unknown to them, but it was very clear that the ideals of a Royalist and those of

356

a child of the Revolution were as far apart as the poles. Love alone might in time have bridged over the distance, but alas! as Madame Mignet remarked to her son one day when they talked the matter over together, there is no love between them on either side. Womanlike, she put the blame for this on Aurore.

"She is beautiful," was her comment on the situation, "but I am afraid that she has no temperament; and André ought to have had either a clinging, affectionate little wife, who would have mothered him, or else——"

The old lady paused and put on a demure expression. She knew what she meant, and so did her son, and between them they decided that Aurore of the wonderful eyes and the cherry-red mouth did not possess any of the attributes which would have made André happy.

"Unless——" Madame Mignet added, who was nothing if not enigmatic. And then she said with a hopeful little sigh, "One never knows."

And Aurore, sitting in the large-winged chair by the window in the pretty room at Nevers, watched the snowflakes slowly fluttering down from the leaden sky. She also watched other things from that pleasant point of vantage—people hurrying by with heads bent against the cold wind, the poor little half-frozen children hurrying home from school, the gossips at the street corner, and the itinerant menders of tin pots or earthenware, and, once a month, when the diligence came in from Paris, her husband, André Vallon, with a small valise in his hand, pausing a moment at the door to ring the bell.

Chapter 35

It was on one of the first days of March that Aurore had the surprise of her life. André, in the course of his visit, announced to her the early arrival of her father at Nevers.

"He will be safer here," he explained, in response to Aurore's little cry, half of joy and half of alarm. "The people in the villages suffered terrible privations during the protracted winter, and tempers over there are none too placid in consequence. Some few hotheads might engineer a regrettable *coup*."

"But——"

"But what?"

"This will not entail any unpleasantness?" she suggested tentatively.

"Unpleasantness?"

"For you, I mean, or——"

"No, why should it?"

"Or danger?"

"Danger? For him? Certainly not. He will be much safer here."

"I didn't mean for him."

"For you, then?"

"Of course not!" she retorted, and then added with a shrug, "As if I mattered."

"Then I don't understand what you do mean by danger. Danger to whom?"

"To you."

He said nothing for a moment or two, but she felt that those searching eyes of his were seeking to find some hidden thought, some unexplainable motive in those two words which she had murmured below her breath. After a few seconds' silence he gave a light shrug and said drily:

"I can but echo your own words—as if I mattered!"

He turned to go out of the room. Involuntarily she called out:

"André!"

The first time, the very first time that she had called to him by name. He paused at the door with his hand already on the knob and half turned to her:

"At your service, *citizeness.*"

His voice was quite harsh and his tone cold, so cold that the impulse which had made her call to him seemed frozen suddenly into a kind of miserable shyness. He was not the sort of man to whom one could offer sympathy or comfort. Nevertheless, Aurore was conscious of an intense pity for her husband. All of a sudden, he appeared to her so lonely! Introspective, too, probably through being so very much alone. And young, scarcely older than herself, and with all his hours spent amid the afflicted, the blind, the deaf and dumb, the miserable poor! In constant contact with everything that was most wretched and most squalid!

And with all his ideals of a regenerated world lying shattered around him! Lonely and disappointed! And she, his wife, could do nothing to comfort or cheer him. When she tried to find the right words with which to touch his heart, she was stupid and tongue-tied. Even now, when she felt so desperately sorry and so deeply grateful, she could not find those words which perhaps might have brought a faint gleam of pleasure to his eyes.

All she could do now was to murmur a few words that were quite unintelligible and apparently failed to reach him. She made a great effort to control herself and her voice and finally contrived to say fairly steadily:

"I only wished to ask you about the arrangements for my father. When does he come?"

"Tomorrow," he replied equally steadily, "by *cariole*. I have secured a nice apartment for him close by here in the Rue de la Monnaie. Pierre will drive him over, and he and Jeannette will look after him as they have done all along at Marigny."

"You are very kind," Aurore murmured. "I wish——" she paused and then went on more glibly "——I wish I could show you in some way that I—that I am not ungrateful."

"There is no question of gratitude," he said drily. "I made you a promise that while you are my wife your father's safety would be my care. I am trying to keep my promise, that is all."

"You are ungracious," she rejoined. "Does not the English poet say that 'Rich gifts wax poor when givers prove unkind'?"

"I would not for the worlds have you think me unkind."

"Then tell me."

"What?"

"How I can best repay you for the trouble my father has been to you."

"I assure you——"

"André," she insisted, "please!"

Again, his name on her lips. Once upon a time she had hit at him with a moral whiplash and she had also struck him in the face. Neither morally nor physically had she hurt him then, and he had not even winced at the time. Then why, at sound of his name on her lips, did that frown appear upon his brow as if he were trying to keep back something, to control some movement—or was it words?—while an unmistakable look of pain crept into his eyes? Only for an instant, though. Within the space of a second the look of pain as well as the frown had vanished, and there was that mocking smile—that hateful, hateful mocking smile which she so dreaded, curling again around his lips.

"Since you desire it, *citizeness*," he said drily, "I will tell you that you would earn my deep gratitude if you refrained from listening too patiently to your father's diatribes on the present political situation. Believe me, we all know it to be terrible. But words won't mend it, not just yet. Your father very naturally hates me, he will——"

"I shouldn't allow him——" she broke in hotly, and then paused, her impulse once more check by that miserable, unexplainable shyness. He put up his hand as if to deprecate anything else that she might say.

"And now," he said, "I am more than repaid."

He went out of the room, and she was left standing there with a big, big ache in her heart, an ache that she could not very well account for, but it forced tears up to her eyes. Tears of anxiety? Of pity? Of regret? She did not know. She only knew that she was desperately miserable and that not even the prospect of seeing her father again so soon had the power to console her.

But had her eyes been gifted with the power to see through material objects she would have made her own heartache seem light and easy to bear. She would have seen a man, strong of will and of iron purpose, broken down by the force of a passion he could no longer control. Gone were resentment and bitterness, pride was torn to shreds. Here was just a man madly—passionately in love. Slowly he fell on his knees; his arm rested against the door; his face was buried in the crook of his arm; and a mighty sigh came from the overburdened heart and broke in a convulsive sob.

Chapter 36

Charles de Marigny arrived the following afternoon. Aurore had been full of eager joy to see him. All morning she had been busy in the apartment of the Rue de la Monnaie, putting it to rights, making it look as comfortable and as gay as she could. The house was at the end of the street, and the windows of the parlour commanded a beautiful view over the Grande Place, the Ducal Palace, and the river beyond. The room was flooded with sunshine.

After an exceptionally severe winter the spring had come in early, with warm days and an absence of cold winds. The shrubs in the gardens of the Palace were covered with tender green. Lilac, syringa, and jasmine were in bud. Aurore went about her task humming the old *chansons*:

"*Il* était *une Bergère, et ron—et ron, petit Patapon!*"

and

"*Nuage, beau Nuage, qui passe Triomphant!*"

She couldn't sit still. At every sound of wheels or clatter of hoofs she ran to the window to see if the *cariole* was in sight.

But at sight of her father her high spirits quickly sank. Looking down on him from the window, as he got out of the *cariole*, he appeared to her to be years older. She ran down, and he embraced her with passionate effusion, but the very next moment he pushed her away from him as if the sight of her horrified him. He followed her upstairs, however, leaving Pierre and Jeannette to deal with the *cariole* and luggage. He did not so much as give a glance round the sunlit room but threw himself into a chair like a man wearied to death. He had not yet uttered a single word.

Aurore came and knelt down beside him. She would not admit to herself how appalled and disappointed she was. She, who had been the apple of her father's eye, felt as if he were a stranger to her, a stranger whom she almost feared. Her anxious glance searched the face that she had loved so dearly, vainly seeking for that expression of almost passionate tenderness wherewith he had been wont to regard her. But now there was a kind of fierce glitter in his eyes which would suddenly die down and give place to a dull, vacant stare. Aurore felt intensely sorry for him, for his face betrayed the suffering which he must have endured throughout this long autumn and winter, brooding over his wrongs, all alone up at Marigny, and seeing the horrors and the outrage of this terrible revolution pass like a nightmare before his eyes.

He said very little that first afternoon, and never once touched upon his daughter's marriage or asked either after her husband or the kind friends in whose house she was staying.

But the next day he appeared more loquacious, was apparently happy at the thought that he would no longer be parted from his darling little Aurore and fell in with all her plans for spending as much time together as possible. They would drive out into the country, or go up the river, and they would spend long evenings together, talking over old times.

He spoke quite rationally, but Aurore could not help noticing that his movements were jerky and that while he talked his hands kept on shaking and his fingers fidgeting with anything that was handy. And suddenly he mentioned André Vallon by name, quite dispassionately at first. Aurore was at her favourite place on a low stool beside his chair, with one arm over his knees. He took hold of her hand, and she noticed that his was burning hot. Carefully, insidiously, he invited her confidence.

"Tell me, my little Aurore," he said, and his tone was gentle and soothing. "Don't be afraid to tell me how unhappy you are. I know you are unhappy, my beloved child, but our troubles always seem less, you know, when we tell of them to a sympathetic ear."

"When you were little," he went on, as Aurore made some evasive reply, "I was your mother as well as your father. You used to tell me everything—all your childish troubles. Tell me your troubles now, my darling. Tell me everything. That cruel, inhuman beast! I'd like to know to what lengths his brutality could go."

And as Aurore still continued to parry his direct questions he put down her reticence to the desire to spare him pain. His tone became more insinuating still, and a look of deep cunning came into his eyes. He leaned forward in his chair till his mouth nearly touched her ear.

"I'll rid you of him, my little Aurore," he whispered. "I have thought it all out. That's why I consented to come to this miserable hole. You trust me. I know! I know just what to do. You needn't tell me anything. I can guess. The brute! The beggarly knave! I know! But I'll rid you of him. Never fear!"

Aurore did all she could to soothe him, but, in spite of herself, her heart was filled with a great and nameless dread. There was something dangerous in the fanaticism of her father's hatred, and although the Mignets and André himself did all they could to reassure her, she had the growing conviction that there was method in her father's apparent madness. He took to roaming about the streets for hours at a time, and Jeannette told Aurore that when he returned he usually brought back with him a lot of news sheets over which he pored and pondered for the rest of the day. Jeannette and Pierre both said that *Monseigneur* slept very little; they heard him pacing up and down the room half the night through and muttering to himself. Aurore questioned the two faithful souls as to what *Monseigneur* said when he muttered like that, but it seemed that those mutterings were mostly unintelligible; the only words they ever heard clearly were: "Quite simple—quite easy! That is what I must do," which certainly did not tend to reassure Aurore.

One day, when she came to see the old man, Jeannette told her that he had just gone out, but had spent all morning poring over some news sheets. One in particular he had been intent on for more than an hour, Jeannette said; it was still lying on the table beside his chair. Aurore went into the parlour and had a look at the news sheet. It was an old number of the *Moniteur*, bearing a date in September of last year. It contained the full text of Merlin's abominable "*Loi Relatif aux Gens Suspects.*" The Law of the Suspect! Obviously, De Marigny had been perusing it; the page with the text lay uppermost; there were notes in the margin in his handwriting. Certain passages were underlined; for instance:

Art 1: Immediately after the publication of this Decree, all suspected persons on the territory of the Republic who are still at large will be arrested.

And below that there was:

Are reputed suspect 1: Those who, either by their conduct or by their relations with former tyrants or *aristos*.

And the last have dozen words were underlined.

Chapter 37

At what precise moment the first dart of a horrible suspicion entered her heart Aurore did not know. All she realised was that an awful danger threatened her husband at the hands of her father.

The horror of such a thing!

She knew, as did everyone these days, that one denunciation, even if it came from an irresponsible person, was often sufficient to bring about the arrest of a fellow creature—arrest which almost invariably was the precursor of death! And with her mind fixed upon this fact she recalled her father's wild rambling words: "I'll rid you of him—I know what to do—Quite simple—That is what I must do—"

Quite simple!

Now Aurore's mind worked more quickly. Something had to be done and done at once. But what? Firstly, where was the unfortunate madman now? Had he already set out on his proposed trail of treachery and crime? Aurore called to Jeannette and to Pierre. She questioned them and questioned them. Where was *Monseigneur*? They did not know. Where did he go when he went out aimlessly like this? Just about the streets, sometimes in one direction, sometimes in another. He was fond of the river bank. The river! Great God in heaven!

For one moment Aurore caught herself almost hoping that he had courted the river in a mad desire to put an end to all his misery. Almost hoping! Heavens above! was she going mad, too? She was, unless she could get a more definite idea of whither her father had gone. But for the moment, since they knew nothing, Pierre and Jeannette must go back to their work. She, Aurore, wished to be left alone to think, to find out something—something!

She looked about her in the small sunlit parlour, feeling helpless and her soul in darkness. She beat her hands together in a wild long-ing for inspiration. What about money? Had he taken any with him? Aurore knew where he kept it—in the drawer of the small *escritoire*. She had often seen him take out a *livre* or two to give to Jeannette. Now she went to look. The pocketbook that was usually in the drawer was no longer there. There were two packets instead. One was ad-dressed to Pierre and obviously contained money, paper and coins. The other was addressed "To my little Aurore." She opened it. There was a letter written in his familiar careful hand. It said:

> My Darling Little One
> I promised you that I would rid you of the inhuman monster who has blighted your young life, and I am going to do it. By the time you get this I shall be on my way to Paris. That arch-rogue Talon, who is as useful fortunately as he is servile, has made all necessary arrangements. His wife has relatives in Paris, and I shall stay with them. For the first time in my life I shall accept hospitality in a plebeian house, but I have no alternative. What I want to do can only be done in Paris, but there it can be done quickly. Do not try and find out what I am about to do or how. Wait patiently for a further letter from me. Talon will bring it you. I may be caught in my own toils, but I care not so long as I have made you happy and free.
> Your devoted Father.

Aurore read the terrible lucubration until the end. Then she re-folded the letter and slipped it in the bosom of her gown. She had no doubt now as to what she meant to do, but she wouldn't leave any-thing to chance. So, she hunted through the drawer again and through the whole of the *escritoire* for some written trace of Hector Talon, that awful, miserable, obsequious Talon! So, it was he who was at the bot-tom of this abominable treachery! Aurore hunted for a letter, a sign of him, as a careful gardener would hunt for the trail of the slug that had impaired his plants. But she found nothing. Talon was a man—no, a worm—who worked underground in the darkness and left no trace of his slimy way.

Then Aurore once more questioned Jeannette and Pierre. Had they seen—did they know anything of Hector Talon? And she wrung the truth out of them, poor miserable wretches! Talon had been in Nevers two days. He had visited *Monseigneur*. He had bribed them to say nothing to *Mademoiselle* of these visits. He had been here early this morning, and he and *Monseigneur* then went out together, Talon carrying a small valise which Pierre had packed with a few necessities at *Monseigneur's* orders.

And then Aurore saw red. She felt like a tigress in a fury, would gladly with her two feeble hands have seized those two fools by the throat. They had taken money, money to hold their tongue, while Monseigneur le Duc de Marigny, who bore one of the greatest names in France, and was own cousin to her martyred king, accomplished the vilest act of treachery that had ever disgraced a *canaille*.

But what was the good of fury, what the good of vituperations, now that the crime was on the point of accomplishment? One fact she did wring out of the trembling lips of Pierre. Lucile Talon's relatives lived in No. 67 of the Rue St. Honoré. Well, that, at any rate, was something. Aurore knew now where she could find her father.

She was half-dazed when she reached the Mignets' house. Without circumlocution, straight to the point, she told them what had happened. "I must go to Paris," she concluded calmly, "at once. How can I do it?"

"My dear child," the old lady protested, "you cannot go to Paris like this, all in a moment."

"I have my papers, money, everything," she said. "Help me to find a conveyance, as the diligence does not leave till next week."

"But what can you do, child?"

"Warn my husband before it is too late."

To every protest, every objection she gave the same reply: "I must go to my husband before it is too late."

And then she said at last, "If you will not help me I will find a way somehow, but I am going before the day is out."

Help her? Of course, they would help her! Were they not the kindest people on God's earth, and was not André Vallon the beloved friend of their heart? Doctor Mignet would, of course, accompany Aurore as far as Paris, and while she went to put a few things together he set out to find coach and horses which would take them as far as Auxerre, where they could pick up another conveyance to take them on to Melun and to Paris. That was probably the route chosen by Talon for *Monseigneur*, and Aurore would be close on her father's heels.

Chapter 38

To anyone returning to Paris in this awful year 1794, after an absence of several months, the aspect of the once gay and lovely city must have been appalling. Streets half deserted; furtive, ill clad figures slouching about the open places; aspects of dire poverty in a blatant contrast with brilliantly lighted restaurants or theatre porticoes; sounds of strident laughter alternating with heart-rending moans. Laughter and tears, and words scarcely whispered lest they be overheard.

This great, this sublime revolution which was to bring universal freedom and universal happiness, how immense has been its toll of misery and of crime! Penury is terrible; certain necessities like soap and sugar are hardly obtainable. Bread is more and more scarce; the queues outside the bakeries line up during the small hours of the morning and last all day.

The wolves of the Revolution are busy tearing one another to pieces. After the Girondins, the Dantonists. Danton, the great Georges Danton, the lion of the Revolution, who for five years has held the snarling, screaming pack on the leash, has atoned for his weaknesses as well as for his crimes, on the insatiable guillotine. Too weak to stem the flood which he himself had let loose, he perished as he had allowed others to perish—his king, his queen, his comrades, his friends. Too weak! The great, the virile Danton, with the resonant voice and tempestuous eloquence, too weak to combat his cunning, slimy adversary, the Sea-green Incorruptible with the ascetic face and the pale eyes! Then what chance had others against the all-powerful dictator who with one word hissed through his thin lips could send any adversary without trial to the scaffold?

It was a month and more since the Dantonists had perished on the guillotine, and Maximilien Robespierre was sovereign master of France.

Aurore, sitting inside the diligence which had brought her and the doctor over from Melun, had no eyes for outward things. Whether Paris was changed or not since last she had been in the city, whether the streets looked dismal and the restaurants lively, she neither knew nor cared. It was a lovely day in May: the chestnut trees in the Tuileries gardens were full of blossom; the sun shone and the sky was blue; but Aurore say nothing of these beauties of nature. Now that the time was so near when she would see her husband her febrile impatience was such that it was only by a mighty effort of will that she was able to sit still in the crowded coach and not allow her fellow passengers to become aware of the state of her nerves. They might have thought her demented. Doctor Mignet sat beside her and now and then gave her hand a slight pressure, which comforted her for the moment.

At last the lumbering coach came to a halt at the Cheval Blanc, the posting inn close to the Pont Neuf. The Quai de la Ferraille was quite close. Aurore elected to walk while Doctor Mignet would look after the luggage. He announced his intention of putting up at the Cheval Blanc, if he could get a room.

"I shall be within five minutes' walk," he said kindly, "so you can call on me, my dear, whenever you want me."

It was then three o'clock in the afternoon. The usual crowd swarmed round the Palace of Justice, waiting to see the prisoners being hustled out after their condemnation, or the well-known advocates or members of the Convention sally forth after the grim work of the day was done.

Aurore paid no heed to anything round her; wrapped in her travelling cape with the hood pulled over her head she walked rapidly, looking neither to right nor left. But suddenly the crowd surged along the bridge, and she found herself hustled and pressed against the parapet: a couple of tumbrils surrounded by men in uniform were forging their way through the throng. They were the prisoners who had just stood the mockery of a trial and were being taken back to La Force or the Temple for their final toilette before their ultimate journey to the guillotine. A few tattermalions in the crowd shouted: "À la guillotine!" Others hurled insults at the prisoners, but the bulk of the people looked on with a kind of stolid indifference, showing neither joy nor horror.

Aurore, pressed against the parapet, saw the tumbrils pass along quite close to her; she saw the prisoners standing with hands tied behind their backs; and suddenly the full force of the horror which she saw reached her consciousness. She searched those faces in the tumbrils, realising for the first time that perhaps she had come too late and that André might be standing there in the tumbril—standing there on his way to death.

When the tumbrils had passed and the crowd drifted away in their wake she remained for a long time there, leaning against the balustrade with eyes blind to everything save to the vision that had just passed by, and lips parted by the cries of horror which she had been at such pains to repress. André had not been one of those poor wretches that were being dragged through the streets of Paris for the delectation of the mob: but the vision of that ghastly exhibition had conjured up the possibility of another, so awful, so terrible, so infernal that Aurore was left wondering if she was not indeed going the way of her father and losing her reason at the foresight.

After a little while she recovered herself, and without glancing to right or left she hurried along the quay. Soon she reached the house wherein she had spent the first few months of her married life! What peace there seemed to be in it! Aurore felt it almost as soon as she passed under the *porte-cochère* and made her way up the familiar stone staircase. She rang the bell of the apartment as she had done so often in the past, and the same pleasant middle-aged woman opened the door to her.

The woman's eyes looked ready to fall out of her head at sight of Aurore.

"But, *citizeness*—!" she exclaimed, and clasped her hand together in amazement.

"Citizen Vallon? Is he in?" Aurore almost gasped and staggered into the vestibule.

The semi darkness indoors after the dazzling sunshine of the street dazed her and made her feel as if she were blind. The woman ran to her and put her arms round her.

"You are ill, *citizeness*," she murmured. "What can I get you?"

Aurore shook her head: "Nothing!—I am not ill—Where is Citizen Vallon?"

"At the Blind School, *citizeness*. He does not usually come home before evening."

"You expect him home, then?"

"But of course, *citizeness*."

The woman, with gentle solitude, relieved Aurore of the heavy travelling cape. She was obviously puzzled and not a little frightened but tried to speak as unconcernedly as she could.

"We were not expecting you, *citizeness*," she said: "at least the *citizen* said nothing to me."

"No," Aurore replied more calmly: "he does not expect me. I came with Doctor Mignet."

The woman opened the parlour door. How inviting it looked! The bright sunny room with the muslin curtains, the armchair and her own work table beside the window; the books, the footstool, the chessmen ranged on the board. Aurore's tired eyes roamed round the room and, in spite of the agony of dread which was gnawing at her heart, an infinite peace seemed to descend on her soul. With a weary little sigh, she sank into the armchair, and a wan smile lit up her face in response to the woman's anxious, puzzled gaze.

"What would you like, *citizeness?*" the woman asked, a little reassured. "A glass of wine, or some hot coffee?"

"Coffee, please, Marie. Some of that lovely coffee you used to make for my breakfast."

"It won't be quite so nice now, *citizeness*," Marie said with a sigh; "and we have no milk."

"Whatever it is, Marie, I shall love it," Aurore assured her. The woman went away, and she snuggled down into the big chair. How lovely and peaceful it was! The quay below was half deserted; hardly a sound came to disturb the quietude of this serene abode. Leaning her head against the back of the chair Aurore felt a flood of tears rise to her eyes—tears that were not wholly of sorrow.

She drank eagerly the coffee which Marie presently brought her. After which the kind woman persuaded her to lie down on the sofa and saw her comfortably settled with a couple of pillows under her head. Poor little Aurore! She was so tired, so infinitely weary! Physically and mentally weary. Her limbs ached, and her head. And she had a great big heartache.

And lying there snugly against the pillows she presently fell asleep.

Chapter 39

The sound of the door and a murmur of voices roused Aurore from sleep.

The next moment André came into the room. She sat up on the sofa, her hands clasped tightly together, her fair hair slightly tousled, and her cheeks flushed after sleep. The shades of evening were drawing in, and the rosy light of sunset had crept into the room. André, at the door, had not yet moved. He was looking his fill on the exquisite vision which had transformed this simple room into a mansion of paradise.

At last he asked the obvious questions:

"Why are you here? Has anything happened?"

"Yes, André," she replied, "a very great deal has happened. My father, poor wretch, has completely lost his reason!"

"Heavens above!"

"No," she said, "I don't mean in that way, though I do think Doctor Mignet would actually pronounce him mad."

She paused a moment. Her throat felt so dry that she could hardly speak. There were a carafe and a glass on the side table. André filled the glass with water and brought it to her. While she drank he stood beside her, and when she was about to put the glass down he took it from her, and his hand touched her fingers, which were trembling and cold.

"You are overwrought," he said gently. "Don't try and talk now. I will call Marie and she—"

"No! no!" she broke in quickly. "I don't want anyone. I am only tired from the journey, and I must tell you—"

"Yes? What is it?"

"Spurred by his insane hatred against you, my father has denounced you—"

"How do you know that?"

"Never mind how I know: I know it. I swear to you that it is so. One day I will tell you just how I found out, but not now. There is no time. I came to warn you before—before—"

"You came to warn me?" he asked, frowning, evidently puzzled.

"Yes."

"Why?"

They looked at each other, he uncomprehending, not daring to comprehend, and she, seized with that awful shyness which almost paralyzed her will and her tongue.

"Why?" he insisted, but this time he came nearer her, and his voice was hoarse and broken like that of a man gasping for breath.

"Because," she murmured, "because—"

It was her eyes that answered him. Her lips refused her service.

"Because you cared?"

Was there ever a cry uttered by man more exultant than this which rose like a *paean* of joy from André Vallon's throat? In a moment he was beside her on one knee, not daring to touch her yet, but with ardent, passionate gaze trying to read the secret of her soul.

"Because you cared?" he insisted. "Tell me."

"André!"

"Because you cared what became of me? Say it! Say it! Say the word, *ma mie!* Tell me that you came," he entreated, "because you cared."

How could she speak? The whole world, the sordid, ugly world, lay suddenly shattered at her feet, and in the gaze that sought and held her own she had a glimpse of such a vision of Elysian fields as human mind could scarcely conceive. She returned his gaze and her eyes, which had always seemed unfathomable, revealed to him the secret which she had thought would remain forever buried in her heart. It was Love that had spurred her to come. Love that had so often made her heart ache almost to breaking point. Love! and the longing to feel once more that dear strong arm around her, to pillow her head against that loyal breast, to hear that great and simple heart beat only for her. He loved her, and she did not know it! And now that the heavenly knowledge had come to her at last it came hand-in-hand with the agonising dread for his life.

"André!" she said suddenly, all the joy in her heart smothered in this awful dread, "you must leave Paris at once."

He did not seem to hear. He had had his answer from her eyes, and his soul was no longer on this earth. It had gone a-roaming in paradise.

"You came," he murmured, "because you cared."

But, womanlike, she thought only of him, of the terrible danger which every minute as it sped by brought nearer and nearer to their door.

"You don't understand, André," she insisted. "My father is in Paris. It was only after he left that I suspected—"

"And then you came because you cared."

"André, at this very hour, perhaps—"

"At this very hour I am adoring you, Aurore—"

"There's time to get away," she entreated feverishly.

"And I want eternity in which to tell you how I worship you—"

"In God's name, André!" she cried. "It may mean death if you stay—"

But his hand was buried in her hair and forced her dear head closer and closer to him.

"My exquisite Aurore!" he whispered in her ear, "you are the most perfect being God ever made. I was a fool not to tell you this before, but I will not die, Dawn of my Soul, before I have taught you how good it is to love, how sweet it is to kiss."

He held her so close that she could no longer struggle. His lips were on hers, and she could no longer warn, and he asked the great, the immortal question which lovers have asked since the beginning of time, and the answer to which will open for them the gates either of paradise or of hell.

"Do you love me, my wife?"

And Aurore's eyes and lips answered softly, "Yes."

Chapter 40

The hours flew by on the wings of an overwhelming happiness, and Love reigned supreme while evening faded into night. The awakening came when the two lovers scarce had finished dreaming. The tramp of feet on the stairs, the knock on the door, the raucous call: "Open in the name of the Law!"

It was quite dark in the room now—quite dark, only through the chink under the door there came a narrow streak of light from the candle which Marie had put on the table of the vestibule, and through the thin muslin curtains over the window the pale flicker of the street lamp cast the objects in the room into deeper gloom.

"Open, in the name of the Law!"

And Aurore, waking from her dream of happiness and love, was suddenly thrust out of the gates of her paradise and hurled back into the hideous world of grim reality. In a moment she was on her feet and across the room. Like a statue of despair, she stood against the door with arms outstretched and head thrown back—a statue of despair but also of fury—a woman in defence of her lover.

"Come and kiss me, Aurore!" came a happy voice, broken with yearning, and in the gloom the arm she loved was stretched out in longing to her.

She babbled hoarsely, incoherently, like one half demented:

"You must fly, André! you must—you must—for my sake—there's time—through the window in the next room. The back yard—no one will see you—André—André—you must!"

"Come to me, Aurore—one more kiss," he said slowly; "ten more if there's time—"

"But they are here," she insisted. "André, can't you hear?"

Just then there was a timid knock at the door, and Marie's trembling voice called aghast: "In the name of God, Citizen Vallon, tell me what to do."

"Why, open the door, Marie," André replied quietly, "else they will break it open."

Then, as Marie's hesitating footsteps were heard shuffling across the vestibule, he murmured softly:

"There's time for one more kiss—Come to me, Aurore."

Obviously, she could not move. Horror, despair, had paralyzed her will and her limbs. The woman defending her lover! how could she move from that door, from that thin, futile barrier, the only thing that stood between her lover and death? The next instant André was beside her; she felt again that dear, strong arm around her, her head once more lay upon his breast, she felt the beating of that heart which she knew now was filled with her image. His lips eagerly devoured her eyes, her throat, her hair, and then in one long, impassioned kiss their lips met once more in enduring, all-conquering immutable love.

Outside in the vestibule there was bustle and noise and tramping of feet; hoarse commands and a murmur of voices, and Marie's wailing sobs. Then a knock at the door. A terrible cry rose to Aurore's throat, but it was smothered before it reached her lips, for André's hand was across her mouth.

"Open, in the name of the Law!"

"Three minutes, Citizen Soldiers," André replied glibly, "while I get a light."

And Aurore, clinging to him with convulsive hands, her face bathed in tears, her voice broken with sobs, whispered hoarsely:

"Kill me, André!—For mercy's sake kill me—I cannot live without your love."

"Look at me, sweet, and listen," he murmured hurriedly; and obediently she opened her eyes and looked up at him.

It was quite dark in the room, quite dark; but the feeble light of the street lamp faintly illuminated his face, and she could see that it was irradiated with a wonderful happiness.

"What you want now, my sweet," he said more slowly, "is courage."

"I have none, André," she murmured feebly.

"You will have when you remember that God in His mercy will give you someone else to care for, perhaps, instead of me."

"Someone else? I don't understand."

He pressed his lips close to her ear and whispered a few words very low, so that she could scarcely hear, but which brought a rush of colour to her pale cheeks. Then he looked once more into her eyes and smiled: the happiest, lightest of smiles.

"And if it is a boy," he said earnestly, but still with that happy smile, "do not teach him to hate all those Frenchmen who were his father's friends, with whom he dreamed dreams of making this old world new and happy, and who died for their ideals because they were men and not gods."

He raised her gently from the ground as he had so often done before, carried her into the next room, and there laid her down on the bed. She had partly lost consciousness, but her arms were twined round his neck, and her fingers so tightly linked together that he had some difficulty in getting them apart. She lay very still, but her eyes were open and her lips parted; her body was shaken with heart-rending sobs. He knelt down beside the bed and kissed her once more on the lips, drank the salt tears that lay upon her cheek; he kissed her ice-cold hands, her throat, her feet above the shoe, then slowly rose and went out of the room, closing and locking the door behind him.

She gave one terrific cry: "André!" and jumped up from the bed, her senses alert; she ran to the door—it was locked; with her hands she beat against the panels, she fell on her knees, clinging to that cruel door which hid him from her view, and calling, calling insistently, piteously, like a bird that has lost its mate. And all the while she heard the murmurs of voices, André's calm response: "Quite ready, Citizen Captain." A loud cry from Marie. The opening and shutting of the front door; the tramp of feet slowly—slowly—slowly dying away down the stairs.

And then—nothing more.

Marie coming in a few moments later found her in a dead swoon across the floor.

Chapter 41

She became known as "Our Little Lady of Sorrows"—*Notre Petite Dames des Douleurs.*

She could be seen daily wending her way from the Quai de la Ferraille to the Palais de Justice in the early morning, waiting in the queue until the gates were opened, and thereafter taking her place in the vast hall, always in the front row of the balcony that faced the prisoners at the bar. At first the other *habitués* of the grim spectacle looked on her as one of themselves, fond, as they were, of watching the prisoners file in, seeing them take their place on the benches facing the judges, with the chief prisoner in the iron armchair in the immediate centre. Women in ragged shawls and tattered kirtles, with dishevelled hair under soiled lace caps, or scarlet berets, who had brought their knitting with them to while away the waiting hours, would nudge Aurore when a well-known name was called out or if they recognised a noted prisoner.

"That's Amisal over there, *citizness*, the third from the end. He tried to assassinate the patriot Collot in the Rue Favart, you remember? Lucky, he missed fire, the brigand! Oh! and if it isn't that young scrub Cécile Renaud! She was for murdering the Incorruptible himself. They found two knives in her market basket, you know. Well, her way to the guillotine is clear enough."

But soon they found that she was not interested in their talk. She didn't listen: she only looked. She had great eyes of a colour impossible to define and wore a dark travelling cape with a hood over her fair hair. She would look and look while the batch of prisoners filed in, but as soon as they were seated and the Prosecutor Tinville began his indictment, she would lean back in her seat and take no more notice of what went on in the hall below.

Until another batch was called, when she would sit up and again look on each face as the prisoners filed in. She never spoke and she never cried, but she looked so sad that a woman one day, seeing her come in rather later than usual, made a place for her by squeezing her fellow spectators and said at the same time, "Here comes the Little Lady of Sorrows. Come and sit by me, my dear. You'll get a splendid view, better than the one you had yesterday."

And so the name stuck to her. And she came, day after day, to the Palais de Justice to watch the prisoners file into the hall, there to receive their sentence of death. There was no alternative. The very fact of being suspected of treason, of being denounced by an enemy or a fool, of being brought to the bar of this travesty of justice, was tantamount to a sentence of death. And Aurore came, day after day, to watch this grim spectacle, because she could not find out to what prison they had taken André and could find no other way of knowing what became of him. The prisons were crowded, the jailers overworked and harassed. Vainly had she tried to get sight of the list of prisoners in every House of Detention in and around Paris.

"We've no orders," was the response she invariably got from the concièrge or the captain in command. "Get an order from the Committee, and you can see the list."

"What Committee?" she would ask insistently. "And how can I get such an order?"

"Bah! Leave me in peace!" the man—whoever it was—would reply with a savage oath. "You don't think you are the only female who comes bothering us in this way, do you? If I had to attend to all of you—"

He would then turn his back on Aurore and have her ejected from the room and the door slammed in her face. The rules governing prison discipline had become very severe of late. The visits from outside, which used to be allowed and were a great feature of prison life in the past, were now strictly forbidden. The government had persuaded itself that plots of all sorts were being hatched in the Houses of Detention, and prisoners, in consequence, were not allowed to see anyone. Thus, frustrated at every turn, Aurore took to haunting the Palais de

Justice. There, at last, she would be bound to see André when he was brought to trial. She would see him when that awful tumbril took him to his death.

She had no hope. None. Though she held but little communication with anyone except, of course, Marie, she could not help knowing that the fate of every prisoner these days was a foregone conclusion. It was only a question of time. Some languished weeks in prison, others even months, some few were hurried through the ghastly process of arrest, trail, condemnation, and death in a few days. Aurore knew that and watched in the Palais de Justice every day.

She had written him a letter, just a few words in which she had poured out her every soul. They were words which, she knew, would give happiness to his heart and bring a smile to his dear lips. This precious paper she inserted in a heavy gold locket which she always held tightly in her hand ready to fling it to him if such a blessed opportunity arose.

May had long since yielded to June. June passed on, serene and warm, with its wealth of blossom in the gardens and a bird song in the summer air. All nature seemed to smile while men hated and destroyed one another and dared to mock God with their horrible Mumbo-Jumbo, the feast of the Supreme Bring, with the arch-murderer, Robespierre, parading in azure-blue coat and white breeches as the arch-priest of the new deity.

That was on the 8th of June, less than a fortnight after André's arrest. Doctor Mignet, who had been with Aurore during the first few days of her misery and had attempted the impossible in trying to find out wither they had taken André, had been obliged to return to his duties in Nevers. She hardly noticed his absence. Her heart was dead to all save to an infinity of grief.

It was in the early days of June that she saw her father again. She was walking across the Pont des Arts when suddenly she found herself face to face with Hector Talon. She thought nothing of the meeting at the moment; indeed, she hoped that he had not recognised her. But what he did was to halt for a minute or two as soon as she had passed by and then to follow her.

The next afternoon, when she came home from her daily pilgrimage, she found Marie bursting with what she thought was gladsome news.

"An elderly gentleman has come to see you, *citizeness*," she said mysteriously. "He is waiting in the parlour."

"Oh, Marie!" Aurore exclaimed involuntarily. "You shouldn't have—"

"Not admitted him!" Marie retorted with the easy familiarity of her kind. "But it's your father, *citizeness*, your dear old father!"

Aurore listened no further. With a heavy heart she went through into the parlour and saw her father sitting there on the end of the sofa close to the window, the sofa beside which André had knelt that late afternoon when first he had told her of his love. It seemed like a supreme insult, this old man sitting just there complacently gazing out of the window. When she entered he put out his arms and exclaimed with joy and tenderness:

"My little Aurore! At last! At last!"

She had not moved from the door. At sight of him her gorge rose in horror. What kind of a miscreated daughter was she that she should hate her own father? Would she, at least, have sufficient will power not to allow the full flood of her loathing to surge out of her overburdened heart? He, on the other hand, did not appear conscious of her enmity. As she did not rush into his arms he let them drop and went on talking in a glib, matter-of-fact way:

"You have no idea, *ma chérie*," he said, "how anxious I have been. I suppose your letter in answer to mine miscarried. I never received it, you know."

"What letter?" she asked.

"I wrote to tell you the joyful news. You never replied. But it was a good idea to come yourself instead."

"What joyful news?"

"Why, that I have fulfilled my promise, *ma chérie*, to rid you of the inhuman monster who had blighted your life."

"You mean that you wrote to tell me that you had committed the most loathsome act of treachery that ever called down the vengeance of God on a miscreant's head."

Even now he looked surprised, bewildered at her vehemence, thinking that his beloved daughter, like so many women in these terrible times, had perchance lost her reason.

"Aurore, my child!" he exclaimed soothingly.

"I am not your child!" she retorted coldly, "no longer the child of so vile a worker of iniquity as you. You have brought upon me such immeasurable sorrow as no man has ever brought on woman since the beginning of time. The very sight of you turns my heart to stone, and I can but pray to God that I may never set eyes on you again. And now, I entreat you to go before I quite forget that you are old and that you are my father."

She threw open the door and stood aside, pointing to it. De Marigny tried to speak. He rose and came a step or two towards her.

"Do not come near me," she said hoarsely. "My God! Can't you see that I am at the end of my tether?"

"You are overwrought, Aurore," he rejoined coolly. "Heaven knows what is going on in your poor distracted mind at this moment. You have spoken words that I shall find hard to forgive, but a father's heart is full of indulgence. I cannot, of course, stay now and plead with you, for the devil apparently has possession of your mind. It will take all our good *abbé's* piety to exorcise him."

Marie was hovering in the vestibule. She looked scared to death as De Marigny came out of the parlour and took up his hat and stick.

"Has she been long like this?" he asked her, indicating Aurore and then touching his forehead.

Marie was indignant.

"There is nothing wrong with the *citizeness's* brain," she said hotly. "It is her heart that is broken because she worshipped her husband, and he is like to perish on that awful guillotine."

De Marigny shrugged. How ignorant, how unobservant were people of that class! He looked back once over his shoulder. Aurore had not moved. The hood had fallen back from her head, and her delicate profile, with the wealth of fair hair above it like a golden aureole, looked like an exquisite cameo against the dark *portière*. She looked a living statue of high breeding, of blue blood and age-old descent—the perfect aristocrat. De Marigny shrugged again. Worshipped her husband, indeed? What nonsense! What a lie! Her mind was slightly unhinged, he concluded, that was all. Once all these horrible times were over and he had her back at Marigny she would be the first to laugh at this woman's foolish talk. And he went away entirely unperturbed.

Chapter 42

It was on the 26th of July that the last blow fell. Aurore sitting at her accustomed place in the Hall of the Palais de Justice saw the prisoners file in, and the first to enter was André.

Our Little Lady of Sorrows! She gave one gasp—a sob that rent her heart and caused even those deadened hearts around her to beat with sudden pity.

"Thou hast seen him, eh, my cabbage?" the woman next to her

asked. "Which is he?"

Two or three of them put down their knitting. They were interested. They meant to be kind. Their hearts were dulled by all the miseries and the horrors which they had witnessed—dulled but not dead. Our Little Lady of Sorrows! They were very, very sorry for her! She was so pretty and so young! And she had been watching here day after day for well-nigh two months to catch a last glimpse of her man.

"Don't try and point him out, my pigeon," the woman went on softly; "only nod 'yes' if I guess right."

The woman on the other side said:

"I believe it is that handsome fellow with the one arm. Well, it is a shame that such a fine soldier-"

"Hush, *citizeness*," someone at the back broke in, "you are talking treason."

That was so. No one was allowed to express pity for the prisoners at the bar, for such pity was a sign of counter-revolutionary tendencies and, as such, punishable by death. Even so, one woman said pointing to André: "He taught the blind to read and the dumb to speak. My daughter, who is blind—"

"Hush! Silence!" came from the rest of the crowd.

Our Little Lady of Sorrows sat and watched, her whole soul in her eyes. She saw André as the chief prisoner of the batch sitting in the iron chair immediately facing the judges. His face looked perfectly serene. He looked older, of course, and wan; prison life had no suited his vigorous temperament; but his dark eyes shone brightly, and around his mouth there was that mocking smile which Aurore had so dreaded once, but which since she had learned to love. Unlike his fellow prisoners André had obviously taken great pains with his appearance. He wore his old military tunic, which, though very worn and shabby, had been carefully brushed. He was neatly shaved, and his chestnut hair was tied back with a bow at the nape of his neck.

Our Little Lady of Sorrows watched him and marvelled that God in His mercy did not allow her heart to break. She listened to the indictment read by Prosecutor Tinville. She heard every lying word, every monstrous accusation. She listened and watched, drawing his soul to hers with the magnetism of her eyes. She threw back her hood so that he should see her better. And suddenly he looked up and saw her. Such a look of joy and happiness and love came into his face, as surely only shines on the faces of the blessed. Thereafter he looked neither to right nor left. Only at her.

The Prosecutor finished his indictment, the advocate began to plead. Obviously, André heard neither. Yet the advocate pleaded with fervour, even with passion. Even the crowd murmured approval at the defence, but what was the good? Prisoners were condemned long before they faced their judges. The advocate was silenced even in the very middle of his peroration, cut short when he was halfway through an eloquent sentence; and the prisoners were not allowed one word in their own defence.

They were all condemned in a body. Traitors all to the Republic! Conspirators against the State! The sentence was that they be guillotined. And that was all! The mock trial was at an end. They were ordered to rise and make way for others. Some of them screamed and wrung their hands; some called loudly to the people and to the Supreme Being to witness their innocence, some took the blow in sullen silence. But André took it with a gently mocking smile. It had to come, and he was prepared. Death these days was stalking every man: it was bound to be his turn one day, and he was prepared.

From the hour when Robespierre and his horde of jackals had attacked Danton the Lion and brought him down, from that hour André, the child of this revolution, knew that he, too, would be its victim. For two months he had languished in prison waiting his turn for the only possible release and dreaming of that wonderful afternoon when first he knew that the woman he worshipped, worshipped him too. So happy, so entrancing had been those hours of supreme joy and love that he felt that Fate and he were quits. God had given him everything, every joy, every happiness, supreme contentment when He gave him this perfect mutual love. So, what did anything else matter? Death would only mean a union more perfect—more enduring than anything that Life could give.

All this he tried to convey to Aurore with the last glance which he was able to cast on her. "Do not grieve, my beloved! The happiness which you gave me was too perfect for this earth, too perfect to last."

Aurore watched him until he too disappeared down the stairs that led to the guardroom. Then quickly she rose. There was one more hope of seeing him, when that awful cart took him back to prison. She could follow the cart, she could see him again, she could throw him her last message of love in the gold locket which she always carried—perhaps, even, she could touch his hand. Hastily drawing the hood back over her head, she rose to go. The others made way for her, helped her all they could. They murmured sympathetic words as she stepped over the tribunes to find her way out:

"Our Little Lady of Sorrows! So young! So pretty!"

"And that handsome husband!"

"Ah, me!"

"Where will it all end?"

There was a great crowd outside the gates, greater than usual, Aurore thought, as feverishly she forged her way down the great staircase and into the courtyard. The carts were there, ranged in a file to the left of the gates which were wide open. The crowd was dense round the carts. One had just gone with its batch of condemned: the other was waiting by the postern gate. It was round this one that the crowd was thickest. Aurore, with the determination and courage of despair, pushed and struggled to get near. But it was impossible: she was jostled and elbowed out of the way until she found herself pressed against the iron railing, on the stone base of which some of the throng had scrambled to get a better view. The open gates were close by. From such a point of vantage it would be possible to get a view of the prisoners in the cart over the heads of the crown, and then, when the cart moved away, to slip out by the gate in its wake. Some kindly person helped Aurore to hoist herself up on the stone parapet.

There she stood and waited, all eyes, and with the locket grasped tightly in her hand. She heard the people about her talking.

"Those are the ones from the Blind Institution."

"And those from the School for the Deaf and Dumb."

They were pointing to a small group of men and women, two or three score of them, who were gathered close around the cart.

"One of the prisoners taught in those institutions."

"Citizen Vallon. I knew him. A nephew of mine is blind. Vallon did wonders with him."

"He taught the blind to see."

"And the deaf to hear."

"I suppose they have come to see the last of him."

"Poor creatures! What will become of them now?"

"Hush! Here they come!"

The prisoners were filing out of the building and were being hustled into the cart. There were eight of them, five men, three women. The men's coats were tied by the sleeves round their necks. All had their arms tied with cord behind their backs. André was the last to step into the cart: at sight of him one part of the crowd set up a cry, weird and inarticulate, the cry peculiar to the tongue-tied and the dumb:

it was taken up by the blind, who had not seen but could guess. The blind called out piteously: "Do not leave us in darkness, Citizen Vallon!" but the dumb could only utter their hideous, inarticulate shrieks.

André stood up in the cart with his old military tunic tied round his neck; his one arm was tied behind his back to the empty sleeve of his shirt. His glance swept the crowd in search of his beloved, and like a magnet her eyes drew his and held them for an instant. Only a few seconds, though, for the next moment he saw those poor afflicted wretches about him, and for the first time his aching heart drew tears to his eyes.

"Vallon!" they moaned and cried. "Vallon!" like children calling in distress to their mother.

The soldiers jostled them, tried to silence them by threats, but they would not be moved, nor would they be silenced, until suddenly out of the crowd behind them there rose a louder cry:

"You scurvy knave! You abominable hypocrite! At last, at last you get your deserts! Scoundrel! Hellhound! Take that in remembrance of those whom you have outraged!"

Aurore saw it all! It was her father, and Hector Talon was with him. Charles de Marigny seemed to have cast all weakness aside, to have suddenly found the vigour of youth through the power of his hatred. It was amazing how he pushed his way through the crowd, right up to the tumbril, and then, with a sudden spring, he put on foot on the hub of the nearest wheel. He was brandishing a stick with the obvious purpose of hitting at André, when the crowd, taken aback for the moment, seized him and dragged him down.

Aurore put her hand up to her mouth to smother a cry. Her father had fallen backward, dragging Hector Talon down with him in his fall. She could see nothing more than that, for the crowd was all over him, and everything seemed confusion—confusion made hideous by weird cries and imprecations. The people in the rear of the crowd declared: "*C'est bien fait!*" It served the miscreant right for trying to hit at a brave soldier who had lost one arm in the defence of his country. The soldiers tried to restore order and only succeeded in keeping back the crowd—the poor afflicted—at the point of the bayonet.

Aurore's eyes wandered back to the tumbril in search of André. She clutched the gold locket with her last message of love, ready to fling it to him. But she couldn't see him; he must have been struck by the old maniac and fallen down, perhaps, on the floor of the cart. She fingered the thing in her hand feverishly—and suddenly was aware that the thing she fingered as unfamiliar in shape and in weight. She looked down upon it. The gold locket was not there; she had instead a crumpled, soiled piece of paper in her hand; it was wrapped around something hard and rough, possibly a stone. She couldn't think what it meant. What abandoned thief had dared to filch her locket? And then a swift recollection went through her mind like a flash. When she saw her father spring up on the hub of the cart-wheel she had tried to smother a cry of horror and had felt a firm, kindly hand grasping hers.

She had thought nothing of it at the moment, merely thought that some gentle soul was trying to express mute sympathy. Instead of this mysterious substitution! What could it mean? Was it? Could it be from André? Oh! if she could only see him. But there was the crowd, the poor, miserable, afflicted crowd, trying in a futile way to avenge an insult done to the man they revered. The soldiers, reinforced by comrades, had pushed them well away. Aurore could not see what had become of her father. Had he been trampled underfoot by the infuriated mob? Had punishment overtaken him at the very culmination of his treachery?

Just then there was another commotion. A wild, terrified shriek, and Hector Talon was hoisted aloft by half-a-dozen strong arms and then flung, still yelling, into the cart. Some people laughed. The deaf and dumb who had seen gave a weird cry of content. The sergeant in command cast a final glance on the tumbril.

"*Allons!*" he called with stolid indifference. "The batch is complete! Eight sheep for Citizen Samson tomorrow."

Then he gave the word of command: "*En avant,*" and the cart-wheels creaked on their axles as the horses began to move.

And André! Aurore could not see André! Not even now when the tumbril turned out of the gates so close to her. The crowd surged in its wake, mostly in silence, though the poor blind who were nearest to the cart continued to call on Vallon, while the tongue-tied, uttering unintelligible sounds, hung on to them and tried hard to explain that Vallon, Vallon, their father and their mother and their friend, was no longer there.

Aurore, more dead than alive, had scrambled down fro the parapet. The crowd was perceptibly thinner. A few soldiers were rounding up the poor afflicted. The others, for the most part, hung about waiting to see the next batch of prisoners file out. Only a few followed the tumbril, from which could still be heard the agonised yells of Hector Talon. In a few more minutes the vast courtyard seemed almost peaceful. Just a few people waiting about in small groups here and there. The spectacle of the day was not yet over. There would be at least another five tumbrils to watch. The blind and the deaf and dumb, the wretched and the poor, had drifted away. Wither? No doubt this fraternal government knew. Was this not the millennium so confidently foretold?

The soldiers had restored order. They had done it at the point of the bayonet, driving the afflicted away like useless sheep unfit even for the knacker. They had also apparently dragged away the inanimate and lifeless bodies of those who had been unfortunately or luckily succumbed in the *mêlée*. Among these was the body of a man who had once been styled Monseigneur le Duc de Marigny, one of the proudest names in France, who once had power of life and death over his fellow men and could toy with the honour of any poor wench who happened to please his eye. His mangled body lay now in the guardroom of the Palace, so-called of Justice; the naked feet of a score of unwashed rabble had trampled the life out of him. Not even decently covered with a sheet, the illustrious remains of a descendant of kinds was destined for a pauper's grave.

But all this Aurore only found out later. Her thoughts, for the moment, were far enough away from her father who had done her such a great—such an irreparable injury. She had found a deserted corner in an angle of the building, and here, unseen by prying eyes, she unfolded the paper which had so mysteriously been thrust into her hand. And this is what was written thereon:

André is safe! Go home and wait for him. Silence and discretion above all.

And below there was the device of a small five-petalled flower roughly tinted scarlet.

And that was all. Aurore, dazed and puzzled, marvelled if she were dreaming now or if the rest of this day had been a hideous nightmare. If, when she woke *anon*, she would find herself inside the gates of an earthly paradise or of an unendurable hell? André's safe! Where? When? How? By whose agency had he been snatched from out the jaws of death? How and why had God interfered to prevent the monstrous holocaust?

André safe? Could it be true? Did such heavenly things happen in these days of darkness, of doubt and misery?

And all the while that these doubts, fears, conjectures, alternated in Aurore's mind, with the wildest, most unbelievable hope, she was running home, running like one urged by hope or driven by despair.

André safe! And Paris looked just the same! The quays, the river, the pavements, the people passing by as if nothing had happened. Was life going on just the same, then? If so, surely it could not be true that André was safe.

Marie wondered what had happened to the *citizeness*. Her habitual sadness had given place to a febrile restlessness. She seemed unable to sit still. For hours she wandered from room to room, up and down, taking no rest. She tried to eat, but food, apparently, choked her.

Marie asked questions but received no answer. She feared, indeed, that the *citizeness* was sick with the fever. She suggestion bed, and toward ten o'clock Aurore agreed to lie down, but only on condition that Marie herself went to bed. She certainly was in a fever then, with cheeks aflame and hands cold as ice. But she did make pretence to go to bed, drank the orange-flower water which Marie had prepared, and promised to go to sleep.

She waited, quiet as a mouse, until no sound save a comfortable snore came from Marie's room. The good soul had taken to snoring of late, and many a time had the sound set Aurore's nerves on edge. But tonight, she welcomed it. Half-past ten. She crept noiselessly out of bed and put on her clothes again. She lit a candle and with it tiptoed out to the vestibule. She set the candle on the table, and she drew the bolt of the front door, leaving it ajar. She pulled a chair close to the door, sat down and waited—Waited, wide-eyed and expectant, as she had waited, day after day, these two months past in the Hall of the Palais de Justice.

A few minutes after midnight she heard a footstep on the stairs. No need to make a guess as to whose it was: she would have known it among hundreds of thousands. She left the door ajar and went back into the parlour. She sat down in the big armchair. The room was all dark save for the dim light cast in by the flickering candle in the vestibule.

And thus, he found her, waiting for him and ready, with arms held out so that he could pillow his tired head against her warm bosom. She gathered him in her arms with that loving tenderness which is the essence of a good woman's passionate love. Her first kiss was on his hair; then only did her lips find his.

Of danger and death, of rescue or safety, there was no talk. All that he said was, "*Ma mie!*" as, cheek, to cheek, they sat there in the big armchair, forgetful of the world, forgetful of everything save of their love.

Chapter 43

Two days later Maximilien Robespierre and his satellites perished in their turn on the guillotine; that 26th day of July which had meant life or death to Aurore and André had also meant life or death to the most bloodthirsty tyrant the civilized world has ever known. It was the first eclipse of his power and of his popularity. Swift as had been his rise, his fall from the giddy heights of dictatorship was swifter still. The same throats, which less than a couple of months ago had yelled themselves hoarse with praise of Robespierre as second only to the Supreme Being, now shouted execrations on the fallen tyrant.

Terrified for their own lives his enemies had made a super-human effort to drag him down. It was he or they, his head or theirs. In the pocket of his coat taken off at the club because the night was very hot had been found a list of names to be indicted on the morrow, names of men to be accused, tried, and condemned. They were the names of the most influential men in the National Convention, Tallien's at the head. It was their life or his, and they put forth all their strength, all their terror, and all their eloquence to bring him down. And they succeeded. On the 26th of July the tyrant was indicted for treason against the Republic; on the 27th, he was dragged, wounded and almost dying, to the bar of the accused; on the 28th, at even, he died on the guillotine.

His death was inglorious and sordid, but it marked an epoch. As if by a magic wand the whole aspect of France was changed. Terrorism died in as many days as it had taken years to maintain itself. Within twenty-four hours the Convention, free from tyranny and from fear of death, passed a law that every man or woman indicted for treason and conspiracy must be served with a Writ of Accusation so that they might know of what they were accused. Prisoners were liberated by the hundred. Houses of Detention were emptied. Justice once more put on the semblance of a bandage over her eyes and held the scales with a steady hand.

And while André and Aurore dreamed their dream of love in the sunny apartment of the Quai de la Ferraille, the aspect of France was changed. Life went on, but no longer the same, for there was hope in every heart, even though hope was often linked with incurable sorrow.

And that is the end of the story which Sir Percy Blakeney, Bart., told to His Royal Highness that evening in the Assembly Rooms at

Bath.

"A fine fellow, your André Vallon," His Royal Highness remarked. "What became of him?"

"He was duly served with a Writ of Accusation, brought to the bar, and acquitted. He has taken up his work again with the blind and the deaf and dumb."

"And he and your lovely Aurore spin the thread of perfect love in their apartment on the Quai de la Ferraille, is that it?"

"I should say as perfect as I have ever seen, sir," Blakeney remarked with a smile.

"Outside your own, you lucky dog!" His Royal Highness rejoined with a sigh. "But what happened to that rascal, Hector Talon?"

"He was indicted for false accusations against a patriot. His name appeared below that of Charles de Marigny on the letter which denounced Vallon to the Committee of Public Safety which has now ceased to exist. He died a very inglorious death just a week after he had hoped to see his old enemy go up the steps of the guillotine."

"Did the daughter ever recover her father's body for decent burial?"

"I believe so."

"Ah, well!" His Royal Highness concluded. "I'll grant you, Blakeney, that for a child of that awful revolution, your friend Vallon has come out of the flames unscathed."

LEONAUR

ALSO FROM LEONAUR

AVAILABLE IN SOFTCOVER OR HARDCOVER WITH DUST JACKET

THE COMPLETE FOUR JUST MEN: VOLUME 2 *by Edgar Wallace*—*The Law of the Four Just Men* & *The Three Just Men*—disillusioned with a world where the wicked and the abusers of power perpetually go unpunished, the Just Men set about to rectify matters according to their own standards, and retribution is dispensed on swift and deadly wings.

THE COMPLETE RAFFLES: 1 *by E. W. Hornung*—*The Amateur Cracksman* & *The Black Mask*—By turns urbane gentleman about town and accomplished cricketer, life is just too ordinary for Raffles and that sets him on a series of adventures that have long been treasured as a real antidote to the 'white knights' who are the usual heroes of the crime fiction of this period.

THE COMPLETE RAFFLES: 2 *by E. W. Hornung*—*A Thief in the Night* & *Mr Justice Raffles*—By turns urbane gentleman about town and accomplished cricketer, life is just too ordinary for Raffles and that sets him on a series of adventures that have long been treasured as a real antidote to the 'white knights' who are the usual heroes of the crime fiction of this period.

THE COLLECTED SUPERNATURAL AND WEIRD FICTION OF WILKIE COLLINS: VOLUME 1 *by Wilkie Collins*—Contains one novel 'The Haunted Hotel', one novella 'Mad Monkton', three novelettes 'Mr Percy and the Prophet', 'The Biter Bit' and 'The Dead Alive' and eight short stories to chill the blood.

THE COLLECTED SUPERNATURAL AND WEIRD FICTION OF WILKIE COLLINS: VOLUME 2 *by Wilkie Collins*—Contains one novel 'The Two Destinies', three novellas 'The Frozen deep', 'Sister Rose' and 'The Yellow Mask' and two short stories to chill the blood.

THE COLLECTED SUPERNATURAL AND WEIRD FICTION OF WILKIE COLLINS: VOLUME 3 *by Wilkie Collins*—Contains one novel 'Dead Secret,' two novelettes 'Mrs Zant and the Ghost' and 'The Nun's Story of Gabriel's Marriage' and five short stories to chill the blood.

FUNNY BONES *selected by Dorothy Scarborough*—An Anthology of Humorous Ghost Stories.

MONTEZUMA'S CASTLE AND OTHER WEIRD TALES *by Charles B. Cory*—Cory has written a superb collection of eighteen ghostly and weird stories to chill and thrill the avid enthusiast of supernatural fiction.

SUPERNATURAL BUCHAN *by John Buchan*—Stories of Ancient Spirits, Uncanny Places & Strange Creatures.